Harry touched the funny little bun on top of that so-precious head and breathed, "You are sadly . . . unchaperoned, ma'am."

She raised her head slowly, her eyes meeting his with the sweet shyness that whispered to him of a promise he must not acknowledge. "Yes, Harry."

"And . . . all alone," he sighed.

"Yes—Harry."

Surely one little kiss would not be so very improper . . . ? But conscience said sternly that it would be most ungallant, wherefore he muttered, "I must not— take advantage of you, little one."

"No . . . Harry," she whispered, her voice incredibly caressing.

"I . . . will not," he vowed, taking her in his arms.

"Nor I . . . Harry," she breathed, lifting her face for his kiss. He bent toward her.

"Sir Harry! Sir Harry!"

The familiar bellow blasted that enchanted silence. Astounded, Harry released her and swung around.

Fawcett Crest Books
by Patricia Veryan:

THE LORD AND THE GYPSY

MARRIED PAST REDEMPTION

THE NOBLEST FRAILTY

SANGUINET'S CROWN

WAGERED WIDOW

NANETTE

Patricia Veryan

FAWCETT CREST • NEW YORK

A Fawcett Crest Book
Published by Ballantine Books
Copyright © 1981 by Patricia Veryan

Library of Congress Catalog Card Number: 80-51854

ISBN 0-449-21150-9

This edition published by arrangement with Walker Publishing Company, Inc.

Manufactured in the United States of America

First Ballantine Books Edition: December 1986

*For Allan
and
With thanks to D. M. Stuart*

PROLOGUE

THE APRIL MORNING HAD BEEN SUNNY, BUT TOWARDS afternoon a light mist crept in from the Channel to ooze stealthily along Dover's cobbled and bustling streets. An inquisitive mist this, for its damp intrusion missed no carriage, cottage, mansion, shop, nor place of business; invading each with silent but stubborn persistence as though determined to pry into every nook and cranny of the ancient town. Coming at length to that venerable inn called "The Ship," it seeped through open casements and unlatched doors, curled about the tap, and slyly insinuated itself into the coffee room. Not until it reached two adjoining chambers on the upper floor was it held at bay by windows tightly closed, curtains drawn despite the early hour, inner doors snug and bolted, and a brightly burning fire upon each hearth. In vain did the mist writhe, twist, and contort itself; it was at last obliged to acknowledge defeat and swirl sulkily upon its thwarted way. And how furious would this pervasive vapour have been (had it indeed possessed reason and curiosity), to learn that of all the many secrets harboured in old Dover town on that spring afternoon, one of the most intriguing was unfolding in the very rooms to which it had been unable to gain access.

The first of these, a private parlour, was occupied by a tall gentleman of middle age and grim aspect. The cut of his coat and the set of his shoulders hinted at the military, and the restlessness of his manner hinted at extreme anxiety. He stood with hands clasped behind rather broad hips,

1

his thinning brown hair rumpled by reason of having been clutched in desperation several times during the past half-hour. His pale blue eyes held a frown, and turned constantly to the closed door of the adjoining bedchamber. Increasingly exasperated, he began to pace up and down, and by one o'clock his pacing resembled that of a healthy Siberian tiger chafing against imprisonment. Drawing forth his timepiece, he consulted it, groaned aloud, and glanced once more to the closed connecting door, his lips pursing in frustration. Animadverting to the chuckling flames upon the unfailing inability of all females (however ravishingly lovely they may be) to be prompt, he voiced his suspicion that his ladies were doubtless happily engaged in idle gossip, then resumed his pacing.

A gallant and intrepid gentleman was Major James Stroud, but in this instance, his vexation was unwarranted. In the adjoining room the ladies in question were in fact disrobing with almost feverish haste. The elder of the pair, a neat woman with soft brown hair and kindly grey eyes, was very obviously an abigail. That she enjoyed the familiarity with her charge that only long service can bestow was as obvious, for ignoring a flood of adjurations that she attend to herself, she continued to unbutton the fine lawn bodice of her young mistress's petticoat, while wailing softly that it "would never do . . . *never* . . . do!"

The recipient of this dismal verdict was a vibrantly lovely brunette. She was small of stature, standing not above five feet in her stockings, but having a generously curved figure that forbade her being classed as 'petite'. In a husky little voice that betrayed a barely contained agitation, she now exploded, "Have done! Oh, have *done*, Lindsay! Your petticoat—off with it! *Vite!* One glimpse of Brussels lace beneath your round gown and I am betrayed. Ah! Thank heaven we are much of a size!" She shrugged her way into the sensible cotton (and lace-less) petticoat, emerging with curls sadly awry and the discovery that she and her abigail were less of a size than she had fancied. "Supposing," she amended, peering ruefully at her somewhat flattened bosom, "only that I do not breathe too deeply!"

2

Lindsay came to slip her blue round gown over the dark head, then knelt to fit her brogues onto the girl's smaller feet. "Oh, *dear* Miss Nanette . . ." she said distractedly, "*must* we? What the *ton* will say I scarcely dare to think! And—your *papa* . . ! Oh, ma'am! I dassn't . . . I just dassn't!"

Paling, Miss Nanette checked, then reached forward to caress the woman's sallow cheek and say wistfully, "but—you would not have him take me back . . ?"

Lindsay gulped, pressed clasped hands to her lips, and blinked tears away. "As God be my judge . . . I *know* it's against all law and reason! Your dear sweet name must be sullied! You'll ruin yourself, my dearie . . . But—oh, I *must* help you!"

She was swooped upon, kissed, and thanked profusely; then Nanette stood and, stepping up and down experimentally in the strange-feeling shoes, said, "You will not forget, dear Lindsay? Keep the hood well forward until Major Stroud has you safely into the cabin on the packet. When you reach Calais he will at once take you to the home of his cousin. There, you will change clothes and be sent to stay with his cousin's old nurse until I call for you."

Lindsay said nothing, and discerning a glittering droplet on the averted cheek, Nanette gathered her close and murmured emotionally, "Never weep, my faithful one. We shall be together again—very soon."

"Oh, miss," sobbed Lindsay, clinging to her. "But—suppose . . . just *suppose* he catches us! Major Stroud is such a . . . fine gentleman! He would be as good as dead! And—what your papa would do to me . . ! While, as for *you*— Oh, my poor little lamb!"

Nanette's hazel eyes lost their fond glow and acquired a defiant flash. "He shall not catch you!" she asserted fiercely, "for you will have quite disappeared. Major Stroud will rejoin his regiment. And—me . . ." She did not finish but, turning to the mirror, began to take down her hair. The distraught Lindsay was urged to hasten "for time it is of the essence. I must board the Accommodation

Coach at two o'clock if I am to reach the convent and my dear Sister Maria Evangeline before dark.''

Moaning her dismay that her adored and highly born charge must submit to the horrors of such crude transportation, Lindsay stepped gingerly into a rich travelling gown of beige linen, fastened high to the throat with brown velvet frogged buttons. A matching silk-lined brown velvet pelisse was placed around her shoulders and the hood drawn closely about her face. For a few seconds, awed by such finery, she scanned the stranger in the mirror. Then, catching sight of her companion, she gave a yelp of shock. Miss Nanette had vanished: in her place stood a girl who appeared to be a halfwit. The luxuriant tresses had been twisted into a tight and untidy knot atop a head that had exchanged its proud uptilt for a forlorn droop. The erectly carried shoulders sagged, and as she watched in astonishment, the hazel eyes, usually so full of fire or laughter, slowly crossed, the firm little chin lolled stupidly, and a lacklustre voice with a decided country accent asked, "Does ye think as how me friends would know me now, ma'am?"

"Good . . . gracious . . !" gasped Lindsay. "I wouldn't have known you myself—me that's cared for you since you was in the schoolroom! Oh, miss! We just might do it! We really *might* escape him! All of us!"

But wrapping Miss Nanette in her own neat cloak, she thought prayerfully, "May God help us if we don't!"

4

CHAPTER I

SIR HARRY REDMOND'S LONDON RESIDENCE WAS NOT SO much situated on Hill Street as hidden there. It was a tall, thin house, and the landlord having indignantly denied his tenant's blithe request that the trim be painted red ("to perk up the old shed a trifle"), its black-and-white façade remained, and was so discreet as to render it even less noticeable. Despite this anonymity, however, and the puny dimensions that were dwarfed by such great edifices as Hilby House, several doors distant, it was comfortable and adequate for the present needs of its occupant.

Having survived to the age of seven and twenty without becoming leg shackled, Sir Harry was also blessed by the accolade of 'Corinthian'. He was a notable whip, a bruising rider to hounds, was said to have once knocked Gentleman Jackson off his pins—although he never bragged of that achievement if it was truth—and was generally acknowledged to be a jolly fine sportsman. He did not demand a surfeit of elegance in his surroundings, a fact that proved no deterrent to his many friends. Nor was Anderson, his major domo and former batman, dismayed by the litter of riding crops and thongs, spurs, newspapers, periodicals, and old copies of the Racing Calendar that were wont to clutter the lounge. Only when Joseph, the butler at Sir Harry's country seat, came into Town did Sergeant Anderson become implacable. On these rare occasions his master was obliged to refrain from allowing his friends to mar the tables with their spurs or contribute their debris to his own, and the house took on an awesomely tidy lustre that prevailed until Mr. Joseph took himself and his supercilious nose back to Hampshire.

The kitchen was located in the basement of the house and was another kettle of fish entirely, and it was to this spotless domain that Sergeant Anderson made his way shortly after eight o'clock one rainy May evening. The Sergeant was a husky man in his early forties. He enjoyed robust good health, but had been so unfortunate as to lose his right leg below the knee at the Battle of Talavera, and it was not easy for him to negotiate the winding iron staircase. He appeared neither disgruntled nor downcast by this circumstance, however. His eyes were bright and he whistled cheerily as he thumped down the steps anticipating his evening cup of tea with the housekeeper—an event which had, over the past year, become the highlight of his day.

Mrs. Thomas heard both thump and whistle approaching. She smiled a knowing smile at the gleaming tea kettle, adjusted the lace cap upon dark hair that showed only a few streaks of silver, and cast a swift and critical glance around the room. Surely, had they been aware, the objects she scanned must have trembled before that keen scrutiny, but with little cause. For the pots and pans hanging in a neat row above the stove winked and sparkled in the glow of the candles; the tiles had a mellow gloss; plates, cups, and saucers shone upon their shelves; and everywhere was order and neatness. Mrs. Thomas gave a nod of satisfaction, and added boiling water to teapot. The Sergeant was early tonight, just as she'd hoped he would be. It was her custom to have both cook and housemaid ousted by nine o'clock; but tonight, knowing Sir Harry would not dine at home, she had made her plans accordingly, and the balance of the evening would not be disturbed by Mrs. Ford's gloomy prognostications of the Doomsday she felt imminent, or the housemaid's tittering laugh that never failed to bring an harassed look to Anderson's strong countenance.

"Come in, Sergeant," she called, turning to smile at him as he beamed his way through the door.

He thanked her, pulled out her chair, then sat down himself, saying politely that he hoped he did not inconvenience her by arriving at so early an hour, and delightedly aware that the tea tray was ready and the pretty woman prepared for just so early a visit. Mrs. Thomas's colour was heightened a little as she poured him a cup of tea and handed it across the table. She assured him that it was no slightest inconvenience and, setting sugar and milk where he might help himself, observed that it was a terrible night for a wedding. "Not that anything could mar the joy of Lord St. Clair and his lovely bride, I've no doubt," she went on, preparing a cup for herself. "And didn't Sir Harry look dashing? You must be so proud of him, Sergeant, for he does you credit. Such a handsome young man. I find it hard to believe when people tell me his brother is the best looking of the pair, and more closely resembles his late papa."

The smile died from the Sergeant's loyal brown eyes. Had anyone else addressed so unfortunate a remark to him, he'd have set them down proper. His plans for Mrs. Thomas, however, did he ever muster sufficient courage to mention them, did not include a setdown. Therefore, he merely muttered that Sir Colin Redmond had been an exceptionally well-favoured gentleman, God rest his soul, and prepared to direct the conversation toward music, and thence, hopefully, to the concert in Hyde Park on Sunday afternoon. Unfortunately, Robert Burns once again proved all wise and, together with countless other mice and men, Sergeant Anderson's best-laid plans 'ganged aglie'. His brow darkened as the front door bell began to ring stridently, and excusing himself, he left the cozy kitchen and began to toil reluctantly upstairs again.

Swinging the front door open to the accompaniment of a barrage of pounding, his resentment was increased as he beheld the tall, drenched young man who stood on the doorstep, a valise at his feet, and the overcoat he should have worn instead wrapped around an armload of heavy volumes. "Mr. Mitchell . . ." said the Sergeant hollowly. "We thought you wasn't coming."

"Oh, no. Did you?" smiled Mitchell Redmond.

"Wouldn't miss St. Clair's wedding for the world. Is my brother from home?"

Anderson nodded. "Gone to the wedding, sir."

"What—another? Egad! Regular epidemic."

"Same one," Anderson said woodenly, making no move to admit the dripping figure before him. "St. George's s'arternoon. Reception at the Earl's house on Bond Street s'evening."

Redmond blinked through the streams that trickled from his bare head. "But—St. Clair's to be shackled on the *fifteenth*."

"Today," Anderson imparted, the barest trace of scorn touching his voice, "*is* the fifteenth." He peered towards the flagway as a distant and impatient bellow apprised him of the fact the jarvey had not been reimbursed.

"Oh, blast!" Redmond slipped past the guardian of the door. "Be a good fellow and pay him, would you?" This request encountering only a bleak stare, he shrugged and added an apologetic, "Cannot seem to find my purse."

Anderson's lips tightened and he turned up his collar.

"Here!" Redmond tossed his coat and said solicitously, "Mustn't get wet."

To his sorrow, the Sergeant instinctively grabbed the garment. He now held it at arms length and looked with disgust to his sodden waistcoat, to the puddle the coat was rapidly depositing on the floor, to Redmond. "Oh, dear," sighed that promising young scholar. "Well, it kept my books dry. That's the important thing, isn't it?" His smile was dazzling; his long grey eyes alight with mischief.

An answering smile was not forthcoming. Sergeant Anderson's response, fortunately, being lost as he thumped out into the rain.

Whatever his personal opinion of the younger Redmond, Sergeant Anderson was devoted to the elder. He knew all too well what would be his Captain's reaction was his brother neglected, and knowing also that Mr. Mitchell was subject to inflamations of the lungs, lost no time in seeing to it that a roaring fire was lighted in his room, a hot bath provided, and the wet clothing removed. Nor was Mrs. Thomas idle, and Mitchell, shivering no longer, was seated before the fire, warmly clad in Harry's new quilted green satin dressing gown, and finishing a bowl of Flemish soup and a mushroom omelette, when a familiar whoop sent up his dark brows and caused him to lay his fork aside and come to his feet in surprise.

The door burst open and Sir Harry Redmond, hatless but still wearing his wet greatcoat, ran in. "Mitch! You slippery cub! Where in the deuce have you been?"

They shook hands heartily and scanned one another with undisguised affection. They were much alike, and each a splendid example of British manhood. Mitchell, some five years the younger, was rather startlingly handsome, but to a lesser degree Harry also enjoyed the lean good looks that had characterized their late father, having slightly curling dark locks, a firm chin, somewhat hawk nose, and a generous, sensitive mouth. They both stood a shade under six feet, but Mitchell's was the lighter build, his posture already inclining to a scholarly stoop, while Harry's broad shoulders and well-shaped legs proclaimed the athlete. The main difference between them was most clearly expressed in the eyes; Mitchell's being grey, well opened, and full of dreams, and Harry's slightly narrowed, perhaps from long exposure to the Spanish sun, but of an intensely vivid green, and full of the laughter that concealed his underlying strength. "You missed the wedding, you clodpole!" he grinned, pounding at his brother's shoulder. And all too aware of Mitchell's exasperating absent-mindedness, asked, "Did you forget it was to be today?"

"Forgot today was the fifteenth," Mitchell admitted wryly. "And then I got on the wrong stupid coach when we stopped to change horses at High Wycombe, and was halfway to Bath before I discovered I was on the stage—not the Royal Mail!" He assisted his brother out of his great coat, flung the garment carelessly over an armchair, and said, "You may be done laughing now, *mon Sauvage*, and tell me how the wedding went off."

"Jolly well." Harry removed the coat from the chair,

9

hung it on the floor, and occupied the chair himself. "Lucian is hopelessly besotted, you know, but acquitted himself quite well. Deirdre, of course . . ." he kissed his fingertips, "looked angelic. Ain't at all sure he deserves her. Neither is he."

Turning his chair from the table, Mitchell sprawled in it and said, "What, after that incredible fracas he stirred up last autumn? I'd say he'd well earned his reward! D'you know the Dean himself asked me to tell him of it, and remarked Lucian had brought the war home with him— though I doubt even Wellington could have conjured up such a witch's brew."

Harry smiled reminiscently. "Ironic, isn't it? From Talavera to Waterloo with hardly a scratch, and after he returned to England he was ambushed, damn near blinded, shot, and forced into a duel with the Devil himself."

"From which you rescued him," said Mitchell, and as his brother burst into a shout of laughter, added, "at least, that's what I told the Dean."

"Single-handed," Harry nodded. "Only for lord's sake don't ever let Vaughan, or Rich Saxon, or Bolster hear you say that! I'd never live it down! And—why the Mail, cub? You should have hired a post chaise." Mitchell, who had risen as he spoke, was searching anxiously through his valise, and Harry added with a grin, "What've you lost this time?"

"Don't say that! It's something I bought for Deirdre. I found it in a little shop in The High. The most fantastically wrought piece of jade I ever . . ." He paused, frowned, and murmured, "No . . . come to think on it, I put it in my coat pocket . . . Only—Anderson turned my pockets inside out when he took my clothes away . . ." His dismayed gaze lifted. "Jove! Not *again* . . !"

"It's likely in Bath by this time," chuckled his brother. "I vow it astonishes me you've not walked onto a ship bound for Tasmania or some such place long since! 'Ware Mitch! You'll wind up in some chieftain's cooking pot yet!"

"No, really, Harry, this is dreadful! Whatever will Lucian think?"

"Nothing he don't already! But—I wish you *had* come

in time, Mitch. It was a grand wedding. All the girls were asking for you, and Mandy said—''

''If it was so grand,'' Mitchell interposed, returning to his chair, ''why are you come home at this ungodly hour?''

His grey eyes were keen all at once, and for the briefest second Harry's green ones fell away before that searching look. ''Grief,'' he said brightly. ''Cannot bear to see a good friend become a benedick. And instead of your having the unmitigated gall to loll about in my new dressing gown and question the actions of the Head of your House, be so good as to tell me the meaning of the letter your tutor directed to me.'' Seeing that his evasion had increased the suspicion in his brother's eyes, he went on hurriedly, ''He says you shall have to cram hard, old lad, if you're to cavort off to Italy this summer. What the deuce you do with your time up there I cannot imagine. Or I could, did I think you the type to hang about the fancy houses!''

''What makes you suppose I am not?''

There was a deep bond between them and Harry had long since discerned the shadows beneath Mitchell's eyes and the slight hollows in the cheeks. The smile left his eyes as he said, ''I'm inclined to think if you've been in bed, it has been very much alone.''

It was Mitchell's turn to look away, but he stood considerably in awe of his brother and he knew that grave stare too well to dissemble. He admitted that he'd had ''a spot of bother'' with his chest again. ''Put me on my back for upwards of a month, and they wouldn't allow me to study. Curst nuisance.''

''And why,'' demanded Harry, his long fingers tightening a little on the arm of his chair, ''was I not told of this?''

''Don't tell you everything,'' replied Mitchell indistinctly, around a piece of the omelette. ''No more'n you tell me . . .''

They locked glances for an instant. Harry got up, walked to the chest of drawers, and poured himself a glass of the sherry Anderson had left there. Sipping it appreciatively, he threw a thoughtful look at his brother. ''And what am I to gather from that remark, my bantling?''

Instead of objecting to a form of address that never failed to irritate him, Mitchell shrugged, "I've heard a few things. Funny sort of rumours." He pushed the remaining piece of omelette around his plate with careful precision and murmured, "Not in the basket, are we?"

"Lord—no! Who the devil told you such a Canterbury tale? My father left the estate practically untouched—he never was a gamester, thank God! Moiré Grange awaits you, child, whenever you will."

"It does?" Mitchell captured his much-travelled piece of omelette and conveying it to his mouth, mumbled, "I'd thought perhaps you intended to occupy the Grange yourself. With your lady . . ." He glanced up from under his lashes and, seeing Harry's smile bland and his eyes very empty, said, "You *are*—fond of the fair Dorothy, aren't you, old fellow?"

"'Course I am! I've been pursuing the lady any time this last year and more. Whatever did you think I was about? She's a lady of quality."

"Pursuing . . . yes. But somehow I wasn't sure you— ah . . . wanted to catch up." Mitchell flushed under his brother's sardonic grin and said awkwardly, "All right, I don't know much about such things, but—it didn't seem to me you had the same look. Not like old Lucian, I mean. Or Damon, come to that."

Harry laughed. "Silly gudgeon!" he said.

"Here . . ."
Sergeant Anderson was startled to find Mrs. Thomas removing the empty cup from one hand and the spoon from the other.

"Good gracious, Sergeant," she smiled. "You are in a state. Whatever is the matter? Is it because Mr. Mitchell has come home?"

He had thought he was concealing his worries and apologizing for his inattention, confessed he'd known there would be trouble the minute Mr. Mitchell "showed his pretty face this evening! He's always trouble, that one is!"

Pouring him another cup, Mrs. Thomas said carefully

that he seemed a tiny bit prejudiced. "If I may say so, Sergeant, I thought him a fine-looking boy. Very much the gentleman. And Sir Harry would, I have gathered, lay down his life for him without an instant's hesitation."

"And da— er, very nearly did!" growled the Sergeant. He accepted his tea with a mutter of thanks, and glared down at it in silence. So she thought he was prejudiced, did she? He scowled. "You'll mind I was the one what found him after the Battle of Ciudad Rodrigo, ma'am?"

"I was not at this situation then, Sergeant, and never have presumed to ask about it. But Mrs. Langridge once told me that poor Sir Harry's back was fairly riddled!" She shook her head, her eyes reflecting sincere distress.

"Not quite that bad," said the Sergeant. "But the Captain was proper mauled by two shell fragments. His horse was all cut up, which is why the beast bolted. Me and the Captain's men searched every inch of that bl— er, that miserable town for him. Everyone said he was killed. Blowed up with poor Colonel Mackinnon, they said, or been buried accidental-like. Some of the men took it awful hard." He stared blankly at the spoon in his powerful hand. "But—I found him . . .

"In a farm, was it not?" prompted Mrs. Thomas gently. "And the dear man near death? How very fortunate that those people helped him."

"Been lying there for days," Anderson nodded, his eyes bleak. "And he'd had precious little in the way of help. You wouldn't believe that filthy hovel! And him in such pain he couldn't even talk to me. But—held out his hand, he did. And give me a grin."

Mrs. Thomas gasped a faint, "Oh . . . my . . ! Poor soul! So you were able to bring him back after all, Sergeant. How very grateful his papa must have been."

"Yus," said the Sergeant, himself rather overcome by that harrowing memory. "Sir Colin thought the sun riz and set in the Captain. It was months though 'fore we dared put him on a ship, and months of illness after he got home, but never a whimper out of him. We was at Moiré Grange, a'course, and Mr. Mitchell come down for the Long Vacation. A fat lot he cared for his brother! Always had his head stuck in a book. Sir Harry was on the mend, and fidgety. Always asking me for news of the war. One morning he says to me, sad-like, "We should be back in Spain, Andy. With the old 43rd . . ." The Sergeant clenched his fist and growled, "I should've kept me eyes on him. He got to feeling so sprightly he asked Mr. Mitchell to go for a ride with him. Mr. Mitchell said later that he heard what he said, but "it didn't really sink in!" Anderson drew a deep breath, his disgust very evident. "I don't think you've never been to the Grange, Mrs. Thomas. From the time he was a little shaver, Sir Harry loved to gallop through the high meadow and up around a path that skirts the Home Wood. The path takes a sharp turn around the edge of the trees, right at the top of the hill, and there's a wooden footbridge over a place what got washed away in a storm once. Well, there'd been heavy rains again that past winter. A whole piece of the hill had give way and took the bridge with it." He said fiercely, "Mr. Mitchell *knowed* how dangerous it was. Only he *didn't bother* to warn his brother!"

"My heavens! Didn't Sir Harry see the bridge was gone?"

"Wasn't no way he could've, ma'am. If he'd been riding slow—perhaps. But Sir Harry don't ride slow. The mare broke her neck. The Captain was set back where he'd been months before. Had to go through all that misery—all over again . . !" He stared at his spoon, his eyes very angry.

Mrs. Thomas was well aware of the Sergeant's devotion to his 'Captain'. She hesitated and, choosing her words with care, ventured, "How awful! But—have you never been so lost in a book, Sergeant, that you did not hear what was said to you?"

"Can't say I has, ma'am. To my mind there ain't no excuse for what he done. No matter how interested he was in that there book, his brother shoulda come first! If he'd really cared, something in his head would've woke him up. Truth is, Mr. Mitchell don't care for nothing nor no one, 'cepting Mr. Mitchell!"

CHAPTER II

"Is the Reverend from home, Baines?" Shivering in the stark and chill hall of the Rectory, Harry allowed the elderly butler to assist him in the removal of his wet coat and hat, and appropriate his whip and gloves.

"The Reverend is composing his sermon," announced Baines, his tones so ponderously singsong they might have emanated from his mistress rather than himself. "If you will step into the withdrawing room, Sir Harry, I shall pour you a glass of wine and then advise him of your arrival."

Harry accompanied the faithful retainer with impatience rather than the boredom this large, dull house and its solemn occupants usually aroused in his irreverent breast. "My aunt is well, I trust? And the children?"

"Mrs. Langridge is in Harrogate, sir. Visiting of her sister, this being May. Master William and Miss Martha went with her and have since, so I understand, contracted measles."

"Dear, dear!" Sir Harry had a mental picture of his aunt Ada, who enjoyed her own imagined ills to the hilt, being suddenly visited by her sanctimonious sister and two sick children. He suppressed a grin and remarked that he trusted Lady Edgar was bearing up under the strain. Mr. Baines fixed the young baronet with a reproving glance and responded that since Mrs. Langridge had taken along some copies of her husband's more recent sermons, he rather suspected they would provide the needed inspiration. He shook his head at Harry's amused wink, and made his dig-

15

nified way from the room having first placed a glass of sherry beside the sinner's cold hand.

Harry sipped the wine and grimaced; it was of a poor vintage, and sour, and the oppressively over-furnished room like ice. He paced to the fireplace and stirred up the wretched remains with his booted foot, then bent to add another log and poke hopefully at it.

"Waste not . . ." came the mournful intonation from behind him, "want not!"

"Afternoon, Uncle." Harry straightened and put out his hand. "You're likely right, but it's freezing in here. With Aunt Wilhelmina sporting about in Harrogate, I'd think you could live a little more comfortable."

The Reverend Mordecai Langridge was what Harry had once, in a moment of total frustration, described to Mitchell as a 'neither man'. Neither fat nor thin, tall nor short, dark nor fair, young nor old, clever nor stupid. "In short," he'd grumbled, "a compromise in every possible direction!" "Until," his brother had smiled, "you come to 'strong nor weak'," and they had both laughed, if perhaps with a twinge of conscience at such harsh criticism. In his youth, Mordecai Langridge had taken a tall lady of unexceptional birth and moderate fortune for his bride, deeming her lofty moral values an asset to his calling. As the years had passed, however, his Wilhelmina's preoccupation with morality had become an obsession to which had been added a frugality bordering on the nipcheese and a self-righteousness that had deepened into pompous sanctimoniousness. Despite these questionable attributes, she was not one to stint herself at table, with the result that girth had combined with height to render her a formidable figure. She was possessed of a sharp tongue, a booming voice, and a growing scorn for her gentle and ineffectual husband. Sir Colin Redmond had been wont to remark that there was good stuff in 'poor old Mordecai,' did he only exert it. And that if he should ever do so it would be better for both of them. Harry and Mitchell, fondly tolerant of their parent's unfailing ability to find the good in everyone, had exchanged amused smiles at such kindly observations, and privately

16

chuckled to think of 'Maude,' as they irreverently dubbed him, daring to stand up to his terrifying spouse.

Now, Langridge drew closer to the fire, holding out his pudgy hands to the warmth and, for an instant forgetting himself, murmured, "Baines watches me like a hawk, y'see, and—" He stopped abruptly, pulled his heavy woollen jacket closer about him, adjusted the knitted shawl he wore over it, tugged at the nightcap on his head, and said a hurried, "I do not find it in the least bit chill. But how generous in you to visit me. You knew perhaps that I am lone and lorn?"

"Are you going to shake my hand or not, sir?" asked Harry briskly.

"What? Oh." The Reverend obliged, his grasp neither strong nor limp, and, shaking his head, mourned, "How swift you are to take umbrage. Pride, Harry, goeth before—"

"Goeth before mystification in this case, sir. Your pardon if I am unmannerly, but—might we sit down?"

"Oh dear! We are upset. We are rude and angry. And anger, my dear boy, is such a wasted emotion. I used to tell your poor father . . ."

Since his uncle was now seated on one of the straight-backed red velvet chairs beside the fire, Harry eased his own long length onto a similar monstrosity and, having waited dutifully but unavailingly for the sentence to end, said, "Uncle Mordecai, my father—"

"My own dear sister's husband! God rest his poor sinful soul!" groaned Langridge, clasping his hands and casting an anguished look at the ceiling.

"I have little doubt, sir," Harry bridled, "but that my father's soul was well-received!"

His uncle's gaze drifted sorrowfully downward, and he was so moved by what he saw in that stern young countenance that he clasped a hand over his eyes. "Poor boy! The innocent victim! Truly—the sins of the fathers . . ."

"For heaven's sake, Uncle!" Harry sprang to his feet. "My greatest regret, and my brother's also, is that our father is not alive today! As for sins—I've no doubt he had

17

some, being human, but he was a great-souled, warm hearted gentleman, with not an ounce of prim and prosy hypocrisy about him!"

"You seek to come to points with me," sighed Langridge. "And I had so hoped we might talk together. That I might, at last . . ."

Again Harry waited, nerves taut. Exasperated, he at last burst out, "Sir, what in the *deuce* is my bank about? I particularly wish Mitchell to take that Italian tour this summer. He had the bronchitis twice last year, and again only recently. A few months in a milder climate might do him good. I sent funds up to Oxford to cover the costs, and the draft was returned from the bank together with a note explaining that my account is closed!"

"One cannot expect a great banking house to deceive, my boy," the Reverend sighed. "I have protected you for as long as I could. Now you must—"

"You . . . have . . . what . . ?"

Langridge jumped. "How like him you are." He shook his head chidingly. "Poor Colin . . . Poor Harry . . . How may I tell you? What can I say?"

"You can start by telling me what the devil all this Friday-faced ranting is about! And why my bank claims my account closed when my father left me very well to pass!"

The Reverend stared up into a blazing anger and, thinking to read accusation there, his mouth fell open a little, a tide of crimson suffusing his features. He stood also, and cried dramatically, "Do I detect base suspicion, sir? Do you dare to accuse a gentleman of the cloth of—thievery?"

Despite his seething frustration, Harry was struck by this pose. Poor old Maude looked so totally ridiculous striking an affronted attitude while swathed in all his wools and with that awful nightcap sagging about his flabby face . . . "Of course I do not, sir," he said with considerably less force. "But something very odd is afoot, and I want to know what it is. Wherever I go I am the recipient of what I'd swear are sympathetic looks; Mitchell also has heard what he termed 'funny rumours'. I've been courting a charming lady for over a year, with her brother's full knowledge and sanction, yet he has suddenly decided I am not worthy of her hand." He scowled and muttered half to himself, "Though Reggie Haines-Curtis was ever a starchy court card, I'll own."

"And—the Lady Dorothy?" enquired Mordecai timidly. "Has she promised to remain—constant?"

Harry flushed. The Lady Dorothy Haines-Curtis had, in point of fact, wept distractedly but announced that although she was "excessively fond of him and ever would be" she intended to wed Roger de Tornay—a man twice her age, with a perfectly vile reputation, but also possessed of an earldom and a vast fortune. And because that rejection still smarted more than he cared to admit, he evaded, "I put it to you, Uncle, that here's too much smoke for there to be no fire. I demand to be told the truth."

"The truth! Dear Lord!" Outrage faded into anguish and, wringing his hands, Langridge paced to the fire, stood surveying the squandered log apprehensively for an instant, then swung about. "My dear boy, your— But—no! I must not rush my fences! The truth is . . ." And rushing to his fences with a vengeance, he blurted, "Far from leaving you very well to pass, your father gambled away everything he owned! You and poor Mitchell are—absolutely *destitute*!"

For a second it seemed to Harry that the walls dissolved, that the two of them stood in a limbo wherein colour ceased to exist save for a jet black and blinding white. He put out a hand and groped for the mantel, thinking with a terrible wrench of fear, "Moiré!" "Don't be so . . . so damn ridiculous!" he stammered. "My—my father never gambled . . . in all his days!"

"Ah—but that was the trouble, you see, lad. Come now—sit down. I'll send for some brandy. Poor fellow—you are pale as death."

"Devil take the brandy!" Harry stood very straight and, managing somehow to control his voice, demanded, "Tell me what happened. And with no fancy frills, if you please."

The Reverend sat down. Surely the boy would not strike him if he was sitting down . . . "I want you to know," he

19

began earnestly, "that I investigated with the greatest of care, for it seemed so foreign to my brother-in-law's character. Colin was not seen in Church as frequently as I would have wished. But I do not believe he was a gamester, and a more devoted husband and—"

"Dammit!" Harry exploded. "*Will* you come to the point? *What* happened? *When?* And *Where?* And why in God's name was I not told?"

"There is no call to bring the name of our Heavenly Father into so sordid a mat—" Langridge here perceived from Redmond's murderous expression that discretion was the better part of valour, and said a hurried, "Your papa sat down to cards with some other gentlemen, and—"

"Name them!"

"Wh-What? Oh—well, there was Sir Barnaby Schofield, Sprague Cobb, Lord Howard Cootesby, and . . ." Langridge hesitated, slanting an anxious glance at his nephew's white-faced rigidity. "And—M. Parnell Sanguinet." Harry's scowl, which had deepened with the first name, did not waver and, stifling a sigh of relief, the Reverend ventured, "Fine gentlemen, all."

That was true of the first three, thought Harry. He knew nothing of Sanguinet, but Cobb was often in White's, and Cootesby—although something of a hermit—had a splendid military record. Barnaby Schofield had been one of his father's closest friends—a fine gentleman indeed, honest to a fault, soft-spoken, courageous, and next to his adored wife had rated Colin Redmond highest in his affections. Had anything been wrong, good old Barney would have put a stop to it at once. "Go on, if you please, sir," he said frigidly, feeling as though the ground was being cut away from beneath him.

"Yes . . ." muttered the unhappy cleric. "Well, as I said, Colin became very—er—inebriated— I am sorry, Harry! But I *swear* it is so!"

"The hell it is!" snarled Redmond. "My father seldom drank heavily!"

"I know—but, dear boy—they all testified—"

"Then they lied, damn them! They were likely bosky themselves, and—"

"Lord Belmont was not bosky," Langridge interposed desperately. "He is one of the finest surgeons in London, you will admit. His examination proved your papa to have been very drunk, and he swore at the Hearing, that—"

"*Hearing?*" Harry fairly pounced on the word. "*What* Hearing?"

Langridge moistened suddenly dry lips and croaked, "The Hearing I demanded. As—as your papa's representative."

"My papa's *representative*," Harry thundered, "was *me*! Why in the devil, sir, was *I* not called?"

Groaning, the Reverend left his chair and began to wander distractedly up and down. "If you but *knew* how I strove with my conscience! It—it all happened so fast, dear lad. You were barely recovered from a long and painful illness, and had already suffered one relapse. When word came of your papa's . . . death . . ." He drew a hand across his sweating brow. "I feared that alone was enough to send you into a final decline! Had you learned about—about his losses, as well!" He shook his head, his eyes fastened pleadingly upon his nephew's livid face.

Harry uttered a clipped, "I should not have shouted at you. I collect you meant . . ." How could he say the man had meant 'well' . . ? He felt choked with rage and grief but, unwilling to abuse his uncle's calling by resorting to the barracks-room language he was burning to indulge, instead rasped, "Be so kind as to tell me what transpired at this alleged Hearing from which my father's sons were barred."

"Harry—do not . . !" beseeched Langridge. "Your regimental surgeon and Dr. MacBride both said you were in no condition to withstand such a double shock. Mitchell was under age and, besides would certainly have told you. Be reasonable."

Reasonable! Were he reasonable he'd likely choke the life from this blundering, addlepated doddipoll! Harry closed his lips tightly over a boiling response, but reading his expression correctly, Langridge stepped back a pace and went on miserably, "I have no doubt that is why poor

Colin had the . . . accident. You will recall how he would sometimes attempt to jump the stream at the wall beside the old ruins. So foolhardy . . . When he—went down, his hunting rifle was fully loaded on the saddle, and—but you already know that part.''

"To my sorrow. Let us have the part I do *not* know, if you please.''

Flinching to the brittle tone, Langridge responded, "Each of the gentlemen who took part in the game was called upon. And they each testified under oath that at the time of the play my brother-in-law was very foxed. That they sought to prevent him from continuing, but even Schofield's efforts were in vain.'' Harry interjected a low and scornful, "What gammon!'' but the Reverend swept on, "Finally, Monsieur Sanguinet was the only other player. Your papa lost heavily. He tried to recoup, and put up first his ring . . . then his horses. And finally,'' he shrugged helplessly. "Everything. Moiré . . . all the furnishings . . . the acreage and farm . . . the carriages . . . Everything!''

His world crashing about him, Harry rasped, "Where was this game? And when?''

"At Sanguinet Towers. It is in Kent, near Chatham. And the game was on the very night of his death. He—he was, in fact, on his way . . . home.''

Harry swung away, strode to the fireplace and, resting clenched fists on the mantel, for an instant bowed his head between them. He could well imagine his beloved father's state of mind. Probably, utterly distraught, he'd ridden too fast . . . too hard . . . To have taken that devilish jump when even a trifle foxed must have been fatal—even without the rifle. He wrenched his head up. "I never,'' he growled loyally, turning back once more, "heard such a stupid lot of damned gibberish in my entire life! You knew my father! Yet you would have me believe this?''

"Not *me*, Harry. The gentlemen who were there! Would you dispute the word of Barnaby Schofield?''

And there it was. The immovable object. Barney Schofield—his unimpeachable honour the *force majeur* against which none could argue nor hope to prevail. "I'll sure as hell hear it from *him*! And even, sir, do I accept this poppycock—which I do not!—How is it that for *eighteen months* I have heard not one whisper of it? A conspiracy of silence?" He saw at once from his uncle's downcast eyes and drooping shoulders that this was the case and, striding to confront him, raged, "You must have been totally shatter-brained, by God! Oh, I can understand your original motivation. But to continue keeping it from us was little short of criminal!"

"Criminal!" Flushing hotly, the Reverend looked up and blustered, "I did the best I knew how! I sought Divine Guidance! And," he added, in an effort to strengthen his backers, "I discussed it with your aunt!" He saw Harry's lip curl and, knowing what he was thinking, went on frantically, "My dear boy! Do not think badly of me. Truly, I longed to be able to bring you about. Oh, if you but *knew* how I struggled to keep things afloat somehow—through all your extravagances!"

Harry riposted savagely, "Had we known where we stood, our 'extravagances' would have been curbed!"

Langridge gave a helpless gesture and bowed his head into his hands. Watching him in wrathful silence, Harry knew that he himself was also much to blame. Colin Redmond had established the Trust with Langridge as Executor, when Harry was believed killed after Ciudad Rodrigo, Mitchell then having been under age. Once the first shock of his father's death was past, Harry had several times discussed the dissolution of the Trust with Crosby Frye, but the solicitor had always some plausible excuse for delay. The 'end of the quarter,' or the 'close of the fiscal year' or such impressive nonsense. All faradiddles, he now apprehended, to keep him from learning the truth. He should have pushed harder, but in his heart he had suspected his uncle derived some sense of importance from administering the Trust. On the one occasion he had mentioned having it set aside, Aunt Wilhelmina had observed caustically that he should do so at once, adding, "else you and your brother may find yourselves badly dipped by reason of your uncle's 'expertise'." Poor old Maude had looked so crushed he'd not had the heart to persist with the matter, and like a total fool had let it ride. A fine mess his compassion had landed them in! A disaster not only for himself but for Mitch! Squirming under that knowledge, he demanded, "If my father lost all our funds, how were you able to keep us going? Are we in your debt, also?"

"I—I used your grandmama's legacy, which was not affected."

"Good God! So that is gone . . . too . . !"

"M. Sanguinet has, I must say, been all consideration," Langridge offered placatingly. "He was in no hurry to take what was—rightfully his. He had constantly to be out of England on diplomatic affairs, and—"

"And so you stood by and allowed Mitchell and me to go our merry way while our inheritance, our home, all we had in the world was snatched away! And we doing *nothing* to preserve what we might from the wreckage! Did it not occur to you that as his sons we had the right to conduct our own investigation into the reasons behind our father's death? How in the devil can we discover the facts behind that damned game at this late date? Can you not see that your well-meant idiocy has effectively prevented us from finding out *anything*?"

The Reverend edged back fearfully from this wild-eyed rage. "Do but th-think, dear boy! The—the awful *scandal*! We *must* think of—the Family!"

"*Scandal?*" Harry exploded, his eyes slits of passion. "*Scandal*—is it? Now if I do not take you by the throat and—"

The Reverend gave a gasp. Sure he was about to be murdered, he folded his hands and stood his ground. He was shaking violently, but somewhere within him was a measure of courage whereby, although his head was bowed, he was enabled to utter a fairly steady, "I so prayed that this moment would not come until Mitchell was finished at Oxford. I sought only to spare you more pain—when you had endured so much. I know you think me a . . . a weak and stupid . . . man. And it is true that I shrank from—

24

from telling you all this, but . . ." His voice broke. He looked up, his face working, the gleam of tears on his cheeks, and, throwing both arms wide, pleaded, "Harry . . . as God is my judge . . . I only meant for the best. I do—*truly* . . . love you both. Forgive me, I beg you. Forgive me . . !"

"Damn you!" groaned Harry. "*Damn* you! How *could* you be so . . . stupid?" But he threw his arms around the Reverend Mordecai, shawl, nightcap, and all.

And never dreamed that the last truth had still been kept from him.

The rain was sheeting down now, drumming on the roof to fill the voids between drowsy bursts of conversation in the old tavern, and driving impatient fingers against the casement windows as the gusting wind shifted. Making her way past the locals, the barmaid carried a glass of brandy to the settle close beside the great hearth and eyed the sprawled and solitary occupant curiously. The handsome young Corinthian had caught her eye when he'd first come in. He had paused an instant on the threshold, creating a dramatic picture, his dark hair wet and windblown, the many capes of his long driving coat whipping about him, his white, drawn face illumined by such vivid green eyes. He'd stalked to the fireplace without a word, ignoring the cheery greeting of the proprietor and the respectful nods of the men gathered about the bar, and had scarcely moved since, his shoulders motionless against the settle, one hand loosely clasping his glass, long and exquisitely booted legs thrust out before him, chin sunk on his chest, and brooding gaze fixed on the flames. Occasionally, as she'd approached he had held up his glass, but although she had replaced it several times, he gave no sign of becoming 'up in the world'.

She had stopped before him and now blushed as he lifted his head at last to look up at her. The despair in those narrow eyes was replaced by bewilderment. "Where the—?" Harry broke off and in response to the instinctive sympathy that had crept into the girl's comely face leaned to take the glass and smile, "Where is this place, m'dear?"

"Why, it be 'The Dirty Drummer,' in Kensington, sir." And his smile winning her, she asked, "Be ye lost, my lord?"

"Neither lost not yet a lord." Harry took out his watch and discovered it to be half past nine o'clock. He declined the girl's suggestion of a cozy room for the night, and when she disappointedly warned him that there were many on the bridle lay 'twixt here and Lun'on, assured her that any member of the High Toby would regret having stopped him. He then called up a plate of cold beef and fresh-baked bread and, while he ate, considered the results of his long battle with despair. Mostly his thoughts turned on his father. He could recall so well his own return from Spain. Through the long weeks that he'd been confined to bed, not one day had passed but that the vibrant man had dropped in for a little while—often a great while—always brightening the sickroom with his presence. He had been full of plans. Mitchell, of course, must finish his studies. Harry and his father would care for the estate. Moiré Grange was a fine old seat surrounded by two square miles of parkland and woods, and Sir Colin had intended to turn much of this acreage to more profitable account. Smiling nostalgically into his mug of coffee, Harry could all but see that intense face, the eagerness in the fine eyes, the love that reached out to say, "I need you, my son. You and I shall accomplish this—together." Scarcely the man to fritter away the home they loved—all their hopes for the future, and merely on the turn of a card! Colin Redmond had loathed cards, such a pursuit constituting a total waste of time in the opinion of so energetic a man. It was wrong! the whole damnable thing was—

"We do be closing now, if it please y'r honour . . ."

The innkeeper was bowing beside him. Shocked at how time had slipped away, Harry paid his shot, was assisted into his still-damp coat, and soon rode through the stormy night once more.

Oblivious to cold, wind, and rain, his mind returned to his problems. He was ruined, no doubt of that. From what old Maude had said, he'd be lucky to be able to raise sufficient lettuce for Mitch to remain at Oxford until he took his degree. Somehow it *must* be done. And the Italian trip was a necessity also, for Mitch was definitely down pin, though he'd never admit it. Harry's lips tightened in the darkness. The knowledge of their disaster must be kept from him or he'd be out of the University within a week. Old Mitch felt things so very intensely—never had forgiven himself for that stupid accident at Moiré. And it had been no more his fault than—

The blasting roar of a gunshot deafened him. Lace reared with a scream of fright. A less notable horseman must have been thrown. As it was, his lithe, loose-limbed body swaying to counter the mare's frenzy, Harry pulled her down and stared in astonishment at the dark figure blocking the road ahead. Dim, but unmistakable, a large pistol was aimed squarely at his heart.

A coarse voice barked, "Stand and deliver!" the time-honoured words followed by a faint but continuing sound, reminiscent of the whistling of an ostler while currying a horse.

"Deliver what?" Harry demanded indignantly, his hand caressing the neck of the nervously dancing Lace.

It was an unfamiliar response and the highwayman, obviously taken aback, echoed, ". . . what . . . ? Why, you blasted well knows, damn yer ears! Now fork over the dibs! Smart like! Or I'll 'ave yer 'eart out!"

"Devil I will! I cannot afford it!"

The whistling hiss came to an abrupt stop. Recovering his shaken sensibilities, the highwayman leaned forward, brandishing his pistol threateningly. "Look 'ere! I got this 'ere pop! You blind or something?"

"No, but you fired it," Harry pointed out. "Rather spoils your threat, you know. Wherefore . . ." He bowed and started Lace on her way.

"*And*—I got *this 'n*!" cried the highwayman, revealing a second pistol.

Harry had suspected as much, which was why he'd not grabbed for his own weapon. For an instant he was silent, the highwayman watching him smugly and whistling faintly through his teeth. "In that case," Harry decided, "I can waste no more time with your nonsense!" Saying which, he applied the spurs hard to Lace's wet sides. It was a measure to which he seldom resorted. Already nervous, she shot forward and the astounded highwayman, instinctively swinging his mount clear of the charging mare, was thus put off his mark.

Bowed low in the saddle, Harry heard a deafening roar. The ball whipped through the hair beside his right ear and a scream of profanity arose from the frustrated member of the High Toby. "You're crazy is what! Don'tcha know better'n to ride at a cocked barker? You just wait me fine bucko! I'll teacher 'ow to behave with Devil Dice! I'll getcher yet!"

Devil Dice! Harry's brows shot up. A narrow escape, indeed! That villain was fond of shooting his victims once he had robbed them, having explained to several onlookers that he never shot first if he could help it because he didn't like to mess up his valuables! Patting Lace's neck, Harry conveyed his apologies for his harsh treatment, then sent her galloping towards the lights of the distant city. Recalling Dice's threat, he smiled grimly. If the affronted highwayman ever did come up with him in the future, he'd probably garner very little for his trouble . . .

"But—you must have been up at the crack of dawn!" exclaimed Mitchell, considerably astonished as he eyed the fat roll of flimsies in his hand. He lifted his curious gaze to his brother, seated across the table from him in the small, sunlit breakfast parlour.

Harry shrugged, allowed Anderson to pour him another cup of coffee, then nodded to the grim-faced man to leave them. "Had to get some cash for my own journey," he said easily. "Jolly good of Harland to invite me to Paris; although I suppose the old boy's lonely, now that Lucian's gone."

"I'd thought Moulton was going with him." Mitchell frowned down at the roll of bills. "Wouldn't a bank draft have been more—"

"Gad, no!" Harry stirred his coffee briskly, then dropped

28

his hand into his lap, hoping Mitch hadn't noticed he was not wearing his signet ring which, together with several other articles of value, had been purchased by a shrewd jeweller. "After that last mix-up with my draft, I thought it simpler for you to take the cash with you. *Please* do not leave it in the chaise! There is sufficient for the balance of the term, and for your trip to Italy."

"I'd no idea you meant to see Harland yesterday . . . in addition to Maude." The grey eyes lifted once more to fix his brother with that troubled stare. "How is poor old Maude? I really *should* like to have gone with you, *Sauvage*."

"Oh—you know Maude." Harry's pulse began to accelerate, but he chuckled, "I wish you *had* been there! He wore the most dashing nightcap and shawl I ever saw."

"Poor old fellow . . ." Mitchell tightened the roll of flimsies and dropped it into his purse. "So you go to Paris with the Earl of Harland—and I am rushed back to my studies . . ."

"By God, you young whelp, but you're getting uppity! One would think *I* was the younger!"

Mitchell eyed his feigned resentment for a moment, and then said with a shy twinkle, "Sometimes, I think you are . . ."

Fearing that his absent-minded scholar might wind up in Shanghai rather than Oxford, Harry hired a post chaise to return him to the University. He walked out to the flagway with him, reminded him patiently whither he was bound, asked to see his purse, and then sent Anderson into the house to search for it. The family fortune was discovered reposing in the hearth, where Mitchell had apparently laid it while pulling on his boots. With a few fond remarks anent the possibility of having it chained to the end of his brother's slim nose, Harry closed the door of the chaise, nodded to the postboy, and waved him off.

For some moments after the vehicle had rounded the corner, Harry still stood on the steps staring after it. If he joined up, there was no telling how long it might be before he saw the young cub again . . . Mitchell had seemed totally unaware, fortunately, of the fact that their handshake had been more prolonged than usual, and must have been astonished had he known how close his brother had come to sweeping him into his arms for a proper farewell.

Dear old Mitch . . .

Heavy hearted, Harry went back into the house.

CHAPTER III

THE NEXT FEW DAYS PASSED IN A FEVER OF ACTIVITY. Informing his dismayed servants that he intended to travel abroad for several years, Harry instructed a worried Anderson to dispose of all the furniture, and a glum Jed Cotton to sell the horses he kept in London, plus his curricle and chaise. He himself repaired to the office of an extremely disdainful Crosby Frye, who professed himself no longer interested in handling Sir Harry's affairs but condescended to grant him a short interview. There was, he imparted frostily, no slightest chance to dispute the outcome of the card game at this late date. Further, M. Sanguinet was now in England and would be more than justified in taking immediate possession of the property he had won eighteen months previously. Did Sir Harry have bills of sale or receipts that might be acceptable in a Court of Law, he should unearth them at once and present them to M. Sanguinet's man of business, or his bailiff. "Devil I will!" raged Harry, thrown into a fury. "My brother's and my own belongings will be removed from the Grange whether the curst Frenchman likes it or not! And if he don't like it, I'll show the fella my Mantons by way of a bill of sale!"

When Anderson and Jed Cotton had discharged their tasks in Town, Harry sent Major Domo and Head Groom next to Moiré to convey his horses by easy stages to Tattersall's. They also distributed the letters that he had directed to each of the servants. Anderson returned with word that most of the staff had packed up and departed the Grange that same day, but the butler—who had been at Moiré when Colin Redmond was a child—would await Sir Harry's arrival, as would one or two other long-time retainers. Of M. Sanguinet or his bailiff there had been no sign, a state of affairs Redmond could only pray would continue until after his final removal from the old house.

Between the sale of his belongings and hunters, Sir Harry now found himself able to cover his few debts and bestow a generous amount upon each member of the staff of his Town house. His farewell to Mrs. Thomas was miserable, but vowing he'd given her enough to keep her comfortable for a year, that steadfast lady declared she would stay with her sister in Mitcham and wait until dear Sir Harry came to fetch her.

Next morning, glancing around at the two valises and three portmanteaux packed and ready in his now-empty bedchamber, Redmond marshalled his rather tattered nerves and summoned Sergeant Anderson. It was of no use, he knew, to employ his 'foreign travels' tale. Andy knew better. Therefore, to an extent he told the truth. His father had invested in a venture that had failed disastrously. All their possessions had been swept away in the resultant chaos. He himself was returning to the military, but had made provision for Anderson to enter the service of the Marquis of Damon at Cancrizans Priory. "You know Lord Damon," he smiled. "Poor fellow was living like a hermit, but now he's about to be married and must spruce up the old place. I shall rely upon you, Andy, to give him all the assistance you can."

Anderson took up Redmond's best beaver and, brushing it carefully murmured, "We going back to the old 43rd, sir? I could easy get—"

"Dammit, man! You do *not* go with me! I may not be *able* to get in! They're cutting back the Army, you know, now that the war's over. You must fend for yourself." A gaze of such injured reproach was then turned upon him that he cried, "Oh, gad! Do not look at me as though I had sprouted serpents' teeth! I cannot *pay* you—you clunching looby!''

''Sorta like a bank account, it'll be,'' grinned the Sergeant, undaunted. ''You hang onter me wages 'til you *can* pay me then—''

''Blast you! *Will* you get it through your thick skull that I am discharging you? I do not need a major domo! Andy—'' he put out his hand, his face suddenly haggard. ''My good friend, I—''

''Cor!'' ejaculated the Sergeant. ''Lookit that! Don't need a man, indeed! Helpless as a newborn babe you'd be without me!'' Evading Redmond's hand, he straightened the immaculate sleeve and tidied the lace cuff beneath it.

Furious because his eyes were growing dim, Harry swung roughly away. Anderson's face fell and he watched the broad shoulders with an expresson it was as well his much-tried employer did not see.

''I am deeply appreciative,'' Harry said gruffly, ''of your loyalty. In the event my finances improve I shall certainly take you back into my service. But meanwhile—'' he turned short about, ''I have told the Marquis you will go down to Dorset, and a post chaise has been ordered for eleven o'clock. You had best pack whatever you will need.''

Anderson, stretching out one hand appealingly, begged, ''But—sir . . .''

''That is an *order*, Sergeant!''

Anderson snapped to attention. ''Orl right, Captain! I'll go. And I'll ride the post chaise what you had *no business* a'calling up seein's we're going to have to practice strict economies from here on out! When I'm done with his lordship, I'll come back. Tomorrer. On the Accommodation Coach!'' Saying which, he tossed a sharp salute and thumped his way out.

Looking after him, torn between tears and laughter, Harry groaned, ''Oh . . . hell . . !''

He ate lunch alone in the kitchen, that being the only room having a table, then wandered back into the quiet saloon. Staring down at the rich carpet, he decided to start for Moiré immediately and put up at ''The Silk Purse'' overnight. As soon as Norrie, their old nurse, was snug somewhere, he'd remove his belongings and Mitchell's and dump them at the Priory, or at his cousin Whitthurst's house in Kent. Then he'd be free to track down the gentlemen who'd participated in that fateful card game. He'd seek out Schofield first, of course. He frowned. What in the deuce *was* he to do with Norrie? Papa had given her a cottage on the grounds of Moiré, for the balance of her life. But now—

"Bonjour, amicus, humani generis . . ." Camille Damon limped in from the kitchen, and with only the lift of one black brow to express his surprise at the bare room, disposed his elegant self in a window seat.

"Blast you, Cam," said Redmond with a show of indignation. He crossed to pour his friend a glass of the excellent brandy he'd placed on a tray in the empty bookcase. "I've troubles enough deciphering your French! To pair it with Latin just ain't fair!" Camille, widely held to be the most handsome man in London, merely flashed his brilliant grin and held up his glass in a silent toast. Joining him, Harry asked, "Why am I the 'friend of the human race'?"

"Because, dear my *Capitaine*, I am in a—er—spot of difficulty. You can assist, will you be so kind, by selling back to me your shares in the Spa of the Swallows."

Lord Damon was the major stockholder in the spa, now a thriving success. But it was unlikely he was being pressured into acquiring more shares. Knowing which, Harry exploded, "The whiskers you tell! You're as bad as ever, Cam! I wonder my cousin Sophia dare contemplate a lifetime with you!"

The Marquis's rich laugh greeted this sally, but during the ensuing conversation he sensed that Harry's trouble was not to be shared, and understanding that some things may only be handled personally, did not press the point. He agreed to provide a place for Anderson, and enquired blandly whether Harry might be aware of a motherly type of woman who would consent to remove to the spa. "We need," he said, apparently unaware of Redmond's searching gaze, "such a lady to assist guests with small indispositions."

Whatever he might suspect, Harry could only gratefully suggest his former nurse—on a temporary basis. Damon gave every appearance of delight and begged she be urged to consider the position. Having refilled his lordship's glass, Harry rested his hand for a brief instant on the peerlessly clad shoulder of this man who had himself known too well the depths of despair and loneliness. Camille looked up at him. It was a look that spoke volumes and, turning away, Harry felt humbled and asked huskily, "During your wanderings about the Continent, did you ever hear of a chap named Sanguinet?"

The glass that was idly turned between the Marquis's strong fingers became suddenly motionless, the clear eyes very still. "To my sorrow," he drawled. "Matter of fact, he's one of the fellows I called out. Do you speak of Guy?"

"No. How many are there?"

"*Trois*. Claude, Parnell, and Guy. I called out the youngest."

Damon's marksmanship was legendary, wherefore Harry enquired if the remaining Sanguinets sought vengeance. With a faint smile Damon said that Guy had refused to meet him. "Did he, by Jove!" Harry gasped. "Yellow?"

"*Mon dieu*—no! He said that he had no intention of committing suicide so as to oblige me. We therefore settled the matter with a target shooting match. I would be happy to report he was at once dropped by the *ton*, as you obviously suppose. I gather you know little of the breed. Attend me, *mon cher*. Few men would dare give a Sanguinet the cut direct. Are you, by some unhappy chance, involved with one?"

"Parnell." And Harry added eagerly, "Nasty?"

Without a trace of amusement, Damon answered, "They call him M. Diabolique. And with excellent reason."

"Drunk as a duck!" The familiar tones brought Harry swinging around to run back down the stairs. "I resent that, Jerry," he grinned, proceeding to shake hands with his lifelong comrade. "What the devil are you doing here?"

"Come t'tell you I'll take Cotton into my service, as

you asked." Lord Jeremy Bolster tossed hat, cane, and gloves onto the window seat Damon had vacated some twenty minutes earlier and, sitting beside his belongings, ran a hand through his straight yellow hair. "Hear you're off to Paris. D-dashed good idea. London's positively bare of company! Mandy's in Brussels with Lucinda Carden . . ." Mention of his beloved brought worry to cloud his eyes briefly, but he went on as blithely as ever, "Cameron's been posted to Dundee; St. Clair's off honeymooning; Vaughan and Saxon are in Vienna. Blasted desert. I'll go with you, Harry, dear old boy."

Redmond thought a horrified, "Lord!" They knew each other like brothers and had few secrets, this making it the more difficult to lie, "Wish you could, but it's an invite, y'see. And they wouldn't—it's no one you—ah—know."

"Oh." Bolster took up one of his gloves, inspected it, and, his pleasant features guileless, murmured, "Ain't nothing wrong, is there? I m-mean . . ." He poked all the fingers of the glove inside out while stammering, "If you ever n-n-needed help, you w-w-w you'd come to me . . . I trust?"

"Naturally—you cawker!" Harry turned to the window and, looking rather blindly into the grey afternoon, asked, "Shall you go to Newmarket?"

There was no reply. He glanced around. Bolster was standing and removing his jacket. His face was angry, a determined light in the hazel eyes. "Been f-f-friends a long time, Harry," he said quietly. "Don't expect whiskers. Sorry—but . . ." He started to roll up his sleeves.

It was an odd demonstration of loyalty, but it was Jeremy. And perhaps for the first time the enormity of his personal disaster broke upon Redmond. For the first time he faced the fact that there would be no more pleasant gatherings with friends at White's or Waiter's; no evenings at Drury Lane, or Ranalegh, or Vauxhall; no more riding to hounds, or summer boat parties and picnics: No improvements at Moiré Grange—in fact, no Moiré Grange! His entire way of life was vanishing forever. Henceforth, he would be a man alone, and near destitute. He sat on the window seat and bowed his head.

"Here . . ." The kindly voice seemed very far away but recalled him to his surroundings. Bolster, his expression grave, proffered a glass of cognac. Very red in the face, Harry gasped, "Good God, Jerry! Your pardon! I just—er—"

"Clodpole!" said Bolster unequivocally. "Drink your damned wine, and—tell me about it."

So he did. He changed a few of the essential details, but basically he told the truth. When he finished, Bolster glared at him. "If I'd be-be-be-acted like that, you'd have punched my head!"

"Yes," admitted Redmond humbly. "Likely I would."

"Roses," Bolster observed after a short silence, "don't grow on cabbages."

Harry looked at him blankly.

"Your papa," Bolster clarified. "Very fine g-gentleman. Dashed f-fond of him, y'know. Wouldn't have done it. It's very mingle-mangled, Harry. We'll simply have to get to the b-b b-b—we'll have to come to the root of it."

"The Silk Purse" was a charming old hedge tavern midway between Guildford and Godalming. The proprietor, a proud veteran of the 95th Rifles, was an old friend of Redmond's, both having served with the peerless Light Division, and Harry invariably broke his journey here en route to or from Moiré. On this brilliant May morning he emerged from the inn with slow and laggard step, heedless of the fragrance of the roses that bloomed about the door; of fluffy clouds sailing in a deep blue sky; the cheerful cackling of the hens scratching in the yard; or the saucy glance of a milkmaid, foaming pails a'swing from the yoke across her dimpled shoulders. He came to a halt and stood stubbing one splendidly shod toe at the dust, lost in thought.

Bolster's words of yesterday kept coming to mind . . . "Your Papa—very fine gentleman . . . Wouldn't have done it." Jerry was right, for it made no sense. But what made even less sense was the motive. Behind every cheating hand at a game of chance was the lure of money. Yet, having won a rich prize, Sanguinet had made no least attempt to claim his spoils and had allowed a year and a half to drift by, having apparently not even bothered to view the property he now owned. Such generosity was unheard of! The uneasy suspicion dawned on Redmond that he might well be faced by a gentleman so kind as to have deliberately held back from causing him more grief. It would be a trifle difficult to blow his head off were that the—

A rapid tattoo of hooves broke through his reverie. An ostler was attempting to hold Lace, but she had glimpsed her beloved master and was frisking about with much flirting of ears and rolling of eyes. "Lace!" called Harry. "Quiet, girl!" At once she was motionless. Grinning, the ostler looped the reins over the pommel and stood with arms folded, watching. For a minute they stood like so many statues, then Harry whistled sharp and clear. The mare tossed her head, galloped to him, and circled daintily to stand behind him, her velvety muzzle whuffling at his left ear. Laughing, he swung into the saddle, then leaned forward to stroke the glossy arched neck.

Applause surprised him. Three carriages had slowed in the lane to watch the little byplay. Handkerchiefs waved from the windows and several pretty faces smiled upon them. Harry bowed theatrically, doffing his hat and urging the well-trained mare into an equine bow that won more clapping. Straightening, he froze, his attention riveted upon one window and the vision who leaned from the shadowed interior to smile upon him. He viewed the face of an angel. The fur-lined hood of her pelisse draped softly over hair as pale as morning sunlight, the gleaming tendrils curling about delicate features and an exquisitely fair and clear complexion. Her nose was small, shapely, and only very slightly uptilting; her mouth a rosebud above a dimpled little chin. The sweetly proportioned forehead was adorned by finely arched brows, subtly darkened, and the eyes— never had there been such eyes . . . large and blue as cornflowers in that bewitching face. She said something, and although he was too stunned to distinguish the words, he knew that her voice was sweet and pure as the notes of a nightingale. And then a soft pink flooded those dewy cheeks, her lashes swept down shyly, she drew back and was lost in the shadows as the coach pulled away.

For a moment Harry was too stunned to move. Recovering his wits, he attempted to follow, only to be thwarted by the arrival of a noisy group of young Bucks. They had been a nuisance during the night, and now crowded around Lace, their drunken and loud-voiced admiration hampering his efforts to escape. When at last he was able to elude them, he turned the mare onto the lane and galloped in pursuit of the carriages. It was a good three miles before he came up with them, but at last they were ahead. As he drew closer, the coachman looked around with obvious apprehension, then grinned and slowed a trifle, and Harry waved his gratitude. He came up with the window, hat in hand and eyes eager. Inside, he could see smiling young ladies and, closest to the window, the object of his admiration, turned slightly away, her hood concealing her features.

"Ma'am . . ." called Harry brazenly, "may a gentleman offer a gift to a lady whose name he does not know . . . ?"

The concealing hood was turned shyly towards him, but still he could not see her face. The other girls, far from appearing shocked by this outrageous impudence, seemed vastly amused and, encouraged, he beseeched, "Have pity, fair one . . . your name—I beg . . . See—I bring you something lovely . . ." He tossed the large pink rose he had gathered (at the expense of a thorn in his thumb), through the window, ". . . though it hasn't an iota of your loveliness." She took up the rose—he saw her little hand reach for it, and urged Lace closer in an attempt to see her countenance. "My Fair—forgive me, but . . . I . . ." He faltered into silence. She looked up at last and thus revealed far different features than those he so longed to see. A small face, with wisps of dark hair straggling untidily about it; eyes hopelessy crossed; and a mouth that hung open in a lunatic lack of comprehension as she gazed dully at him. The shock was a near physical thing, like a blow to the midriff. He knew his jaw had dropped; he knew those wretched girls were all but hysterical. With a tremendous effort he recovered himself. He must not allow his revulsion to become apparent. By her plain round gown of coarse dark blue stuff, he guessed her to be an abigail. Poor creature—how cruel of them to serve her so! He waved his hat and said merrily, "Alas—that you show no mercy to a poor swain! Ride safely, my Fair!" and slowing Lace's smooth canter, tried not to hear the squeals of mirth that came from the rapidly departing carriage.

Staring after them, his smile vanished, leaving his pleasant face rather grim. Those girls should be spanked! But—perhaps it was as well, for what was the use of pursuing that golden vision? He was possessed of neither fortune nor expectations. He was, in fact, the kind of man hopeful mamas would dub a fortune hunter and instruct their daughters to avoid like the plague! That peerless little beauty was undoubtedly en route to Town—perhaps to be presented at the next Drawing Room. The lateness of the Season would be no deterrent to such as she, and many a lucky Corinthian and Buck would worship at her shrine before she'd been in London a week. He turned Lace back towards the "Silk Purse," smiling wistfully at the thought of the consternation the lady's arrival must cause among Almack's debutantes. How he'd love to see it . . .

The wind came up while they were still in the coffee room, and by the time they were journeying up the last hill, Bolster was very depressed. He was fond of Moiré Grange, his memories of the old place going back as far as memory served him. Harry seemed to be taking it well enough, but aware that his feelings must be harrowing at this moment, Bolster glanced at his friend uneasily.

Harry drew rein at the top of the hill and sat perfectly still. Why did one never really appreciate anything until it was lost? He let his eyes travel slowly along the winding path of the river, past the lodge gates, through the pleasant park, and around the foot of the low rise whereon stood the house itself. Even on this grey morning the spreading half-timbered old building looked warm and welcoming, with smoke drifting from several chimneys. The wind stirred the trees and riffled the surface of the river, and the ducks and mudhens darted busily about. The flower beds were bright with daffodil and hyacinth; the shrubs ablaze with yellow, pink, and white. His gaze lingered on the enormous and venerable oak shading the library and Mitchell's room, from whose branches so many impromptu swings had swung. How many tree houses it had supported . . . how many Redmonds had it seen come and go . . .

Bolster asked mildly, ''Ain't that Old Joseph?''

Harry blinked, and his jaw hardened. The butler's head was white now, but he was not too frail to put up a good struggle against the stocky man who sought to thrust him down the hill. Even as they watched, Joseph staggered and fell, and the other man tossed a valise after him, made a show of dusting off his hands, and started back toward the house.

''Jeremy,'' said Redmond. ''D'you recall that fat damn Spaniard in Cádiz?''

''Yoicks!'' cried Bolster joyfully.

Side by side, they thundered down the hill. In a blaze of speed the bay mare and the grey gelding raced up the rise and were upon the stocky man even as he turned a startled face to them. Two splendid horsemen leaned down. Two strong hands grasped.

'' 'Ey!'' howled the stocky one, legs thrashing at the air.

''Put that man down''' bellowed an infuriated voice from the front door.

They obliged at once, and their burden soared, screeching, from their mutually relinquished hold, to splash into the river. Two laughing young faces turned to one another; two hats were doffed; two heads, one golden, one dark, bowed low.

''Wot the 'ell d'ye think you're blasted well a'doing of?'' roared the individual in the doorway.

Harry dismounted and led Lace toward his butler, who had scrambled to his feet.

"Sir Harry . . ." gasped Joseph, eyes glistening suspiciously. "I am so very glad . . . to . . ." He broke off as Redmond's hand went out and, gripping it firmly, could not continue.

"I know, old friend," said Harry gently. "It don't look too bright just now. But you must not—"

"I said," yowled that irate voice, now almost upon them. "Wot the 'ell—"

"Be quiet!" frowned Lord Bolster. "Sir Harry is talking to his butler. Are you blind, fellow?"

"*Fellow?* 'Ere! 'Oo you callin' of a fellow?"

Harry turned, smiling faintly. A large individual wearing a much-too-tight jacket and a waistcoat that could not begin to cover his ample paunch regarded him balefully. "Bolster," he said curiously, "What d'ye suppose it is?"

The heavy features darkened, but into that small mind had crept a familiar name, and from crouching slightly as he made toward Harry he checked, straightened, and said a cautious, "Bolster . . . ?"

"It knows me!" cried Bolster, ecstatic. "I am f-famous, Harry!"

"I s'pose as you're Lord Bolster. In which case, *you* must be Sir 'Arry Redmond, wot useter own this old ruinated—"

"I have neither the desire nor the time to further our acquaintance." Harry's voice dripped ice. "Remove yourself and that person." He gestured toward the river bank up which the stocky man crawled with much spluttering.

"Can't do that, sir. Josiah Plum—Mr. Sanguinet's bailiff, I is. Come ter clean out the old broken down—"

A distant scream rose on the chill air. Harry returned to the saddle with a running leap that brought admiration to Mr. Plum and alarm to Bolster, who had just dismounted. Lace was whirled about and Harry was off at the gallop, Bolster rather tardily following.

A wagon was pulled up on the lane before Mrs. Norah Bacon's cottage, and two men were filling it with trunks, boxes, and articles of furniture while exhibiting a marked lack of either interest or care. They paused, looking up as the pretty bay mare flashed towards them across the velvet turf. "Cor . . ." breathed one. "Lookit him go!"

Harry continued to go, setting Lace at the picket fence without an instant's hesitation, effecting a sliding dismount while the mare yet ran, and leaping with hardly a check into the front hall of the pleasant old cottage.

A tiny woman, clad in a gown of black bombazine with a torn but snowy collar, her white lace cap sadly askew, her silver hair tumbling, clung defiantly to one sturdy beam from which a tall man attempted to dislodge her. Another shriek rent the air, cut off abruptly as Harry, the capes of his coat flying, exploded into the room, launched a right that sent her attacker soaring backwards, and had her in his arms in a whisper of time. "Norrie, dear," he began tenderly.

A strong hand grabbed his shoulder. He was wrenched around and staggered by a left to the jaw. Shaking his head, savage with delight at this opportunity to vent some of his frustrations, he plunged at the two who awaited him confidently. A few moments later, confidence gone, the second man, sprawled and groaning, was so unwise as to raise his head. Mrs. Bacon applied her frying pan to it with gusto, then, surveying the bent handle, murmured, "I never dreamed that wretched pan would be useful. The bottom was warped y'see, my dear Mister—er—Sir Harry. And . . ." Her lip began to tremble. She put down the pan, walked into his arms, and wept.

Lord Bolster rushed into the hall, surveyed the mayhem, scanned his somewhat battered friend, then went outside, closed the door and, leaning against the wall, folded his arms and waited.

Moments later a howl interrupted Harry's explanations to his nurse. He opened the front door hurriedly. His own travelling chaise stood behind the wagon. A new arrival was staggering about, bent double and clutching his middle. Bolster, pale with fury, strove mightily against two men who held his arms. Mr. Plum, reaching for the door handle, jumped back, threw up his hands, and leered, "No trouble, Sir Redmond. We don't want no trouble!"

Mrs. Bacon hurried onto the step and uttered a small cry, one hand flying to her chest. She had suffered a slight heart seizure some years earlier, and Harry knew he must get her out of this. He bit back a pithy response, therefore, and said sharply, "Bolster, don't mess about there! You know perfectly well the Marquis of Damon expects Mrs. Bacon!"

As he'd hoped, the dropping of Camille's famous name was effective. The bullies restraining Bolster let him go, then ducked as he swung on them, brandishing his riding crop furiously. The rest of Norrie's belongings would, Harry assured her, be carefully placed in the wagon, and he would soon deliver them, along with his own, to the Priory. Meanwhile, Lord Bolster would convey her to Cancrizans. There was a small dispute between himself and Mr. Plum as to his appropriation of the chaise, but since the vehicle was plainly marked with his initials, ownership was reluctantly conceded. When Plum triumphantly ordered Monsewer's horse freed from the poles, Jeremy just as triumphantly desired Joseph, who had now come up with them, to assist him in harnessing his fine grey gelding to the chaise. At length, Mrs. Bacon was ushered inside. Harry wrapped a warm travelling rug about her knees, quieted her anxieties with a kiss, sprang down, closed the door, and turned to Bolster.

"Harry," said that worthy in a troubled undervoice. "I don't like leaving you in this damned mess!"

"Get her the devil out of here!" Redmond murmured urgently. "I shall follow you with the wagon just as quickly as I can."

All afternoon Sir Harry strove doggedly against Mr. Plum and his leering sycophants. With the aid of the faithful Joseph, a footman, and a groom who had also refused to leave, the wagon was loaded with the belongings to which he was able to prove ownership. His progress through the house provided excellent entertainment for

Plum and company, who did all possible to harass and impede him, nudging one another, shouting mockery, and howling their amusement. When Harry crossed to the drawing room sideboard to pour a glass of Madeira for himself and his three helpers, a swaggering lout snatched up and deliberately dropped the decanter. The lout was neatly floored for his insult, whereafter the rest of that uncouth crew took care to stay clear of Harry's deadly fists.

In the study, a hurried search through his father's desk brought forth a notepad carefully inscribed with their various birthdates, evoking a pang he could barely hide. A crude comment from one of his tormentors so infuriated him that he wrenched the next drawer too hard. The resultant cascade of papers, old quill pens, broken pencils, and all the litter that accumulates in desk drawers over a period of years added immeasureably to the amusement of his audience. Among the debris, he came upon a packet of letters half under the drawer lining, neatly tied and inscribed by a female hand. Curious, he stuffed them into his pocket.

Shortly after six o'clock, friends of M. Sanguinet began to arrive. An ill-assorted lot, clad in a miscellany of garments ranging from morning clothes to one magnificent fellow in full Ball dress, they prowled the house and engaged in furious altercations over various items of value. Choked with fury, Harry stalked through the uproar, head high, as they wrangled over his father's beloved clocks and miniatures, sterling, china, paintings, and rugs. Watching him with the eyes of love, Joseph fought to emulate that fiercely proud demeanour but stumbled along, barely able to see through his tears.

Sir Harry's intention to depart without further violence almost came to naught when he was forbidden to remove several fine old books Mitchell had purchased from a private library sale the previous summer. The more he argued with the adamant and insulting Plum, the louder and more hilarious grew the comments of the crowd, and he was urged to take his case "to ol' Parnell" at Sanguinet Towers. Through teeth gritted with fury he smiled, "I shall."

Joseph insisted upon driving the wagon, adding his few belongings to the contents, and they departed, profanely bidden adieu by Mr. Plum, his minions, and the guests.

At the top of the hill, Sir Harry drew rein. For a long, aching moment he looked back. Then, without a word, he rode on.

It was cold that evening, the wind moaning through the trees, a new moon peeping occasionally from behind racing clouds and casting shifting shadows across the narrow, deserted road. Lace was fidgety and, having seen Redmond twice glance back, Joseph turned also and voiced the fear that rank riders might be about. He had no sooner uttered the words than one of Harry's travelling pistols flashed into his hand as a horseman galloped after them.

An arm was waved vigorously. "It do be I, sir!"

The footman hove into sight, mounted on his old cob, a carpetbag slung behind the saddle. Thankfully, Harry restored the pistol to his deep pocket. Braggs announced his intention to go with them as far as the Priory, and although Harry was vehement in his protestations, the man said stubbornly, "Give me too much pay you done, sir, and well I knows it. I'll find myself another situation prompt-like with that letter you writ. I owes you more'n this, Sir Harry, so let me help, do!"

Harry was both touched and pleased. He'd had no intention of leaving Joseph alone on the roads with the wagon, but his need to confront the man who had so carelessly allowed his friends to plunder the Grange was a consuming flame. He gave one of his pistols to Braggs and insisted they should pass the night at "The Georgian" where he was well known. Promising the worried Joseph that he would travel to the Priory the following day, he funded them, waved a farewell, and was away at the gallop.

Looking after him, Braggs smiled admiringly, "A reg'lar out'n outer, our Sir Harry, eh Mr. Joseph?"

"Who's about to get his head blown off!" Joseph worried. "I know plenty about the Sanguinets, Braggs. Let me tell you . . . Poison, they are! Poison!"

CHAPTER IV

IT BEGAN TO DRIZZLE SHORTLY AFTER NINE O'CLOCK, AND by eleven was coming down in torrents. Lace was tired, Harry was cold, and the darkness had become so absolute that only his familiarity with the road enabled him to go on. To journey any farther tonight would be folly, but although he was well known in Tunbridge Wells, it appeared there was to be a large wedding on the morrow and that every available hostelry was filled to overflowing with those guests the bride's parents were unable to accommodate. Shivering after his third rejection, Harry made enquiries at the nearest stable, where an obliging ostler directed him " 'fust right, second left, dahn the lane. Missus Burnett's. Can't miss it, guv!" Harry had never been adept at recalling directions; he could and did miss it, and was drenched and half frozen when at last he came upon an inviting looking three-storey house set back from spreading lawns, before which a lantern illumined a swinging, rain-beaded sign that read "Mrs. Burnett's" and beneath this disclosure, "A Refined Boarding House for the Genteel Traveller."

Harry dismounted wearily and bestowed Lace and his instructions for her care, together with a shilling, upon a lad who ran up, poorly protected by a square of sacking. He strode up two steps, across a small porch, and opened the door into a warmly lamplit vestibule giving onto a parlour wherein several people sat about a leaping fire. They looked very genteel, indeed, but the thin and neat little lady behind the desk scrutinized the newcomer from sodden beaver to muddied boots and with folded arms and chilly mien informed him that regrettably she was "Full Up! And—what's more—"

Harry snatched off his hat as she spoke, and now, pushing wet locks back from his brow, said ruefully, "And what's more you run a respectable house and do not take in stray travellers with neither valise nor valet to recommend 'em, eh, ma'am?"

She eyed him warily, but the cut of the coat was awesome; his clumsy efforts had sent his dark hair into wet curls that made him show beguilingly youthful; the deep voice was gentle and cultured, and she liked his wide mouth and the set of his chin. A good deal of the starch had gone out of her voice, therefore, when she said, "S'right, sir!"

"Don't blame you at all, ma'am." He looked wistfully into the parlour, encountering the eyes of no less than six pretty young ladies who had been surveying his tall figure with interest. "My loss, for I can see your establishment is the kind we used to dream of in Spain. Oh, well . . ." He shrugged. "Best be on my way."

Hostility reeled before the full impact of his dazzling smile, and she said feebly, "You'll likely find . . . somewheres . . . sir."

"Not tonight, I'm afraid. Been just about everywhere. Though nowhere as home-like as this." He patted her hand. "Now take that worried look from your pretty eyes. I shall do."

His own green eyes were making Mrs. Burnett's heart beat faster than it had done for many a day and prompting the wish she was twenty years younger. "And—you was in Spain, sir? Oh, my! To send one of our fine young fighting men out on such a night . . ! It do seem downright cruel."

"I've slept under a hedge on many a worse night, I do assure you . . ."

"Hedge!" she cried indignantly. "For a gentleman such as yourself?" She pulled her register closer and, tearing her gaze from his hopeful face, peered at the close-written page. "We must have *something* . . ."

48

Half an hour later, sprawling before the fire that burned brightly in the parlour grate, Harry was almost too weary to pull off his boots. Accomplishing this he settled back, blinking drowsily at the flames and calling down blessings on Mrs. Burnett's head for having discovered that this small suite had just been vacated. A gust of wind sent smoke billowing down the chimney, and the waiter, entering with the tankard of ale he had ordered, observed it was a perishing night. Harry agreed, and expressed his relief that he had been able to find a room. "Did *Mr.* Burnett give you the suite, sir?" the waiter enquired curiously. "I doubt as they've changed the sheets yet." Harry assured him the suite had been allocated by the landlady herself, then desired that his riding coat be cleaned, his shirt and cravat washed and ironed, his beaver dried, and his boots polished. "Better let me take your breeches, too, sir," said the waiter. "All mud, they is." Harry agreed, the waiter accepted his gratuity and, laden with clothing, took himself off.

Despite the fire, Harry's scanty remaining apparel soon reduced him to gooseflesh. He blew out the candle and tottered into the darkened bedroom. He felt no compulsion to search for fleas, but crawled between the sheets and stretched luxuriously. The bedding was adequate, the mattress a soft billow of feathers, the sheets almost perfumed . . .

He awoke with a start. The room was very dark, but he knew suddenly that he was no longer alone. His first thought was of the thieves that were known to haunt hostelries and boardinghouses these days, but then the blankets were pulled back. A sweet fragrance reached his nostrils, and a warm, soft form slid into the bed beside him. Mrs. Burnett's had more to recommend it than he'd dreamed! Delighted, he slipped an arm about her. "Hello, sweetheart," he said by way of welcome.

A smothered shriek rang out. The feminine form struggled frenziedly against his ardent embrace. "Come now," he laughed. "No need to play about, m'dear." Amusement became indignation as nails clawed at him. "I say, now!

That's a bit much!'' His arm tightened. ''What's the difficulty? Wrong gentleman? Well, it's too late now. Here you are, and—''

''Oooh! *Ooooh!* Let me go! You horrid beast! You wicked ravisher! Let me go!''

''Let you *go?* I should jolly well think not! *You* came to *me*—I didn't drag you! How *dare* you call me a ravisher? Boot's more on t'other foot if you was to ask me!''

She fought wildly, but she was soft and cuddly for all her struggling and, from the sound of her voice, was young. ''Come on, puss,'' he said, cajoling if somewhat breathless. ''I'm not such a bad sort. How about a kiss?''

Instead, a hand cracked against his nose. He yelped and held her tighter.

''I shall scream!'' A note of pure terror was in the panting little voice. ''And—and if I do—you will be incarcerated!''

''And you, m'dear, will likely ruin any hopes you may entertain of future business in *this* boardinghouse! Come now—enough is enough. You hopped into my bed, and now you must—''

''This is *my* bed! And *my* room! There must have been some mistake. I should have lit the lamp, but I was so very sleepy, and . . . Oh, sir! Whoever you are, I *beg* of you . . . I do not wish to ruin myself, but if you will not let me go, I shall most assuredly scream and we shall have *everyone* in here!''

The prospect was not intriguing. ''Well, of all the false starts!'' protested Harry, feeling much abused. ''Let's have a little light on the subject.'' He reached for the tinderbox but was stopped by a half-sobbed, ''No! Do not! I should *die* of shame! And you . . . Oh, my dear God! You are . . . *naked*!''

He chuckled. ''Yes, but you aren't.'' To his horror she began to weep in earnest, and he said kindly, ''Now, don't cry, for Lord's sake. Look—you do not seriously expect me to believe all this? Mrs. Burnett gave me this suite.''

''Mrs. Burnett is a great gaby!'' A loud sniff accompanied this denunciation. ''My friend did leave, but I told

Mr. Burnett I would remain. He is half-foxed most of the time, and I suppose . . . Oh, sir! I *know* what you must think . . . what you could not but believe. *Please*—I *implore* you—release me. I am an unmarried lady, travelling with my friends from the Convent.''

Harry gave a gasp of dismay. *Convent?* She really did sound like a well-bred chit. The cultured accents could be imitated, of course, but if she *was* a lady of Quality, he'd be in a fine pickle. And so would she! The deliciousness of the situation brought a curve to his humourous mouth. Not relinquishing his grip, he said, ''Very well. I will let you go—if you will at least leave me with a kiss.''

There was silence. Then a small hand fluttered to his lips.

''No, by God! Your mouth, ma'am!''

''But . . .'' She sounded forlorn. ''No one but my relations . . . has ever kissed my . . . lips.''

''Even so, you must admit I am being most generous,'' Harry insisted. ''I have every right to demand that you—''

''Yes, yes. Very well.''

He bent toward where he imagined her mouth to be. As if she had forced herself to a sudden surrender, she swung up her head. The kiss became a violent collision, evoking a gasp and a sobbed, ''You *horrid* monster. You bit me!''

''I never did! If you want to know it, you near knocked out my front teeth!''

She was making small distressed sounds, and he said, ''We'd best have the candles. I promise to keep covered, and—''

''Please—*no*! I have done as you asked. Now, if you are a gentleman you will turn your face to the other side and remain so until I am gone.''

Harry grumbled and fussed, but did as she requested. When the parlour door closed softly a moment later, he was smiling into the darkness. His nocturnal visitor had been a choice armful, and one he'd every intention of meeting again. Understandably, she had been desperate to keep her identity a secret. Nonetheless, in the morning that secret must be revealed. If she left the boardinghouse he could easily discover her name from one of the servants. If she remained, he had only to find a damaged mouth and he would have her!

Mrs. Burnett had said breakfast was served until nine o'clock. Promptly at eight, bathed, shaved with the razor he'd bespoken from the waiter, neatly dressed, and with his dark hair brushed into a careless style he knew became him, Harry strolled downstairs. Whoever had laundered and pressed his clothes had known what they were about; the shine on his topboots might horrify Andy but was adequate, and he felt himself to be fairly presentable.

The coffee room was already well occupied. Mostly, he noticed, by young ladies. He paused atop the two steps that led down into the room, scanning the guests eagerly. His heart missed a beat. Three ladies were seated at a table beside the far windows. It was ridiculous, of course—the coincidence too far-fetched. Yet he had learned long since that life has many coincidences, some so incredible as to be beyond belief. The golden curls of one head were the colour of winter sunshine; the slender back indicated youth. Breath held in check, he watched her, and as though she sensed his presence, she turned slowly to face him. Could it be—it *was*! The golden little beauty who had hovered in his thoughts from the moment he'd seen her in the carriage yesterday morning! The great cornflower blue eyes held a measure of reproach, but dimples peeped about that rosebud mouth.

And at the very centre of her upper lip was placed a small patch!

Scarcely aware that he moved, Harry stepped towards her. Another young lady sat at the table, a dark girl wearing a plain round gown and with her hair pulled unattractively into a tight bun atop her head. She turned to look at him and, even as he stared, her big eyes crossed and an expression of vacuous stupidity settled onto her face. The poor half-wit! Stunned, he blinked at her.

And upon her upper lip was placed a small patch!

Baffled, he stood there, and one by one the other ladies turned fully to confront him. Many an eye held a roguish light, and many a smile was kind because he was young and good to look at, and so totally bewildered.

But upon each and every pretty mouth was a small patch!

A slow grin spread over Harry's face: "Gammoned, by God!" he murmured.

The third lady seated at his Beauty's table was very fat and rather elderly, and she wore the sober black habit of a nun. She stood and started towards him. He drew back uneasily, then gawked at her.

In the centre of her upper lip was placed a small patch!

Shrieks of feminine laughter rang out.

The nun folded her hands and shook her head in gentle reproof.

Shattered, Harry flushed to the roots of his hair and fled, their mirth following him.

His precipitous flight ended in an encounter with two friends he'd not seen since the Battle of Ciudad Rodrigo. They were decidedly bosky, having obviously been celebrating all night, and alerted by Mrs. Burnett's ominously jutting chin, he hurriedly conveyed them up to their suite, settled them comfortably, and finally overcoming their tearful pleas that he not turn his back on 'ol' comrades 'n arms,' ran downstairs. His fears that he'd been gone too long proved justified. The nun and all her young ladies had departed. Mrs. Burnett allowed him to peruse the guest register, but he learned only that Suites 3 and 4, and Rooms 6, 7, and 10 had been assigned to Sister Maria Evangeline and "Eight Young Ladies". He raced back to his room and, staying only to shrug into his riding coat, clap his beaver at its customary jaunty angle upon his head, and snatch up his gloves and whip, hurried downstairs, paid his shot, and repaired to the stables. To have found his Golden Goddess twice must surely be an indication that Fate had ordained them to meet. And if he dared not presume to enter the ranks of her suitors, he could at least discover her name and direction. Someday, perhaps, when Fate had allowed him to improve his lot he would seek her out, lay his heart at those dainty feet, and hopefully find her not indifferent to him.

Unhappily, the stableboy could not quite recall whether the nun's carriages had headed north or west. He was quite sure, however, that they had not journeyed to the east, and in desperation Harry turned Lace northward, banking on the likelihood that the good Sister had been conveying her charges to the City. He rode as far as Sevenoaks with no sign of the carriages he sought, nor did his enquiries prove fruitful. Ostlers, innkeepers, and sundry pedestrians could, and all too often did, provide him with a list of equipages and travellers they *had* seen pass their way, but a nun and eight young ladies had not been among them. The afternoon was far spent when Harry at last found a groom who recalled seeing three such carriages heading towards Reigate not an hour since. Harry turned westward at once but three hours later, in a gathering dusk, was forced to admit defeat. He had found his little perfection only to lose her again. As well, perhaps, for she'd likely make a brilliant match long before he could approach her. He sighed, reined Lace around, and headed to the east once more, his heart heavy.

The skies were clear that night, the moon high. He procured a satisfactory but dull meal in a small hedge tavern and, when he was assured that Lace was rested, resumed his journey. At ten o'clock he followed the deserted highway to the crest of a sprawling rise. The moon gilded a distant pond to silver and painted the winding road ahead so that it shone like a white ribbon. The wind was busily rattling the branches of trees and bushes, and far off he could hear the notes of a fiddle, expertly played, rising from some snug farmhouse or cottage. His keen eyes searched the dimpled hollows of valleys, the soft sweep of hills, and the denser darkness that was woodland, but discovered no sign of a great house. The tavern owner had directed him to this road and said Sanguinet Towers was just beyond the Lowland Woods. To be sure, a dense stand of trees bisected the road below, but there was no mansion visible, unless . . . Beside a nearby hill the black and slender arm of a chimney rose against the sky. A gatehouse, perhaps. He started Lace down the road.

It was a lonely spot, especially at night, and Harry first tightened his grip on the pistol, then, driven by an odd unease, drew it from his pocket. He was almost to the trees when he heard the faintest breath of a sound he'd heard before: the closed-teeth whistling an ostler emits while currying a horse. Too late he jerked the pistol upward. The last thing he saw was a flash that split the night and scattered it into countless whirling fragments . . .

The dark rider moved slowly from the shadows, calling to the mare so as to calm her. Dismounting, he took up her reins, tied them to a branch, and then bent over the crumpled form of his victim. Harry lay face down, and the man turned him with one rough boot, his pistol at the ready. There was no attempt at reprisal, however, the slim body limp and unresisting. The white face was darkly blotched and stained, the ominous streaks spreading even as he watched. Curious, the man bent closer. "I'll be gormed!" he exclaimed. "So *you're* Redmond! I'd've said 'ello, me fine flash cove, if I'd knowed we was acquainted, like. Oh well—too late now since I've gone and blowed yer brains out! Let's see whatcher got fer old Dice . . ."

He dropped to his knees, his practiced hands swift and sure. Watch and cravat pin were soon removed. The lack of rings or fobs was disappointing, but the cardcase sported a fine ruby in the crest, and the purse drew a gratified "Aha!" from the big man. The many-caped riding coat was next to go; then Dice stood and, having deposited his loot in the saddlebags and slung the coat across the horse's withers, he pulled Harry's lax form to his shoulder, then slung him face down across the roan's saddle. Crossing to Lace, he stroked her, talking gently and admiringly for a minute or two before he ventured to mount up. He rode on for a short distance, leading the roan, keeping to the shadow of the trees until he came to a deep cut full of bracken and fern that fell away to his right. He leant over, shoved Harry from the saddle, and watched him tumble down the steep bank until he vanished from sight.

Considerably richer, Devil Dice rode away whistling merrily, well pleased with his night's work.

* * *

Harry's first impression was that he lay in the mouldering Spanish farmhouse. It seemed to him, lost in the swirling mists of half-consciousness, that he heard the man and woman wrangling over him, trying to decide how much he would be worth to the British and whether it would justify the exertion of riding to Ciudad Rodrigo and notifying his regiment that he still lived. And for what must be the thousandth weary time he pleaded, *"Digale a ellos que estoy agui . . . Le suplico! Digale a ellos . . . que estoy aqui . . ."*

"It's all right, matey," mumbled a deep and very English voice. "We *knows* you're here."

Peering up eagerly, Harry made two discoveries: firstly, that the sharp edge of pain was this time in his head; and secondly, that a blurred round glow hung over him. He blinked, and the glow began to resolve into the thin face of a man with drowsy, heavy-lidded eyes deepset under extremely bushy brows. Untidy brown hair curled thickly under a battered old straw hat. The chin was an unyielding jut, belied by the kindly gaze that was fixed upon him.

Glancing to the side, the man said in that lazy drawl, "Here we go again, Mr. Fox. That's what y'get, y'see? Fish a cove outta the River Styx, as y'might say, and what's he do? Jaws your ear off all night—and foreign jaw into the bargain! Now, does I look like a Spanisher, old friend? I asks yer! It's enough t'try the patience of a honest man what likes his privacy and as little jaw as maybe!"

Harry had been looking about him while he listened to this monologue. It was night still, and he lay in a clearing in the woods. A fire leapt and crackled merrily nearby and above it a large iron pot hung from a trivet, giving off a fragrant aroma. To one side was a tent, crammed with all manner of articles, among which he discerned books, shovels, coils of rope, a ship's wheel, a violin case, numerous cooking implements, several large bottles, blankets, a ladder, and what looked to be one end of a rowing oar. A small donkey grazed beside the tent and a cart, poles up, was close at hand.

His companion was talking again. "What y'reckon he's going to dream up this time? Are we going to get Spanish again, or will he be calling me his Golden Goddess? Cor, luvvus! Wouldn't I look fetching wrapped up in yards o'stuff like them Greek ladies! Diccon the dryad! Cor!"

His search for another man having failed, Harry's gaze shot back to this 'Diccon'. He was probably about five-and-thirty, and his clothes, although much worn, were neat and clean. But he was one of the most cadaverous individuals Harry had ever beheld, and the prospect of that tall figure clad in a Grecian gown so amused him that, being quite light-headed, he broke into an involuntary laugh, choked on a groan, and clapped one hand to his brow.

"Rejoice, Fox," quoth the long man. "He is restored!"

"Not . . . appreciably," gasped Harry. "What the devil . . . happened? Did Lace throw me?"

No answer being vouchsafed he looked up to find that gaunt face only inches away, a calculating light in the pale blue eyes. There was no doubt but that they were quite alone, and the unhappy suspicion dawned upon Harry that not only was he completely knocked out of time, but that his rescuer was a raving lunatic. It might well, he thought, become necessary for him to defend himself, which at the moment would be difficult. His knees felt weak; his head, in addition to throbbing brutally, was full of cobwebs; and he could not seem to remember anything with much clarity. He was in great trouble, but—what it was . . .

The voice was rumbling on. "I am called Diccon, sir. And you'd likely feel better if you was to take a bite o'my stew. Can you sit up and tell me your name? I couldn't fine no cardcase, nor nothing."

His long arm slid under Harry's shoulders. The struggle to move was wracking, and his best response was a gasped out, "Thank you. I'm . . . Harry Allison . . ." which was all he could manage.

"Harry Allison." Diccon propped his uninvited guest against a convenient tree and, having noted that the pale lips were tightly compressed and the fists clenched, he crossed to the cart, returning in a few minutes carrying a tin cup. "Took a real wisty rap you did, your worship. But your head's not broke less'n I mistake it, and I seen a'plenty in me time. Have a swig o'this."

The brandy was mellow and potent, the quality such that Harry's eyes widened in surprise, but it also made him cough, the resultant chaos in his head rendering him so sick and dizzy that Diccon's words reached him as from a vast distance, and he lay very still, listening.

"Stay low and keep your mouth shut," his host offered. "That's what me mum told me when I was a little shaver, and that's about what I does. Not much of a talker be I. A gentle, peaceable cove, what likes quiet and a good book, and the backwaters o'life, as y'might say. So you'd likely think that was I a'sitting here with Mr. Fox, minding of me own business, and with me stew starting to smell fit to eat, nothing could move me. But I found out something else during me travels, milord, and that is that if trouble comes a'sniffing around, it's best to go and take a look at *it*—'stead o'waiting t'let it come slithering up to look at *you* when you ain't nowise ready. So when I—"

"I am not," Harry frowned, vaguely irritated by this flow of narrative, "a lord." He raised one hand as he interjected this crucial statement, and Diccon was silent a moment while his shrewd eyes fastened on that white hand with its slim, tapering fingers and well-kept nails. "Well, that's a sad thing, I grant ye," he commiserated. "But then neither is I, so there y'are. And here was I when I heered that there shot—"

"Shot?" Harry clutched again at his brow while he strove painfully to remember.

"Ar," nodded Diccon. "And up I creeps to the holler and sees you come a'flying down the bank and a big cove riding off with two horses, and—"

"Lace!" Starting up, aghast, Harry winced but, pushing away Diccon's restraining hands, struggled to his knees. "That dirty . . . bastard! He's taken my Lace!" He gained his feet and, reeling, was steadied by a strong arm.

"Easy, Sir Harry," said Diccon, watching him narrowly. "If your Lace be a showy little bay mare, he took her all right."

"Well don't stand here chatting about it, blast you!" cried Harry furiously, gripping his head with one hand and pushing at Diccon with the other. "Get after him! Dammit—*will* you move! *Sergeant*!" And then, staggering, went to his knees and groaned a febrile, "What in thunder am I saying? How long ago, man? Can you not follow and see where—"

Diccon allowed as how it had been a half-hour back and wasn't no use t'go rushing off like some chawbacon, and that if Sir Harry didn't lie down and stop jumping about like a flea in a skillet he'd do hisself up proper. Since Harry was by this time beginning to feel the benefit of the brandy, his response was, if thready, so lengthily explicit that awe came into Diccon's eyes. He restored his guest to the tree and waited until at last the distressed man ran out of breath and groaned an anguished, "Damn, damn, damn! If he spoils her pretty mouth, I'll . . ." His voice broke and Diccon nodded sympathetically. "Know how you feels, sir. I'd be the same if 'twas Mr. Fox."

Harry leaned his pounding head back against the tree trunk and surveyed his benefactor for a moment, thinking only of his pretty mare and the affection they had shared these last two years. But the gloomy countenance that was now bent over the savoury pot intrigued him, and he asked at length, "Mr. Fox?"

A loud and hideous response shattered the silence of that sylvan glade. Startled birds twittered, owls hooted in fright, and two confused rabbits shot though the clearing and all but ran into the fire. Throwing his hands over his ears, Harry stared in astonishment to where the little donkey tossed his head about, that cacophonous blast issuing from between his open jaws.

Diccon waved one arm toward the braying ass. "Meet my friend—Mr. Fox."

The morning was brisk and cool. A slight breeze stirred the yellow green of new leaves, and birds sang blithely to welcome the sun which sprinkled an ever-changing dapple of light into the clearing and awoke diamonds from the hurrying stream.

Sir Harry Redmond, late of Moiré Grange and Hill Street, known to most of the *haut ton* as a Top o' the Trees, a proud member of the Four Horse Club, and an undisputed Corinthian, knelt beside that chattering stream working carefully and with an occasional muttered expletive, at the bandage about his brow. He had already shaved, thanks to the loan of Diccon's razor and soap, and washed himself to the waist in the icy water—a sight that had so unnerved his host he'd withdrawn in horror. Now, with the smell of frying bacon driving him to distraction, Harry could not seem to succeed in freeing the bandage from the wound short of starting it to bleed again. He was in the midst of a lusty burst of profanity when something thudded into his back, sending him head first into the stream.

Howling his indignation as he emerged hurriedly from that chill immersion, he glared up at a raucously amused Diccon and a head-swinging Mr. Fox.

"Shoulda warned you," Diccon snorted. "He's got a rare sense of humour."

"Does he, by God!" snarled Harry, shivering. "B-B-Blasted damn ass!"

Mr. Fox laid his ears back, stretched forth his neck, and fluttered his upper lip in an idiotic grimace that could only be a laugh. Forced to a reluctant grin, Harry swore to even the score but was then pleased to discover that his plunge had soaked the bandage clear. Diccon, inspecting the gash, pronounced it closing nicely but allowed as how Mr. Allison likely had "a right headache, s'morning." Not too bad," lied Harry between chattering teeth. "And I've to thank you for being in no worse c-c-case. Gad, but that smells delight—" and he stopped. Diccon was obviously not a rich man and he himself now poverty stricken.

"Hungry, is ye?" asked Diccon sympathetically. "Come on, then."

Harry "came on" and, wrapping a blanket about himself, stood by the fire trying not to notice the tin plate piled high with crispy bacon, eggs cooked to perfection, and crusty bread, thick with fresh butter.

"Well, sit down," said Diccon impatiently. " 'Fore it gets cold."

Harry thanked him but said he was not in the least hungry and seldom, in fact, ate breakfast. Diccon gave him a measuring look, turned aside and, seating himself, took up another and even more heavily laden plate. "Awful waste," he said sadly. "Doubt I can eat it all. But—Mr. Fox won't consider hisself too flash to eat with the likes of I."

Mr. Fox was doomed to disappointment. A short while later, leaning blissfully against a tree, a steaming mug of coffee in his hand and his headache much lessened, Harry allowed that there wasn't a coffee house in Town to equal Diccon's cooking. "Never," he opined, "have I tasted such food."

"Or not since Spain, eh?" murmured Diccon, sprawled lazily nearby, the remains of his disreputable straw slanted over his eyes.

"Spain . . ." Harry gave a reminiscent grin. "We were lucky sometimes, I grant you. But there were many days we ate only acorns—*if* we could find any! I remember—" He stopped, a frown puckering his forehead. "How the deuce did you know I'd served in—"

"Talked a lot 'fore you woke up proper yestiddy," said Diccon.

A blast from the donkey shook the clearing. Harry winced and held his head. "Good God! What does he want?"

"Breakfast." Diccon made no attempt to gratify this need, however, and regarding his apparently exhausted benefactor, Harry demanded, "Do you not feed him first?"

"Had to feed you," said Diccon indignantly. " 'Sides—he bites."

Harry, who had started to his feet, was given pause by those words.

"Less'n you gives him something first," Diccon amended. "He's allus grumpy first thing of a morning. Like some people."

"But he's been chewing on that bush ever since I woke up."

"Ain't the same. Likes something of a more personal nature." With a great and noble effort, Diccon reached over to pick up a folded letter. "This'll do."

Harry snatched it away. "It will not! That's mine!" Diccon slumped back but found the energy to sigh a few instructions as to oats and tubs. Following these, Harry eventually approached the donkey bearing a laden tub. Mr. Fox eyed him malevolently. Sure that Diccon was watching with amused anticipation, Harry retrieved a fragment of newspaper fluttering in a nearby bush. It seemed ridiculous, but he proffered it with a few low-voiced remarks of rank flattery. Mr. Fox appreciated both the approach and the news and, accepting the offices of this promising newcomer with becoming grace, settled down to his breakfast. Amused, Harry asked, "Why do you call him Mr. Fox?"

"Looks like him," said Diccon drowsily. " 'Specially when he's got his hat on. And any man what looked like Charles James Fox and had a pretty lady in keeping for years without wedding her was a worse donkey than that'n!"

Harry laughed. "A moralist! Yet Charles Fox *did* eventually wed the lady, you know. And he was a very great man."

"Well," yawned Diccon, "my donkey's a very great donkey."

Harry turned a curious gaze on the tent. "Are you a tinker, Mr. Diccon?"

"Never mind the mister. And—tinker? Cor, bless you, sir—no! A tinker's a victim o'folks' whims. Spends all his days hauling a lot of stuff folks *might* want—but seldom does! *I'm* a trader. That is t'say, Mr. Fox and me is. When we comes to a place, folks comes and sees what we got, and shows us what *they* got, and we trades. Sometimes we trades for tools and the like. Sometimes it's just for lunch with say a tankard o'home brewed."

"Never mind the 'sir' . . ." Diccon raised his hat at this and, peering upward, grinned broadly, and smiling in return, Harry next regarded that solitary oar. "And—do you enjoy a good business, may I ask?"

"Most times. Sometimes it's hard to part with what we get. I traded a scythe once for some books o'them Greek philosyphers."

Harry returned to his tree, lowered himself cautiously, and noted with a twinkle that this seemed a practical exchange.

"Was for that there farmer. He couldn't read. Terrible shock for me, though."

"Were you not able to trade them?"

"Started to *read* 'em! Awful!" the battered straw stirred agitatedly. "I allus thought them Greeks was a pure and high-minded lot. Cor! Such carryings on as I never dreamed of! Fellas seem to've spent most o'their time seducing their mums, or their sisters, or whacking off their dads'—" He paused, and uttered, "Shocking!"

Harry, eyes alight with mirth, pointed out that the Greeks were nonetheless noted for great thoughts. "Euripides, for example—"

"Ah—he's the one Mr. Fox liked. Easy to see why. He was a 'ristocrat. And just look at our nobility, would you! The way they carry on is fair disgraceful! I heered as that there Lady Melbourne had nine children, not no two of 'em having the same father, and," here he lifted his straw the better to direct a righteously outraged glance at his companion, "—and not a *one* by her own husband!"

"Six," Harry corrected, his lips quivering betrayingly. Lady Melbourne, the product of an earlier and lustier generation, had been wont to address him as her 'darling boy'. He had been devoted to her for as long as he could remember and, knowing her lively sense of the ridiculous, could appreciate her delight to learn of this conversation between an itinerant trader and an impoverished ex-soldier in a lonely Kentish wood.

Diccon replaced the hat and after a moment said sleepily, "I 'spect as ye'll be wanting t'get back to your own people."

Harry was silent, watching Mr. Fox with troubled eyes.

To go back now must be to beg for help and generosity. And how willing they would be—how eager to help. Bolster, bless his old yellow head, was so very well breeched, as was Damon—or St. Clair, for that matter. They would, in fact, be furious with him for not asking their assistance. But the very thought made him cringe. He had no wife to consider, and Mitch, thank God, was provided for—at least for the immediate future . . .

A loud snore interrupted his musings. He looked at the long, sprawled shape of his somnolent host and wondered how Diccon ever mustered the energy to be about his 'trading'. To share this inactivity, at least for a little while, was most pleasant. Harry settled back and contemplated swaying trees, rippling stream, the contentedly grazing Mr. Fox, and the deepening blue of the sky. The sun was getting warmer and he was dry now and felt surprisingly well despite his head and sundry bruises and abrasions. He took up one of the letters he'd found in the desk drawer and unfolded it idly. It was addressed in a neat, copperplate hand to Sir Colin Redmond, Moiré Grange, Near Haslemere, Hants., and read:

Sir Colin:

Your testimony at yesterday's Enguiry left me both baffled and distressed. It was very evident that you are concealing something. I can only implore you to not be intimidated. My beloved brother is dead, and with your help, it will be proven MURDER.

I beg you will reconsider, and shall await your reply with the greatest anxiety.

> *Yours, etc.,*
> *Annabelle Carlson*

Astounded, Harry sat up straighter, folded the letter, and reached quickly for the next.

Sir Colin: (he read)

Do you seriously think to fob me off with such nonsense? I am not a child, sir, and know bribery and

corruption when I see it! If you have accepted his money,
I will pay you more! If, however, you are afraid of him,
I will hire guards to watch you day and night until he
is brought to trial. Search your conscience and write as
soon as you can to,

Annabelle Carlson

This letter had been inscribed with obvious agitation, since the writing was nowhere near as neat as that of the first and beneath the signature, as if in desperate afterthought, was scrawled, "Please, *please*—help me!"

"The Devil!" muttered Harry, and took up the third letter.

Villain! (this began abruptly)
 So he has terrified you into silence! I had heard you
were an honourable man. I know you now for the cring-
ing, fawning, lying servility that you are!

("By God!" Harry growled, and his hand tightened furiously on the page.)

 I write this reminder, well knowing it will merely af-
ford you laughter. A gallant young man was murdered
before your cowardly eyes—and you turned away! A
helpless woman is victimized—and you care not!
 Day and night my prayer is that someday you may
reap the bitter fruits of what you have sown!

Annabelle Carlson

"Well . . . I'll be damned!" gasped Harry.

From behind his hat Diccon murmured, "Reg'lar fire-spitting shrew, ain't she?"

"Devil take you!" Harry exploded. "You read my letters! How *dare* you, sir? You'd no right!"

"No more did you," shrugged Diccon. "You ain't the—as y'might say, addressee."

"Sir Colin Redmond was my father!" Harry flashed, coming to his feet and glaring down at his benefactor.

Diccon poked up the brim of his hat. "Is that a fact—
Mister Allison . . . ?"

Harry's face flamed. Diccon grinned and allowed the
brim to flop again. Not until then did it dawn on Harry that
yesterday the big man had once addressed him as 'milord'
and later as 'Sir Harry'. Between his injuries and the shock
of losing Lace, it had slipped his mind. "How did you
know?" he demanded.

"Tried t'find out who you was," Diccon murmured.
"Said you wasn't a lord. Hands wasn't calloused. Handkerchief had three initials. Then I read them letters." One
bright eye was visible through a large hole in the brim.
"Curiosity. Y'might say I'm like them Greeks. They had
their faults. I got mine."

"Yes," said Harry, tight-lipped. "You have, indeed!"

CHAPTER V

BY REASON OF A BRUISED KNEE HARRY LIMPED SLIGHTLY
as he followed the winding lane. Diccon had given him
directions reluctantly, having warned him to "stay clear
o'that lot!" but he'd already lost much time and had set
out determinedly for Sanguinet Towers. The sun was hot
now, and he began to wish he had his hat. He had taken a
courteous but cool farewell of the Trader. Regarding him
through the hole in his hatbrim, Diccon had bidden him
take care but had not bestirred himself to shake hands.
Fuming, partly because of that omission and partly because
the man should have been so ungentlemanly as to have read
private letters, Harry had politely expressed his thanks for
Diccon's kindnesses. Trading in turn, he had then placed
his hat on a fallen tree, observed that it might not fit, but
the buckle was of silver, and departed.

Now, his pique having cooled, he reflected that it was
quite ridiculous to have expected Diccon to have behaved
any differently. The man was a simple wanderer—and a
good-hearted fellow . . . Harry's steps slowed. There had
been something oddly likeable about him and that hu-
mourously inclined donkey. And perhaps it *had* been logical enough for Diccon to attempt to discover his identity.
Yet the name and direction should have sufficed, instead
of which he'd admitted to having read all three letters.
Unforgivable!

He came at length to a rise, atop which stood a gate
and gatehouse, with a long brick wall stretching off to

either hand. A meadowlark soared upward carolling blithely, the pure notes recalling a never-to-be-forgotten voice of sweet purity, an angelic face, framed by hair of palest gold . . .

"Wot you think you be a'grinning at?" A leathery-looking man, arms akimbo, stood before the gate. He wore the green of a gamekeeper and had a narrow face, ferrety eyes, and an expression of sneering vindictiveness.

"I have business with M. Sanguinet," Harry advised coolly.

The eyes of the leathery man drifted with slow impertinence from hatless and bandaged head to scratched, dusty boots. The cut of those boots and the set of the jacket across the broad shoulders spoke of the Quality, as did the tilt to the chin and the cultured accents of the deep voice. But the condition of both man and clothes told their own story, wherefore the thin lips of the gamekeeper twisted into a mocking grin. "Well, 'oity-toity! Does yer now? Down on yer luck, is yer, me royal 'ighness?" Harry frowned and stepped a pace closer. The gamekeeper jerked his thumb toward the woods and said a contemptuous, "Go on! Out've it!"

"In view of the fact that I am not yet *in* it—I cannot very well get *out* of it. And since neither your manners nor your face commend themselves to me, you will be so good as to stand aside."

The gamekeeper proving unwilling, it became necessary for Harry to be more explicit. Massaging his skinned knuckles, he then stepped over his antagonist, climbed the gate, and went upon his way.

The drive wound upward through scattered trees, and as he strode along, the letters haunted him. ". . . My beloved brother is dead . . . bribery and corruption . . . the cringing, fawning, lying servility that you are . . ." And most ominous of all, "Day and night, my prayer is that someday you may reap the bitter fruits of what you have sown . . ." Was this the answer to his father's untimely death? Had this demented woman, whoever she may be, so hated Colin Redmond that she had contrived his destruction? To what

Enquiry had she referred? And who was the man she obviously feared and believed responsible for her brother's death?

Pondering thus, he came at last to where the drive wound around a high bank, after which the trees fell away to reveal a great house below, rising squarely from a moat-like pond in the centre of an expanse of green lawns. Starting down the slope, Harry's appraisal was not approving. Constructed of grey stone, the mansion was even larger than he had imagined. It was four storeys in height, but appeared taller since the corners were rounded off and lifted into towers with conical roofs. Despite its size, however, it presented the appearance of being huddled together, as though it hugged itself jealously and regarded the outside world with eyes of cold suspicion.

The sudden thud of running feet alerted Harry and he swung around, prepared for conflict. His late antagonist, reinforced by three comrades and armed with a businesslike looking club, bore down on him. Harry dodged the first man, grassed the second, ducked as the club swung at his head, drove home an uppercut that sent a chubby fellow staggering backward, and was himself knocked sprawling by a solid right to the jaw.

The whirling kaleidoscope of green and grey slowed and settled into two sturdy legs, one foot drawing back. Indignant, Harry raised his aching head. "Do not dare to . . . kick me. Damn . . . your eyes!"

The movement of the boot was arrested. Four angry faces, two of them quite damaged, glared down at him.

" 'E don't *talk* like no poacher, Fritch," observed the owner of the foot. "Sounds more like me old Colonel."

"Well, 'e don't *look* like no old Colonel," pointed out the ferrety-eyed gamekeeper angrily. "Planted me a facer, 'e done, an 'aint got no business 'ere, of that you may be—"

"What are you men about?"

Harry dragged himself to one elbow. The man who had ridden up on a magnificent black mare hooked one booted leg casually over the pommel and leaned forward, scanning him with disdain. It would have been difficult to say whether he was nearer to thirty-five or fifty. Dressed in jet, relieved only by the snow of cravat and cuffs, his clothes were superb and he wore them with assured grace. His hair was a glossy blue-black, curling about a dark-complected face. The nose was slim and straight; the bones of cheek and jaw finely chiselled, and the skin over them having an almost stretched look. The mouth, full and sensual, was smiling, but the smile went no further than the lips; and it was the eyes that caught and held Harry's attention. For in that darkly beautiful face were set eyes so light as to be almost colourless; large, brilliant eyes, holding an expression of hungry ferocity barely held in check, and of themselves so alien that for the first time in his life the mere appearance of another human being caused Harry, at least inwardly, to recoil.

"This 'ere intruder hassaulted me, Monseer Sanguinet," said Fritch aggrievedly. "Tipped me a leveller, so 'e did!"

"In which case," purred Sanguinet, his accent barely discernible, "you failed. And failure you must know displeases me."

"But . . . sir . . . !" whined Fritch.

Sanguinet lifted one gloved hand. A lazy movement, but the fingers might have gripped a crossbow to judge by the speed with which the Ferret slunk away.

"My estate," smiled Parnell Sanguinet, "bears signs. And the signs read—in English, mark you—'trespassers . . . will . . . be . . . shot!' " His gaze slid to his men and his shoulders shrugged in a Gallic gesture that reminded Harry of Camille Damon. "*Eh bien*? So—shoot him."

Harry stared, then laughed scornfully. "*Coûte que coûte . . . ?*"

The pallid eyes widened a trifle and returned to him. "It shall cost *me* nothing, sir." He gestured once more and Harry was hauled to his feet. The scene blurred, but he kept his head up and from an echoing distance heard Sanguinet demand, "How are you called?"

"Harry . . . Redmond. I have come—" His rather indistinct utterance was checked by a startled, "*Pas possi-*

70

ble!'' and Sanguinet leaned forward, his eyes glowing slits as he scrutinized Harry intently.

"He was with that there trader fella, Monsewer," put in the fat individual. "I seed 'un s'marnin.'"

Briefly, Sanguinet remained rigidly still. Then, his breath hissing through shut teeth, he relaxed. "You have come down in the world, monsieur," he sneered. "And as to *why* you have come here—this to me is of *peu d'importance*. I would be much wearied to discuss either the loss of your ancestral estates, or . . ." the shapely mouth twisted mockingly, "or the so-nonsensical death of your papa."

Harry swore and lunged forward, but was restrained by strong hands.

"Since you are nobly born," Sanguinet went on, "I permit that you leave. But—be warned. If upon my property you again set your feet, I *shall* have you shot. And—"

"And thrown to the dogs?" mocked Harry. "You are the one who is nonsensical, Sanguinet! This is 1816—not the Dark Ages! And you are 'monsieur'—*not* 'monseigneur'! I tell you now that I intend to discover what happened at that damnable card game and why my—"

The Frenchman's black brows had met during this defiant outburst, and now one hand flung imperiously upward. To his rageful astonishment a hand came from behind to clamp hard across Harry's mouth.

"I have a dislike to be interrupted," announced Sanguinet. "Your papa was so foolish as to challenge me when he was—how do you say this . . . ? In his cups? He lost—*logiquement*. That his whelp comes whining to me for mercy, I find disgusting. Besides which . . ." He grinned suddenly. "Mercy is a commodity of which I have none." He pointed his riding whip at the struggling Harry and said with deadly intensity, "Offend me once more, Redmond, and you will discover me to be—*vraiment*—a monseigneur!" He twisted in the saddle with lithe ease, drove home long spurs, and rode toward the house, calling over his shoulder, "Rid me of him . . . *tout de suite!*"

Half strangled and all but sobbing with fury, Harry was

71

spun violently about. A large and knotted fist drove at him. There was no chance to avoid it. The beautiful spring morning exploded, and ceased to be.

His head was filled with merciless gnomes, each pounding at his skull with cruel pronged hammers. And as though this were not torment enough, his boots had never been intended for long hikes over rough country lanes on very warm afternoons. Harry began to feel sick and, weaving onward, did not allow himself to think of what he would do if he did not find the friendly pedlar and his humorously inclined ass. At last he approached a copse that looked vaguely familiar, but it seemed to shimmer oddly before his gaze and he put out one hand to steady himself against a tree . . . He flinched to an ear-splitting blast of sound and was surprised to discover not only that he had fallen to his knees but that he was all but nose to nose with a droll and familiar countenance, topped by long ears threaded through a forlorn beaver hat. "Mr. Fox . . ." he muttered thickly, and then was puzzled to discern dark skirts approaching, together with a ripple of feminine laughter. He peered upward and struggled to his feet, brushing impatiently at his clouded eyes.

She wore the same round gown as when he'd last seen her, and her dark hair, although still pulled into the tight know atop her head, was even more unattractive since strands and wisps had come loose and straggled down untidily. It was the poor half-witted girl who'd sat beside his Golden Beauty at Mrs. Burnett's genteel boardinghouse! "You . . !" he gasped. "But—how—"

She was already running to him, crying sympathetically, "Oh, my goodness! They *have* been rough with you!"

"Serves him right," said Diccon, slouching up to scan Harry's battered self judicially. "I told him to stay away from that lot!"

"Yes," Harry admitted. "You did. But—" He blinked at the girl, wondering if he was dreaming. "I do not understand . . . how—"

"Of course you do not," she said, seizing him by the

arm. "And you will please to sit down on this tree stump before you fall upon your face, for it is much too warm to carry you about. There—that is better. If you will be so kind as to bring water, Diccon, I will contrive to repair your friend. I am, indeed, relieved that you found him, since—"

"Diccon did not find me." Harry glanced curiously at the tall man who now rummaged through the cart. "Were you looking for me, Diccon? I—er—I thought you would be gone about your trading."

"Was." Bowl in hand, Diccon wandered towards the stream.

"Do be still," the girl adjured, wiping at Harry's head with a wisp of cambric. "If you will refrain from speaking all the time, I shall try both to attend to you and answer your curiosity, which is, I can see, setting you all on end."

Ten minutes later, however, he had gathered only that "the good Diccon" had rescued her from a Horrid Fate, that her name was Miss Brown, and that she had "left" Sister Maria Evangeline and her friends and been brought this far by a kindly young clergyman who was very shy and very stupid since he had taken her many miles out of her way and then become 'calf eyed' so that she'd had to leave him and would have been stranded—save for 'Good Diccon'.

Harry was feeling much better now than he had upon regaining consciousness outside the Sanguinet estate, but his head still pounded so savagely as to make thinking a sad effort. Unable to unwind the tangle of her words, he reverted to a previous, and unanswered, question and was promptly told to hush.

"I only asked," he said with faint indignation, "if your friend was—"

"Be quiet!" she frowned, working gently at a cut on his lip. "All you do is talk while I try only to help you. Instead of all this . . . chatter about my friend—Oh! I am so sorry! But there is a little speck of gravel. I must get it out."

Submitting, he could only marvel she had not fainted. The water Diccon had brought from the stream was now

73

crimson; his hurts must have been a frightful mess. Yet she had bathed them kindly, albeit with frowning concentration and an apparent disinclination to answer the few questions he had managed to slip in when she did not have him in such a grip that talk was impossible. Now, he again seized his opportunity. "She was sitting with you at the table, and—"

"Oh—Sister Maria Evangeline. Well, of course she is not here! Where do you suppose we should have hid her? Beneath the cart?"

The picture this conjured up drew a laugh from Harry, followed by a spasmodic clutch at his ribs; but before he could comment, she went on, "Still, she is a good woman, and I am glad you found her so fascinating."

"Er—yes . . ." He eyed her uneasily and thought to glimpse the flicker of a dimple at the side of her mouth. Her eyes were quite large, he noted, and flecked with little splashes of blue. Actually, she wasn't so bad looking, if only . . . She moved her head a trifle, glanced at him, and those big eyes slowly crossed, her chin sagging in the vacuous expression of stupidity that quite appalled him. "I'm sure she is estimable," he said, blinking and looking away hurriedly. "But, I really meant the other—" He gasped and flinched back from her hands, and she cringed a little, her eyes returning to normal.

"*Tiens!* Your head—it is very bad . . . I think."

"And you are very brave," he said comfortingly.

She looked down at her bloody hands and fluttered, "I am not . . . missish . . . if that is . . . what . . . you . . ." She swayed. Harry jumped up and caught her, and she leaned against him weakly.

"Here." He guided her to the tree stump on which he'd been sitting. "Please rest a moment, Miss—er, Brown. I'm not like to bleed to death, you know."

She tried to smile but her face was paper white, her eyes lacking focus. Harry had seen that look before and at once swung her head down between her knees. She gave a resentful squeal and punched him on the thigh, and he jumped back. Regarding him with indignant and watering eyes, and

74

touching her snub nose, she wailed, "Oh! How bad of you! I think you have broken it!"

Harry explored the afflicted area. It was idiotically small but appeared intact. "I am sorry ma'am," he said penitently. "I thought you were going to faint."

"A poor sort of creature you think me!" She stood, bade him be seated, and resumed her repairs. After a moment, he tried once more. "Your friend—"

"I have no friends," she snapped. "I am all alone in the world. With no one who cares a tiny piece for me!" Diccon, an interested if supine observer, made a small sound of protest, and she flashed a tremulous smile at him and amended, "Except my very dear, kind Diccon."

Weeping women terrified Harry, wherefore he maintained a discreet and fearful silence. Nonetheless, in a little while he saw that tears crept down her cheeks and, aghast, burst out, "Oh, Lord! I beg you will not weep, ma'am! I am really feeling much better thanks to—"

"I shall weep if . . . I wish . . ." she asserted, her lower lip trembling. "And I do not cry for you, at all events, but because . . . because I am such . . . a great stupid!" She swung away, and sobbed, "Oh! How I hate myself! I was so *sure*—if I had gone to Spain . . . I would have been able to . . . But I see I am just a—weak and foolish . . . girl . . . after all! Juana is worth ten of me!"

Harry, who had listened in bewilderment to this uneven speech, now interposed an eager, "Juana? Do you refer to Juana Smith?"

"*Oui*—I mean—yes!" She wiped away her tears with the heel of one hand, leaving a crimson smear across her cheek. "She is my very dearest friend. But I hate her. She did what I am too weak and vapourish to be able properly to do. And—" She turned to him intently. "Why? Do you know her, also?"

"I do, indeed. Her husband and I saw service in Spain together. Juana is the dearest girl, and as for old Harry Smith—" "*Old* Harry!" she snorted, resuming her task. "I doubt he is a day older than you! And Juana is the world's most dreadful spitfire. Except for me. But she is brave . . . There—I am done. And you may have a black eye, sir, which shall give you less opportunity to look at the ladies.''

"God forbid!" grinned Harry. "Speaking of which—the lady I sought to describe had hair the colour of sunshine in the morning, and—"

"And eyes of the cerulean blue," she cried, waving her arms dramatically. "And a shape beyond the dreams of mortal man. While her voice—ah! the trill of a nightingale! *N'est'ce pas*?"

At first taken aback, Harry had become lost in reflection and sighed a dreamy, *"Mai oui . . . absolument . . ."*

"Pah!" she snorted rudely. "It is as I have think! You are just like all the rest, and have fallen in love with my Lady Nerina Tawnish!"

"Nerina . . ." he breathed. "What a beautiful name."

"It means nymph of the sea," said Miss Brown. "And if you love her you had best be able to swim very fast, for there are many big fish after that one!"

The dreams fading from his eyes, Harry looked up. "You are exceeding outspoken, ma'am. Why would you think I should presume to have a *tendre* for the lady? I only ever saw her twice."

"The more fool you, to have fallen in love so quickly! And least of all with Nerina. But you have the look—much good it will do you! She knows where she is going, and what she wants. And it is not the likes of *you*!"

Flabbergasted by such blunt rudeness, Harry stared at her speechlessly. The scorn died from her eyes to be replaced by a look of dismay that as quickly became defiance. "I have shocked you, I collect. Well—" her voice scratched a little, and her lips quivered, "do not expect me to behave as one of your sickly sweet ladies of Quality, for I am not!"

"Of course you are," frowned Harry. "You are Convent educated and should be spanked for—"

"Oh, and have been, I do assure you, sir," she flashed. "More times than I could count. But all have despair of me. Even Sister Maria Evangeline . . ." Her voice softened and a wistful look crept into her eyes. "She was used to say that I am more shrew than saint, Convent or no . . ." She sighed, then her chin went up and she snapped, "And so be warned!" nodded fiercely, and started off with her nose in the air.

Harry recovered himself in time to stand and catch her arm. "Even so, I thank you," he said politely. "I am most grateful, Miss—er, Brown."

She wrenched away; then, as if disconcerted by the violence of her reaction, dropped him a swift curtsey. "I would let you kiss my hand, Mr.—er, Allison, did I not know the kind of man you are."

He comprehended at last why she spoke to him with contempt. At the boardinghouse she had affected a patch on her mouth, and she likely considered him an immoral man. He flushed and drew back, whereupon she went to the stream and, kneeling, began to rinse out the rags, singing softly to herself in a rather scratchy soprano.

The pride that had sustained Harry during the girl's ministrations ebbed away. He was not quite sure whether he sat down or his knees gave out under him. He leaned his head back against the tree with a weary sigh and closed his eyes for a minute . . . Opening them, he was astounded to see the sky flushed with sunset. A blanket had been spread over him, and despite the sensation that he had been ridden over by a cavalry regiment, he felt a little less miserably uncomfortable. Mr. Fox grazed nearby, still wearing his hat. It was a rakish beaver, although the crown was now somewhat crushed and the brim drooping. Perhaps it was the angle at which it sagged, or the faintly whimsical look in the large dark eyes beneath it, but there was a distinct resemblance to the great statesman and Harry muttered, "By George! He really does look like Charles James Fox!"

"Told you so." Diccon appeared at his side as if by magic and, scanning him a trifle anxiously, said, "You look properly dished!"

"I shall come about, never fear. But—I do apologize for causing you all this trouble. And for leaving you in such a . . . er—"

"Top lofty?" Diccon suggested.

Harry coloured faintly. "No, was I? Well then, I certainly—" Here, his gaze straying to Mr. Fox once more, a surge of resentment put humility to flight. "Dash it all! That's *my* hat!"

"Well, it's been a hot day." Diccon sat down beside him. "Mr. Fox—he feels the heat something terrible."

There was a brief silence. Almost, Harry fell asleep, but memory stirring, he looked up again to ask, "Were you really seeking me, Diccon?"

"Wanted to give you your share." Diccon dropped two coins onto the blanket.

"Two shillings! Wealth for a sultan! But—why give it to me?"

"Your hat buckle was silver, like you said. Sold it to a tinker."

"Even so, I have been eating you out of house and home, besides being a confounded . . . nuisance." Harry roused himself and held out the coins with one hand even as his other moved to touch his pounding temple. "Take them— please. I owe you much more than—"

"Don't owe me nothing," Diccon intervened gruffly. "Bought enough vittles to keep us eating fer a week—if you want to come along."

"Please." Harry managed a smile. "Now I'll feel less of . . . a burden . . ."

"You keep on like this," observed Diccon with mild severity, "I'll have to charge you more'n buckles! Terrible strain on Mr. Fox t'see you all banged about. Took a real fancy t'you, he has, and he worries dreadful."

His voice droned on, but the words became indistinct and Harry drifted into a slumber haunted by dreams of eyes that glowed like diamonds in a darkly handsome face.

The next time he awoke it was full dark, and the sounds of heaven were filling the clearing. He lay very still, scarcely daring to breathe. The sparkle of the fire dazzled his eyes, the air was soft and balmy, and the music soared and rippled through the stillness with an incredible beauty. Gradually, he realized it was a violin he heard, and in the hands of a master. What the melody was he had no idea, but when at last it stopped he did not move for a while, hoping it would resume. At length, turning carefully, he lifted himself to one elbow.

Diccon sat on the tree stump, fiddle in one hand and bow in the other, gazing into the fire.

Astounded, Harry settled back, and drifted into sleep while pondering the incongruities of this most unusual trader.

CHAPTER VI

DURING THE COURSE OF HIS LIFE, HARRY HAD NOT COME in the way of many people cursed with afflictions, but those few he had encountered had been unfailingly self-effacing and of a pronounced humility. His earlier suspicion that Miss Brown possessed neither of these traits was borne out the following morning. He awoke feeling renewed and, intending to repay Diccon in whatever way he was able, left his blankets so as to start the fire. Miss Brown, however, was before him. Not only was the fire blazing merrily, but water was heated, and Harry was immediately pounced upon, made to sit on the convenient tree stump and have his head inspected, bathed, pronounced healing satisfactorily, and rebandaged. He was grateful for this kindness and made some courteous enquiries about her background. These were most harshly repulsed. His attempts at polite conversation were ignored, but when he gave up and lapsed into silence. he was promptly accused of sulking. Miss Brown, he perceived, was a hopeless case. Far from attempting to minimize her pitiful handicap, she accentuated it by a hostile manner that frequently deteriorated into outright rudeness. It was possible that did she attempt to improve her appearance a trifle she would not be totally repulsive, but instead her hair seemed even more untidily tangled this morning, and her face not only lacked any trace of cosmetics but was defaced by several smears of dirt. His incredulity that a gently born girl could have plunged herself into so shocking an adventure faded before the realization that she was as wanting in sensibility as in conduct. If she saw anything improper in having spent the night alone in the woods with two strange men (an event that would have reduced most gently bred ladies to despair), she betrayed no sign of it and was even now, in fact, glaring at him belligerently.

"How dare you frown at me in that haughty fashion?" she demanded, and before he could answer said, "And I am *not* a fast lady!"

"I never said you was!" Flushing guiltily, Harry turned to Diccon who stood before the fire stretching, and appealed, "Now did I say anything of—"

"Well, you were thinking it," grumbled Miss Brown. She gave the fresh bandage a little pat and scowled at him. "Merely because I accepted the ride the poor old carter gentleman offered, you think—"

"Poor *old—carter* . . . ?" Harry interposed. "Yesterday you said you were brought here by a shy *young clergyman* who had 'calf eyes'! If you want to know what *I* think—it's a lot of slumgullion that you make up as you go along! Chances are you wasn't offered a ride at all but stole one! Dashed if I—"

Miss Brown set her hands upon her hips and, leaning over him, said furiously, "If I did not think you would bleed all over me again, I should tear my fine bandages from your evil brain! And scratch you, besides! You are a horrid man, Mr. Harry Allison! I shall go away and wash my hair, and you shall not have to thank me for all I do, so bother yourself not!" And snapping her fingers under his dismayed nose, she turned and flounced off.

"Wait!" cried Harry, scrambling to his feet. "I *do* thank you. And I am sorry if I . . . was . . ." But she put her small nose into the air, snatched a towel and soap from the tent, and moved with her supple swinging step into the trees.

"Now you done it!" Diccon's voice shook suspiciously. He had collapsed into his customary sprawl, the hat shielding his eyes, and his shoulders propped against a tree trunk. Harry crossed to lift the brim of the old straw and discover a grin. "I c'n see why you're always getting y'self bashed about," the Trader went on. "You'd oughta learn a little taking ways."

"It would seem you've enough for both of us. Whatever are you about, man? She's a lady of Quality. You've a head full of maggots if you think—"

"But that's just it, y'see." Diccon raised the hat to scan Harry earnestly. "How could I leave her alone by the road? She'd only got tuppence in her purse when I come on her. And she'd been crying her eyes out, poor little thing, though she never would admit it. Running away from home, and—"

"Allow me!" groaned Harry. "Her papa is an evil monster who squandered his fortune and now seeks to bring himself about by forcing her into wedlock with some rich, lecherous old man, the very sight of whom sends her into a decline!"

Diccon regarded him with awe. "That there Oxford really puts a head on a fella's shoulders!"

"Cambridge! And I would hope I've enough in my head to spot a hoary old whisker like *that*! More likely it's that poor nun who ran away! You should properly have put Miss Brown on the first stagecoach, and—"

"Didn't have enough money. I spent near all the dibs on food. Likely it'll come in handy now but— Have *you* got any, Harry?"

"Only the two shillings you gave me. But, even so— Good God, man! She *cannot* stay with us! You surely must realize!"

Diccon eased the straw to its habitual slant. "Why? I wouldn't harm the lass. No more would you."

"*Harm* her? Of course I wouldn't harm her! But—dash it all . . ." Harry peered around the clearing cautiously and murmured, "A single lady? Unchaperoned? Not so much as her abigail, and roaming about the countryside with two strange men? Blest if I *ever* heard of such a shocking thing!"

"I 'spect you're right," Diccon acknowledged slowly. "Well—what shall we do? She says as she wants to go to her aunty's house in Devonshire, which is along my way, so I thought—''

''*Devonshire?* You're going in the wrong direction.''

''Had to make a turnabout on account of a good trade in Hawkhurst what I heard of. Just as well or I'd not have come up with you, so you could help me.''

''The best way I can help *you* is to send her back to her papa!''

''I dunno.'' Diccon pursed his lips doubtfully. ''I've heard o'poor young females being as good as sold to old men afore this. And—the lass is under age. If her papa's as bad as she says, he could easy force her to—''

''Under . . . age . . .'' Harry echoed in failing accents. ''Oh, my God! We'll land in Newgate, is what! You must face the fact that the girl has taken advantage . . . I mean—well, I doubt she was telling the truth. She does seem a bit—er . . .'' He stumbled into silence as the hat was lifted and Diccon stared at him trustingly. Feeling a total villain, Harry stammered, ''Don't you think she's—sort of . . . ?'' He tapped his temple.

''Looby?'' said Diccon, baldly. ''Oh—is *that* it, y'reckon?''

''I don't really know, of course. But—sometimes she does look rather . . . ah—afflicted, wouldn't you say?''

''Poor little thing,'' Diccon sighed. ''Well, you're the gent, a'course, and knows about things like chivalry. Sight more'n me. You saying we should kick her out, 'cause she's all about in her attic?''

His face hot, Harry said, ''What? No! Of course not! Dreadful thing to do. But—oh, Lord! It just ain't *proper*! She's a girl, and—''

''And a fine one *you* are to talk of propriety, Mr.—er—Allison!'' The scowling little face was at his ear, and when he turned to her, those big eyes were crossed again, her face so contorted that he barely repressed a shudder. ''Or—*whatever* your name is,'' she added caustically as he all but jumped back.

''At least I gave Diccon my own name,'' he countered. ''It would seem to me that if you are to trust us—''

"Do pray disabuse yourself of *that* notion! I trust *no* man! For all I know you may be acquainted with my papa and would at once deliver me up to him!" Her eyes were normal again, her demeanour regal.

Harry hardened his heart. "Be assured of it, ma'am! As any gentleman of honour would, if only to protect your good name."

"Gentleman of honour!" she mocked. "*Is* there such an animal, I wonder? Mr. Fox there possesses more honour than most 'gentlemen' I've met. Except—" Her eyes clouded suddenly, and her scornful mouth trembled. Harry, who had been on the verge of an angry rejoinder, checked, seized by the terror that she was about to cry once more. "Come now, Miss Brown," he began bracingly, then shook his head. "The devil! That just don't suit you!"

"I cannot think why it should not." She blinked rapidly and wiped at her eyes in her unaffected little-girl fashion. "But," she sniffed, "if that is all that disturbs you . . . How does 'Nanette' suit?"

"Much better," Diccon nodded.

"It is *not* all that disturbs me," Harry pointed out. "I am far more—"

"Though, I'll admit" went on Diccon, still considering the matter, "as I'm very partial to 'Diana'."

Harry chuckled. "You and your Greeks! The goddess who hated men. Most apt!"

"But I am not a goddess," sighed the ex-Miss Brown, watching him from under her lashes. "Not like your golden Nerina."

"No," he agreed, with a wistful smile. "Still—"

"Oooh!" she gasped, at once livid with rage. "You are even *horrider* than I had thought! Had I a title, as she has, or was I an heiress, I collect—"

"Well, you ain't! I've no designs on your fortune which, from what Diccon tells me, consists of tuppence." Harry gave her his most engaging grin, uncomfortably aware he'd been clumsy and hurt the poor chit's feelings. "Now there's what I should call you—Tuppence!"

For a moment she continued to frown at him. Then she

gave a sudden little gurgle of laughter, and when Diccon demurred that 'Tuppence' didn't sound very lady-like, she said pertly, "Then you may improve it to 'Lady Tuppence'."

"I think not." Harry fixed her with a suddenly stern gaze. "For a lady would not risk her reputation by jauntering about the countryside. Nor cause her loved ones to grieve and worry for her safety!"

At once her fists clenched and her eyes grew stormy as she thrust her chin at him. "Much *you* know of it! And at all events, *you*—Mr. Allison—have naught to say in the matter! The tent, the cart, *and* the donkey—all are Diccon's!"

He bit his lip, silent in the face of these home truths.

"Aye, lass," Diccon put in gently. "But Mr. Allison's got a say, 'cause he bought all our food." His eyes twinkled as he met Harry's grateful glance. " 'Sides, Mr. Fox likes him."

"Oh . . ." She looked deflated, and to cement his position, Harry said firmly, "Yes, and that's my hat he's wearing."

Her scorching gaze passed from ex- to present owner. "Indeed? I had thought it created especially for—a donkey."

Harry threw up one hand and laughed a rueful, *"Touché!"*

A mischievous answering smile danced into her eyes but was swiftly banished. "I came back," she informed him sternly, "to take pity on you both and cook your breakfast. But since you are feeling so full of spirit this morning, Miss Nanette will defer to you the privilege of cooking." She curtseyed quite gracefully, and left them.

"Sounds t'me," murmured Diccon as he lay watching Harry wrestle with the frying pan, "like what your poor papa was drugged." The chef, looking very much the worse for wear with his bruised cheek, swollen jaw, and the bandage about his brow, shot a grim glance at his exhausted host. Diccon shrugged. "Only way. If all them fine gents said he played—he must've. Couldn't've *all* been Captain Sharps. And you said one of 'em was his best friend. Name of . . . who was it?''

''Sir Barnaby Schofield.''

''Hmmmnnn.'' Diccon sat up, accepted his plate, prodded at his eggs, and threw Harry a reproachful look. ''I don't like me eggs cooked too much, and our coffee's boiling over!''

With a soldier's fluency Harry consigned his eggs to perdition and his coffee along with 'em. Diccon was unmoved. He waited for a break in the tirade then allowed as how the Captain had a rare gift o'language but that he never could abide grounds in his mug.

Harry covered Miss Nanette's breakfast with a saucepan lid, tended the offending pot, and settled himself upon a convenient root with his own plate. For a while, he devoted himself to business, then enquired, ''How did you know I was a Captain? And don't tell me I talked about it in my sleep.''

''Got a funny sorta memory,'' Diccon nodded, cleaning his plate efficiently with a piece of bread. ''Prob'ly heard it—or read it somewhere. Mentioned in dispatches, wasn't you?'' He smiled at Harry's astonished expression. ''I'm allus reading. Finds old newspapers along me road, and some of me friends saves 'em for me. Things tend t'stick in my head. Like that there Schofield. I read as his poor son come home blind after Waterloo. Terrible thing fer a young fella like that. Still—he done his duty for his country. It wasn't a waste. Not like that poor Lieutenant Carlson. Now *that* was a odd thing, and t'think your papa was caught right in the middle of—Hey! That ruddy bacon cost me ninepence-ha'penny!''

Harry managed to scoop the bacon back onto his plate. ''You *know* about that Enquiry? Good God, man! Why didn't you tell me?''

''Didn't ask.'' Diccon set his plate aside and resuming his customary attitude, pulled his hat over his eyes, only to have it snatched away and a grim young face thrust

86

within inches of his own. "I will take it kindly," breathed Harry, "do you tell me whatever you may recall of it."

In that moment he was all aristocrat, the humourous sparkle gone from the narrow eyes and a set to his jaw that brooked no evasions. A tentative bray arose from the direction of the tent. "That's my hat you're a'crushing off . . ." Diccon hauled himself to a sitting position. "And you're upsetting Mr. Fox."

Harry returned the wrecked straw and cast a glance at the donkey. Sure enough, Mr. Fox peered at them with an oddly apprehensive attitude. He sat back, therefore, seething with impatience but schooling himself to calmness.

"I dunno," Diccon began thoughtfully, "as I can remember it very clear. As I recollect, you papa had been visiting friends and started home later'n what he'd meant to. Sudden-like, his coachman turned a corner and they was a big carriage in front, coming up fast behind one o'them there fancy coaches the young Bucks drive nowadays—you know the kind; very fast, with the body slung right atop the front axle . . . ?"

"A high perch phaeton?"

"That's it. Anyway, the carriage and that there phaeton goes a'shooting off on a side road. Your papa was a sportsman, so natural enough, he looks back, thinking it's a race and hoping to see who'd win. But they're driving like they was on a pike road 'stead of a bumpy country lane, and they goes up into the hills—too wild and lonely for your papa. He thinks to hisself they're a couple of booberkins and goes on his way. Well, it's a bright moonlit night, and after a bit he looks back again and sees that there phaeton sail right off the top o' Satan's Perch!"

"Good . . . God!" gasped Harry. "I knew nothing of this! When did it happen?"

"Let's see . . . Musta been somewhere in early '13, I'd say . . . No! Come to think about it, it was in the summer time."

"While I was ill . . ." Harry breathed, half to himself. "So *that's* why he didn't tell me."

"Thought they brung you home in the summer of '12."

87

"Yes. I'd an accident later, but never mind about that. Please go on."

"Well, there was a flash young cove in that there phaeton, name of Frederick Carlson. Dead as a doornail when they found him. His sister would have it was murder. Proper heartbroke she were, and kept insisting as your papa knowed more'n he was telling—that he'd seen who was in the carriage."

"What fustian! I collect the poor woman must have been deranged by grief. If they were racing they probably came too close to the edge, is all. Had it looked like foul play, I do assure you my papa would never have rested 'til he came to the root of it." He was silent for a while, puzzling at this new and unexpected development, and thinking he *must* talk with Barnaby Schofield as soon as possible.

Diccon summoned all his forces and managed to saunter to the cart. He rummaged among the miscellany, muttering that he'd best have a look at his 'tradeables,' and Harry watched, curiously. The first item to be removed was the battered violin case.

Shocked, Harry expostulated, "You're never going to trade *that*?"

"So you heard." A half-smile touched that gaunt face. "Thought as how you was all wore out."

"You have a great gift," said Harry earnestly. "Why in the name of heaven do you live like this when you could play before the crowned heads of—"

"Thank you, sir," said Diccon, his face inscrutable.

"There's a story here," thought Harry. It was quite obvious, however, that Diccon did not wish to speak of it, and being much too well bred to pursue the matter, he said no more.

"Now, this here," Diccon announced, pulling out the oar, "I *am* going t'trade." He sighed and added despondently, "One o'these days."

"Where did you get it?"

"From a nun. On Salisbury Plain. Traded her a pistol for it."

Harry's jaw dropped. "A . . . *nun* . . ? What in the—Why would a nun—on Salisbury Plain . . . have an oar?"

Diccon looked at him pityingly. "All them years you was at Oxford . . ."

"Cambridge!"

"An' ye c'n ask such a foolish question. She had the oar for a boat, a'course. What else?"

Harry closed his sagging jaw. To verify his utter stupidity by venturing to enquire what a nun would want with a pistol was more than he dared do!

"Dead?" Sir Harry stared blankly at the magnificent being who stood in the open doorway of Sir Barnaby Schofield's big house. "B-But—when? How?"

"My late employer was killed when 'is curricle hoverturned two week ago," said the footman to some invisible giant who apparently towered behind the morning caller. "Hi should think has 'ow you'd know that hif you was hindeed acquainted wiv him. Good day, sir."

"Is there some difficulty here?" A soberly dressed man of vast dignity appeared in the doorway. His indifferent gaze abruptly resolved into horrified dismay, and Harry was urged to come inside at once. Closing the door and dismissing the pained footman with an impatient wave of the hand, the butler cried, "Sir Harry! Good gracious! Whatever has happened to you?"

"Bit awful, ain't it, Dyer?" said Harry ruefully. "D'you think I dare offer my condolences to Lady Barnaby—in all my dirt?"

"I am very sure she would rather have it thus, sir—than not at all. However, she's in Devonshire with Mrs. Manderville. I am instructed to close the house for the balance of the year and to dispose of as many of Sir Barnaby's effects as would cause his widow pain." The faded brown eyes that had been scanning Harry throughout this small speech had become more and more anguished, and now, forgetting protocol, he burst out, "Oh, sir! I heard you had closed your houses, but—I never dreamed . . ! And—your poor head!"

"A highwayman, I'm afraid. Blasted fellow got my mare, which is what really puts me into the boughs. And all my effects are in Dorsetshire, unfortunately. I'd not have stopped, but I chanced to be near Maidstone and knew Sir Barnaby was often here at this time of the year . . . Lord, but I cannot believe this! I must seek out Lady Barnaby."

"But, sir! You *cannot* step outside in that condition!" The well-kept hands wrung in agitation. "I shall instruct your groom to take your coach around to the stables and you can borrow some of Major Bertram's garments—you're much of a size, I think."

"Didn't come by coach, Dyer." Not having the heart to further distress the man by informing him that a donkey had drawn his conveyance as far as the end of the lane and that he'd walked the rest of the distance he said, "Since my mare was stolen, a friend was so kind as to drop me here."

It was odd, thought the worthy Dyer, that Sir Harry had not been given the loan of a mount and that the friend had not waited. His suspicions deepening, he said earnestly, "My late master and your papa was bosom bows all their lives, sir. And I know what Sir Barnaby would wish me to do. You come along with me, Sir Harry, and we'll have you neat as a pin in no time!"

Pride demanded he refuse. Necessity, and the burning need to discover what had happened to Schofield, prevailed.

An hour later, bathed, dressed in clean linens and clothes that were a close enough fit not to amuse, Harry leaned back in the wing chair beside the saloon fire, accepted the wineglass that was handed him, and gave a sigh of gratification. "Dyer," he said as the butler took the chair on the other side of the fireplace. "I always knew you were a prince of a fellow. I feel human again! Thank you. And now, if you will, pray tell me what happened to poor Sir Barnaby."

"He'd been very low in spirits for well over a year, sir," sighed Dyer. "I always thought it was your father's death that started it all. He never seemed to quite get over it.

Nothing Lady Barnaby could do would seem to cheer him. He was . . . like a man haunted. Many's the time I heard him say, "Poor Colin . . . dear old Colin . . ." over and over again, even when there was no one nigh him. For a while I really feared for . . . for his reason. But then Major Bertram came home from Waterloo, and—well . . . we had our hands full."

"Yes. I heard. How does the poor fellow go on now?"

Dyer stared at his glass. "He's blind, sir. And he never was the kind to—er . . . That is to say—I hope he may improve."

"Took it hard, did he? Cannot say I blame him." And having been well acquainted with the pompous display that masked Bertie Schofield's weak nature, Harry asked shrewdly, "The bottle?"

The butler nodded. "And I'm inclined to think that was the last straw for Sir Barnaby. He took to doing such—odd things. Things a man of his constitution had no business doing, if you'll excuse me for saying so. He was, for example, driving a four-in-hand, and quite—er—bosky, when he turned over."

"A *coach and four? Schofield?* But your footman said it was a curricle!"

"We felt . . . the family felt . . . it sounded less ludicrous, sir."

"Gad! Had he become one of these looby amateur coachmen, then?"

"That, and worse." Dyer leaned forward, hands clasped between his knees, his eyes full of sadness. "Sir Harry, I mean no disrespect to the dead, but you being such a close friend . . . There wasn't *anything* he wouldn't do! Nothing too wild or too reckless! I used to go to bed at night with the candle set out on the hall table, and Sir Barnaby having told me not to wait up for him. And I'd lie there waiting for the Watch to come—or the Runners . . . to tell us he'd killed himself. Because—I think that's what he wanted. I think poor Sir Barnaby *wanted* to be dead!"

* * *

Before leaving the Schofield house Harry imposed on the butler for the loan of pen and paper, and these being made available, he dashed off three quick letters. The first was to Bolster, thanking him for his help at Moiré and explaining that he'd been unavoidably detained but would reach the Priory within a few days. The second was to his Hill Street residence, desiring that Anderson come at once to Chichester, bringing some of the meagre funds he'd left in Town, together with a valise containing sufficient of his clothes for a week or so and his new drab greatcoat. His third letter was directed to Mordecai Langridge, asking what he knew of the Carlson affair and requesting that his reply be addressed in care of the Marquis of Damon at Cancrizans Priory.

Dyer having promised to send the letters to the Receiving Office at once, Harry shook him by the hand, thanked him fervently, and refused his anxious offer to call up a hackney. His remark that 'his friend' had promised to swing by and pick him up brought a look of relief to the butler's worried eyes, and Harry took his leave, pledging to return Major Bertram's garments, duly cleaned, at the very earliest opportunity. He strode off down the lane at a brisk pace. The two golden guineas Dyer had shyly begged to loan him would assure him of a meal and a ticket on the stagecoach. He had no idea where Sprague Cobb lived, but he'd heard that Lord Cootesby owned a small seat outside Chichester, and to that lovely old cathedral town he intended to repair as swiftly as possible. Schofield's death had come as a sad shock, for he'd been deeply fond of the genial man. It had also delayed his hopes of learning more about that fatal card game. Still, with luck he would be in Chichester by early evening, and Cootesby, having been a friend of his father, would likely be willing to put him up for the night, or perhaps— He frowned at the sight of a drunkard weaving along the lane before him, quite obviously scarcely able to navigate. Even as he watched the man blundered into a tree and slid loosely downward. There were no ladies within sight, fortunately, and he went over to help the individual to his feet. ''A trifle early in the day to be in that condition, ain't . . .'' The scornful words died in his throat as a pathetically emaciated young face was lifted. The boy was obviously ill and on the brink of collapse. Harry's concerned enquiry elicited the information that he'd been wounded at Waterloo and had only recently managed to work his way home. When it was revealed that he'd served under the command of Timothy Van Lindsay (with whom Harry was sure he had once dined in Madrid), there was nothing for it but to help the poor fellow.

By easy stages and the benefit of Harry's supporting arm, the youthful veteran was enabled to reach a small coffee shop near the stagecoach office. He was, he imparted when the first pangs of hunger were eased, Billy Ernest, and with the flicker of a smile he said it had always been a joke with his mates that he had two first names. His health was gone, the long battle to recover from a shattered hip not likely to be won. But he said with quiet courage that he was nearly home now, and if he could just reach Winchester and see his family, he'd not so much mind dying. He looked as though he would probably do just that and, his heart wrung, Harry said sternly that he couldn't picture one of Van Lindsay's chaps selling out so cheap. A sudden spark in the hollowed eyes encouraged him. He left Ernest rapturously tackling a large slice of custard pie and hurried to the stagecoach office. The coach from Chatham to Southampton departed in ten minutes; it would stop at Chichester, and there was one seat left—outside. The coach from Canterbury to Guildford would arrive in half an hour, and connections could be made at Guildford with a stage that would pass through Winchester. There was no way that Harry's gold pieces would stretch to cover both journeys; nor was there any doubt in his mind. He returned to Ernest and chatted with him until the last of the pie was tucked away and a trace of colour had returned to the drawn young face. Then he escorted him to the coaching station and, having exchanged a few words with a sympathetic guard, left Rifleman Ernest, the ticket clutched in one thin hand and tears of gratitude shimmering in his eyes.

* * *

What had him fairly into the hips, thought Sergeant Anderson glumly, leaning back in the uncomfortable chair in the solicitor's waiting room, was where was the Captain? When the hackney had rattled to a stop in front of the house an hour ago, he'd thought Sir Harry was come back and his heart had fairly jumped through his ribs. Never had he been so put about as to find that little twiddlepoop, Mr. Mitchell, had slipped his leash and slunk back to Town. And what a roll of flimsies he'd flashed in that purse of his! The jarvey had all but fell off'n the box waiting for some of it to be put in his greedy paws! Good thing *he'd* been there or nodcock Mitchell would've give him a pound note 'stead o' the two shillings he warranted for the journey from the coaching station.

Anderson rested his brooding gaze upon the frail, balding little man who laboured at the tall desk just outside Mr. Crosby Frye's inner office. Poor scrawny little chap. A nice life he must lead with that cantankerous solicitor to bow and scrape to all day. A slippery customer, Crosby Frye, with his smiles and subservient bows for the Quality and snarls for common folks. The Sergeant could not help but grin a little to recall how breezily Mr. Mitchell had strolled straight into the inner office, without so much as a by-your-leave. The clerk had seemed mesmerized by the young man's easy manner and pleasant smile, not realizing until it was too late that Redmond had no intention of stopping at his desk.

One thing, Anderson thought grudgingly; Mr. Mitchell had taken the news of their changed circumstances calmly enough. When he'd walked into the house and discovered the rooms bare of furniture, he'd paused for the barest instant and drawled lazily, "Has my brother removed, Sergeant?" And when he'd been told straight out that the Captain had no more lettuce in the bowl, he'd looked only mildly surprised. Not until he'd learned that his brother had been gone for five days and no word, had the smile left those grey eyes. They'd come here 'tooty sweet' then, as the Frogs would say. Though what for, he—

A small bell over the door commenced to jangle violently. Sergeant Anderson stared in astonishment as the clerk literally leapt into the air and, with his tall stool toppling behind him, scurried not for the office of his employer but for the outer hall. Lord, how the chap ran! Like a scared rabbit!

The inner door opened and Mitchell exited briskly closing the door behind him. "Come on, Andy," he said, striding past. "Cannot wait all day."

"Andy!" thought the Sergeant furiously, standing and thumping after him.

Their driver had taken his hack for a walk up and down the street; a logical enough procedure yet one that put a small crease between Mitchell's brows as they hastened to the vehicle. He snapped something to the jarvey and sprang inside. Climbing in after him, Anderson barely had the door closed before the hackney plunged forward. Flung down, he glared at Redmond as he righted himself. "Where we orf to now?"

Mitchell ran long white fingers tenderly over his right wrist. "Into the country," he murmured. "London's noise distresses me."

Anderson's disgust was as eloquent as it was silent, but it was also very brief, for as they rounded the corner they all but collided with a black, enclosed carriage racing past at great speed. He peered after it curiously. "Bow Street. Looks like the Runners is after a hot one." Mitchell made no reply, and glancing to him, Anderson asked indifferently if he had hurt his hand.

"Think I must have sprained it," Mitchell yawned. "Probably picked up something too heavy."

The Sergeant snorted. "A book, most likely."

Mitchell's response to this barb was to appear to go to sleep, not stirring again until they had left the metropolis behind. Rousing at length, he looked absently out of the window but, feeling his companion's scorching stare upon him, enquired, "Have you ever noticed, Andy, how magnificent a creation is a tree?" Well aware of the tightening of that grim mouth, he went on drowsily, "I know of few things more restful than to watch the flutter of the leaves."

"Flutter of the leaves . . ." muttered Anderson, *sotto voce*. "Luv a duck!"

"You prefer to contemplate birds? Well, you've a point. Ducks, though . . ." Mitchell wrinkled his brow. "I'd not thought . . ."

"Gawd!" snarled the Sergeant. "What we a'doing of in this ruddy, stupid wilderness, Mr. Redmond, while Sir Harry's up to I dunno what all by himself?"

"But you said he was with Jeremy Bolster. And if ever there was a fighting fool, it's old Bolster. I remember once . . ."

He continued to remember in lazy detail while they headed northwest towards the hillside cluster of habitations that was Hampstead. It seemed to the infuriated Anderson that the driver wound about as fancy took him, and they came at last to a charming district of large homes set along winding, tree-lined lanes. Leaning from the window at the junction of two such lanes, Mitchell murmured, "Tranquillity Avenue—is it not delightful? Stop here, driver." He opened the door and sprang down, not troubling to lower the step. "I think I shall take a short stroll—you may wait here, Anderson. Just look at that acacia! I simply must have a closer view of it . . ." And he was gone, leaving the Sergeant to glare after his tall, slim figure and consign him, his Tranquillity Avenue, and his perishing acacia to the hottest area of Hades. Within a few moments, however, rather cramped from the drive, Anderson also alighted from the vehicle. There was no sign of Redmond, but the air was warm and fragrant, the lane inviting, and the beauty about him not lost upon Anderson, despite his frustration. He began to wander along, admiring the fine houses in their spacious, well-landscaped grounds. He was not the only one thus engaged; a buxom nursemaid, her perambulator at a standstill, was staring at a dwelling of Grecian design with a fine portico across the imposing front. Following her gaze, Anderson's eyes became fixed and glassy. High at the side of the house, a gentleman clung precariously to a vibrating trellis. Even as he watched, Redmond launched himself sideways and barely caught the edge of a

96

second-storey windowsill. "Gawd!" gulped the Sergeant. The nursemaid turned a pale face and shocked eyes towards him. He touched his hat. "No n-need to be alarmed, Miss. He's a student and a bit forgetful-like. Always losing his doorkey. And—it's the butler's day orf."

She recovered sufficiently to gasp out, "Cor . . !" and hastened along her way, her journey marked by many a backward glance.

Anderson held out little hope of escaping arrest but sped across the lane and made his horrified way to the criminal. "Mr. Mitchell!" he cried in scandalized accents. "What in the devil is you about?"

"Do be quiet, Andy!" And hanging by both hands from the window ledge of the residence of Mr. Sprague Cobb, Mitchell pointed out, "You are attracting attention!"

CHAPTER VII

BETWEEN BADLY BLISTERED HEELS AND THE RECALCI-
trant kitchen pump of a kindly farm wife, it took Harry
two days to reach Tunbridge Wells again. His success with
the pump earned him a fine breakfast and the loan of the
farmer's razor, but otherwise it was a lonely two days,
affording all too much time for contemplation of Past, Future, and—more depressingly—Present. He passed the first
night under a haystack, and the second less successfully,
discovering that the leaves and bracken he piled over himself provided neither warmth nor protection from the drizzle which, by the time he awoke from a fitful doze, had
become a steady downpour.

He reached the Wells in mid-morning, in so disreputable
a condition that it was doubtful any friend or acquaintance
would recognize him even did they chance to be abroad
before noon. Encouraged by this thought, he ventured into
the Constable's Office and reported the theft of Lace. His
story created a sensation. He was compelled to remain and
add his impressions to a pile of sketches and descriptions
of Devil Dice that were as diverse as they were inaccurate.
His hilarity over one lady's tale of the dashing young highwayman who had kissed her hand even as he gently slid
the rubies from about her throat irked the stern minions of
the law. An indignant Harry was interrogated at great
length. It was obvious that his appearance and lack of identification caused them to doubt his veracity and he was
required to dictate a detailed account of his experience to

a dim-witted youth who seemed barely capable of discerning one end of a pencil from the other.

It was late afternoon before he escaped and continued upon his journey, eating the roast beef sandwich he had purchased from a small clean ordinary. And although the rain continued drearily and his heels hurt, it was not these discomforts that gradually caused his spirits to become depressed. On the Peninsula he had cheerfully endured conditions a hundred times less pleasant, with lashing rain and icy wind; bones that ached with exhaustion; a stomach cramping from near-starvation; and the deadly crack of rifles echoing across the Spanish hills. But also there had been the merry laughter of comrades; the badinage of fellow officers who would die before admitting their own misery; the cheerful profanity of the rank and file, their courage undaunted by hardship, their loyalty fierce and inflexible. He sighed, wishing he'd not told Diccon to go on and not wait for him at Maidstone. He'd been so sure Barney would be able to provide him with many answers . . . poor old Barney. Now, he must get to Chichester—a matter of sixty miles and more, and the munificent sum of two shillings and threepence halfpenny could not be stretched to include a warm bed en route. Once at Chichester, of course, he would be very close to the unfailing hospitality of Lucian St. Clair's Beechmead Hall, or the Earl of Harland's Hollow Hill Manor. But regretfully, he knew he could not go to either of those gracious homes, or to Lord John Moulton's lovely old Greenwings. His friends would press him to stay. They would look at him with affection—and sympathy. And sympathy he found he could not endure.

He scowled and pulled his sagging shoulders erect. What a gudgeon to be lumping along like this! Fate may have dealt him a leveller, but although he could not call on them he *was* blessed by friends! Many, loyal, and good friends. And he had Mitch and Mordecai and the numerous other members of his family. He walked on at a brisker pace; and because the wind was colder and blew the trees mournfully, because the rain grew ever heavier and the leaden skies were no whit gloomier than his prospects, he whistled cheerily.

The hoofbeats that came up behind him were those of a single animal and proceeded at a leisured pace so that he knew he would neither have to jump for his life as the mail coach flashed past, nor guard against the sheeting mud and water flung up by racing carriage or chaise wheels. With luck it might be some good-natured carter, willing to let him ride along for a while. But even as he started to turn around, he heard the hooves quicken to something almost approaching a canter, while a great rattling and clanking was accompanied by a shout, a feminine squeal, and an outburst of wild braying. Harry's heart gave a joyous leap, and he ran to meet as royal a welcome as ever he had known.

Mr. Fox brayed and butted at his ribs; Diccon swung down from the cart to seize him in a hug; and even Miss Nanette, shielded from the rain by a man's greatcoat and with a piece of oilcloth held over her head, exclaimed with apparent enthusiasm that it was like meeting a long-lost comrade and urged him to get into the cart, "For you look," said she, "like a drowned rat."

Harry's protests that it would be too much of a load for Mr. Fox were overruled. Diccon insisted that he had been riding all day and it would do him good to stretch his legs. He waved Harry to the driving seat beside Miss Nanette while he went to Mr. Fox's head, and they started off once more.

"How glad I am that we met again," said Harry with real sincerity. "Does Diccon take you to Devonshire now?"

"Yes, for he has no more trading to do for a little while and promises we shall go straight there. Indeed, we thought we would have come up with you before—" She checked, then finished rather lamely, "Unless you got a ride."

He raised the flap of the oilcloth Diccon had tossed him and eyed her curiously. "You were looking for me?"

Miss Nanette's attempt to reply evidently imposed a severe strain, for her eyes slid into the crossed position once more, and Harry turned quickly away, feeling sorry for the poor little chit that so simple a question should overwhelm her. "Not . . . exactly," she managed at length. "But Diccon plans to go through Chichester, so we—that is, Diccon, thought—"

"Does he? Oh, but that is famous! We can all go on together!" His exuberance faded and he finished humbly, "At least, if he don't mind . . ."

"How should he mind?" she said, her pertness restored. "The time it hang heavily on his hands when he has not to occupy himself tending to your cuts and scrapes."

Harry laughed, and she laughed with him. Diccon turned and grinned back at them, and Mr. Fox emitted a small bray for pure companionship's sake.

And if the rain pattered down as dismally as before, and the breath of the wind was as cold, Harry noticed neither and thought only how much brighter was the world than it had been these past two days.

"Oh, my lor' . . . Oh, let me die! Quick!" Trapped in the small cabin of a packet that wallowed in heavy seas, Sergeant Albert Anderson, who had uttered not a whimper when his leg was amputated, now clung to the rail of the bunk and moaned cravenly.

Mitchell, sitting on the other bunk, feet braced against the side, scarcely heard the heartfelt wails, his full attention upon the unfinished letter he had purloined from Sprague Cobb's deserted house in Hampstead.

> *"My Dear Old Coot,"* (this read)
> *"I scarce know how to tell you what I learned yesterday by purest chance. If it is truth, then you and I—"* This half-sentence was lined through heavily, and the letter went on: *"You have by now heard of poor Barney Schofield's tragic death. I wonder if your thoughts, like my own, have—But perhaps it is best that I do not set my fears onto paper. I leave today for Dinan. I will come to see you as soon as I return. If I find—"*

Here, the disjointed missive had been abandoned, and an echo of the Sergeant's anguish penetrating his consciousness at last, Mitchell looked up. "Poor sailor, are you, Andy?" he asked sympathetically.

"Ain't . . . sailor . . . 'tall!" gulped the unhappy sergeant. "And what in the name of . . . What I'm a'doing of in this lot . . . I dunno . . !"

"I told you," Mitchell explained patiently. "It is quite typical of Sir Harry to go charging off to Brittany like this, but—"

"Don't know as . . . he has . . ."

"I think it highly probable. And when you went round to Lord Bolster's flat they said his lordship feared Harry might've gone after Sanguinet, don't you remember?"

"Don't remember . . . me own . . . name!" Anderson groaned, looking wretchedly away from the porthole and the grey seas that heaved upward until they blotted out the sky.

"Poor fellow. It is Anderson, and you—" Here the Sergeant's baleful glare deterred him. "I'm sorry," he smiled. "But you surely know how hot at hand Sir Harry can be. I must stop him before he gets into trouble. But there was no need for you to— Oh, dear!" He crossed swiftly to hand the sufferer a bowl. "You need this, I fear." That he was right was unhappily evident, and a short time later, wiping the Sergeant's pallid features with a wet rag, he said, "Think I'll take a turn about the deck. Always did love a storm at sea."

"Yus," moaned Anderson, eyeing him without delight. "You would. Sir."

Mitchell turned back and pointed out that he should have stayed in England, a sentiment Anderson fervently echoed, but then observed he'd not dared to let Mitchell come alone. "Not once I found what a horrid streak . . . y'got in yer, sir."

"Me?" blinked Redmond, injured. "But I am a very quiet individual. I love my books and my music, and to commune with nature. I would never—"

"Never have the Bow Street Runners *and* the Watch arter us in one day? Wouldn't dream of it! Oh, no! I'm sure!"

"I cannot imagine whatever gave you the idea that the Runners were—"

"Oh, can't yer! That there little wisp of a clerk of Mr. Frye's goes—" Anderson groaned and tightened his clutch on the bunk as the room tilted slowly to one side. "Goes shooting orf like a . . . scared rabbit. And we hop it, just as the Runners comes tearing past! The next thing I knows you've took to milling kens . . . breaking and entering! Robbing houses what's got the knocker orf the door! And we're running like hell with half of Hampstead's Watch, popylation, and dogs howling arter us! And I'll tellya what else I think, Mr. Redmond! Oh, Gawd—oh, fer dry land! . . . I think . . . as you hurt yer hand picking up that greasy little Crosby Frye! I think . . . as you took him by the neck and shook him . . . like a rat. And that's why there's prob'ly warrants out fer us, right this here . . . minute!"

"Well, there you really *do* mistake it!" Mitchell's tone was grave, but his eyes danced, nonetheless; and as Anderson watched that sparkle suspiciously, he clarified, "Crosby Frye is a weasel. Not a rat." Here, Anderson uttering another groan, he said, "You really do have my sympathy. My brother's not a good sailor, either. Must be awful. You know, Sergeant, what you should do is lose yourself in a good book." He crossed to the small wall bookcase, opened one of the glass doors, and threw up an arm to ward off the catapulting volumes. He picked up *The Corsair* and glanced at the rugged, if greenish features that were turned toward him. Lord Byron and Anderson could have little in common. The next book, happily a small one, was entitled, *The Treacherous Custom of Bathing*. Intrigued, he turned the first pages and beheld the subtitle: 'Being a Learned Humanitarian's Discourse on the Dangers and Frequent Fatalities Resulting from the Ill-Advised Practice of Dabbling in Water.' He grinned but set it aside. The third volume was entitled, *The Mysteries of Udolpho*. He considered it thoughtfully. Ann Radcliffe. Not the book he'd have chosen but undoubtedly the likeliest of the three. He carried it to the sufferer and placed it within reach of his palsied hand. The scornful snort that greeted this gesture was a pitiful echo of the usually bull-like rebuff. "Try it," Mitchell urged gravely. "It might take your mind off the—ah—heaving pitch and roll of the seas."

Anderson informed him faintly that he was a vicious young gentleman. Mitchell chuckled, fought his way to the door and, having assured the Sergeant he would not be buried at sea, left him.

The door closed and drifted nauseatingly to where the ceiling had been. Outside, the wind howled through the rigging, and spray splattered against the port. His insides quaking, Anderson recalled Mr. Mitchell's sadistic words, ". . . might take your mind off the heaving . . ." Desperate, he snatched up the book. A romance! As if he wanted that tripe! He cast it aside with loathing. The packet hung atop a giant wave, then slid down a green wall into the trough. Shuddering, Anderson groped for Mrs. Radcliffe. Anything, he thought, would be better than this!

The dark clouds were beginning to thin out, adding drama to a magnificent sunset when Diccon announced they would stop for the night. His choice of a campsite was excellent. They were sheltered by great oak trees, a stream ran close by, and the rain having stopped at last, their fire was soon bringing warmth and cheer to dispel the cold dampness of the evening. Miss Nanette had become quiet and withdrawn, and by the time Harry went to help Diccon put up the tent, her crossed eyes and dull-witted expression had so repelled him that he was glad to escape her. The exertion, however, brought on a recurrence of the occasional blinding headaches he suffered since Dice had shot him, and although he believed he was concealing his discomfort, Diccon's shrewd eyes were quick to detect his deathly pallor. "That's done," he said cheerily. "You go and rest a bit, Mr. Allison." Harry's opposition was of a token nature only; but not until he stretched out beside the fire did he realize how very weary he was, and he raised few objections when he was refused permission to help with preparations for dinner.

His philosophical musings on how terrible a thing was

loneliness were banished by amusement as he watched the girl. She approached each task with an eager intensity—as though it were all very new and exciting. Teasing her because she cubed the meat while holding the tip of her tongue on her upper lip, he was flashed a sparkling glance but begged not to disturb her until "this beef is subdued." Her encounter with onions had her in tears which she found both uncomfortable and hilarious, and her watery-eyed resolve that "this beast of a bulb will be dealt with!" led to a spirited exchange that left all three weak with laughter. Harry was convinced Miss Nanette knew little of cooking, but her movements were graceful, her step swift and light, and she had a way of coming abruptly from gravity to total merriment that was really quite taking. Her affliction, together with her belligerence, seemed less evident, so that he began to wonder if both were not largely caused by nerves.

Dinner was a jolly meal. Harry's headache had abated, and Miss Nanette joined eagerly in the conversation which turned often to Moiré Grange and the Redmonds. The subject seemed to enthrall her, and she bombarded Harry with questions that he found rather pathetic by their eagerness, leading him to suspect that her own unhappy childhood must provoke this rampant curiosity regarding the lives of others. When the meal ended, he insisted upon helping to wash and put away the dishes but, claiming a reward for these noble efforts, asked that Diccon play for them. The Trader hesitated, but Miss Nanette also pleaded until the old fiddle was brought forth. When Diccon began to play, she exchanged an astonished glance with Harry, then leaned forward, hands clasped, listening with breathless concentration. Diccon played superbly and for a moment, when he finished, neither of his audience moved. Then Miss Nanette jumped up and ran to hug him. He was clearly taken aback by this impulsive gesture, but if it was improper, Harry also felt it an apt tribute, and said so.

It had been agreed between them that for so long as they travelled together, Miss Nanette would occupy the tent. Tonight she left them when Diccon's battered old watch indicated the hour of ten, and the two men wrapped themselves in their blankets and settled down beside the fire. For a little while they engaged in desultory conversation, but Harry was too tired to be rational and fell asleep listening to the girl singing softly to herself in her funny little voice.

Some hours later a small but dismal sound awoke him. Diccon snored softly, the wind had died down, and save for the occasional hoot of an owl, or the rustling progress of some small creature through the wet bracken, the night was quiet. Harry rolled over and glanced to the tent. Miss Nanette's candle was extinguished, but his keen hearing had not misled him, for soon he heard another muffled sob. He pulled himself to one elbow and frowned at the tent uneasily. She was an odd little thing, but he felt a kinship with her—perhaps because they both faced so uncertain a future. She was undoubtedly of gentle birth, yet there was not an ounce of affectation to her, and even in the brief time of their acquaintanceship he'd come to feel as comfortably at ease with her as though she were a younger, and rather naughty, sister. There was little wonder that she should weep. She had certainly led a sheltered life up to now, and her present circumstances must evoke fears that would be nigh crushing. If she were to be discovered before Diccon could convey her to her aunt, or if the gossips learned of her flight, she would be totally ruined and must consider herself fortunate if the suitor she so disdained consented to wed her.

At this point, a shuddering sob so wrought upon Harry that he started up, resolved to try and comfort her; but despite his happy-go-lucky demeanor, he was not without sensitivity. Miss Nanette was, he knew, trying very hard to be brave and resourceful. To reveal that her weeping had been overheard might but add to her distress. He lay back, torn between sympathy for her despair and vexation with her foolishness. Frowning into the darkness, he could not but wonder how many sheltered girls would have possessed the courage to take so gigantic a step, however ill-advised. He wondered also if her father was wakeful tonight, plagued with fears perhaps, and his heart breaking for his errant daughter, poor old fellow . . . Determined that he would make every effort to restore her as quickly as possible to the bosom of her family, Harry fell asleep.

His resolve was heightened the next morning when he discovered the eggs to be like nothing so much as rubber, the toast charred, and the coffee boiled over. He ate lightly and, keeping a cynical eye on Diccon's plate, saw it wiped clean, while not so much as a murmur was raised over coffee in which grounds floated murkily. He was startled when the Trader said they would rest today, and protested the waste of time with vehemence. Diccon waited patiently through this tirade and then pointed out that it was Sunday, and he never travelled on Sundays. Harry felt like a clod and looked guiltily toward Miss Nanette. She was staring at him with what he had come to think of as her witless look. They had, she then remembered, passed an old church a mile or so back, and perhaps Diccon would escort her there, since Mr. Allison was quite obviously not a God-fearing type. This snide attack brought an immediate protest from Harry, and he proceeded to recount how he and his father and brother had rarely missed Sunday services. At once all interest, Miss Nanette was full of questions which he answered willingly enough for a while. Inevitably, however, such memories engendered sad thoughts of his father and of the task in which he appeared to be making very little progress. He fell silent and was gazing despondently at the fire when he heard the mellow call of a cuckoo.

"Listen!" Nanette tilted her head to one side. "How very pretty it is."

"A bit early in the season, isn't it?" Harry glanced to Diccon, but the big man no longer sprawled in his customary fashion against an obliging tree. Instead, wearing a fairly presentable hat and carrying a gnarled walking stick, he pronounced himself ready to escort Miss Nanette to church. If, he added, she felt it wise. The girl, who had started up brightly, hesitated, drew back, and shook her head.

"In that case, I'll be back soon. Keep a sharp eye on Mr. Fox, Harry." A twinkle crept into the light eyes. "And I hopes as how you'll both remember it's Sunday and a day of peace and rest. Let's not have no trouble."

Not a little astounded by Diccon's purposeful stride, Harry walked a little way with him and returned to discover the girl industriously folding the blankets. His offer to help was rebuffed and he was urged to instead shave himself because "your chin looks like my hairbrush!" Amused, he began to gather his borrowed shaving impedimenta but paused when Miss Nanette got into a terrible muddle with the blanket. His chuckles set her cheeks aflame with mortification, but again disdaining assistance she swept past him, her nose in the air, only to trip over a trailing end. He sprang quickly to restore her. Part of her bun had fallen over her eyes, and she knelt on hands and knees amid a welter of blanket. She scowled up at him, but her chagrin faded before his gallant attempts to restrain his mirth, and her own lilting laugh joined his as he helped her to her feet.

Harry then retreated to a secluded spot beside the stream, but shaving proved difficult. Attempting to maneouvre around the half-healed cut on his lip, he raised his arm in such a way as to wrench his bruised ribs, and swore.

"Would you wish *me* to help *you*? enquired a sweet, feminine voice.

Stiffening at this blatant invasion of his privacy, he turned away and buttoned his shirt hastily while informing her in no uncertain terms that she wanted for conduct. At once, her swift temper flared. "I helped my brother once when he broke his arm and his valet was ill," she said hotly. "And as for conduct, your own is atrocious! Did you perhaps imagine I creep down to the stream to view your body?"

He tried to picture Dorothy Haines-Curtis uttering such a forthright remark and, a quirk tugging at his lips, admitted he had indulged in no such flight of fancy.

"I came," she went on, "only because you are taking all day and I thought perhaps you had difficulties. And instead I hear your frightful swearing."

He pointed out that she would have heard a lot worse on the Peninsula. At once sadness filled her eyes, and he probed curiously, "Why did you want to go? An *affaire de coeur*?"

"*Affaire de coeur*, indeed! Love! Is that all you men ever think of?"

He grinned. "Don't like us much, do you?"

"I hate men!" Her eyes flashed fiercely. "They are all the same! Animals!"

Harry blinked before such vehemence and said with dry logic that in that event he'd have thought the Peninsula the last place she'd have wanted to be.

Her anger vanishing as swiftly as it had come, she knelt close by and gazed down at a lupin she had plucked from the bank of the stream. "My brother was there," she sighed. "Had I only been with him, we could have had a little more time together."

"What was his regiment? Perhaps I knew him."

She made no answer, her sad gaze fixed on the lupin. She looked very small suddenly, and very helpless, and with a pang of sympathy, he asked, "Did you lose him, Tuppence?"

The bowed head nodded. "Yes," she whispered huskily. "I—lost him. And he . . . he was . . ." She turned away, her voice breaking, "so very . . . dear."

Touched, he said softly, "My sympathy ma'am. But—were he alive, do you think he would countenance this? No—" he lifted one hand in a graceful fencing gesture and smiled, "don't eat me! But *do* think on it. Surely, he could only be horrified to see you here. Alone, with two strange men, and—"

"Strange, indeed," she frowned. "A Trader who is too lazy to work. And a rich young man who pretends to be penniless!"

Harry's kindly concern vanished. "Pretends!" he ejaculated. "D'ye think I am in this sorry case because—"

"I think," she interrupted, "that you are engaged in some silly dare. One of those stupid bets you men so enjoy and that are such childish folly."

Infuriated, he spluttered, "Well! If *that* don't beat the Dutch! Can you seriously imagine that for the sake of some idiotic wager I would allow myself to be shot and beaten and starved, and half-frozen? Why, you wretched girl, do you suppose I *enjoy* tramping about in the rain with blisters on my heels? I collect you fancy it all a hum and that I've *not* swallowed a spider, nor—"

A horrified expression coming over her face, she intervened breathlessly, "You have not . . . *what* . . . ?"

"Swallowed a spider. But—"

"Harry Allison! You *never* did!"

She looked so awed that he could not restrain a chuckle. "It's just cant. I beg pardon; I should not have said it."

"Cant? Oh—let me guess! It means . . . to be without funds? To borrow? To be, as my brother was used to say, In Dun Territory?"

"More or less," he nodded.

Clapping her hands, Miss Nanette laughed delightedly. "Oh, how quaint! Now this I have never before heard!"

Considering that animated little face, Harry decided that she might look quite pretty in a nice frock, with her hair neatly brushed, and a ribbon around it . . . But almost at once the mindless emptiness filled her eyes and her chin lolled. He took a deep breath and, recovering his senses, waited until she was restored to normalcy, then asked gently, "Forgive me if I presume, but you've a slight accent—are you French?"

"My mama was French."

"I see. And your father is—"

Her head flung upward, her eyes blazing at him. "We will not speak of my papa, if you please! Instead, I shall now ask *you* the questions. You are the fine aristocrat, why—"

He started. "So you knew who I was, all the time."

"You are Sir Harry Redmond. And your papa left you, among other things, a great house in Hampshire. You are very far from penniless." The sudden bitter twist to his mouth stopped her. Her eyes narrowed. "Unless . . ." She leaned forward. "Are you truly without funds, Sir Harry?"

"Unfortunately, ma'am."

She drew a long, deep breath, then snorted, "Disgusting!"

"Wh-What?" Addlebrained or no, she was impossible!

His brows lowering, he grated furiously, "*Now* what are you saying?"

"That you should be ashamed! Not two years since your father's death and already you have squandered his entire fortune! *Men!* Pah!"

"By . . . God!" raged Harry. "This is too much! I wish *I* was your brother! You should be soundly spanked for making such snap judgements!" His fury cooled, however, as he perceived the approach of a newcomer. Miss Nanette did not. She sneered, tossed her nose into the air and turned from him, bending nonchalantly to pick another lupin. Retribution, thought Harry with wicked joy, was at hand.

Mr. Fox was in a humorous mood. His lowered head caught Miss Nanette well and truly. With a shriek, she dove head first into the stream. Her reaction was quicksilver. She sprang, dripping, onto the bank and her hand flashed out to slap across the donkey's face. "*Odious!* Wretched brute!" she shrilled. "*Donkey!*"

Harry leaned against a weeping willow and laughed until the tears flowed down his cheeks. Mr. Fox, braying his distress, trotted to the tent and cowered behind it. Soaked, her hair a wet straggle, her dress clinging about her, Miss Nanette stood on the bank, trying to wring the water from her skirts, and all but weeping her fury.

"You . . . you look a fine . . . sight . . ." gasped Harry, holding his ribs with one hand and wiping his eyes with the other. "A fitting chastisement!"

"Horrid wretch of a—a gamester!" she retorted.

"Oho! What a temper! You were right; I think you're worse than Juana! She, at least, would never slap a little donkey's face and make him cry."

She ceased her efforts and regarded him with dismay. "Oh . . . I did not do this. Did I?"

"Look—at him," he gasped weakly. "Poor little fella's breaking his heart over there."

She all but flew to put her arms about Mr. Fox. "*Mon pauvre!* I did not mean it! You were just playing, I know this. Although—it was very naughty of you. Ah—do not weep!" She kissed his neck and stroking him tenderly,

111

pleaded, "You will forgive your wicked Nanette—yes? I am an odious girl and should not be heeded!"

Harry, who had followed to watch this exchange, was fixed with an anguished gaze and a whimpered, *"Mon Dieu!* The poor little thing is inconsolable. I am the greatest beast in nature! Whatever shall I do to make up with him?"

He was touched to see tears in her eyes and, crossing to the cart, groaned, "Don't start weeping again, for heaven's sake!" He rummaged about and found amongst many papers a crumpled reward poster for Devil Dice. It seemed apropos. "Here . . ." He returned to hand it to her surreptitiously. "Give him this."

She stared up at him in astonishment, and he noted that this morning the flecks in her eyes were green; also that her teeth were beginning to chatter and the end of her little nose to turn blue. "Hurry up," he urged. "He has a literary taste. And you are breaking out in goosebumps."

The little donkey eyed her reproachfully but finally accepted the paper and, having devoured it, leaned his head against her. "Ah . . . !" One cold hand clapped to her heart and she closed her eyes with a sigh of relief. "He has forgiven me! Thank goodness!" She hugged Mr. Fox, and sneezed.

"And you, little one, are taking a cold. Come over by the fire and take off those wet clothes. We can—"

Instead, however, she made a mad dash for the cart and began to pull frantically at the oar. Watching her sadly Harry thought that there could be little doubt but that the poor chit's intellect was disordered. What a pity.

Meanwhile, Nanette had succeeded in releasing the oar, and grasping it in both hands, she swung to face him, panting, "Stay back! Filthy villain! You think to ravish me now we are alone, *hein*?"

"Good God!" gasped Harry, considerably taken aback. "I wouldn't ravish *you* were we alone on a desert isle for the rest of our days!"

For some odd reason this did not appear to please her. "Crudity!" she screamed. "Foulness!" She swung the oar, but it was much heavier than she'd suspected and so cumbersome as to take her off balance. Her eyes widened as she was pulled sideways. Her swing had been lusty; the oar gathered momentum, and before she could relinquish her grasp it whammed into the tent, drawing her after it. The tent promptly collapsed and with a muffled shriek she disappeared from view.

It had been quite some time since Harry had so hugely enjoyed himself. He wiped the tears from his eyes and sobbingly unearthed her. "Are you . . . hurt? By George, but you're a fire-eater!"

Miss Nanette, lying with arms wide-tossed amidst the wreckage, refused the hand he reached down to her. "I have not . . . the breath . . ." she gasped. Her gaze searched his mirthful face and whatever she read there appeared to calm her fears. "That . . . beast of . . . an oar!" She began to giggle and Harry was undone. His hilarity exploded and he sat beside her while they laughed until they held their sides with exhaustion.

Mr. Fox, meanwhile, had discovered the pot of gold at the end of his rainbow and happily devoured all the papers in Diccon's cart.

Miss Nanette's gown was still not quite dry when she pronounced herself bored with sitting in the tent wrapped in a blanket and insisted upon it being brought to her so that she might don it again. Harry had worked hard to restore the tent and would have been glad to relax for a while. However, although the morning had become warm, it was cool in the shade of the trees, and fearing the girl would take a chill, he suggested they go for a short stroll. He quickly discovered that while her intellect might be disordered, she yet possessed an extremely high level of curiosity. Their 'short stroll' was constantly lengthened by her discovery of some new interest to this side or that, and her dartings off to investigate a flowering shrub or a hovering butterfly had a tendency to make conversation erratic. In the midst of a sentence describing the lily collection in the greenhouse at Moiré, he turned to discover himself alone and could discern no sign of that small, untidy head.

113

"What the devil!" he muttered in exasperation. "Tuppence . . ?"

The only response was the echo of his own voice. Cursing under his breath he hurried down the hill and came upon her standing very still amid some small trees, a warning frown upon her face, and one slim finger held to her lips. He slowed and peered curiously. A squirrel was advancing with much caution along a low-hanging branch toward the acorn she offered. A twig snapped under Harry's boot and the squirrel was gone in a blur of speed.

"Oh!" Nanette exclaimed with the stamp of one foot. "What a great, blundering creature you are to be sure!"

"Your servant, ma'am!" He bowed his most graceful, flowing bow and, as they walked on together, murmured, "Such enthusiasm for flora and fauna! One might think you'd never been for a country walk."

"Not at my home," she sighed. "Always, my papa insisted I must ride in the carriage. Walking, he says, is for servants and street women. And my brother was a formidable horseman so with him I rode also. You, I suppose, having been blessed with a very kind father, learned much of the countryside?"

Before Harry knew it, he was deep in a discourse upon Colin Redmond. Miss Nanette's interest was both intense and flattering, and not for some time did he realize that he was doing all the talking. As soon as that fact dawned on him, he turned the conversation deftly until he at last came to his opportunity and enquired as to how long she had been acquainted with Lady Nerina.

"For about five years, I suppose." She headed for the brow of the hill and sat beneath a spreading old oak, gazing out across the countryside. "How very lovely it all is . . . so green, and just look at all the chestnut trees . . ."

"Yes," he said shortly and, having cast a swift and unseeing glance at the verdant panorama, persisted, "did you meet her at the Convent?"

"Mmmmn. What is that great castle in the distance?"

"Bodiam. Were—er—were all of you young ladies leaving the Convent?"

"Why, yes. We could not bring it with us, you see, sir."

He frowned, but the dimple that peeped forth beside her mouth disarmed him.

"Little shrew!" he laughed. "You know what I mean."

"*Oui.*" She yawned behind her hand. "You wish to know if the Lady Nerina is returning to the Convent. She is not, for we were only visiting. We took Sister Maria Evangeline out for her birthday party, and then we journeyed to Park Parapine to see Nerina's cousin Yolande, who also attended the Convent when she was young. And on the way back we stayed at Mrs. Burnett's boardinghouse, which is where you laid eyes upon your vision of paradise."

Harry felt his face become hot and said hurriedly, "Yolande Drummond must have aged very rapidly since last month she was, as I recall, one and twenty."

Watching him with grave intensity, she asked, "Did your papa have such very green eyes?"

"No. His eyes were grey, like my brother's."

"Ah, yes . . . your poor brother. I suppose he can no longer stay at Oxford now that you have gambled away all—"

"You mistake it," he intervened coldly. "My brother will take his degree."

"*Bon!* Your papa used to say he will become a famous scholar someday, and—"

"Good God!" Harry dropped to his knees beside her. "You knew him?"

"No. But my uncle spoke of him. He is making a book about interesting things in the law. So he goes often to the Courts. And he was most surprised by the funny way your papa acted at some trial or hearing . . . or something."

His heart beginning to pound rapidly, Harry probed, "Do you mean the Hearing about the accident my father witnessed?"

"She shrugged. "I do not recall."

The witless look had crept over her face again so that

he could have shaken her, and it took all his control to remain outwardly calm and wait.

"Very well," she sighed at length. "Since you are burning to ask me about your Goddess, we had as well get it over. She lives in Berkshire most of the year, at her father's country estate."

His mind riveted to the other matter, Harry scarcely heard her, and when she paused, asked, "What did you mean—'funny way' . . . ?"

"I said no such thing! Nerina is not funny at all. Indeed, one has only to tell a joke for her to stare blankly and say she does not understand. Which is because although she is beautiful, she is a stupid, and—"

"No, no! My papa!"

"Your papa—was *stupid*? Oh! What a dreadful thing to—"

"Vixen!" He took her by the shoulders. "Must I shake it out of you? The *Hearing*! Your uncle said my father spoke in a 'funny way'."

"If you do not this instant remove your hands from my body, Sir Harry Redmond, I shall tell you nothing at all! How do you dare to lecture other people about propriety when you yourself are a wicked gamester with libertine propensities, who—" At this point, the look of molten rage in his eyes caused her to say hastily, "That is better. My uncle said your papa saw an accident in which a young man was killed. Your papa was the only one who saw it, but he would say nothing although the coaches passed close by him and he must have seen who was in the big one. But this is all so very foolish, for you certainly know more of it than I, so why—"

"I wish to God I did, for I feel it is important, somehow." He paused, worrying at it, then tossed up his head. "But if my father said he did not see who occupied the big carriage, then he did not. He never lied, and—"

"And very obviously did not confide in you about the matter. So since he did not trust you with that, it is scarcely to be expected he would—"

"*Trust* me?" he scowled. "Of course he trusted me."

"Then he must have told you of it. Unless . . ." She gave an empty little laugh. "Ah . . . I see. It is something you wish to keep quiet—yes? Well, if you were so compulsive a gamester you were ruining the poor man, I suppose he had to raise funds somehow. One could not blame him, and if the other driver was very . . . rich . . ." And she stopped again, quailing from the dead whiteness of his face, his eyes flames against that pallor. "He did not tell me," grated Harry, "because I was very ill at the time! And since you have the incredible affrontery to suspect his integrity, madam, let me advise you that he was far and away the finest—"

Nanette's eyes slid past him and he checked and glanced over his shoulder.

Unnoticed, Diccon had approached and was perched upon a large boulder. "What you done with all them papers what was in my cart?" It was the first time Harry had ever seen anger written upon that lugubrious countenance, but it was written there now, effecting an odd change in the man.

Their dispute forgotten, the culprits exchanged guilty glances. "I am truly sorry, Diccon," Harry said contritely. "I only gave him one, and he—"

"Harry did not give it to him, dear Diccon." Nanette crossed to smile at the Trader with a rather startling degree of charm. "I am the naughty one."

"But I told you to give it to him," Harry argued.

Diccon folded his arms. "I 'special asked of you to keep a eye on Mr. Fox, Harry. Some of them papers was important t'me. Very important."

Nanette hung her head, and Harry stepped closer to her. "It started when Mr. Fox pushed Miss Nanette into the stream," he explained.

"And then I tried to hit Harry with the oar," she said with a dimple.

"Only she knocked down the tent instead," grinned Harry.

Diccon looked from one merry face to the other and sighed.

CHAPTER VIII

ASIDE FROM HIS MORNING FITS OF THE SULLENS, MR. FOX was a good-natured beast, perfectly willing to pull the cart and exhibiting few of the signs of mulishness associated with his kind. On one point, however, he was most stubborn, and this was a disinclination to hurry. It was partly due to this trait, and partly because Diccon had stops to make along the way, that their progress was not rapid. Two days later, in fact, they had only travelled as far as Lewes. They camped in late afternoon, to the west of that pleasant little town, in a glade bright with wildflowers, blessed by the proximity of a small stream, alternately shaded by trees and warmed by the sunshine.

Nanette hummed softly as she carried flour and lard from the large food box in the cart to her cooking table. Harry put up the tent and Diccon sat leaning against a birch tree, writing laboriously in the small leather-covered book he always carried and that he called his business book.

"Harry . . . We need more wood," called Nanette.

Harry had walked beside the cart for much of the day and had hoped to rest for a little while, wherefore he gave an irked frown.

"Unless, of course," she added innocently, "you are not hungry, sir?"

He was ravenous. He placed one hand upon his heart and bowed low, and waving the wooden spoon airily as she did so, she sank into a graceful curtsey. He grinned, finished his task, gave Mr. Fox a friendly pat, and started on his next assignment as the mellow call of a cuckoo lingered on the warm air. He became quite heated in the process of gathering an armful of firewood and, sitting on a boulder, put down his branches and stared at them glumly. They should reach Chichester tomorrow and heaven knows it was past time, yet the thought saddened him. These past few days had been touched by a rare lustre difficult to identify but vaguely associated in his mind with his campaigning in Spain. Perhaps it was the clean open air and the long hikes beside the cart that made food when it came beyond words delicious. Perhaps it was the long philosophical discussions he enjoyed with Diccon as they followed the sunlit ribbon of lane and track and highway—discussions that never failed to leave him impressed by the Trader's breadth of knowledge. He sighed. He would miss the drowsy chatter around the campfire at night, capped by Diccon's superlative music. He would miss Nanette's consuming interest in everything, that opened one's own eyes to little sights long overlooked—the beauties all about that busy days in Town rendered invisible. He smiled faintly as he thought of his indignation that very morning when he'd awoken to the tugging of her impatient hands and been dragged to the brow of the hill whereon they had camped, to view a sunrise of such surpassing beauty that his vexation had been swept away by the wonder of it . . .

"Harry . . . ? Ha . . . rrry . . ."

The imperious summons made him start up, grab his harvest, and hurry back to the clearing. Yet once there he found Nanette standing at the table gazing upward, her hands covered with flour, flour on the tip of her pert nose, and her eyes following a flock of birds that wheeled and dipped across the turquoise skies. He halted, watching her upturned face and the sheen the mellow sunlight awoke along her profile. In her own way, he thought, she was not unattractive. Her body was certainly beyond reproach; small she might be, but her curves were just as they should be and, although much more pronounced than the fine-boned perfection of Lady Nerina, were nonetheless the type that many men would find delightful. Her snub little nose and the proud tilt of her chin had a way of growing upon one; and her eyes—when they were not crossed—were large and the more interesting because the flecks amid the hazel tended to vary according to the colours around her, or the time of day, so that in the early morning they were the clearest blue, and at this moment, closer to green. A little touch of feminine fal-lals could work a vast improvement, though she stood in dire need of instruction in the proper behaviour for a lady of Quality.

"How wonderful to be able to fly," she murmured, her gaze still fixed upon the soaring birds. "Just think of all they can see. The cities and towns . . . the people . . . the beautiful countryside . . ."

"The burning stew," grinned Harry, "and the dumplings that had best not be as leaden as those cannonballs you gave us last night, my girl, or I shall take the oar to you!"

Her gaze lowered, wrath bringing a flash to her dreamy eyes. "Peasant! Have you no romance in your soul? I show you a small miracle, and all you think of is your stomach! Men!" And she kneaded the dough with a violence that caused him to suspect she wished his throat was between her fingers.

"If your birds could talk," he said, "they might tell us where Diccon wandered off to. Do you suppose he has abandoned us?"

"Of course not! He'd never abandon Mr. Fox. But if he does *not* come, it will be Nanette who commands the oar, sir!"

Tossing down the branches, he looked at her in mild surprise. And realizing that if Diccon did not come they would be alone together, an odd tension raced through him. Nanette looked down, a crimson tide sweeping up her white throat and into her cheeks, her lowered lashes hovering upon that blush like dark fans. Harry, unaccountably finding breathing become difficult, was irritated by such rank stupidity and asked with commendable aplomb whether Sister Maria Evangeline was the nun from whom Diccon had acquired the oar.

She nodded, her eyes still downcast, and went on kneading her dough although with considerably less vigour. Harry chopped a long branch neatly in half and, dropping both pieces onto the fire, said, "He told me he traded it on Salisbury Plain. Why on earth would you have had an oar in such a spot?"

"One of the wheels came off our coach, and we went into a ditch. The driver said he needed something for leverage. A gypsy came along, and we bought the oar from him. He made a great fuss about parting with it, but . . ." Her hesitation was brief. "He was persuaded, at last."

"Nerina, probably . . ." thought Harry wistfully. Who could refuse that sweet vision anything? He sighed, and when he glanced up met such a baleful glare that he demanded, "Now what have I done?"

"You are a foolish young man," she observed rudely. "And you have a foolish face which I do not at all like. And when you think about—her—it becomes even more foolish. Which is quite as it should be because you know nothing of the matter whatsoever."

Feeling his offending countenance become hot, Harry wondered how she could possibly have guessed his thoughts and responded, "Know nothing about—what?" And at once wished he'd treated her remark with the haughty silence it deserved.

"Love."

"Oho!" he sat on a convenient root and leaning back, grinned, "While *you* are an expert on the subject, I take it."

"Sufficiently to know I want none of it. Yet sufficiently to know that you stand in abysmal ignorance of the very meaning of the word." She busied herself in shaping her dough and dropping it onto the simmering meat and vegetables in the big iron kettle, but when Harry began to whistle, deigning her no reply, she scowled and demanded, "Well? What *do* you know of it, Don Juan?"

He shrugged and said lightly, "I suppose it is for a man to find someone so beautiful, so pure, so perfect that he would want to spend the rest of his life shielding her.

Keeping her safe and happy . . . and—loving and caring for her." And, embarrassed because he had become serious, he looked down and was still.

Nanette gazed upon the careless and unconscious grace of him; the long legs, the strong, slender hands, the broad shoulders . . . She sniffed and looked away. But her eyes slipped back, irresistibly drawn to that downbent head. His thick dark hair was a little shaggy, yet infinitely more attractive than that of any Bond Street beau she had ever beheld. The bruises were fading from the lean face, and the deepening tan made his green eyes seem the more vivid. And those eyes were lifting to her rather shyly, wherefore she sniffed again but said nothing.

"Come now, Madam All-Wise. Your turn."

The laughter in his voice steadied her. "I think it is . . . oneness . . ." she said, frowning at the dumpling she had fashioned. "It is finding someone with whom to share your joys and sorrows, someone you know will be amused by the very things that make you laugh. It is pride because he is brave and strong, and honourable. And feeling safe when he is beside you. It is like . . . like being an empty picture frame if he is gone, and only complete when he is near. But above all—it is giving . . . and wanting ever to give . . . to make him happy." She stopped, for she had said far more than she'd even known she thought, and for a moment her hands were trembling and she, in turn, scarcely dared look up.

Staring at her, Harry wondered how he could ever have thought her plain, for in that moment she seemed all feminine, and quite lovely. And in that same instant she did look up, and beholding his expression, her eyes crossed, her chin lolled . . . And he knew, and springing to his feet cried furiously, "You do that *deliberately*! Why you wicked little shrew! It is all a hum!"

She had panicked and employed her defence once too often. She backed away, one hand stretched out in a gesture of restraint. "Do not—dare . . !"

"Why would you *do* such a hideous thing?" he de-

122

manded, striding angrily towards her. "To win sympathy?"

"*Sympathy!*" Pride restored her, and she halted. "Why would I want *your* sympathy?"

Halting also, he frowned, "Then—why? To keep away the men—is that it?"

"It is a trick I have always been able to do. And—" her chin came up. "I am a girl—alone. And men are—"

"Lustful brutes, eh?" he grated, his eyes savage with anger. "And is this why you employed your 'trick' with me? Do you hold me the kind of libertine who would abuse a helpless girl? Am I so crude as to force myself on—"

"You are a *man*!" she flashed, teeth bared. "And *all* men are obsessed—"

"By God!" the infuriated Harry exploded. And he leapt forward and soundly boxed her ears.

For a second Nanette froze, her face livid as she stared in astounded disbelief. Then, her hands flying upward, she sprang at him. "Filthy beast! Loathsome *monster*! How *dare* you strike me! How *dare* you!"

"You deserved it!" Harry held her wrists, his eyes glaring wrathfully into her own. "How dare *you* believe such evil of *me*?"

She said nothing, her entire energy directed to fighting, kicking, and struggling so that of necessity he gripped her tighter. She swung her head down, white teeth darting for his wrist, but he wrenched her away and, a little breathless and aghast because of this unseemly brawl, cried, "Have done, woman! Gad, but you need a firm hand! Tomorrow you shall be taken to your papa, and—"

As he spoke her hair tore loose from its bun and fell like a dark cloud about her, rippling down far past her shoulders. Her eyes had widened at his words, her fury replaced by horror. "You *would* not! Harry, please! He is—"

"*Another* 'loathsome monster,' I suppose," he sneered.

"He is vile," she said unequivocally. "And—cruel . . . and—"

"And beats and starves you, and keeps you locked in an oubliette?" He gave a short, mocking laugh and, still smarting with hurt and anger, frowned. "A fine way to speak of your father! No, spare me the drama, I pray, for I believe none of it." He loosed her and stepped back, saying in a cold voice, "You've scarce uttered one word of truth since I met you."

"And who asked you to come with us? Not I. Not Diccon! So why do you not at once leave us and resume your . . . your sacred quest?"

All too aware of how his real quest had been neglected, he said nothing.

"Go on!" she taunted. Her lip curled and, folding her arms, she regarded him with contempt. "Go and search for your Golden Goddess!"

"I shall leave here in the morning. And you—Miss Nanette, or whatever in the deuce your real name is—will go with me. If you refuse to give me your father's direction, I shall take you to the nearest constable, and—"

"Yes!" she hissed, crouching a little. "You *would* do that, you unfeeling wretch! Well, your concern is as unwarranted as it is unwanted! I shall be perfectly safe, I assure you. Once *you* are gone!"

"I've a very good mind," grated Harry, "to put you across my knee, madam!"

She straightened, shook back her hair, and faced him with proud disdain. "You will find your Nerina at "The Star" in Alfriston. Do not look so astonished. She waits there for me. Have you forgot she is my friend? And have no fears that I shall tell her of your crude, ungentlemanlike behaviour towards me. I promise, my poor lovesick stupid, that—"

"Sister Maria Evangeline was perfectly right," snarled Harry. "You are indeed more shrew than saint!"

"—that it will not need this for her to send you packing," she went on, as if he had not spoken. "So—go, sir! Run—to your vision of delight!"

Now as she spoke thus she gave a mocking laugh, and her manner was almost regal in its scorn. But her hands were tight clenched, her cheeks deathly pale, and a quiver came and went beside her mouth so that had he not been blinded by his own rage, Harry might have behaved differently. As it was, he responded with a crisp, "I shall! Be so kind as to tell your knight errant that I had to leave! And thank him for *his* hospitality, at least!" Having uttered the which gallantry, he snatched up his few belongings. His fury increased when he dropped one of the neckcloths he'd purchased in Horsham. He retrieved it and found Miss Nanette standing close by, offering his jacket between thumb and finger as though the garment were contaminated. He whipped it from her grasp and stamped off. Only this morning she'd sung as she sat in the cart, sewing a button on that jacket . . .

He turned back, marched up behind her, rasped, "Thank you for sewing on the button!" and stamped off again.

He'd gone a little distance before he realized he was headed in the wrong direction. Fuming, he shot a glance toward the glade. Luckily it was out of sight and if he circled wide, she would not see him. He began his detour. Had there ever been so perverse a female? To think he'd felt sorry for her 'affliction'! And the barefaced gall of her—to stand and shriek like a veritable fishwife that he was a man and, therefore, implicitly a crude and lusting savage! Where in the devil had she gathered such an impression of males? She'd said of her father, "He is vile, and cruel . . ." Harry's steps slowed. More of her gammoning. Still, he must not leave her all alone. Whatever had come over him to do so ungallant a thing? He moved slowly back towards the clearing. He'd stay just close enough to keep an eye on things . . .

The scream paralyzed him. But even as a wild outburst of braying followed he had tossed his belongings aside and was running. A five-barred fence loomed up. He placed one hand on the top, vaulted it with a fluid leap, and raced up the gentle slope.

Nanette, a scratching, writhing wildcat, was being dragged away by two men who swore with her every movement but made no attempt to strike her. They were both well over six feet in height and impressively clad in livery of black, trimmed with gold, and having large crested gold buttons.

"Hey!" cried Harry. And his rage was such that he scorned to take up a branch or anything with which to wage his uneven struggle, longing only to smash at them with his bare hands.

They spun about. In their cold eyes he read brutality and viciousness, and his heart leapt with joy.

" 'Old 'er . . ." growled the younger of the two and started forward. He was muscular, with a mop of crinkly brown hair, and he crouched a little as he advanced. Laughing softly, Harry ran at him. A knotted fist flashed for his jaw. He danced to the side, jumped in and landed a right and left to the midsection that brought the crinkly man doubling over, a great "Oooff!" escaping his gaping mouth. Harry struck with his right again, and that whistling uppercut straightened out his antagonist and deposited him on his back amid the clover. In the nick of time, Harry spun around and ducked the knife the second man slashed at him. He gripped that flailing arm, added to its momentum, and sent the man heels over head down the slope.

"Harry!"

He started to turn too late. Something thudded across his back and the all-too-familiar lance of pain was sharp and blinding. The clearing dissolved. He sank down and lay there totally unable to move, his brain reeling, while a terrible weakness turned his bones to water . . .

"Ah, *mon pauvre! Mon pauvre* . . ." The grieving words penetrated the mists. Soft arms were about him, and he lay in them gratefully and tried to breathe without groaning. The nausea eased a little, and he saw eyes filled with tears and a new glow that puzzled him so that he said stupidly, "Tuppence . . . ?"

"Yes, my brave one. Are you better?"

"I am—very well . . . thank you." He endeavoured to take stock of the situation. Down the slope the knife wielder was dragging the crinkly one to his feet, and close at hand a red-faced bully sprawled on his back, his mouth as wide as his eyes were closed. Harry turned in amazement to Nanette.

"I hit him," she nodded and, touching his brow anxiously, asked, "Are you all right? You look so pale."

"Perfectly . . . fit. What did you hit him with?"

She held up a small, nobby club. Harry took it and with a great effort clambered to his feet and tottered to where the knife wielder was tugging at his groaning friend. Harry raised the club.

"Don't 'it me, guv!" An arm was flung up to shield the bullet head. "Don't you 'it me no more! We'm a'goin'. Just give me a chance ter get me mate."

'Well, devil take you—hurry up!" growled Harry, managing to sound threatening as his head cleared. He waited until all three went weaving off, then crossed to the tent, from behind which came a soft, distressed braying.

Nanette was attempting to console Mr. Fox with a shopping list. It was accepted with reluctance, the donkey fixing them both with a reproachful gaze. Harry stroked his neck and explained matters to the best of his ability, and after a while the eyes closed, the shaggy head butted against his chest, and a gusty sigh of contentment accompanied the retreating hoofbeats that proclaimed the departure of their unwelcome guests.

Harry turned to Nanette and found her regarding him with a smile, half-amused, half-tender; but recalling the manner of their parting he frowned "I wonder you did not cross your eyes and slobber at 'em."

She lowered her lashes and said meekly, "You came back."

"And had no business leaving you, though as God is my judge, little one, I'd not have done so had I any notion you would be attacked. Filthy swine!"

"They were from my papa," imparted Nanette softly.

He gave a gasp of dismay. "*What?* Why did you not—"

"Tell you?" She said sadly, "You would have let them take me."

Would he? Those crude louts? What manner of man would send such after a loved daughter? Confused, he muttered, "Put up your hair—before we have the rest of Sussex here."

She searched his face and, finding the deathly pallor gone from under his eyes, stifled a sigh of relief. "Yes, Harry," she said, again with that uncharacteristic meekness, and started to search in the cart. Watching her, he said worriedly, "Tomorrow, you will come with me to . . ." Here, Nanette leaning far over, he caught a glimpse of a trim ankle and finished with a grin "—to Lewes."

"No, but I cannot." With swift movements of her white hands she began to wind her hair into two long braids. "I must go to Alfriston to meet Nerina."

Harry's heart gave a jump, but he said with forced nonchalance, "Very well—to Alfriston. But I warn you, I intend to make enquiries for your papa." He could not like to see how the colour left her face, and lowering himself cautiously onto Diccon's folding stool he said, "Now pray do not enact me another of your tragedies, miss. I'll admit those three ruffians might have been better chosen, but likely your poor father is worried and desperate."

"Oh, of that I have no doubt whatsoever," she nodded bitterly.

She looked like a pretty child with her hair dressed so, the bright red ribbons binding the shining ropes she had fashioned. But—she told such awful whiskers! "Little one," he sighed, "do you really *have* a papa?"

She smiled and, coming to kneel close beside him, confessed. "He died when I was two. I cannot remember him, but he was a fine English gentleman."

"Aha! I might have known!"

"I believe," she went on, knitting her brows ferociously, "my stepfather contrived his death so as to be able to marry Mama!"

She was off again! "Oh, egad! So it is your wicked *step*father who seeks to force you into marriage for money—and with a man you loathe?" She nodded, and he pointed out with the quiver of a grin, "But you loathe all men."

"This one especially. For he complicates my life most unfairly."

"He is old and ugly and lecherous," he ventured tentatively.

"He is young and handsome, and a perfect gentleman." She sighed, a wistful light in her eyes, then scowled, "And I *hate* him!"

Harry shook his head in reluctant admiration. "And what does this young, handsome, perfect gentleman think of you?"

"He loves me, of course." She bit her lip. "But—he has not offered."

"If he loves you," said Harry, still striving, "why hasn't he offered?"

"To spite my papa. *He* hates him, too."

"Oh—of course," he added gravely. (Whatever else, she was good at it!) "And why does your papa seek to force you into marriage with this handsome young gentleman who hates him and whom you hate? Surely there must be other and less reluctant wealthy prospects? One you might find—er—acceptable."

She frowned at him, her eyes becoming very hard and bright. "I do not want someone 'acceptable'. I want to marry for love. Like you and—Nerina."

Harry's head came up slightly, and he met her challenge coolly. "You mistake. Even were I acquainted with the lady I could not offer. I *have* nothing to offer."

"What matter? Nerina has lots of money. And since you gambled all yours away, why not—"

"Be still!" he commanded angrily. And when, much to his astonishment, she closed her lips and knelt there in humble silence, he persisted, "Does your papa know you hate this handsome young suitor?"

"Yes."

"And does he know the suitor hates him also?"

"Well, of course he does!" She looked at him as though he were touched in his upper works and added, "He is his brother."

Harry gawked at her, then went off into a peal of laughter. "Oh, you've done it up rather too brown, my girl! You could at least have made him a cousin!"

Nanette sprang up and glared at him. "I do not *make* him anything, Sir Harry Horrid! Could I make him into something else, I would make him without the taint of my stepfather's evil blood. And then I *would* marry him!"

"But—you hate him!" pointed out Harry, standing politely and wiping his eyes.

"Only because he is my uncle. If he were not, I would love him. In point of fact, I *do* love him. Save only for . . . Papa."

"Oh." His laughter faded. "Well, you certainly cannot marry your uncle. I should think even your wicked papa would see that!"

"My wicked papa," she said, low voiced, "holds there is no blood relationship." She clasped her hands imploringly and begged, "So you see, Harry, you must *not* force me to go back to him! I beseech you to save me!"

Unmoved by this dramatic performance, he said, "Save yourself."

"Peasant!" she raged, stamping her foot at him. Then asked, "How?"

"Simple. Marry someone else."

"Oh . . ." The dark lashes drifted down again to the soft glow that warmed her cheeks. "I—dare not."

"Your villainous papa would kill him, I collect." He could not hold back a laugh and tugged gently at one of her fat braids. "What a rasper!"

"You are a stupid!" she flared, clenching her hands as she railed at him. "I hope your Nerina *does* marry you! It would serve you right to spend the rest of your life listening to her foolishness—when you were not gambling away *her* fortune!"

Harry brandished the small club and warned, "Now you listen to me, my girl! I have endured about enough of—" And he stopped, gazing in stunned disbelief at what he held. "Where did you get this?"

Struck by the change in his manner, she replied, "It was

in the cart. I found it when I was searching for the rolling pin. Why?''

He tore his eyes from the crown atop that truncheon and asked, ''Do you know what it is?''

''But of course. It is a little bludgeon—or club—with a knob on one end. It is quite heavy. I suppose Diccon carries it for protection. He does not care for firearms, you know. And I am glad I hit that beast, for he struck you with a great branch. Most dreadfully hard. I wish I had killed him!''

''Killed who?'' asked Diccon, ambling into the clearing. His eyes flashed to Harry. ''Trouble? I see you found my baton.'' He reached to take it, grinning broadly. ''Didn't know as how I was a Runner, did you?''

''What I'd *like* to know,'' smiled Harry, ''is how you came by it.''

''Three of my papa's men found me!'' Nanette interposed urgently. ''Hideous great smelly ruffians! They sought to drag me off, but I screamed, and Mr. Fox shouted, and Harry came. And he fought them! Oh, Diccon!'' Her hands clasped, her small face suffused with a flush of excitement. ''If you could have but *seen* him! So brave! And so terrible! He knocked the biggest one down, and then the other also, but another came and crept around behind him, and—''

''She crowned him with your baton,'' Harry laughed. ''Like a regular Amazon!''

''Amazon!'' she expostulated with a flash of her big eyes.

''Oh—well, I mean, with incredible courage,'' he amended hastily. ''Whilst I was like so much dead meat.''

''No! Do not heed him, Diccon. He was splendid! Only when the other pig hit him across the back with a branch, he could not jump up right away.''

Diccon's faint amusement gave way to concern. ''You all right, Harry? You took a nasty one at Rodrigo.''

Harry had no recollection of having mentioned that fact and frowned his perplexity. Before he could speak, however, Nanette cried, ''Ah! Now this I did not know!'' She grasped his arm and pulled him towards the tent. "In with you! You shall rest, mighty warrior, while I prepare your victory feast."

Her program sounded delightful but he said gravely, "I fear our victory feast must wait, little one."

"Right," sighed Diccon, relinquishing his plans to settle down beside the fire. "What we got to do now is to move camp. Less'n we want more unexpected visitors. I think we'll let our military gent drive the cart. He's likely had a bit of experience at leaving no tracks behind."

The 'military gent' smiled grimly. "Do our three valiant girl snatchers pass this way again, they'll think Mr. Fox grew wings!"

The sun was almost down now and the purple shadows of dusk were creeping into the little glade beyond Alfriston where they had at length decided to halt for the night. Harry accepted the tin cup Diccon brought to him, rose from the stool beside the fire, and lifting his cup, saluted "A lady who is as brave as she is lovely."

Nanette glanced up from her kettle in pleased surprise. Harry took a sip of the brandy and, watching her over the rim of the cup, knew with a touch of nostalgia that he would always remember her like this, the flames lighting her face with a dancing glow, her eyes very bright, that half-smile hovering about her lips. Lowering the cup, he smiled back at her. And at once she blushed, while her thick, curling lashes dropped in confusion. His heart beginning to beat very fast, he took an instinctive step towards her.

"*Does* ye think she's pretty?" Diccon asked softly.

Harry, who had completely forgotten the Trader was present, checked and sat down again hurriedly. "Why, yes. In her own way."

"Aye." With a sigh of contentment, Diccon at last assumed his favourite position and, stretching out his long legs, murmured, "A man'd have t'be a blind fool not to see it." A faint smile lurked in the blue eyes, and Harry reddened and said defensively, "Yes—er . . . well, Jove! That *awful* face she pulled!"

Diccon chuckled. "Near split me sides each time she done it. If you could've seen your expression!'

"I saw hers!"

"Aye. Well, she'd reason enough, poor lass."

"Indeed?" flared Harry haughtily. "Against me, sir?"

Diccon raised one hand in a conciliatory gesture. "Don't frizzle your ears! If I'd thought that, I'd never have let you come along."

"I'm glad you did. Lord, but I wish you could have seen her! To think of a tiny girl like her having the nerve to whack that hulking lout on the noggin!"

"She's a rare one, all right."

"With a rare imagination. You'd not believe the whiskers she spun me! One would suppose her father to be a veritable prince of darkness!"

Diccon's gaunt face became unwontedly grim. "There's things walking about on two legs, Harry, as I'd be downright ashamed to interduce to Mr. Fox as men!" He took a healthy swallow of his cognac and was sufficiently strengthened as to sit up and lean forward. "Way I sees it," he said softly. "She's a spirited little thing and fighting as best she knows. But her papa's got the law on his side, and he ain't the kind to care fer public opinion; nor her the kind to get her friends mixed up in it 'less'n she must. Only thing I can think to do is get her to her aunty, like I promised."

Troubled, Harry's eyes followed the girl as she bustled about, singing happily to herself. Was the poor little shrew really a victim of brutal avarice? If so, he'd been a perfect clot! Totally lacking sympathy and understanding. Squirming inwardly, he found Diccon's twinkling eyes upon him and said, "I only hope she is not seen with us. It would, I fear, put her into a most unhappy situation."

Diccon turned also to look at the busy cook and muttered, "If her papa comes up with us, friend Harry, you and I will have a deal more to cope with than a unhappy sityation!"

* * *

Harry had come to love dinner time and their easy conversation as they ate around the fire. Tonight, however, although he took his part in the talk, he was preoccupied, his thoughts turning ever to the morrow. He would see Lady Nerina again! Anticipation made his heart race. Would she remember him at all . . . ?

"Troopers and special police all over the place," Diccon grumbled.

Harry gave a start. "Where? Lewes?"

"Aye. More excitement than you'd've seen in a month o'Sundays in the old days. They was even some young bloods from London. All after the reward."

"Reward? What reward?"

"Some child's been stole, and the poor family has put up a tidy sum for information."

"And so the greedy vultures gather," frowned Nanette, standing and taking the empty plates.

"I could use a reward myself," said Harry thoughtfully. "And if there's one thing I despise it's anyone who would harm a child. A girl, Diccon?"

" 'Fraid so." He shook his head. "World's losing it's morals, so it is."

Nanette was singing as she carried the kettle to the pan on the table and began to wash the crockery. Her voice was not strong, but she carried the tune truly. She had tied a red shawl about her shoulders, the rich colour matching the ribbons that held her braids. Harry went over to help and urged her to go on singing. She did so, shyly at first, but gathering confidence until she faltered, unable to recall the words. He prompted her in his rich baritone, ". . . thy neighboring hills . . ."

"What a nice voice!" she exclaimed, putting the plates into the box. "Sing with me, Harry!"

And so they sang together and were soon joined by another voice—the pure, soaring notes of Diccon's violin. Nanette clapped her hands delightedly when the song was finished, but the evening air was growing cool, and as they went to the fire, she shivered a little. Harry took off his jacket and wrapped it about her. She looked so absurdly small that he said she was more like a little bird than a girl and, swinging her off her feet, deposited her on the stool and sat close beside her as Diccon launched into a rousing version of "A'Hunting We Will Go"!

And so the pleasant hours passed. The fire leapt and crackled; the air was brisk and clean, full of the sweet smells of earth and blossoms and wood smoke; and the moon crept higher until the trees stood like black etchings against a silver sky. The violin, Nanette's husky soprano, and Harry's deep tones entwined through one song after another. He also forgot the words in the midst of "The Mermaid," and his improvisation brought a shout of laughter from Diccon, while Nanette yanked at his hair in mock indignation. He threw his head back against her knee and laughed up at her, and when he straightened, her hand slipped onto his shoulder. It seemed so natural, so as it should be. But looking down at his tumbled dark hair, her voice shook a little. And watching her, Diccon's eyes grew troubled.

CHAPTER IX

THE MANY PANED WINDOWS OF THE VILLAGE SHOP POSI-
tively sparkled with cleanliness. The display area was immaculate, the beaded green and white reticule tastefully
placed beside the green sunshade. On the stand, the white
gown of sprig muslin with pale green ribands beneath the
bodice and laced through the tiny puff sleeves, was dainty
and charming. Harry looked through the windowpanes with
not one whit of appreciation for their spotless shine, however, and the rest of the display escaped him entirely, as
he gazed at the muslin gown with helpless longing. How
sweet Nanette would look in that gown. Almost he could
picture her in it. Never before had he so desired anything,
and never before had he been so totally unable to purchase
what he desired. He smiled wryly, recalling the emerald
and diamond necklace he had bestowed on the last barque
of frailty to live under his protection, and the ruby en-
crusted comb that had brought such a sparkle to the eyes
of his little Spanish ladybird. And now, a simple muslin
gown that probably cost five shillings at the most might as
well have been a hundred carat diamond, so totally was it
beyond his reach. He turned sadly away.

Diccon had driven on to "The Star," where Nanette
wished to have a private cose with her schoolfriend. She
had told Harry he was not to come to the inn until at least
eleven o'clock, so he had plenty of time.

He glanced again at the muslin gown. It was quite useless,
of course . . . He strode up the step and entered, bowing his

head to avoid the low lintel. As he straightened, his eyes were level with the chin of a giant of a woman, and he was so startled he all but took a step back. She stood at least five inches over six feet, and there was little doubt but that she indulged a hearty appetite. Several double chins were ranked above the small ruff of her vast dove grey gown; her bosom was of awesome proportions, and the arms that were folded across it would have done justice to a wrestler. Her hair was black and glossy and arranged into tight curls of such profusion as to be suspect, and they framed a face that seemed composed of two round and rosy cheeks, between which a tiny nose, blue eyes, and a little rosebud mouth were all but lost. Instinctively, Harry's eyes shot to the narrow door and, reading his thoughts, she chuckled and said in a rumble of a voice, "There be another door out back, sir. Twice that size. Else I'd have to conduct me business outside!" The folded arms began to heave up and down, the grey gown shook violently, the small mouth widened, and the eyes disappeared. From within this formidable lady came a great wheezing explosion of mirth, a sound so contagious that Harry could only join in. It ceased as suddenly as it had begun and, wiping at the folds of her cheeks, she removed her handkerchief to again reveal those two bright blue slits that were her eyes. "I seed ye look at the muslin. What size be your lady, sir?"

Harry held his hand beneath his chin. "The top of her head comes to here."

"A little'un, bean't she? My husband now . . . he do be just about your size."

"Is he now?" murmured Harry politely. And he thought, "Gad!"

"Ar," she chortled knowingly. "That there frock would be just the right size. Be she pretty?"

"Yes, indeed she is. And—if she had some ribbons for her hair . . ."

Before he could finish, her hand darted out and clasped across the pudgy palm she extended were several loops of ribbon exactly the shade of those on the muslin gown. "Six shillings the lot," she rumbled.

"I should not have come in and wasted your time, ma'am," he said ruefully. "I do apologize," and he turned to leave.

"Cannot always have what we want, can we?" she said sympathetically, her eyes scrutinizing him with an odd intensity. "Take my husband, now. He always longed to go to one o'them there fancy London tailors. Never could, a'course. But he do be a fine figure of a man. Like yourself. That there jacket o'yourn now. Would *that* be from a fancy London tailor—by any chance?"

"Yes, ma'am. Though it has seen better days, I fear." Harry looked down regretfully at Bertie Schofield's somewhat tattered garment.

"Ar—but . . . *which* one?" she persisted.

"As a matter of fact, it is by Weston."

"Ar. Western . . ." She fixed him with a shrewd stare. "And does lots o'lords, and sirs, and honourables—that sort—does *they* go to this here Western?"

"Indeed they do, ma'am. He has, I believe, dressed the Regent, and—"

Her mouth fell open, her arms dropped, and for an instant of sheer terror he thought she was about to faint. Then, "How much?" she demanded feebly.

"What?" gasped Harry. "But—ma'am, it's torn, and dirty. And . . ." he peered at the bloodstain Nanette had been unable to remove from one lapel. "I doubt your husband would want—"

"Not *that* one, my dearie! I can take that all to pieces and make a pattern to sew my Hezekiah a jacket what was designed by the chap what tailors for the Prince. Oh, my! Won't he be took!" She gripped her hands and, seeing how Harry's eyes flashed to the muslin gown, beamed, "Sir—I be very sure as how we can help one another."

The five Corinthians at the large table were very loud and, although it was not eleven o'clock, appeared to have consumed more than their share of wine this morning—unless they'd been at it all night, which Harry deduced was more than likely. He sat in a far corner of the fragrant little coffee shop, a steaming mug before him, waiting impatiently for the clock to strike the hour. His thoughts were on the little shrew and the surprise that would light her expressive face when she saw her presents. He straightened the clumsy parcel on the chair beside him. Mrs. Hawthorne, overjoyed with his jacket, had next convinced him to trade his top boots. Harry had found her husband's old shoes loose and strange to his feet and had warned the proprietor of the dress shop that Mr. Hawthorne might find Hoby's handmade boots impossible to get into. "Fer something as elegant as them," she'd asserted, "Hawthorne'll curl his toes up!" The trades had been sufficient for Harry to purchase the muslin gown and ribbons, plus a small silver locket in the shape of a heart for Nanette, and a used but finely wrought enamelled snuff box with a hound embossed on the lid for Diccon, and still have some few shillings left over.

His sleeve looked dreadful, the ill-fitting brown corduroy jacket rendered the more hideous by its unhappy conflict with his grey pantaloons. Amused, he stretched out one long leg and peered down at that awful shoe . . . Good old Bolster would split his sides if— Again, his musings were interrupted by the uproar, and he glanced at the noisy group. The aura of Town hung about them, and if they were here in an effort to win the reward Diccon had mentioned, they weren't working very hard at the task.

"My turn! My turn!" One of the young men had jumped to his feet, waving a sheet of paper. "Now listen, you bosky booberkins!" He cleared his throat and, as they quieted, watching expectantly, he read in a slurred, nasal voice:

"The maze of Parnell Sanguinet was really very clever.
But Mitchell Redmond liked it not,
To Sanguinet he gave his shot—'

Here, the grinning poet was interrupted by shrieks of hilarity, while Harry sat rigid and stunned with shock. His voice cracking with suppressed mirth, the poet resumed,

"To Sanguinet he gave his shot—
And made that maze so blasted hot
That it will grow back—never!"

He collapsed into his chair, chortling gleefully as his friends whooped and howled and beat upon one another.

Harry sprang up, and his chair went over with a crash. The poet turned to him and the laughter died from his face. "What ails you, fellow?"

With a tremendous effort, Harry held back the flood of questions that trembled on his tongue. It was very apparent from their haughty stares that they judged him a bumpkin. If he behaved like an equal he'd likely get tossed into the street and learn nothing. With a hand that shook, he touched his brow and said respectfully, "If you please, sir—I served with Cap'n Harry Redmond. Be that his brother you was a'speaking of?"

At once a smile lit the flushed face across the room. "Yes, my good man. Mr. Mitchell Redmond fought a duel with a gentleman named Sanguinet a few days back."

Harry's heart seemed to stop. He clutched at the table and could feel the blood draining from his face.

The poet peered at him curiously. "Loyal fella, ain't ya? Don't worry. Your Captain was not involved. Still—pity it—" He was interrupted, encircled, and swept away by his friends. All talking at once, laughing uproariously, they reeled toward the door. Cold with dread, Harry snatched up his parcel and followed them into the pale morning sunshine. Mitchell *could not* have called out Sanguinet! Pray God, not! He didn't know one end of a pistol from t'other!

He was so consumed by apprehension that all thoughts of either Nerina or the little shrew were swept from his mind. He dogged the erratic steps of the rowdy group past whitewashed shops and half-timbered cottages, so intent upon them that he failed to note a closed carriage sweep past, slow, pull to the side of the cobbled street, and stop. The inebriated gentlemen ahead were turning into the smithy. Harry was almost to the open door when a small boy overtook him, thrust a folded paper into his hand, then ran off.

Bewildered, Harry stared from the departing urchin to the letter he held. The inscription was to himself and the familiar scrawl that of his brother. Apprehension gripping him, he broke the seal, spread the page, and read:

My Dear Sauvage—
    Since you read this, I can only beg your forgiveness, for I have deserted you in time of trouble, and you must now be the last, and undoubtedly the most worthy, of our noble line.

Harry's throat seemed to close, and for an instant the words before him blurred. He was unaware that the parcel had slipped from beneath his arm, or that across the street a window of the carriage had been let down and pale eyes, lit with sly laughter, watched him. He fought away the terror that was making him shake, and blinked his eyes into focus once more.

    . . . our noble line.
    Reflection convinced me, best and most honoured of brothers, that you were not only scorched but had deemed me not quite up to the rig. And so I left my 'little schoolhouse' and came home. You had already departed, and I discovered my suspicions to have been correct. I shook the truth from old Frye (what a beastly little worm he is!) and bullied Andy into accompanying me to Brittany. (Incidentally, Harry, your old campaigner has become quite a bookworm. You may have to watch his selections, though. Frightfully racy stuff!)
    I have just met Sanguinet. I cannot say I like him. Nor can I say, however, that I believe he cheated my father: for him to have done so lacks all reason, and I honestly do not think him capable of such perfidious conduct. He has an unfortunate mouth withal, and I find my temper shorter than I had supposed. I challenged the fellow, and I write this as we prepare to face one another at twenty paces.
    With the knowledge that you will be given this letter

only in the event of my death, I am emboldened to say what under other circumstances I would not dare.

I have always loved and respected you—far more than you know. I am aware you love me also and cannot wish you will not mourn me. But I beg that you will seek no redress from Sanguinet. He has behaved quite properly and with scrupulous honour. Live for both of us, Harry. Make it a good life, and be happy. You deserve happiness. If you have a son, and I pray you will, you might perhaps keep in mind the name of a silly chap who let you down, but counted himself extreme fortunate to have been,

> *Your devoted brother—*
> *Mitchell*

Mitchell was dead . . . He had always thought somehow that he would sense it if something happened to his brother, that their closeness would warn him if Mitch was hurt or in trouble. But it hadn't warned him—and Mitchell . . . was dead . . .

Harry's steps slowed, and he realized with dull surprise that he was in the country again, and wandering dazedly along a lane whose hedgerows blazed with a glory of wildflowers. He had a vague recollection of a small girl picking up his parcel and handing it to him and then running back to her mother, calling, "The poor man! See, Mama—he's crying!" But he did not remember leaving Alfriston, and had no notion of where he was now . . .

He heard the clip-clop of hooves on the lane behind him, a rattle of wheels turning slowly on the uneven surface. But it was not these sounds that brought the frown into his stricken eyes but the laugh that, soft and merciless, wound through them.

He knew. Even as he whirled about—he knew!

Parnell Sanguinet leaned from the open window of the luxurious carriage. "Good morrow, *mon ami*! *En effet* I had no thought when into my hands that letter came that I should be so fortunate as to deliver it in the person! Such a pleasure to be of service . . . On a walking tour are you?'' With a dance of enjoyment in his bizarre eyes he leaned back, taunting, ''What a pity your brother cannot be here . . . with you . . .''

And before the enraged Harry could move, the coachman whipped up the team and the four magnificent white horses plunged straight at him. He made a desperate dive for the ditch, was half-stunned by a violent impact, and hurled aside. The rear wheel missed him by a hairsbreadth as he rolled helplessly in the dust. Sprawling, the breath knocked out of him, he heard the sounds of the wheels and the pounding of sixteen polished hooves fade . . . until all that was left was the echo of a sneering laugh.

''Get ye gone! Gert horrid hound that ye be . . . get ye gone!''

The quavering tones were very familiar. Harry lifted his head and as the whirling landscape gradually righted itself, was able to discern the erratic approach of a very tiny man and a very large dog. The man was extremely old and frail, and retreated so often that he tottered almost as much to the rear as he advanced. But the dog seemed quite pleased with this slow progress and leapt and pranced about him, barking joyfully.

The old man halted and turned to stand almost eye to eye with the dog—a well-cared-for animal, having a thick and glossy coat and a waving plume of a tail. One trembling arm was brought forth from behind the man's back. Clutched in his hand was a piece of wood that might once have been a hammer but was now headless, and he brandished this potential weapon threateningly. The dog, however, very obviously placed a different interpretation upon this demonstration and, uttering a bark of joy, turned around three times so as to be ready.

Finding his voice, Harry came to one elbow and called, ''Mr. Chatham . . .''

The dog gave a bark of pleased recognition, bounced over, and proceeded to jump about on this good friend, delighted with the game. The ancient one, however, had given a small and startled leap at Harry's call, and thus launched, he tottered back the way he had come, gasping

143

out, "What be ye a'doing of—a'wallerin' in the dirt, S'Harry . . . ?" the last words fading with distance.

Roused by necessity, Harry restrained the exuberance of Lord Lucian St. Clair's hound with a stern, "Homer! Down, sir!" He then managed to regain his feet and gladly accompanied by Homer, pursued the departing figure, coming up with him a scant instant before Chatham toppled into the ditch. Having flung one arm about the frail form, Harry guided the old gentleman to the low wall that replaced the hedgerow nearby, eased him onto it, and sat beside him.

For a few moments there was silence between them. A comparative silence, that is, broken by the gasps and wheezings of the venerable Mr. Samuel Chatham, whose faded blue gaze was fixed upon his companion's drawn face. "Ye been . . . piping yer eye," he observed at length.

"Yes," said Harry simply.

"Ain't nothing t'be ashamed of," comforted Chatham. "Me father done it when me ma went to her reward, God rest her soul." He pondered for a moment, then added a reinforcing, "I done it meself a time or two." He thought again and, leaning closer, lost his balance and all but fell into Harry's arms so that it was necessary that he be tilted to a less precarious angle. He ignored these procedures while continuing, "Told a lie about'ee 's marnin'. If anyone in these here parts knows as who's here and who ain't— it do be I. An' I said as how *you* wasn't. But that," he added with a disappointed glance at Harry, "was a'cause it never would've occurred to I to go a'looking under hedges for a barrernet o'this here realm!" He shook his head chidingly. "Never would've thought it of'ee, S'Harry. Ain't in keeping with your position. Not atall!"

"No, I don't expect it is," Harry apologized and, striving to be rational, sighed, "I didn't have much say in the matter. Was someone asking for me?"

"Ar. 'S marnin'. Could'a goed to Jarge Brown, 'ee could. Jarge were a'standing there, an' Jarge allus thinks as how *'ee* knows all there is t'know. But yer man come t'me, and asked if ye be up to the Hall, or over to Greenwings. I allus allowed as how your Sergeant had a good head on his shoulders. Though I'm powerful disappinted in him. *Powerful* disappinted! Snails be bad enough. But—*live worms* . . . ?'' He shuddered. "It don't bear thinking on!''

Allowing the incomprehensibilities to sift past, Harry seized upon the one pertinent fact. "Sergeant Anderson was *here*? Looking for me?''

"Ar. Rushing about like a headless duck, he were. Turble upset. Still, 'twarn't no excuse fer 'ee t'tell a trusting old man such a horrid tale!'' He placed one near-transparent hand on his middle. "Fair turned me stummick!''

There could be little doubt as to why poor Andy had been so 'turble upset'. Or why he was so desperately trying to find him. Harry stood and said dully, "If you will excuse me, sir. I'd best seek him out.''

"Ar.'' Chatham floundered about but with little success until Harry leaned down to slip a gentle hand under his arm and assist him to his feet. " 'Ee do have goed t'see yer friend what has them funny-coloured eyes—that there Markwiss of Damon. 'Course, they folk in Dorset be a strange lot altogether. And so I told'un. Your gentleman'll have goed to Lunnon, says I. Wouldn't listen, a'course. Dicked in the nob 'ee do be, I fancy. Poor chap.''

It was borne in upon the stricken Harry that the old fellow was deeply disturbed, wherefore he put his own sorrow aside and enquired, "Whatever did my Sergeant say to so upset you? Something about Spain, was it?''

"Ar. He says . . . as they Spanishers eat . . .'' He glanced around furtively. "Eat—*live worms*! Ugh! Horrid! Why should 'ee tell me such a ugly whisker?''

"I rather fancy Sergeant Anderson meant eels. And some of our customs seem just as odd to them, y'know, Mr. Chatham.''

An awed countenance was upraised, and horrified eyes searched his face. "Ye bean't saying as it's *true*?'' Harry nodded. "Oh . . . my Lor'! I wish as how ye hadn't of told me! Live . . . eels! Wait'll I tell *that'n* to Jarge Brown!'' He gave a whooping cackle of anticipation, slapped his knee, then cherished it repentantly. "Good day t'ye, sir. And if your Sergeant comes up wi' Mr. Redmond afore—"

Harry, who had started drearily away, tensed and swung about, "*What* did you say?"

"Dang me gizzard!" Chatham quavered wrathfully. "Y'don't got no call t'beller an' roar an' make me jump nigh outta me skin! Ain't I been a'telling and a'telling of 'ee all this time as how your Sergeant's lost his gentleman?"

"Y-Yes . . . but—I heard . . . there was a duel."

"Ar. Well there was. That's what comes o' all that book learning d'ye see? As I says to your Sergeant, y'can't hardly blame they Frenchies fer bein' a mite put out and running your brother outta Brittany that way! I'd be—" He stopped, cringing back with a cry of fear as Harry ran to grasp his arm, his face convulsed.

"Mr. Chatham—what are you saying? Sergeant Anderson was looking for—*my brother? Today?* Mitchell is—is safely *home*?"

"Well—glory! Ain't I been a'telling and a'telling—" The old man checked and said incredulously, "S'Harry! Ye're a'piping o' yer eye again!"

"Yes!" gulped Harry, dragging a muddy hand across his glistening but joyous eyes. "I am, by God!"

"How do you do?" Lady Nerina Tawnish, clad in a gown of ivory jaconet muslin, her golden curls clustering delightfully beside each shell-like ear, a trace of shock in eyes as blue as Spanish skies in summertime, extended one hand. Shaking those slender fingers gingerly, Harry was horribly aware of Mr. Hawthorne's frayed old coat and shabby shoes. "I am honoured to meet you, my lady," he said uneasily and flashing a glance at Nanette, saw her brows raised and dimples lurking about her mouth. "Good gracious, Harry," she laughed. "Whatever happened to your clothes? You look dreadful!"

"I fear I do," he said wryly. "And you are most kind to receive me in my—er, tatters, ma'am."

"No, but I think it splendid," the Beauty said earnestly. She disposed herself upon the sofa in this cozy parlour and motioned to Harry to sit down. "Nanette told me how gallantly you volunteered to escort her. I collect you purchased old clothes lest you attract attention. And, indeed, a Dandy *would* call notice to my poor friend in her—her desperate flight."

Nanette went into a squeal of laughter. *"Dandy?"*

Evaluating the benefits of strangulation, Harry smiled tautly and admitted he had seldom been farther from that species. "Indeed, I wonder the proprietor allowed me to enter. Had it not been for his good wife, I doubt I'd have been shown his boot, rather!"

"Another victim of your charm?" Nanette shook her head at him and, noting the glint in his eyes, added roguishly, " 'Ware our Captain, dearest! He's a rascal with the ladies . . . when he's not boxing their ears!"

Lady Nerina's lovely mouth dropped open. Her eyes became like saucers, and in pretty dismay she gasped, "He . . . he never did? *Your* ears, love?"

"Oh . . . gad . . . !" groaned Harry.

"Hard!" his tormentor confirmed, sparkling with mirth. "And threw me in the river, then made me take off my clothes, and—"

"Aaah . . ." moaned Nerina. One hand lifted to her temple, her eyes half-closed and her handkerchief flapped feebly.

"Pay her no heed, ma'am!" Harry leapt to take up that scrap of fine cambric and lace and fan her with it frenziedly. "She is a naughty scamp, and—"

"A naughty . . . scamp . . ." echoed my lady faintly. And having scanned the pleasant face above her with eyes that, hidden behind her lashes, were yet keen enough to discern the familiar look of adoration, she relented sufficiently to acknowledge that it was a great comfort to her to know her dearest friend was guarded by an officer and a gentleman. "Although—" she went on, struck by an afterthought, "Papa has always held that fighting is wicked . . ."

"Yes, I know," Nanette put in. "But—Sir Harry fought with Wellington."

This observation carried little weight with the Beauty,

who shook her lovely head and remarked primly that Papa held Wellington "to be a—Rake!"

Harry's attempts to vindicate his commander were to no avail; my lady embarked upon a softly spoken but lengthily confused denunciation of wars, military men in general, and the Duke in particular, that brought a gleam of mirth to Nanette's mischievous eyes and only concluded when Harry was able to insert a gentle, "I doubt we could have prevailed upon Bonaparte with reason, ma'am, and had we lost the war—"

"Oh, I should not have liked *that*!" Nerina exclaimed, "For then we would have even more Frenchmen in England than we have now. And I do so dislike French food!"

Harry did not comment on this scintillating observation, perfectly content to look at her, and managing to ignore the twitch beside Nanette's lips.

Warming to her subject, Nerina resumed, "There are those, you know, who hold it superior to our own, which I think downright treasonable when you think that they eat the legs of slimy frogs! *And* put intoxicating spirits into their sauces! I—" She stopped, her eyes widening and one hand flying to her paling cheek. "Oh! what a ninnyhammer I am! And you—half-French! Nanette, I *do* beg your pardon!"

With a twinkling glance at Harry, her friend leaned to hug her, but Nerina refused to be comforted. "You see how it is! I say silly things sometimes." She spread her hands and, proceeding from frying pan to fire, said regretfully, "I wish I could be more like you, Nanette. It is only that I am unaccustomed to being deceitful."

As hopelessly dazzled as he was, Harry could not resist turning a speaking look on the indignant Nanette. Then he murmured consolingly, "Of course you are, dear lady. Who could expect you to be experienced at such tricks?"

Nanette gasped audibly. Nerina, however, bestowed a heartstopping smile upon Harry, then turned to her friend. "Dearest—*please* come back with me! I know how miserable your life was, but only think—if ever the truth should leak out, you would be ruined . . . *Ruined!*"

"Well, it shall not leak out," said Nanette firmly. "Who

148

would recognize me in this frightful gown? And—'' she smiled sweetly at Harry. ''In such unsavoury company.''

He acknowledged the hit with a grin and a slight lift of the hand. Nerina, however, apparently found nothing unwarranted in the remark and sighed, ''I suppose you are right. But—what if your *papa* should ask me questions. *Oh!* I should faint dead away! I know I should!''

''You wouldn't give me away?'' Nanette asked anxiously. ''But you are so brave, Nerina. Did you not come and warn me?''

''Yes, that is true.'' Those breathtaking eyes returned to Harry. ''It was so difficult, sir, to overcome my moral scruples and come here, for I have been properly instructed from my cradle, though you might not think so to see me thus—practically alone. Whatever Papa would say, I dare not guess!''

Papa, thought Harry dreamily, could only say that her voice was music; her face and figure sublime; that she was beyond words adorable . . . She should be guarded like some national treasure or perfect work of art . . . He was shocked to realize he was sighing like a callow youth and said hurriedly, ''Why, my lady, I am sure you could do nothing to cause your papa aught but joy. Do not worry about—''

''But I *am* worried,'' she mourned, her eyes still plaintively fixed upon him. ''Everything has gone wrong! Indeed, my life is become—quite a . . . shambles!'' Those long, curling lashes became beaded with glistening drops, so shattering a sight that Harry took an instinctive step closer and begged to be apprised of any way in which he might be of service. With a pathetic quiver in her soft, sweet voice, Nerina lifted one white hand to her brow and confided with fearful apprehension that she had been so overset of late she dreaded lest the result be—Lines! He assured her that nothing could be farther from the truth, and encouraged by his charming smile, my lady launched into a long and tragic exposition of her woes. At the end of a rather baffling ten minutes, Harry was able to deduce that her come-out had been intended for last autumn, but her brother had been feared lost at Quatre Bras and then

149

sent home so gravely wounded it had been delayed. And now, when her Ball was arranged, even to the invitation list, her grandpapa had fallen victim to some kind of seizure, which might well lead to a further postponement. "I cannot think," she mourned, with a tragic little *moue* Harry found enchanting, "why he must become ill now—when he has managed to go on quite nicely for ninety years."

"Utterly selfish," put in Nanette, smiling into the flash of Harry's irked glance. "But then, one can never rely upon old people."

"Have you noticed that?" Nerina asked, amazed at such perspicacity. "It is a sad truth, is it not? To be old must be very unpleasant. I shall die young."

Harry protested against this gloomy pronouncement but was ignored as Nerina went on to remark that old people were not beautiful. Disregarding Nanette's ironic grin, Harry said staunchly that Lady Nerina must be lovely when she was eighty, and doubtless would be surrounded by flirtatious old gentlemen. His effort, alas, was not well received. Papa, said Nerina, much shocked, found flirting disgraceful. She was not that kind of girl and hoped she had not given Sir Harry a false impression. "And yet—oh, my! How could you but harbour such thoughts of me when I am unchaperoned in this *dreadful* place!"

Her patience at an end, Nanette exploded, "Oh, for heaven's sake, stop sniffling and behaving like such a stupid! You have your maid and your groom, and are scarce ruined because you speak with friends in the parlour of an inn!"

"N-No, but Papa will not think so! He has such great plans for me, and if I am disgraced I shall never receive offers from anyone above a mere *baronet* and Papa will be furious! Oh, I wish I had never left Ann's and come here!"

Nanette slanted an hilarious glance at Harry. His answering grin went slightly awry, seeing which she said crossly, "Then return to Ann at once, you foolish girl! I am indeed sorry that I asked you to meet me here!"

At this, Nerina burst into tears. Harry muttered a scolding, "Be still, vixen!" and hastened to drop to one knee beside the grieving Beauty. He took up one small hand

and, patting it, said kindly, "Dear lady, I beg you will not so distress yourself. Miss Nanette spoke in haste, but meant no harm, and—"

"I meant every word!" hissed Nanette under cover of the dainty sobs.

"—and if you will but give me the name of your groom, I shall have your carriage called up and you can soon be on your way home," he finished.

"It—it is . . . Roper," my lady said unsteadily, lifting tear-drenched eyes devastatingly to his. "Thank you, Sir Harry. You are—s-so good."

He stood, bowed, and turned to the door.

"Even if you *are* a mere baronet . . ." giggled Nanette as he drew level with her.

He glared but was undone as her eyes slowly crossed and her chin lolled. Battling a laugh, he whispered, "Shrew!" and stalked past.

When he returned, the two girls were seated side by side on the sofa, chattering happily. They both stood when he came into the room, and having embraced Nanette and vowed to "say exactly" as she had been instructed, Nerina turned to Harry and extended her hand. "I hope you will forgive me if I was silly," she smiled sunnily. "I am not a clever girl, you see."

He bowed over those delicate fingers. "You are delightful, my lady. And it has been my very great pleasure. If I can *ever* be of service . . . I beg you will call upon me."

"You may have to call quite loudly," Nanette advised helpfully. "Especially if he is posted to India."

Harry regarded her without appreciable rapture.

"Oh," said Nerina. "Have you bought a pair of colours, then?"

"Not—ah—yet, ma'am."

"If he cannot, he will likely enlist," offered Nanette.

"In . . . in the . . . ranks?" gasped the Beauty, one hand flying to her throat.

"It is—possible, my lady," nodded Harry, his palms itching to box someone's ears.

"How . . . *dreadful* . . . !" said his Golden Goddess.

CHAPTER X

IT WAS PEACEFUL BENEATH THE OAK TREE, BUT AL-
though he was seated comfortably enough, Harry frowned,
for the echo of a mocking laugh rang in his ears, and pale
eyes haunted him. Sanguinet had tried to kill him, beyond
doubting. Why? Because of his duel with Mitchell? Thank
God old Mitch *was* alive! The intensity of that emotion
brought with it the recollection of his searing anguish. Only
a sadist could deliberately cause another human being such
a depth of grief . . . Some dawn, with a Manton in his
hand, he would avenge that piece of savagery! Some
dawn—and not too far hence . . !

His fingers clenched over an unfamiliar object. He
glanced down and discovered he held Lady Nerina's dainty
handkerchief. His grim countenance softened. Had there
ever been a more bewitching little vision? So sweetly feminine; all gold and pink, and daintiness personified. And
how loyal, that despite her fears she had ventured to try
and help her friend. Looking back, he was forced to the
reluctant admission that she *had* seemed a little more
preoccupied with her own predicament than that of Nanette. Yet who could do any less than worship so exquisite
a Beauty . . ?

He was, he suddenly apprehended, ravenous. Diccon had
said he would come at twelve o'clock, but it must surely
be much later than that. He glanced up and his nose all but
collided with the piece of crusty bread, well-buttered, and
topped by a slice of ham that Nanette thrust at him. Her

eyes, beyond this superb offering, held scorn, seeing which he at once politely declined. She shrugged carelessly and sank her white teeth into the feast. Harry, his mouth watering, turned away.

"Bought it at the inn," she explained rather indistinctly. "I wonder you did not think to do so. Unless—now that you've properly met your Goddess, you intend to moon and sigh and waste away for love."

For once he was able to bite back his furious response. He fixed her instead with what he hoped was a cool stare—somewhat marred by the sight of her second onslaught upon her lunch.

"Had a cousin who did that," she mumbled. "He fell madly in love with an actress—quite beneath his touch, of course, and his papa would not hear of his wedding her. Poor lad would eat nothing for three days! He went about reading Byron—even tied a kerchief around his neck instead of a neckcloth." She gave a callous trill of laughter and almost choked. "I thought it hilarious!"

Longing to throw her to the nearest crocodile, Harry said at his iciest, "Really?"

"So did his papa," she nodded, recovering her breath. "And the actress—well, she was fairly in stitches."

"Is that so?"

She confirmed the fact, quite cheerfully unfrozen although she should by rights have been severely frosted by this time and, waving her lunch with apparent nonchalance under his haughtily elevated nostrils, shrugged, "Of course—*he* was only thirteen at the time . . ."

Between her mischievously dancing eyes and the memory of just such a youthful passion, Harry burst into a laugh. "Wretched little shrew! You may count yourself fortunate there are no alligators lurking about!"

"May I?" she giggled. A ray of sun slanted across Harry's face, and watching him, the mirth faded from her expression. "And—what *did* you think of Nerina?" she asked idly.

He sighed. "That she is as lovely, as gentle, as sweetly mannered as any man could desire." His eyes became wistful and, after a moment, no response being heard, he glanced up and into a withering glare.

"Desire . . . pah!" she said with scathing contempt. "How ghastly to be a man! To be everlastingly and totally—"

"Motivated by lust—no?" Harry interpolated, immediately ablaze with righteous indignation.

Her chin lifted, and with a droop of disdainful eyelids she sneered, "If the cap fits . . ."

"If you did but know," he grated savagely, "how I had to struggle to restrain myself from stripping the clothes from her—right there in the parlour!"

"Good God!" gasped Nanette, horrified. "If you *ever* hope to win her, do not dare to make so crude a remark within *her* hearing!"

"Of course I would not," he said, flushing with guilt. "Do you take me for a flat? I am aware she is a perfect lady."

"I see." She put down her lunch and with a fluid movement stood beside him. "And you are also aware of what I am—eh, Captain Sir Harry Redmond?"

The tone was one he'd not heard before. He was on his feet in a flash and, catching her by the shoulders, shook her gently. "You infuriate me when you speak so cynically of men. But I meant no disrespect to you, little one."

"Why should you respect such as I?" How high her head was held . . . how prideful the glint in her hazel eyes, and with what quelling scorn did she speak now. "I am a wanton, who roams the countryside with two strange men; and had I a reputation to start with, it is certainly trampled in the dust by now."

The ice in her tone struck to his heart, but the knowledge that he had hurt her was a deeper pang; and in an attempt to win her to a smile again, he teased, "Even if one of your fellow wanderers is—a 'mere baronet'?"

Her mouth quivered responsively. Laughter danced into Harry's eyes, and pressing his advantage, he reached for her hands. "I was properly driven against the ropes, was I

154

not? Forgive me, little one. It was an unforgivable thing to say. I *do* apologize.''

For an instant she stood there, gazing up at him. Her hands began to tremble in his clasp, and Harry knew a confusing need to pull her into his arms; but she drew quickly away and, sitting down, opened the package she carried and unwrapped another piece of bread, this topped with a slice of roast beef that drew a blissful groan from him as he again sat beside her. "Mademoiselle," he said, accepting the food gratefully, "you are a diamond of the first water!" She chuckled, and they ate together, chatting in perfect harmony until he glanced down at the tight bun atop her head and asked quietly, "Am I forgiven?"

"Of course. Oh, but I have such a dreadfully quick temper, Harry. You must not heed me when I behave so—or you will not like me at all, I . . . fear."

"To the contrary, miss. I *shall* heed you. And do you become too—"

"Shrewish?" she prompted.

"Shrewish," he grinned, watching that dimple come and go beside her lips. "Then I shall simply have to box your ears again!"

She laughed. "When you first came into ''The Star,'' you looked more ready to do murder than to box someone's ears."

"I was," he said slowly. "I am. I shall. Though it will not be murder."

"Harry . . . do not! It frightens me to see you look . . . Who is this man you mean to fight? Did you see him here? Today?"

He nodded, hesitated, then said, "I have told you of my brother, Mitchell . . ?"

"Yes. Your poor brother who is so forgetful and whom you did not allow to share your troubles but sent back to Oxford as though he were a little child. I think, when he discovers the truth, he will punch your head for this."

His smile was brief and did not reach his eyes. "Probably. Though it seems that he is not at Oxford for he discovered the truth—or some of it, and went rushing off to call out the man he thought responsible. Today, before I came to "The Star," I was told Mitchell had been . . . killed in that duel . . ."

He had expected understanding but was unprepared for the tears that filled her eyes, or for the soft cry of pity she uttered, and the arms that suddenly swept around him, to draw his head to her shoulder. "Ah . . . my poor, grieving boy," she said huskily. "And I have tease and torment you while you suffer such heartbreak! My dear . . . my dear—I am so sorry! I know—too well what it means to lose someone you love."

It was the second time Harry had been clasped in her arms, and for an instant he did not move, delighting in the sweet, fresh scent of her, the warm softness of her little body. He straightened then and with an awed sense of wonder said, "What a very remarkable girl you are. Thank you, my sweet."

Her lips trembled; a tear slid down, and she gulped, "You are . . . so brave. I know how much he meant to you."

Gently, he wiped away that gleaming droplet, then pulled her into a hug and, vaguely surprised that this should cause his pulse to quicken, said, "Do not grieve so, dear child. Mitchell is not dead—thank God!"

She all but sprang back and, dashing away her tears, cried furiously, "You have deceived me yet again! Oh, but you are the horridest man alive! I *hate* you, Harry Redmond! How could you let me make such a great exhibition of . . . of . . ." And she stopped, her flushed cheeks paling once more as he watched her gravely. "Dear heaven," she whispered, her eyes dark with new horror. "Someone told you that—by mistake? And you really *believed* him—dead?"

"I believed him dead, but there was no mistake." His jaw set grimly. "I was meant to believe it, so as to provide entertainment."

Nanette gave a shocked cry, but before she could speak they heard hooves and the rattle of wheels. His cheerful self again, Harry sprang up. "Here's our Diccon at last!"

He assisted her to rise and started toward the oncoming cart only to stop uncertainly. A gypsy was driving; a young man, little more than a boy, but with a powerful pair of shoulders and large, expressive eyes, almost as dark as his tumbled black hair. For an instant Harry stood in mute astonishment; then he gave a shout, "Daniel! What the devil are you doing up there?"

The cart halted. With a lithe spring the gypsy alighted, and for a short while the two men alternately pounded at and smiled upon one another. But watching them, Nanette saw that while Harry said a good deal, the gypsy said nothing at all, although he seemed just as delighted by this meeting.

"Miss Nanette," said Harry. "This is my very good friend Daniel."

She smiled, and the gypsy touched his brow with shy respect.

"He cannot speak," Harry explained. "But he can hear you. He's a splendid fighting man, and hauled Lucian St. Clair out of the river last year when he all but stuck his spoon in the wall . . . You doubtless heard about it. Dan, I suppose you are acquainted with our Trader. Where is he?"

For answer Daniel drew a folded paper from his pocket and handed it to Nanette. She broke the wafer, unfolded the sheet, and scanned it rapidly. When she finished, she looked pale and worried, and said, "He asks that I read you this last paragraph . . . 'Harry, I've got some work I must do, and I will not be able to come back for a few days. I know as you will take care of the young lady and Mr. Fox. I'll come up with you by the time you gets to Chichester. Meantime, you'd best keep to the byways, as I think Miss Nanette's father is looking for her very hard like . . . ' "

"It won't do!" Harry frowned. "Little one, you simply will have to go back with— Now, where in the deuce did he get to?"

Lifting her troubled gaze from Diccon's scrawl, Nanette said a blank, "Your pardon?"

"Daniel—he's gone! Now blast it all, this *will* not do, ma'am! It was bad enough for you to be traipsing about with Diccon, but . . ." His words died away, for she looked so very scared all at once, and so little. He said regretfully, "I'm sorry, but I shall *have* to take you back to Lady Nerina."

"No! Oh, no! Harry—please! Diccon says my papa is close by! I beg of you—do not let him take me back. *Please* . . . !"

"Dear child," he said gently, "be sensible. Lady Nerina was quite right, you know. You are a lady of Quality, and for us to travel alone would most certainly spell your ruin!"

"And God knows," he thought, "what it would spell for me!"

She clung to the lapel of his jacket, gazing up at him like an apprehensive child indeed. "Foolish one! Why do you think I wear this ugly frock? Why is my hair in this hideous bun, except to prevent myself from being recognized? To make sure that Diccon—or you—shall not be accused of . . . of . . ." She blushed and her lashes swept down.

"Compromising you?" And with an impact that was near physical, he acknowledged to himself that she was quite hopelessly compromised.

"Yes. No! Harry—I know you would not harm me."

He patted that small, tugging hand and pointed out with a rather crooked smile that he *had* boxed her ears. She implored him to be serious and to escort her if only as far as Chichester . . . She really was very pretty, thought Harry; and several times of late he had fancied to catch a glimpse of something in her eyes that told him she was not indifferent to him. Not love, perhaps, but certainly a fondness. As for himself, he had been in love so many times . . . Or had he? What was it Mitchell had said? Something about his not having the same 'look' as St. Clair . . ? His love for Dorothy had not been love at all, he knew that now. And Nerina? He admired her, certainly—as one would admire a beautiful painting, or a flower. A flash of defiance asserted, "She is exquisite!" But common sense, recalling her empty chatter and the betrayal of selfishness, whispered, "You love the Beauty, not the girl beneath it . . ." The thought of Nerina coping with life in the train of an army brought a wry grin to his lips. But instantly he could see Nanette, weeping with frustration because his hurts had sickened her . . . envying Juana Smith for having shared her husband's perils during the war. He glanced down at her, so lost in thought he was oblivious to the angry sparkle in the big eyes, the jut of the little chin. Here was a girl whose furies as swiftly gave way to laughter, whose heart was as warm as her mind was bright and enquiring. They might not love one another, yet life with his 'little shrew' could only be a zestful adventure. If he joined up, the men would adore her certainly, as they had adored Juana . . .

"Monster!" she raged, stamping her foot with frustration. "You have heard not one word of all the things I have spoken!"

"No," he grinned. He placed one long finger beneath her chin and, tilting it a little higher, said, "Been practicing a speech of my own. Now do stop scowling so, and listen . . . Little one—you're not in love with me, nor I with you. But it would suit you to acquire a husband, and I must wed sooner or later. I think we might deal quite well together. What d'you say?"

For an instant she stared at him speechlessly. Then her eyes filled, and the glittering drops spilled over. The sweet child was overcome. Smiling his tenderest smile, Harry leaned forward to be staggered by the hand that slapped across his face with all her considerable strength behind it.

"Beast!" she exploded, fairly dancing her fury. "Unfeeling! Pompous! Pedantic! Idiotish! *Oooh!*"

"The devil!" blinked Harry, holding his smarting cheek. "In case no one ever instructed you, ma'am, that is *not* the proper way to respond to an offer!"

"Offer! Is *that* what you call it? That was not an offer, you puffed-up bag of conceit! That was a sanctimonious martyrdom—a sacrificial willingness to save me and to accept second-best from life! Well, I am not *that* desperate, Harry Sir Captain Redmond! Oh—or whatever! Sooner than wed a star-crossed, gushy-eyed, half-blind, maggot-witted chawbacon like you—I'll marry my uncle! And be dashed to you!''

"Good God!" he exclaimed, grabbing her shoulders and shaking her hard. "Here's fine language for a gentlewoman! I should scrub out your naughty mouth!"

"Do you not remove your lecherous hands from my body in this very instant, I shall scream bloody murder!"

A horse was appraoching—and at a rapid trot. Harry cast an unhappy glance to the trees at the curve of the lane and stepped back.

"Go!" snarled Nanette. "Climb into your beastly little cart, with your ugly coat and your great clodhopping shoes, and take yourself off! Go!"

Two boys sauntered toward them, grinning openly. Harry felt a savage urge to rap their loutish heads together. He bent a fierce glare upon them, and they fled towards the oncoming rider. Following their progress, he grumbled, "Then what *will* you do?"

"For your information, sir, the last proposal I received was delivered in a palace, with the gentleman down on *both* knees before me! And there are plenty more where that came from, so spare me your sympathy, I do entreat!"

Flushing partly because of her blazing scorn and partly because of an unhappy feeling it was well-justified, he muttered, "Lord, what a whisker! One of these days your—" He interrupted himself to gasp a disbelieving, "Nerina!"

The Beauty, mounted on a bay mare, waved agitatedly as she rode toward them.

"Go!" repeated Nanette, one outstretched arm pointing dramatically to the west. "You have done what you wished, for she is here to take me back, I've no doubt; and if I must watch you melt all over her silliness again, I shall cast up my accounts!"

"Shrew . . !" he grated. "Why must you use such crude expressions?"

"To describe crude situations! Now begone, sir—else I shall tell your sainted Goddess what manner of *roué* you *really* are!"

With a fuming glare Harry turned from her, swung into the cart, and slapped the reins against the neck of the drowsing Mr. Fox. "I hope you *do* marry your uncle!" he snarled. "It would serve you right to have a nursery full of nieces and nephews for your children!"

Having uttered the which rather muddled insult, he guided the little donkey away without a backward glance.

A mild breeze ruffled Harry's thick locks, and the sun shone benevolently upon him. A meadowlark soared upward, the clear notes of his song rippling through the peace of this beautiful spring afternoon. And aware of none of these blessings, Harry glared at Mr. Fox's ears, one sticking proudly upright through the brim of his old beaver, the other drooping at half mast.

What a shrew! What a bad-tempered, foul-mouthed, wretchedly ungrateful little baggage! He touched his still-tingling cheek. A fine reaction to the first offer he'd ever made! He'd likely have the devil of a bruise. Gad, but she'd dealt him a leveller! And to think he'd almost saddled himself with the vixen! What he should have done, of course, was to have swung her across his knee there and then and paddled her derriere! But recalling that Lady Nerina had seemed upset, he slowed the cart and glanced back uneasily. ". . . a gushy-eyed, half-blind, maggot-witted chawbacon . . !" Scowling, he turned around and jiggled the reins resolutely. Gushy-eyed, indeed! Lieutenant Fowler had been gushy-eyed over that little ladybird in Valencia. A revolting demonstration! He and Bolster had laughed themselves sick over it. Had he *really* looked like that? "I'll marry my uncle! And be dashed to you!" He chuckled despite himself. She'd do it, too, blasted little spitfire! But that had been a good one he'd dealt her in return . . . a nursery full of nieces and nephews. The amusement faded from his eyes, for the thought of Nanette as a mother brought with it the awareness that she would be superb in the role. He could all but picture her with head tenderly downbent over some tiny scrap of humanity. Why that should make him feel so damnably miserable he could not imagine; but, by God, she wasn't going to be pushed into a marriage she didn't want!

He turned Mr. Fox and started back even as two boys tore around the bend of the lane and galloped towards him. They were the same two who has passed earlier, and instead of continuing on their way, they detoured widely across the field, their white, scared faces very plainly betraying a reluctance to encounter him. Harry slapped the reins against the donkey's neck and urged him to "giddap!", but to no avail. Apprehension escalated into fear, and the placid trot became unendurable. He leapt from the cart and began to run. Behind him then there arose an alarming rattling and a distressed braying. Poor Mr. Fox was worrying again . . .

Harry rounded the bend as a piercing shriek rent the air. Nerina's bay mare was bolting towards the village, and at first he thought she had been thrown; but his frantic gaze discovered her standing by the low-barred fence with closed eyes and both hands pressed to her mouth. Samuel Chatham was beside her, and he turned as Harry ran up and waved with tremulous urgency. Lady Nerina raised a pale countenance and moaned, "Thank *heaven* you are come! Oh, why does she do such rash things?"

"Them wicked boys throwed me hammer over the fence, S'Harry," piped Mr. Chatham. "And the pretty little lady goed t'get it fer I . . ."

Was *that* all . . ! A sigh of relief escaped Harry. And then he saw Nanette standing in the middle of the field and, seeing also the reason for her frozen immobility, for a split second could not breathe.

"If only . . ." sobbed Lady Nerina, "her shawl was not . . . *red!*"

"A fine Welsh bull, bean't he? wheezed Chatham. "Willyum Brown paid a purty penny fo'un. But so *mean* natured, 'ee do be . . ."

He was also the biggest, blackest, and most muscular bull Harry had ever seen, with horns that looked a yard long as he stood there, tossing his massive head and pawing at the earth with one impatient hoof. Once, Harry had attended a bullfight in Madrid. The sport had not appealed to him, especially when he'd seen the unfortunate horse of a picador impaled on the bull's horns. He could still remember how it had screamed . . .

He had cleared the fence and was running even as the thoughts raced through his mind, but the bull had also started forward. *"Move!"* he roared. Nanette turned to him. He had a brief impression of huge eyes dark with terror and, beyond the chalk white face, a charging monster. He reached the girl a few seconds ahead of the bull, tore the shawl away, thrust her violently to the side, waved the shawl at the oncoming fury, and ran for his life. That he had succeeded in distracting the brute was evidenced by the nightmare of sound that was all about him: an explosive snorting of such power as to freeze the heart, a thunder of hooves with fourteen hundred pounds of power and muscle behind them. Harry waited until the last possible instant, then launched himself in a frantic dive to the side. A mighty shape brushed past him. He was down and rolling in the dirt, but regained his feet in a lithe spring. The bull was swinging about, midway between him and escape. Without waiting for those hot little eyes to discover him, Harry raced back the way he had come. He had never dreamed he could move so fast. He glimpsed Nanette clambering over the fence and fairly shot towards her. Again that petrifying thunder of hooves—gaining on him with every stride. The ground vibrated to the fearsome pursuit, and the fence looked miles away. "Too close!" he thought, and angled desperately to the side. A razor-sharp horn that would certainly have sliced into his back brushed his right sleeve. A deafening bellow escaped the infuriated animal, echoed distantly by a grievous braying. His lungs bursting, Harry sprinted frenziedly. In mere seconds he could again all but feel the snorting explosive breathing and sensed that death was inches from him. He essayed a mighty burst of speed and flung himself at the fence, his left hand grabbing the top rail as he vaulted into the air. A maddened snorting. An earth-shaking gallop. A dark shape lunging at him. Something thudded against his forearm—but he was clear!

The fence shook and creaked as the bull rammed it in a bellowing frustration. Sprawled on hands and knees in the ditch, his head hanging, Harry sobbed for breath and prayed numbly that the fence would hold. The bull snorted fiercely, then lost interest and trotted away.

"Harry! *Harry!*" Frantic hands were tearing at him. Nanette, on her knees also, was bending to peer into his contorted face. "*Mon Dieu!* Are you all right?"

"Sufficiently so . . ." he gasped, "to give you . . . the spanking you warrant!"

With a stifled sob, she threw her arms about his neck, murmuring a heartfelt, "Thank you! My brave one! Thank you!"

"Silly . . . chit . . ." panted Harry. "Do not—get so up . . . in the boughs . . ."

"Nanette!" Lady Nerina trod towards them, regarding her friend's unconventional attitude with shocked eyes.

Nanette stood and, flushing, said a defiant, "Well, he saved my life!"

"And most gallantly," acknowledged the Beauty, bestowing a dazzling smile on the impromptu matador. Her eyes were a blue stain in her exquisite face; the mellow sunlight turned her clustered curls to spun gold, and the white plume of her riding hat, curling beside her dewy cheek, seemed to emphasize the perfection of her skin. Befuddled, Harry eased into a sitting position and, leaning back on his hands, gasped, "It was a pretty good run . . . if I do say so. But a bit . . . too close . . . for comfort!"

"*Much* too close!" agreed Lady Nerina, watching him admiringly. "Oh, Nanette! Why do you do such madcap things? Sir Harry might have been killed!"

Nanette's lip was quivering, and there was the glitter of tears in her eyes as she looked beseechingly from one to the other. "The poor old gentleman was so upset, you see. I did not dream the bull was in there, or . . . Oh, Harry! If you had been—" She broke off and he grinned at her, but she tossed her head away. "Do not make excuses for me! I am just . . . a stupid! I do it all the time, do I not, Nerina?"

"Yes, truly," sighed my lady. "Nanette is always in a taking about something or other, and it is quite impossible to avoid being drawn into her predicaments. Only yesterday I was happily ensconced in my sister's lovely old house. Today, not only must I endure that awful village where the people stare at one so, and the inn is so *primitive*, but I have again risked Papa's displeasure by riding out alone, for I dared not bring my groom to carry tales." Her brow furrowed deliciously. "It is wicked to disobey one's parents. And yet—one must be loyal to one's friends. What a dreadful dilemma. If only one . . ."

Despite the appeal of that silvery voice, Harry's attention wandered. He was commencing to feel odd and to suspect all was not well with him—a suspicion verified by Mr. Chatham's piping interruption. "Ye'd best stop all the chit-chat, ma'am, and tie up S'Harry's arm."

Harry looked down to find crimson streaking his left hand. "Duece take it all," he said wryly. "Didn't run quite fast enough at that!"

"Idiotish man!" Nanette had paled. "Take off your coat! No—do not get up!" She helped him ease the torn left sleeve free while scolding, "Are you *so* infatuated you dared not interrupt her but sat there and stoically bled like . . . like a fountain? Give me now your little knife."

Scarlet with embarrassment, Harry complied. "I was not being in the least stoical. I knew the brute had hit me, but I thought it was with his confounded snout. I'd no idea the horn caught me. And if you would but learn, my girl, to—" He checked, flinching, as she swung his wrist gently upwards.

"Tiens!" she gulped.

The underarm was deeply gashed between elbow and wrist, and bleeding profusely. Harry flashed a quick glance at Nanette's white face and said calmly, "Well, he really ripped me up, didn't he?"

"You need not be so valiant," she responded, her voice only slightly uneven. "I have not the intention to faint this time."

" 'The road to hell'," he quoted, " 'is paved with good intentions . . .' "

She returned his smile and began to gingerly peel the shirt away, while requesting Lady Nerina to run to the cart and find a clean neckcloth for bandaging.

"Ye got t'be careful o'horn wounds," said Chatham knowledgeably, peering over Harry's shoulder. "It mayn't hurt much now but give it a hour. Say a half hour. Ah—does ye see the bone there, miss?"

Nanette turned even whiter and nodded. Harry nerved himself and clamped his right hand firmly around the gash, holding it closed. Nanette cringed but immediately pressed a piece of the ripped shirt sleeve against the part of the cut his hand could not encompass. He made no sound, but she saw his eyes flicker and, aching with sympathy, exclaimed, "Oh! That must have hurt dreadfully!"

"No," he lied. "Not—too . . ." but then had to stop, breath eluding him.

Nanette whipped her gaze to Lady Nerina. The Beauty stood motionless, with head averted and eyes tight shut. "Good God!" raged Nanette. "What are you *doing*? The neckcloth! Quickly! Poor Harry is bleeding horribly!"

My lady pressed a hand to her mouth. "*Must* you talk about it?" she choked. "You are making me . . . ill . . ."

"If you dare to faint—I shall slap you!" Nanette started up, only to jump back as blood at once pulsed from the wound. "Oh, lud! Go at once, you silly girl!"

Nerina tottered off, sobbing miserably that if she caught so much as a glimpse of Sir Harry's injury she was sure to be sick. Nanette began to mutter beneath her breath, and when at last Nerina crept haltingly towards them, reached out and said a fierce, "Give it me! Hurry!"

In the act of complying, Nerina checked, stared with horrified eyes at her friend's bloody hand, and crumpled into a dead faint.

Dismayed, Harry started up, but sat back hurriedly as Nanette tightened her grip on his arm and ground out, "Do . . . not . . . dare!" She accepted the neckcloth gratefully from Mr. Chatham's wavering hand and added a heartless, "She does it all the time."

Harry directed an indignant glance at her. "Samuel—would you please help the lady? Perhaps—" But again his breath was snatched away, and for some moments he was quite unable to speak as Nanette bound his arm tightly.

Mr. Chatham essayed the trip to the cart, returning via an erratic route but bearing one of Diccon's clean shirts and a flask of brandy. Harry was by this time feeling not at all the thing and thought this an excellent notion, but Mr. Chatham's plans did not include the matador. He knelt instead beside the recumbent Beauty and began to pour the brandy between her teeth.

The bandage was knotted at last, and refusing aid, Harry insisted that Nanette turn her back while he changed into the clean shirt. Buttoning the left cuff clumsily, he asked, "Are you all right, little shrew?"

"Yes . . ." she whispered. He reached out and, turning her chin, said, "Poor little girl. You won't forget you promised not to faint . . . ?" She buttoned the right cuff and answered with a shaky smile, "If I do, you may box my ears, Tyrant!"

He winked jauntily and clambered to his feet. The trees tilted oddly, and he felt breathless again, but fought off the weakness and crossed to where Mr. Chatham sat with Nerina's head pillowed in his lap. "Ah, but she be a treat fer the eyes, don't she?" wheezed the old man. "Just to look at, a'course."

"You wicked old rascal," grinned Harry.

The dark lashes fluttered then, and those enormous blue eyes peered up at him. "Where . . . am I?" asked my lady predictably.

Harry leaned closer. "You are quite safe. Are you better now, ma'am?"

She blinked, managed to sit up, and gulped, "I . . . fainted."

"Yes, but I don't think you hurt yourself. Can you stand if I help you?"

He extended his hand. She scanned it anxiously, put her

167

fingers gingerly into his grasp, and came to her feet, only to sway and clutch her brow. "Oh! I feel . . . drefful. An' I can taste . . ." Her eyes opened very wide and she spun on Nanette, who sat staring rather blankly at her stained hands. "Dear God! You—did nothing! My *frien'*! They have made me . . . drunk!"

"No, no," Harry reassured her. "But since you are better now, you must at once go back to Alfriston."

This ill-judged remark unleashed a torrent of slurred dramatics. Lady Nerina was *not* better! She had, she sobbed tragically, been abandoned by her faithful steed and further betrayed by her alleged frien' who had callously allowed her to be Drenched, Degraded, and Besotted with Spirits! The risks she had taken in Nanette's behalf were itemized and elaborated upon through a veritable tempest of tears. Harry listened patiently, but at length he turned away and, ignoring her protests, went to touch Nanette's untidy head very gently, "Are you all right, my shrew?" She managed a rather shaky smile and said she was perfectly all right. "But—poor Mr. Fox! Harry, you must explain to him!"

The little donkey's bowed head rocked rhythmically back and forth as he uttered his sounds of distress. Harry went to him at once, followed by wails of indignation from the ill-used Beauty. Mr. Fox let it be known that his sensibilities had been deeply offended but was restored, fortunately, by Diccon's letter to Nanette.

Harry joined then in the efforts of Nanette and Mr. Chatham to calm my lady, efforts that were interrupted as a wagon jolted around the bend. The driver of this equipage was a ruddy-faced, middle-aged man of stocky build and a shock of red hair that stood up all over his head, giving him a rather startled appearance. It developed that he was Mr. Chatham's youngest son, and upon being adjured by his sire to "get down here smart-like, and mind yer manners!" he clambered from the high seat. Cap clutched in hand, he nodded respectfully to the ladies, shook Harry's hand while viewing the discarded shirt with eyes that were very round indeed, and enquired if there was anything what he could do.

"Six sons I had," beamed Mr. Chatham. "One died o' the pox; one was killed at Assaye—served under Lord Moulton, he did! And one got blowed ter smitherins at that there Spanishy place where you come a cropper, S'Harry. This here's me Henery, wot's come to stay wi' me and me daughter fer a bit. Landlord over to "The Red Bull" in Cerne Abbas, 'ee be. Though," he grinned broadly, "maybe I'd best not say that—seein's ye've had yer fill o' bulls terday, S' Harry!" He gave a cackle of mirth at this fine joke and dug his son in the ribs. "S'Harry went and got hisself gored by Willyum Brown's bull."

"Did ye now?" Henry's eyes clouded with alarm. "Bull's horns be nasty-like, Sir Harry. Ye'd best come and let me sister have a look at it.'

"Thank heaven!" sighed Nanette. "Then I shall not have to risk going to the village. These gentlemen will take you back to "The Star," Nerina, and—"

My lady, who had been holding her head and staring distractedly from one to the other of them, now cried shrilly that sooner would she be dead than ride into the village like a bumpkin, in that "hideously dirty wagon!" She turned to 'Henery'. "Can you not understand . . . Mr. Red . . . ? They have . . . *ruined* me!"

Harry, torn between amusement and vexation, threw a look at Henry. That worthy, however, was surveying his venerable sire in outright, goggle-eyed disbelief. *"Father . . . !"* he gasped, when he could get his sagging jaws together. "What has you . . . gone and *done* . . . ?"

Nanette clapped a hand over her mouth. Harry, tears of mirth coming into his eyes, fought desperately for self-control. A crafty look creeping into his rheumy eyes, Samuel pulled back his shoulders and, with a markedly jaunty stagger, covered the distance to his son's side and hissed at him to shut his fool mouth afore he let the cat outta the bag!

Blinking rapidly, Harry turned to Nerina and pointed out that her servants must be worried since her hack had returned without its rider, and she *must* go back with Chathams. My lady lapsed into near hysterics and a long diatribe through which he tried in vain to reason with her, at length saying rather wearily that were Nanette to accompany her, there would be little danger of her reputation being impaired.

"Oh, no!" Nanette put in worriedly, "But I *cannot*, Harry! That is why poor Nerina came, you see. To warn me that my father's men are searching everywhere. You escort her and she will feel more comfortable." She turned to the cart. "I will—"

In two swift strides he caught her arm and said sternly, "Do you imagine for one instant that I shall allow you to journey alone, ma'am?"

"No. Of course not, sir." Her tone softened and a smile lit her eyes. "But I can wait for you in those trees over there. Harry, that is truly a dreadful gash. You must see a doctor as soon as possible, and—"

"Bean't a doctor in Alfriston," put in the younger Chatham.

"Nor in Lewes neither," nodded his sire. "We has a foine dentist, though. Jeremiah Maxwell, what does surgicals fer folks in his chair. I seed 'un sew up young Charlie Tanner arter he nigh cut his leg orf with his own scythe."

My lady swayed, and Nanette hastened to put her arms around her.

"Poor Charlie," sighed Henry. "He died in that chair, as I recollect."

"Ar, so 'ee did," Samuel admitted. "Come to think on it, Bill O'Hara died, too, arter Mr. Maxwell sewed him up!" He brightened. "*That* were a bull, ye'll mind, Henery. Old man Dean's bull got him proper. In the stummick."

"I am going to be sick!" sobbed Lady Nerina, pulling away from her friend. "What a dreadful day! I am all dust, and—Oh! My *feather* is broken!" It was, indeed. She held it up and raised her drenched eyes to Harry so tragically that he had to fight a wicked urge to laugh, not mitigated by her anguished plea that he take his pistol and put a period to her. She might as well be dead, she wailed, as to be sent back to the village in a "ebriated condish'n, having been in the wilderness, unchap'roned . . . with an ex-soldier! Word will spread'n spread . . . and who will want to marry me then?''

"Harry will," said Nanette tartly. "Without hesitation! So enact us no more Cheltenham tragedies, I do implore you!''

Harry had begun to appreciate that marriage to the glorious Beauty might be a decidedly mixed blessing and held his breath. Nerina merely uttered another heartrending wail, followed by renewed sobs. Breathing a sigh of relief, he murmured to Nanette, "And that will be just about enough sauce out of *you*, my girl! Lady Nerina, this is quite ridiculous. And—''

"And so are you!" Nanette again took her friend into her arms and, patting her shoulder comfortingly, went on, "It is of no use, Harry. If you try to talk sense to her when she is like this, she will only fall into strong hysterics. Now—Nerina love, you know I care for you . . . Be brave.''

Bravery, however, was noticeably absent as the sobs increased in volume.

"Good God!" Harry grated. "Why do I not simply pick up the foolish girl and toss her into their wagon?''

Nerina's reaction was loud and, having repeated references to libertines, military rattles, and violated innocence, caused the Chathams to eye one another uneasily.

"Hush, dear," said Nanette, drying her friend's tears. "I know this has all been very dreadful, and I am truly sorry. But Mr. Chatham is a good man and well known to Sir Harry. He will be glad to—''

"Stop!" cried Harry, running after the 'good man'.

"Sorry, sir!" called Henry, whipping up his horse. "But we be late for dinner already, and me sister will be powerful upset. Good day t'ye.''

"Oh . . . damme!" muttered Harry, holding his throbbing arm as he watched the wagon disappear around the bend in the lane.

A shout drifted back to him. "Don't'ee let that there cut go too long—else ye'll have some dentist a'hacking at ye!"

Coming up beside him, Nanette said with anxiety, "That is quite right! You should have gone with them—well, you'll have to go into Alfriston."

"And leave you out here alone? Absolutely not! Yet—our foxed Beauty must be conveyed to safety. Jove! What a mess! Where does her confounded sister live?"

"Just beyond the village of East Bourne. But we cannot go there, Harry. It will take you miles out of your way again."

It would do just that, and he was seething with impatience to reach Chichester, where he might, with luck, find both Mitch and Anderson awaiting him. There was little doubt, however, that Lady Nerina was in a difficult situation, and besides, her sister might offer Nanette the chance of a warm bath and a decent bed, and she looked wan and tired, poor little shrew . . . Her dirty face was upturned to his, her eyes wells of tenderness. She seemed prettier than ever, the parted lips softly irresistible . . . He bent to her.

"*Oooh*!" she squeaked furiously. "She is the most selfish girl in nature!"

Harry turned round and gave an involuntary laugh. Lady Nerina had succumbed to the exhausting events of her 'dreadful day'. She was curled up in the back of the cart fast asleep, her head pillowed on Diccon's violin case, a blanket pulled snugly around her. As dishevelled as she was, she contrived to look angelic, but the soft, purring little snores that escaped her would have thoroughly horrified one slightly intoxicated Beauty.

Harry leaned back from the seat so as to pull the blanket closer about my lady's shoulders. Slanting an anxious glance at him, Nanette muttered, "I should not have allowed you to turn back. And *you* are the one who should be resting!"

"Well, I've no intention of doing any such thing," he grinned, straightening, and urging Mr. Fox to hasten. "Do

172

you take me for a little old lady, to have a nap in the middle of the afternoon?''

She giggled. "I shall tell her what you said!"

"Yes, you would, you vixen! As though she has not had enough to bear! Inebriated, and in the wilderness with a 'mere baronet' . . !'' He exploded with mirth. "Gad! What an awful fate!''

Nanette laughed with him but then sighed, "I was wicked to say she is selfish, for she really isn't, you know. Or at least—not very. It's just . . . she is so very beautiful. And—well, she's not very—''

"What you mean," he chuckled, "is that she's thoroughly spoilt, very missish, and a total henwit. Though not *deliberately* unkind.''

"Poor Harry. Are you dreadfully disillusioned?''

"Devil a bit of it! Happens all the time. I paid court to the loveliest little London debutante for over a year, thinking I was fixing my interest, but—*she* thought we were only flirting.''

He had spoken cheerily, slanting his whimsical grin at her, but suspecting that he made light of something that must at the time have been crushing, she looked away and said softly, "It sounds as if you have never met the right one.''

"You're likely right. And if I do, shall probably be too stupid to realize it in time, and she'll be snatched away from under my nose by someone else. Which might be just as well," he added, some of the laughter leaving his eyes, "since I've not a feather to fly with!''

"Nor has Nerina," chuckled Nanette. Harry looked down at her questioningly, and she said, "Hers broke—do you not recall?''

The memory of the Beauty's tragic dismay over that minor disaster properly set Harry off, and they laughed together as Mr. Fox trotted placidly around the bend of the lane.

CHAPTER XI

THE MOONLIGHT FILTERED THROUGH THE TREES IN AN EV-erchanging pattern that Harry found most pleasant, and he lay in drowsy contentment, the sound of hooves and the movement of the cart a pleasantly familiar accompaniment to his thoughts. His arm hurt, which at first seemed odd. But gradually, the events of the day began to drift back to him. He remembered stopping the cart beside a pond and watching Nanette as she washed herself and tidied her hair. At his request she had let down the bun, and he smiled into the darkness, recalling how that cloud of rippling silk had swung down about her face, and how prettily she had blushed when he told her that she was beautiful . . . He'd allowed her to take the reins after that, for he had become so tired he was scarcely able to maintain his position on the seat. He'd been quite determined not to do as she requested and lie down, thus leaving her to drive with only the doubtful assistance of Lady Nerina. He knew she was frightened and had tried desperately to maintain an easy conversation and conceal both his growing weakness and the fact that his arm had commenced to throb abominably, but he'd awoken to find his head on her shoulder and the cart stopped. His immediate bright remark that he "must have dropped off for a minute" had drawn a caustic, "Almost right off the cart, sir!" and she had insisted that her friend be roused. He had a vague recollection of changing places with the complaining Beauty, and of Nanette demanding he swallow some of the brandy. It had certainly helped take the edge off the pain, and he must have fallen asleep almost immediately.

It dawned on him that they should have reached East Bourne hours ago, and he started up. A hand closed over his mouth, and Nerina bent above him. "Oh, Sir Harry!" she whispered. "Thank God you are awake at last! *Please* do not make a sound!"

"What in the deuce is going on?" he hissed as she removed her soft palm from his lips. "Where are we?"

"Indeed, I wish I knew! I thought I did. But I was quite mistaken, and we were lost. Nanette felt sorry for the man's donkey, so we stopped, and she helped him, although it was hideous, and I can never understood how it is that when one is with her one is always becoming involved in such strange happenings. Of course, my French is poor, but it was quite the same with the oar, you know."

Perhaps because he felt decidedly light-headed, Harry responded to foolishness with more foolishness and asked, "What *was* that all about?"

Nerina leaned closer. "We were coming back from Park Parapine. Nanette became overset because some men followed us. She was sure they were her papa's servants, and I expect she was right. She begged Sister Maria Evangeline to instruct the coachman to take a side road, and Sister Maria Evangeline is just as dramatically natured, so we did, and were in no time most terribly lost. Just as bad as now, in fact! Then the wheel came off the carriage and we went into a hole in the middle of that desolate Plain, and who should come along but a gypsy with a caravan full of the oddest things. He had an oar—it was new, he said, and he'd ordered it for someone and could not sell it, nor lend it to our coachman to help raise the carriage. *I* knew at once it was all a scheme to make us pay more, but no one could persuade him—until Nanette, as usual, managed to talk him around her thumb." She sighed and said in a rather puzzled tone, "Everyone says I am much more beautiful than she is. Yet, somehow, the gentlemen always fall in love with *her* . . . I suppose it is because she is so—" She stopped abruptly and then said, "Well, at all events we drove on as fast as we could go, once the wheel was repaired, but then we met the person who owns this donkey and cart, and in some odd fashion Sister Maria Evangeline seemed to know him, so we stopped, and nothing would do but that we trade the oar for a pistol he had. I thought it all strange and most shocking, but Sister Maria Evangeline said something about "needs must when the Devil drives" which did not make any sense at all, for Harold was driving and he is a very respectable individual, I am sure. And it was just as I feared, because when her papa's men came close, Nanette fired the pistol at them!''

"Did she, by God!'' Harry muttered admiringly. "Did she hit anyone?''

"No, thank heaven! But it made me cry for it was the most ghastly noise. Still, they rode off. And when we reached Tunbridge Wells at last, Sister Maria Evangeline insisted we stay at that frightful boardinghouse because Nanette's papa would never dream of looking for us there. The other girls are silly and said it was exciting. I thought it was dreadful *and* improper! And . . .''

Her voice went on and on, but it dawned on Harry that his shrew must be very tired; and as soon as she paused he twisted until he could reach the long hair Nanette had evidently not had time to restore to the bun, and tugged it.

She glanced around, her eyes warming as she saw the white gleam of his smile in the moonlight. "Poor Harry. How are you feeling? Do you remember nearly fainting and with never a word to warn me of it? I vow you are the—''

"Never mind that, miss!'' He could detect the sound of many hooves and a low mutter of conversation. "What have you got us into now? Who *are* these people?'' He started up on one elbow and gave a gasp of indignation as her hand came around and pushed his head down. She admonished. "Lie still, do! You must rest. We are with some very kind—er—travellers.''

"Of all the henwitted things!'' Harry grumbled, pulling her hand away. "You should have woken me at once. Two women—alone! I wonder they didn't—''

"But I told them you were here," she interrupted hastily, "and indeed they were most kind. M. Yves said he and his friends would escort us. Only we have become lost. A little bit. A man was guiding them, but he has gone to try and find a good campsite for the night."

"I *must* get to my sister's house!" Nerina said in a low, scared voice. "If I spend the night in the wilderness with all these strange men, I shall be—"

"Ruined . . ." muttered Harry, and thought that this time she was absolutely correct. He eluded Nanette's restraining hand and heaved himself upward, wincing a little as he peered over the side of the cart. "The . . . devil!" he gasped.

A long line of ponies and donkeys followed, single file, each animal having a large barrel slung on either side of its back. Quiet riders ranged along the train at intervals, ensuring that they stay within the shadows of the trees. He could catch only an occasional word or two, but that they were French was obvious. "Free traders!" he ejaculated. "That damnable little rascal has us leading a consignment of illegal brandy!"

Despite his irritation, he had spoken with prudent softness. The shriek my lady let out, however, would have woken the dead. Shouts and curses rent the air. The cart came to an abrupt stop and Harry was surrounded by grim faces, while no fewer than six even more grim pistols were levelled at his head. A moan and a soft thud beside him acquainted him with the fact that Nerina had fainted.

"*Qu'est-ce que c'est?*" cried one of the smugglers, peering at Harry.

"Precisely what I should like to know, monsieur," he answered in French. "What the devil do you mean by involving us in your unsavoury business?"

A small but villainous-looking man wearing a blue-and-white knitted stocking cap fixed Harry with an intense stare and growled suspiciously, "You have a very youthful papa, mademoiselle!"

"*Oui, en effet,*" Nanette agreed, leaning to pat the indignant Harry's shoulder. "But I am very young myself,

M. Yves. No, *mon père,* you must not be cross. These gentlemen have been too kind.''

''I'll *'mon père'* you!'' he hissed as she planted a filial type of kiss on his cheek.

''Well, I had to make them think we were properly chaperoned,'' she giggled. ''I told them Papa was taking his nap . . . Oh, dear! Did Nerina faint again?''

''Yes—when I told her your 'kind gentlemen' are smugglers!''

Her small jaw dropped. ''Lud . . !''

''You may well be dismayed. D'you realize we could all land in gaol for this?''

''Do you know what is in my thoughts, Yves?'' murmured a stocky man with hard eyes. ''It is that this one is an exciseman!''

This frightful assertion brought forth several exclamations of horror, and the pistols, which had begun to sag, were swung into line once more.

''Well you quite mistake it,'' said Harry. ''Nor am I the lady's papa!''

At once six Gallic faces broke into broad grins. ''By God!'' he cried wrathfully, ''you Frenchmen are all alike! You cannot imagine I should run off with *two* of 'em?''

It appeared they not only thought this likely but variously, conformable, convenable, and desirable. Nanette, who had left her perch so as to minister to the stricken Beauty, was vastly entertained and squealed with mirth.

Rapid hoofbeats announced the return of the guide. ''What's wrong?'' he called in French as he galloped towards the cart. ''I have found us a fine clearing, with a nice stream so that we can—''

Harry had stiffened in disbelief at the first words, and spun around. The newcomer reined up. For an instant, petrified with astonishment, neither of them moved; then two shouts rang out.

''*Sauvage!* What the devil . . . ?''

''Mitch! By thunder! Mitch!''

Harry was out of the cart in a mad scramble. Mitchell flung himself from the saddle. The brothers embraced amid a farrago of questions and counter questions; of beaming eyes, glad smiles, and such a deep rooted joy that being men it must, of course, give way to embarrassment and be concealed beneath raillery. But even as they laughed and teased one another, Mitchell's keen gaze was taking in Harry's pale face and torn and stained coat. And aware of the concern that lurked behind that brilliant smile, a lump came into Harry's throat. He thought of the letter that even now resided in his pocket and which Mitchell, of course, must never know he had read. And gripping his shoulder hard said gruffly, "Jove, you young whelp—but I'm glad to see you!"

The 'clearing' Mitchell had found was actually more of a hollow and to a solitary wanderer must have seemed a forbidding spot, ringed about as it was by rocky slopes and hemmed in by the brooding darkness of the trees. The smugglers, however, had proclaimed it *parfait*, for the fire's glow was less likely to be seen from outside the deep declivity and the hurrying breath of the night wind was happily excluded. With much zestful singing, the men bustled about, erecting the tent, building the fire, and unloading and tending to their animals, while a stout individual named Henri took charge of their combined provender and, with a deal of interference, engaged in the preparation of a meal.

As Mitchell had promised, a stream ran close by and, water having been heated, Lady Nerina retired to refresh herself. Harry, meanwhile, was led to the fireside and required to sit down so that Nanette might replace the dressing on his arm. Mitchell at once hastened to watch the proceedings, and Harry exclaimed impatiently, "At last! Now tell me how it chances that not quite three weeks ago I put you into a post chaise for Oxford, have since confidently imagined you to be toiling at your studies, and instead discover you tonight, leading a band of smugglers through Sussex! Furthermore—" He stopped with a hiss of indrawn breath as Nanette attempted to loosen the last layer of bandage, which had adhered to the wound. She flashed an anxious glance at his face. Mitchell had been given a brief account of Harry's encounter with Willyum Brown's fine Welsh bull and volunteered to dress the arm, "for I am sure you must be tired, ma'am, and would like to join your friend."

"Oh, no you don't!" said Harry. "She has hands like a feather."

Nanette smiled. "Thank you, kind sir. It comes from practice, you see, Mr. Redmond. I have spent much of these past few days tending to your brother's hurts. Indeed, he is a most violent young man!"

Curious, Mitchell said, "You've a lot to tell me, I can see. I—Good God! That's no 'little cut', *Sauvage!* Yves! Over here, *s'il vous plaît!*"

The Frenchman hurried over, a plucked chicken dangling from one hand. He passed the fowl to Mitchell and, acquiring a professional air, inspected the arm. When told the injury had been wrought by a bull, he pursed his lips. "This must be very well cleansed and sewn—*tout de suite!*"

"But," Nanette's voice was sharp with concern, "you are not a surgeon."

He made a grand gesture. "Have no fears, mademoiselle; I have care for the swine of *mon père* many time these ten years and am most skilled."

"Swine!" Harry exploded, then broke into laughter. "Mitch, you coxcomb! A fine respect for the head of your family! Thank you—no. I prefer Mr. Chatham's dentist."

"What—Maxwell?" Mitchell shook his head dubiously. "Last time we were at Beechmead, Lucian St. Clair told me all his patients die."

"Whereas I, my friends," Yves interpolated with simple pride, "have yet to lose one swine."

Harry gave a hoot of mirth, and despite the worry that lurked in his eyes, Mitchell chuckled. Nanette, however, was not amused. "Men!" she exclaimed. "How can you jest about such a horrid great gash? Ah! You cannot! We have no laudanum."

"Got something a da—er, a sight better," said Harry.

"One of the advantages of having a free trader in the family!"

Mitchell nodded, clambered to his feet, and went towards the neatly assembled casks. Yves, meanwhile, having gathered hot water and clean rags, approached his patient and requested Nanette to provide him with a needle and thread. Her horrified expostulation that he had not washed his hands brought an indignant assertion that he had indeed done so. "This very morning, at the first light!" He thrust out two grubby palms in support of his statement. Nanette shuddered, and bowing, Yves said grandly, "Very well, since tonight we dine in high fashion!" and wandered in search of soap.

Nanette's smile was rather forlorn and Harry saw her glance down at her dusty and stained gown. "Oh, what a dolt!" he exclaimed. "There is a parcel in the cart, little one. A small token for Diccon, and something for you."

Her bright eyes came around to him eagerly, and he told her to go and make herself pretty so that they all might celebrate when the surgeon was finished "with this swine."

The half hour that followed was not destined to rate among the high points of Harry's life. Concealing his apprehension admirably, Mitchell sat close at hand, keeping the patient's cup well filled with cognac, and at the first stick of the needle, he launched hastily into the explanation his brother had demanded. It was, he pointed out, all Harry's fault, for had he not from the outset sought to deceive, none of it would have happened. Harry's attempt to protest was foiled by a need to grit his teeth, and suppressing a shudder, Mitchell said, "I returned to Town to discover you already departed. Crosby Frye—er—confirmed my worst fears about my father . . . and when I learned Sanguinet owned a chateau in Dinan, I assumed you'd gone tearing over there to see what he could tell you. I followed, naturally, in a gallant attempt to keep you out of trouble, for in view of your predilection for hare-brained escapades . . ." He laughed. "No, don't eat me, Harry. I was really quite justified in—"

"In . . . in calling out Sanguinet, and—" Harry's vehemence was again shut off, and he leaned back, lips tight.

Mitchell tendered the cup. "Oh, so you heard about it. It was all so damned nonsensical. When we reached the chateau—did I tell you I took Anderson with me? Poor fellow, I'm afraid we became separated in all the commotion after I shot Sanguinet, but—"

"After you . . . *what*?" gasped Harry, sitting up again, while Yves also gaped his astonishment.

"Well, I'd not really meant to, you understand," Mitchell explained earnestly. "But when I first went to the chateau the place was crawling with guards and they were so dashed unfriendly. Wouldn't tell me if you was there or not, and looked ready to cut up rough, so I had to leave. I chanced to meet Jacques de Roule of all people, in Dinan, and it turned out he was to be a guest at a masquerade party Sanguinet was hosting that evening. Drink up, old fellow, you look a bit green around the gills . . . Well, Jacques is a jolly good man, as you know, and to make a long story short, he took me along with him. I'd not told him anything of my father's connection with Sanguinet, of course." He hesitated and, well aware of his brother's unyielding adherence to the Code of Honour, said with a trace of anxiety, "It was a trifle underhanded, but—had I not done so, d'you think he would have invited me?"

"Very likely not," Harry said dryly.

"Precisely. And in view of the attitude of Sanguinet's people, I took the precaution of carrying one of your Mantons in my pocket. Now don't get up in the boughs, for Lord's sake!" His boyish grin disarming Harry's indignation, he went on, "It is the most incredible place, *Sauvage*! They must be so rich as to buy several abbeys! The chateau itself is all gold and crystal and red velvet, and full of art works. And the gardens! The entire hill is divided into separate areas, each landscaped in a given theme so as to—"

"The . . . devil with—the hill! What happened between you and—"

"All right, all right." Mitchell wrenched his eyes from that horrifying needle. "When we came inside everyone was masked, of course, and I could not discover Sanguinet. Nor anyone I knew, save for . . ." He paused and said musingly, "One of the ladies, a charming Puritan, seemed to know me. She beckoned at last, and when I went to her, told me she was a widow from Sussex and begged to know where we'd met before. Oh, laugh then, but she would not be convinced and finally teased me into unmasking. I could see that she was truly baffled . . . Well, at all events, it turned out she *did* know Sanguinet's costume and pointed him out to me. I think the fellow saw her do so, for he came over at once. He was all affability, but when I revealed my identity, at first denied having met my father, and then made a remark . . ." He hesitated, not daring to repeat what Sanguinet had said of Colin Redmond. "Er—to which I took exception. You must admit, I am not the least hot at hand, but . . ."

Beginning to feel sick and exhausted, Harry interposed jerkily, "Did you . . . slap him?"

"I'd intended to, but—unfortunatley . . . Well, we were in the refreshment room, and I had collected a full plate of delicacies for my Puritan, and—" Mitchell flushed and said sheepishly, "Jacques held it was frightfully *gauche* of me, but—I'd quite forgot the plate was in my hand, you see . . ."

"You would!" grinned Harry. "You never threw the lot in his face?"

Yves had again paused in his efforts as though he couldn't believe his ears, aware of which, Mitchell's flush deepened. "No, no! well—not *all*. But—" He scanned Harry's face anxiously. "I fear a few cream puffs did rather . . . sail off."

"Cawker!" Gleefully picturing Parnell's sneering countenance adorned with cream puffs, Harry laughed, "When did you meet him?"

"Half an hour later. For heaven's sake, Yves! Don't gawk at me—you're not done with your sewing! Yes, Sanguinet called me out at once. Lord, but he was furious. I never saw a man white and shaking with passion, yet so terribly mannerly. Oh—that surprises you, *Sauvage*? He was, I assure you. His friends urged that we delay until the morrow, but there was no containing him. I had humiliated him in front of his guests, he said (and I fear he was right!). De Charlet, his second, was concerned that the guests might learn of it, but Sanguinet said we could fight in the centre of the maze where none would see us—they've an enormous one in front of the chateau, and there's a clear space in the middle, about twenty feet across. "I'd choosen pistols, of course." He gave a wry smile. "Poor Jacques was sure my last hour had come. It seems Sanguinet's a renowned shot, and I—er . . ."

"Do not know muzzle from grip," Harry nodded grimly. "Blasted idiot."

"Well, at all events, I was looking around, thinking how beautiful it all was, for it was a lovely night. But then I remembered what he'd said." Mitchell's jaw set, and a fierce light Harry had never seen before crept into the long grey eyes. "De Charlet called 'Fire!' just at that moment." He shrugged and then said with his shy grin, "Jacques held it was beginner's luck."

Harry waved away the cup. "And you actually *hit* him?"

"Just below the left armpit. Horrid mess. But—to give the devil his due, he was dashed decent about it until—" Here, his teeth caught at his lower lip and, eyeing his brother nervously, he finished in a rush, "—until de Charlet lifted him and said, '*Sacré blue!* Is it very bad, Guy?'"

"*Guy . . . ?*" gasped Harry.

Watching him in an agony of apprehension, Mitchell stammered, "You'll not disown me, will you?"

"You . . . shot the *wrong . . . man*?"

"Deuced awkward, isn't it? Guy was a trifle put about when he realized what had happened."

"I . . . should imagine . . . he well might be!" Harry looked at Yves, and Yves stared openmouthed at Mitchell, and they all fell into such a howl of laughter that surgery had to be temporarily suspended.

"Dashed clodpole!" sighed Harry at length, wiping his brimming eyes. "Did you know there is more than one of the breed? I wonder you got away with your skin!"

Mitchell chuckled but, as a tearful Yves resumed his work, said slowly, "Tell you the truth, Harry, it *was* a trifle chancy. Oh, not because of Guy; he was a good sportsman. But when he fainted, his men were not very nice. Jacques and I had to run for it and would never have found our way out of the blasted maze had it not been for my lovely Puritan. She followed us and guided us out. *Sauvage . . . ?*" He leaned forward anxiously. "Are you all right?"

"Devil . . . a bit of it," said Harry dazedly. "I wonder Yves's papa has a single swine . . . left! Continue, Mitch, I beg you. It sustains me. Did no one attempt to stop you?"

"Well, the thing was that the shots brought many of the men rushing to the maze, but luckily they couldn't find their way to the centre. We were stopped once, but fortunately Jacques and I were able to down the fellows and change masks with them before any more came around the corner. We were almost out at last when a shout went up that I had shot Sanguinet. Next, the howl was raised to unmask—if anyone saw a man they didn't know, they were to seize him. I'll admit, I thought we were done for!" He was silent a moment then, his mouth curving to a mischievous grin, said, "Happily—many of Sanguinet's guests were—ah—not well acquainted . . ."

"Oh! Damn it all . . !" Harry groaned. "How I should love to have seen it!" He laughed unsteadily. "And so, while mayhem raged in the maze, you and Jacques made good your escape. But—how did you meet your free traders?"

Mitchell wiped his brother's wet face and held the cup to his lips once more. "Jacques went one way and I another. I stole a horse in the village, but Sanguinet's men were everywhere, and I could not come to the pension where Andy waited and finally had to make a dash for the coast with four of 'em hot on my heels. When my poor hack could go no further I ran until my legs gave out. The moon was down by then, and on the beach I overheard someone talking. It turned out to be this rascally lot carrying their kegs down to the ship. One of them crept up behind me and was preparing to split my skull when luckily—"

"He spoil our Gaston," Yves put in aggrievedly. "Only Gaston have known the ways on this side of the water. And M. Michel he throw Gaston down and spring his ankle."

"Yes, and they all but shot me out of hand," said Mitchell, "until they found out I am English. So we drove a bargain—they would give me passage and I would be their guide."

Mitchell's efficiency as a guide appeared to be questionable, and he and Yves wrangled good-naturedly over his accomplishments, or the lack of them, for the next several minutes.

Between the potent brandy and his brother's drollery, Harry managed somehow to endure without disgracing himself. He had seldom been more relieved, however, than when Yves pronounced his task completed, waved away their thanks, and returned to the group obsessed by dinner preparations.

With a stifled sigh, Harry leaned back against the tree and closed his eyes. To conceal the fact that he was almost as shaken as his brother, Mitchell launched into a vivid description of the grounds at Chateau Sanguinet until gradually Harry's pallor began to be less frightening. When he was at last well roasted for having made mice feet of his first duel, Mitchell's grin held more of delight than repentance. "I have yet to hear *your* story, my revered dotard," he countered. "No sooner is my back turned than you vanish, to turn up in a cart driven by two ravishing beauties!"

Harry chuckled. "My taste is none so bad, eh?"

"Bad! Never in my life have I seen so lovely a sight as The Tawnish! She'll have London by the ears when she comes out! I wonder you did not fall in love with her at first sight!"

"Matter of fact," smiled Harry, "I did, but—" He shoved himself away from the tree, staring incredulously. The girls were leaving the tent, but it was not upon the angelically fair Nerina that his eyes lingered. Beside her was a lady who was all witchery from the top of her shining head to her little slippers. Her lush young body was enticing yet demure in the white muslin gown. Dark curls framed her piquant face, and the ribbon tied about her head awoke green lights in those brilliant hazel eyes. Her gaze flew to meet his, and her slender fingers touched the silver locket that hung upon the sweet curve of her bosom.

The noisy clamour of the smugglers faded to a hushed silence, through which Mitchell breathed an awed, "By . . . Jove!"

"Devil take it!" Harry thought. "My shrew is beautiful!" Her beauty lacked Nerina's fragile perfection; her gaze was more honest and direct; her mouth wider than Nerina's softly petulant rosebud lips, yet holding a sweet curve, withal; and the chin—that indomitable little chin . . . why had he not see how adorable she was? A flood of yearning swept him; he knew an irresistible need to take her into his arms and hold her . . . to tell her what was suddenly, breathtakingly in his heart. His past infatuations vanished and were gone forever, and in that moment he knew with total sureness that his tender, volatile, courageous little shrew had filled his life from the moment she entered it. And God willing, would fill it until the day he died.

Somehow he was on his feet and starting forward. But another was before him. Mitchell was bowing low and saying with a revoltingly charming smile, "Who is this, my lady? Introduce us, I beg of you."

Nerina muttered something, and Nanette laughed up into the young man's handsome face. Harry stood rigid, his breath held in check. Nerina wandered to him and, looking at the two who stood in quiet converse, sighed, "What a pretty couple they make. Truly, your brother is a gentleman of most insinuating address, Sir Harry."

Mitchell? The girl had maggots in her attic, that's what it was! Insinuating address? His absent-minded schoolboy of a brother?

Nanette came to him then, her eyes scanning him anxiously. He looked very tired, she thought, but his colour was improved and when he cheerfully assured her he felt much better, she was vastly relieved. She laughed when he peered around the clearing and said he could not think what had become of the little shrew he'd been escorting to Devonshire. "Alas," she said gaily, "she is as shrewish as ever despite her new finery, but—Oh, Harry, the dress is perfect and I love my locket! Thank you!"

He managed to respond appropriately. But in his mind's eye was the dusty ribbon of the lane that afternoon, and Mr. Fox plodding along it, while Nanette said, ". . . it sounds as if you've never met the right one." To which, like a total knock-in-the-cradle, he had replied, ". . . and if I do, I'll probably be too stupid to realize it in time and she'll be snatched from under my nose by someone else . . ."

Dinner was a memorable feast. The brisk air whetted appetites and the fire painted its dancing light upon faces aglow with good fellowship. Henri had wrought a magnificent repast of roasted chickens, crusty hot loaves spread with butter and sprinkled with cheese, and to wash it down, a hearty ale.

Nanette was a faerie creature that night, sparkling with gaiety and seeming to draw an answering happiness from all about her. Harry's attempt to sit beside her was thwarted when Mitchell slipped into that favoured position and Yves occupied the space to her left. Betraying no trace of the hot flare of his irritation, he turned his attentions towards Lady Nerina. Even the nervous Beauty could not but be charmed by the adulation of the men who surrounded her, and having been promised she would be taken home as soon as they had eaten, she cast off her fears and entered into the conversation willingly, if somewhat inanely.

Harry ate little and tried not to notice the admiration with which Mitchell watched Nanette, nor how expertly the girl used every possible trick to ensnare him. The studious Mitchell's acquaintance with ladies had been slight. He was comparatively new to the art of the shy, upward glance, the soft voice, the demure sweep of downcast lashes, the innocent, parted-lip smiles. But Harry was not, and as the meal wore on, became so infuriated it was all he could do not to seize Nanette's hand and drag her aside to where he could properly spank her. He had thought he was concealing his rage until he tore his eyes from her animated face and found Mitchell watching him with a trace of anxiety. Shocked to realize that this brother he had only a few hours since mourned as dead he now devoutly wished at Jericho, he forced a grin. Relief came into Mitchell's eyes, and he turned eagerly back to Nanette.

My lady was boring on about the friendship between her Dear Papa and the Stirling-Armstrongs. Sir Harry was, of course, acquainted with that noble family? He replied politely, appearing to hang on her every word but with his thoughts elsewhere. What right had he to resent Mitchell's attentions to his shrew? In point of fact, he deserved it, for he had done everything wrong from the start. Having shamefully ignored her while he mooned and yearned for the beautiful rattlepate beside him, he'd been so idiotic as to tell Mitch he had fallen in love with Nerina. He'd been interrupted before he could complete his remark, but Mitchell could not be expected to know that and naturally imagined himself with a clear field. If only the cub wasn't so blasted handsome! He thought defensively that he *had* helped in the matter of the bull, but on the heels of that hopeful recollection came the memory of his clumsy proposal, and he all but groaned with mortification. To think that, in his blind arrogance, he had dared offer her a marriage of convenience! Well, he would offer again! And his brother had better stay clear! He needn't think—

A hand slipped onto his shoulder. Mitchell bent over him solicitously. "Arm troubling you, *Sauvage* . . . ?"

Harry looked into those concerned eyes and felt wretched. "A shade tired," he mumbled. "Nothing to fret about, but—" And he stared, astounded, at the smugglers, who were scrambling madly away from the fire and into the trees. In a flash the clearing was bare of Frenchmen, and Harry was on his feet and rasping, "Quick! Get the girls out of this!"

Mitchell stammered a bewildered, "What . . ? Why the—"

"*Now!*"

Nanette was already standing, eyes big with fear, and Harry fairly dragged Nerina to her feet. Ignoring her outraged squeals, he propelled her into the trees, then whipped her behind him as two dark shapes blocked their way. Her shriek rang in his ears, and Mr. Fox let out a shattering bray that set all the other animals snorting and whinnying with fright.

"Who are you?" Harry demanded, and as Mitchell sprang to his side, a dagger gleaming in his hand, added, "And what do you want?"

"It'd serve you right," drawled a familiar voice, "if I was a Exciseman! I counted twenty kegs, Harry! Downright illegal!"

"Diccon!" Weak with relief, Harry placed a restraining hand on his brother's arm. "It's all right, Mitch."

Nanette ran to welcome the Trader, and the second newcomer proving to be Daniel, they all proceeded to the warmth of the fire where the necessary introductions were performed. Diccon complimented Nanette on her 'fine feathers' but said to Harry in a low voice, "A fine bumble-broth you've made of it! Letting Miss Nanette get herself all pretty and sweet so anyone chancing to ride by might recognize her!"

This aspect of the situation had slipped Harry's mind, and he said uneasily, "This ain't exactly St. James's, you know."

"And putting both the ladies in with a scurvy crew of free traders!" Diccon went on remorselessly. "What it's the duty of a law-abiding man to hand over to the Watch!"

The French contingent was slinking back into view, and it dawned upon Harry that if Diccon should prove a staunch supporter of law and order, they might be in a very sticky situation. There was a reward for informing against smugglers, and it would be logical enough for the man to be tempted.

"You are very right," Nerina proclaimed righteously. "They are smugglers!"

"That they is, ma'am," nodded Diccon, casting a scornful glance at the motley crew. "And a more clumsy, bungling lot I never hope to see!"

"At the least," frowned Yves, folding his arms, "*we* were where we were supposed to be!"

"Then why the devil didn't you stay there 'til I could come up with ye?" demanded Diccon. "Why didn't you lie low like I've allus told ye, and—"

"Because *this* one," said Yves, indicating the flabbergasted Mitchell, "have spoil Gaston so we cannot bring him to show us the way. And he have say he know Sussex, so when you do not come he say he will take us to the Inn of the Black Garter. Instead of the which, he meet a pedlar, and buy a book from him, and ride along reading it, so that we get most into the pickles until we find Mr. Fox and think you must not be far away, so have at the last arrive here!"

Nanette gave a gurgle of laughter. Harry grinned, "Devil take you, Diccon! You nigh scared the wits out of me!"

Eyes alight, Mitchell said, "Fine company you keep, revered gaffer!"

"But," Nerina puzzled uneasily, "Sir Harry said you was a Trader . . ."

Harry shot his brother a warning glance, but Mitchell was already chuckling, "So he is, my lady. A Free Trader!"

Nerina gave a small scream, and admitting the justification for her dismay, Harry said, "The ladies must be escorted to East Bourne at once. Can you guide them, Diccon?"

"No. Sorry I am to say it, but I got to get my clumsy lot here to 'The Black Garter.'" His keen eyes fastened upon Harry's rather drawn face. "Don't look like you're up to a long ride, neither. What happened?"

Harry's attempt to make light of the incident was drowned by Nanette's swift and glowing account of his heroism, which was in turn cut off by Nerina's wailing plea to be conveyed home. Mitchell, who had remained silent, his thoughtful gaze on Nanette, offered to escort the ladies, whereupon Nanette promptly reiterated her determination to go on to Devonshire.

"Obliging of ye, Mr. Redmond." Diccon's gaze flickered over him doubtfully. "But—you'd best let Daniel take ye, ma'am."

"Oh, but—no. Thank you," said my lady swiftly. "We shall be quite safe with Mr. Redmond, I'm sure."

"Doubt it," Diccon argued. "The roads is fair swarming with men hunting fer the poor stole heiress, and—"

"Heiress?" said Harry. "I thought it was a child who was stolen."

"Someone's child, I s'pose," Diccon shrugged. "One o' the wealthiest women in all Europe, they say. Stole from the boozum o' her family, what's offering five hundred pound fer news o' the poor creature."

Harry and his brother exchanged interested glances. Nanette breathed an awed, "Five . . . hundred . . . pounds . . . ?"

"Aye," confirmed Diccon. "And if we don't get Lady Tawnish back to her relations, we'll have the hue and cry up fer her, like as not!"

Nerina was wholly in agreement with this, but when Nanette firmly refused to accompany her, she uttered a wail of distress and implored Harry to "make her see reason!"

Nanette turned a frightened gaze on him. "You will not force me to go with her, my tyrant?"

"No one," he answered, in a tone that brought Mitchell's eyes flashing to his face, "shall force you to do what you do not wish to do, little one. Mitch, do you know the way?"

"Daniel knows," said Diccon stubbornly. Mitchell's frown was not lost upon him and he sighed. "He's a fine fighting man, Mr. Redmond."

"I am well aware of that fact." Mitchell's head was high. "And normally my brother is also. He's a trifle down pin just now, however, and I think Dan should remain here."

"Doubt there's much we could teach Sir Harry when it come to fighting," grinned Diccon.

Nerina wrung her hands and, outrivalling Diccon for tactlessness, blurted, "*Tinkers*, dearest! And—soldiers! And *gypsies*! To say nought of *smugglers*!"

Diccon and Daniel glanced at one another in covert amusement. Harry, however, frowned worriedly; and echoing his brother's troubled thoughts, Mitchell urged, "Lady Nerina is perfectly right, you know, ma'am. Should your flight become common knowledge, you would be completely ostracized."

"And—never," said Nerina in the voice of Doom, "receive another offer for as long as you live."

Nanette watched the play of emotion over Harry's pale face, summoned a smile, and contradicted, "I doubt that, dear. In point of fact, I received another offer this morning."

The Beauty stared, then looked to Harry. Mitchell, having given a slight start at Nanette's words, also turned to his brother with an incredulity that was shattered when Nerina said, "Oh, but I meant a *respectable* offer!"

For once even Nanette was rendered speechless, but Harry, the ready laughter leaping into his eyes, assured my lady that his offer had been refused. Seeing Mitchell about to explode with mirth, he added, "However, I'm promised to see her safe to Devon, and Devon it shall be!"

Lady Nerina dissolved into tears, and when Yves offered her his hack, flatly refused to travel alone with a *gypsy*. Very soon, therefore, she wept over Nanette, tearfully implored Harry to protect her and, apparently made even more despondent by reason of his quiet, "With my life, ma'am," sobbed her way out of the clearing with Mitchell on one side of her and Daniel on the other.

CHAPTER XII

NANETTE HAD TAKEN HARRY'S JACKET TO HER TENT to clean and patch the sleeve; the smugglers quarrelled contentedly while loading up their animals; and beside the fire Diccon and Harry sat talking together. Not once did the Trader's remarks imply a mistrust, yet there was that in his manner which kindled a spark in Harry's green eyes; and at length, his piercing glare fixed upon Diccon's face, he demanded, "Why do you sigh each time you look at your tent?"

Diccon regarded him steadily. "Why, things has changed a bit, I think. When I left, Miss Nanette hated men. Or said she did. And you was halfway in love with the other lady and not no way in love with Miss Nanette. Or didn't think you was. Now . . ." And he sighed once more.

"Now . . ?" echoed Harry. Both eyes and tone held a warning, and Diccon said softly, "Why, I do know as how you'm a gentleman. But she's been put in my charge, don't you see? And—what with you being—fond of her . . ."

"Well, I am not," said Harry, just as softly. "I love her."

"Aye. I thought that was the way of it. Still, you did once tell me that you—er—fall in and out of love. Rapid-like."

Harry's eyes became deadly slits; then he flushed and looked down. "That was because I was a prime idiot, for—to own the truth, I—I've never really been in love before."

"But—excuse me fer asking—how does ye know as ye is now?"

Harry's gaze drifted to the tent and he murmured dreamily, "Once you are, there can be no doubts. It is so—different. So—well, it's sort of . . . holy." He knew he was reddening but, turning back to the grave man beside him, said levelly, "I pledge you my word of honour, Diccon. The lady will be as safe with me as though she were my sister."

For a long moment the anxious blue eyes held to the steady green ones. Then Diccon stood. "Reckon my poor rattlebrained Frogs is ready. How they ever got this far is beyond me! I never let 'em come more'n a mile or two inland but what I meet 'em with me own train." He put out his hand. "I'll be back afore dawn, but if for some reason I don't come, you get on your way. And keep to the byroads, whatever you do!"

Harry had also come to his feet, and their handshake was firm. Diccon grunted, "You'd better get some sleep. You don't look up to snuff at all, and—"

"Wait up a minute!" In belated recollection, Harry crossed to the tent and called to Nanette. She came out in a few seconds and smilingly handed him the small box. He returned to proffer it to Diccon. "Please take it, though it is a very poor thanks for all you have done."

Diccon opened the outer wrapping, and the snuffbox was carefully removed. For a moment he stared at it in silence. Then, slanting a wondering glance at Harry, he said, "A . . . bloodhound . . ." He appeared quite overcome and, without a word, crossed to mount up and soon rode off at the head of the long line of ponies.

Nanette joined Harry in exchanging farewells with Yves and the rest of the Frenchmen, but not once did Diccon respond, or look back. Until he was out of sight his head was bowed as he gazed down at the small enamelled box reverently clasped in one bony hand.

Long after the last sounds of the departing Free Traders had faded into the night, Harry half-lay against the tree,

195

staring sleepily into the fire and struggling to stay awake until Mitchell returned. The events of the day crowded in on him. So many happenings in so brief a time. The most important thing, of course, was that his brother was alive and safe. Then, with a leap of the heart, he thought of his love, but splintering into that happy contemplation came a puzzling memory of Diccon saying, "She's been put in my charge . . ." Put in his charge? Surely he had implied he'd come upon Nanette accidentally and taken her under his wing from pure kindness? Yet—how stupid to be in a pucker over such rattlebrained stuff. The combined effects of brandy and loss of blood must be catching up with him, and his blasted arm throbbed unendingly. He shifted, preparing to stand and walk about for a bit, for Nanette must be guarded . . . he dare not fall asleep . . . before Mitch . . .

"Harry . . . ?"

The soft call brought his nodding head up, and with a pang of guilt he was on his feet.

Nanette said repentantly, "Oh, I wish you will not!" She stepped closer and reached up to touch his brow, while asking in a worried tone, "Does your arm pain you very badly? We must . . ." Her troubled eyes met his, and that warm wave of colour swept up her perfect skin. She turned away, faltering, "Do not . . . look at me . . . so."

He had been thinking that he would only have to drop the merest hint and Bolster would buy him a pair of colours. The loan could be repaid, and then, was he careful, he could support a wife. It would mean she must follow the drum; not the life he would have wished for his bride. But—if she loved him . . . *if* she loved him! And even if she did, it was possible that her papa was not in the basket at all but merely a greedy and ambitious man. Perhaps his brother was a wealthy Cit, or some Indian nabob. Quite apart from the 'Uncle' she loved—yet also despised—her looks and charm had apparently won her some very eligible suitors. Even without her father's interference she could doubtless achieve a far more elevated station in life than would be her lot did she wed a penniless ex-captain, whose

196

future was as uncertain as tomorrow's weather. His heart sank. He had so little to offer her—save his love. And in all honour he must not even offer that until he knew more of her background. Certainly, to address her now, while she was alone, would be reprehensible, wherefore he stifled a sigh and forced himself to say easily, "A man must be a fool not to look at you, for you are exquisite in that gown, my little shrew."

The familiar nickname brought a ripple of laughter. "Thank you, Señor Matador! And I shall always cherish this." She glanced down, fingering her locket gently.

Her bowed head with its dusky silken curls awoke a fierce hunger in Harry. The need to hold her in his arms was nigh unbearable.

Nanette raised her eyes and immediately turned away. "I must . . . go, for I fear—"

"Fear?" He touched her elbow. "Do you still feel unsafe in my company?"

"No." But she trembled and would not face him, though he sought gently to turn her. "Only—we have been thrown together in . . . in most unusual circumstances. I . . . cannot but be aware that your natural impulses must be . . ."

Harry's arm hurt fiercely, and he felt achingly tired; and, therefore, swift and uncharacteristic anger flared. "Had I allowed my 'natural impulses' full sway, ma'am, I'd have spanked you—or boxed your ears soundly at dinner! How dared you flirt so with my poor brother?"

Her own nerves overwrought, Nanette flashed, "*Flirt* with him? I grant you he is a most handsome and charming gentleman, but—"

"Yes. Blast him! And he is also inexperienced, and you teased him abominably, you minx. As well you know!"

Her eyes sparked and she frowned deliciously. "If I enjoyed the attentions of a fine young man, I do not see the need to ask *your* permission! And before you presume to criticize *my* behaviour, look to your own! The way you fawned upon and sighed over and worshipped Nerina, I wonder Mr. Fox did not kick you where 'twould do the most good!"

197

"And further," growled Harry, stepping even closer to scowl down at her, "you have more the vocabulary of a coachman than a young lady from a seminary!"

He was so near, and if his face was set and grim, it also held an expression she had never seen there before, so that her betraying heart raced and her breath hastened. "You . . . do not look at me," she stammered, "as if I was . . . a coachman."

"Perhaps," he murmured idiotically, "because I never saw one wearing . . . so dainty a white gown."

"Did you . . . not . . ?" she breathed, just as idiotically. And with her face upturned, could not look away.

Harry knew only the need to hold her against his heart and kiss those parted lips. "Oh, Nanette," he thought. "My valiant little darling girl . . . my beautiful shrew. I adore you." He reached for her shoulders, and she seemed to lean to him. Struggling for control, he clenched his fists and drew back. "We have been thrown together in most unusual circumstances . . ." He was trembling, so greatly did he long to declare himself; but honour must be served. And, therefore, never dreaming how his eyes betrayed him, he said a raspingly uneven, "Go and get some sleep, little one." And turning away, began with great concentration, to add more logs to the fire.

Harry awoke to find the clearing cold and damp, and so thick with drifting vapours he could scarcely see across it. He lay drowsily for a while, on the edge of sleep, his thoughts turning backward. Mitchell had returned soon after midnight, with word that Nerina was safely restored to her sister. He had refused to answer any further questions, demanding instead to be told of his brother's adventures since they had parted in Town. Harry had yawned his way through most of his tale, having several times been obliged to quiet Mitchell's anger, or hilarity, as the events were unfolded. For the life of him he could not recall whether he'd finished the saga or fallen asleep in the midst of it. He glanced to the side. Mitchell lay close by, sound asleep. The flap to the tent was still closed, but Daniel was up and already had a fire blazing and water heating. Harry went over to join him and was greeted with a bright smile and a note written in the youth's fine, copperplate hand, conveying the information that Diccon had not returned and it would be well for them to take to the road early. Harry agreed, gathered his toilet articles and, with Daniel conveying the bowl of hot water, made his way to a secluded spot where he proceeded to wash and shave. His arm was swollen and throbbed dully, the touch of the air was clammy, and he shivered with increasing violence until he cut himself and swore.

"Did she turn you down again, *mon Sauvage*?" Mitchell, a jug of hot water in one hand, watched him.

"Didn't offer again," Harry smiled. "I'd no right to offer in the first place." He resumed his shaving, thereby avoiding his brother's too-penetrating eyes as he confessed, "But I'd not realized I loved her then, you see. I imagined myself nobly offering her a way out of a difficult situation."

"I see. And now—you do realize. And thus cannot offer?"

"Here? Would you? Under the circumstances we Redmonds have come to?"

There was no answer. By way of the mirror he had propped in the angle of a branch, Harry discovered a wistfulness in Mitchell's lean face. "Perhaps," he said reluctantly, "you should know that I have no claim on her."

"After near a whole week with the lady? Mitchell's smile did not quite reach his eyes. "You must be losing your touch, old fellow."

"Beyond doubting. Now, we've much to discuss, but first—tell me about the Ravishing Beauty. Was her doting sister vastly relieved by her return?"

"Indeed she was. A fine taking they were in. You'd not credit the dramatic tale I dredged up to account for her absence, though I'd time and enough to invent it, Lord knows! How she jabbered! All the way, or at least until we were stopped and—"

Amused, Harry inserted a curious, "Stopped?"

"Four times, actually. By men hunting for Miss Carlson. And had it not—"

"For—*who*?" In the act of drying his face, Harry swung his head up, peering at his brother over the towel.

"That should be 'whom'," Mitchell corrected, shedding his jacket. "When using the personal pronoun, you must—" Familiar with the glint that lit Harry's eyes, he grinned,"Miss Carlson. By your leave, gaffer, I'll borrow the razor." Doing so, he went on, "The missing heiress. Remember?"

There must, thought Harry, be lots of Carlsons in England . . . He slung the towel over his shoulder, retrieved his jacket from a branch, and tossed the packet of letters to Mitchell. "I doubt it's the same woman, but—see what you make of those. I found them at the back of a drawer in Papa's desk at Moiré." He emptied the bowl as Mitchell began to read, and slipped cautiously into his jacket. The left sleeve had been very neatly patched. He touched the dainty stitches tenderly . . .

"It is!" Mitchell exclaimed. "It *is* the same woman! For God's sake, Harry—what does it all mean? Is she totally demented?"

Baffled, Harry sat down and, while Mitchell shaved, told him all that he knew of it. Despite his deep affection for both his sons, it had not been Colin Redmond's habit to confide in Mitchell, whom he had considered not only an impractical dreamer but also a schoolboy. Since Harry had been too ill at the time of the Carlson tragedy to be troubled with such worrisome matters, the brothers were thus equally in the dark. Mitchell, however, attached far more importance to the accident than did Harry. He shared Harry's persistent belief that Colin Redmond had been gulled, but having seen the chateau in Dinan and heard his brother's description of Sanguinet Towers, shook his head over the likelihood of Parnell's having been behind some devious plot to acquire the Redmond estates and fortune. "There is absolutely no motive, *Sauvage*," he said earnestly. "Sanguinet would no more take such desperate risks for Moiré than you would be willing to besmirch your honourable name for—for Diccon's tent! If there *was* anything underhanded about that card game, I suspect it's a case of *cherchez la femme.*"

"What—the Carlson woman?"

"Yes. She held a grudge against my father, and is very obviously all about in her head—poor creature."

"That may be, yet she is scarcely capable of disguising herself as a man and bluffing her way through an evening of cards."

"Of course not, but there are a dozen ways she might have arranged it." Mitchell washed his face and, reaching for the towel, asked, "How well were Cobb and Cootesby acquainted with my father?"

"So far as I'm aware, not at all."

"Aha! Now suppose the Carlson woman had some little dalliance afoot with one of 'em? She persuaded him to arrange the card game, drug Papa's wine, and afterwards they may even have had his mare tripped, or—"

"Her lover must have been infatuated, indeed, to countenance an involvement in murder," Harry pointed out quietly.

"Well, perhaps he also needed money—or hoped to win Moiré for himself."

"I cannot think it likely. Maude said they all sought to persuade my father to *stop* playing, and when he would not they withdrew from the game until only Sanguinet and Papa continued. Besides, Mitch, had such a plot been hatched, surely M. Diabolique would be the last man they'd invite—knowing he is a skillful player and would be hard to handle in such a situation. And if Sanguinet himself was the 'lover,' he'd be far more likely to have simply picked a quarrel with Papa and called him out. No, the plot becomes too thick, I believe. Unless . . . " He paused, his eyes gleaming suddenly.

"What? What?" Mitchell demanded, turning from emptying the bowl.

"Well, the Carlson woman seems to have stirred up quite a bobbery in claiming that Papa withheld evidence at the investigation into her brother's death. Now, suppose one of the players was the man she suspected of that murder? Suppose he also believed that Papa knew more than he'd admitted—or . . ." He frowned thoughtfully, "—or that he might *recall* something. To kill him outright must re-awaken suspicions in the Carlson matter and point to himself. On the other hand, to ruin Papa, send him off so heartsick he could logically be supposed capable of mis-judging a jump, and *then* stage an 'accident' . . ."

"By God!" raged Mitchell, very white. "The dirty hound!"

They stared at one another grimly, but then Harry gave an exclamation of impatience. "And what fustian! For it makes no sense at all!"

"But it does!" Mitchell wrestled with his cravat and argued hotly, "More sense than for Papa to have suddenly changed the habits of a lifetime! Or for M. Diabolique to destroy a man and reduce his sons to penury for no logical reason."

"Because we cannot come at a reason does not mean there is none. But had my neat little theory been correct, Papa must have been a fool to drink and gamble with a man he knew harboured a desperate need to see him dead, or might *possibly* do so. For I'm sure Miss Carlson had told my father whom she suspected."

Mitchell's exuberance faded. "And Papa was no fool," he sighed.

"True. Good God! What a horrid mess you've made of that. Come here, do!" Mitchell meekly submitting, Harry wrought a passable cravat upon him, while cogitating, "Yet consider, bantling. Papa and Schofield are both dead. Cobb appears to have vanished. And now our female suspect has left the scene in macabre fashion."

"The devil!" gasped Mitchell. "You do not think—the poor woman . . ?"

"The devil, indeed." Harry's voice was harsh suddenly, his eyes narrowing to slits and a look appearing on his face that Mitchell had seldom witnessed. "I'd not put *anything* past Parnell Sanguinet! Nothing whatsoever!"

Briefly they were silent. Then Harry looked up from his

efforts and nodded,—"You'll do. You would horrify the Bond Street Beaux, but at least you look fairly civilized." The obvious retaliation that of them both, Mitchell was by far the more presentable, was not forthcoming. Something was being worried at in that scholarly mind. "Wake up!" Harry urged. "Breakfast awaits!"

They started off together, but Mitchell's steps slowed. Stopping also, Harry turned back to regard him with the questioning lift of one eyebrow.

"I rather suspect," said Mitchell in a hesitant fashion, "that I have been sadly indulged all my life."

"And only proper you should admit it."

Unsmiling, Mitchell turned a rock with the toe of one dusty boot and, watching this vital effort, observed slowly, "Habits—are hard to break."

"Oh, egad! You're about to go from Piccadilly to John O'Groats to reach St. James's! Get it said, Mitch!"

"It is only . . ." Mitchell was decidedly flushed, "that I do not think I would care to be . . . all alone in the world, you know."

Harry stared at him, then teased, "Uppity brat! D'you think you've sole hunting rights on the Sanguinet clan?"

Flashing a quick, shy glance at him, Mitchell said, "Jacques de Roule was likely in the right of it when he said I had beginner's luck. You—are not a beginner, *Sauvage*."

"No. But I am a pretty fair shot."

"And Parnell Sanguinet a very different article to his brother, I hear. Harry—" One thin hand came out to clamp onto his shoulder. "Is it irrevocable?"

Harry looked full into the grey eyes. "I'm afraid it is."

Diccon had left two of the smugglers' hacks for their use, and it was decided that Harry and Mitchell would ride while Nanette and Daniel drove in the cart. They were on the road by eight o'clock and progressed cautiously through a silent and sepulchral world in which hedgerows loomed like dark shadows through the rolling vapours, and occasional travellers rushed upon them only to immediately

203

vanish into the encompassing drifts. Mitchell remained beside the cart, gratifying Nanette's insatiable thirst for details of Moiré Grange and their life there; but Harry rode ahead, his mind grappling with his many problems. As the miles slipped away, he formulated and rejected one plan after another, arriving at length at the conclusion with which he had started; Cootesby held the key to their future, for what he would tell them must determine whether they launched a battle for revenge and restitution or abandoned all ties with the past and built new lives for themselves.

"What a snail's pace!" Mitchell spurred to his side. "Three hours and more and I doubt we've gone fifteen miles! At this rate we shall reach Chichester when Cootesby has removed to Brighton for the summer!"

"I doubt Daniel could persuade Mr. Fox to move faster even did he deem it wise. I know it's frustrating, Mitch. But it's safer for Nanette."

"Oh. Yes, of course. How stupid of me." Mitchell was quiet awhile, then murmured, "Do you suppose her papa really is the ogre she paints him?"

"Diccon appears to believe her, and he's a deal more shrewd than he appears."

Mitchell said nothing, but noting how that sensitive mouth tightened, Harry said a noncommittal, "Don't like him very well, do you?"

Mitchell shrugged. "He makes me uneasy. I could not say why."

Despite himself, amusement lurked in Harry's eyes and, knowing him so well, Mitchell said resignedly, "Go on— laugh at my nonsense."

Harry did not laugh, however. Diccon had all but mocked the boy, and it was scarcely to be expected that someone as youthfully defensive and proud as Mitch could forgive that. Therefore, he merely warned that such gloomy imaginings were doubtless the result of hunger, and suggested that Mitchell ride on ahead and find a tavern where he might purchase them all a luncheon. "I presume you still have some of your ill-gotten gains?"

Mitchell grinned, nodded, and seconds later had disappeared into the fog.

Reining back, Harry waited until the cart drew level then kept pace with it. Nanette scanned him anxiously and asked how he was feeling, and when he had answered her blithely, if inaccurately, that he felt 'perfectly fit,' she said, "Whatever do you suppose has become of Diccon?"

He turned to Daniel, but the gypsy youth was concentrating on his driving and appeared not to have heard the question. "I doubt he could find us in this murk," Harry replied easily. "Besides, he may have had to lie low for the night since I hear Riding Officers are on the prowl."

She giggled. "Poor Diccon. His smugglers were not a very experienced set of rascals, were they?"

"No, indeed." Both smile and voice held a caress. She gazed at him, her own eyes soft, then shivered suddenly. Concerned, he said, "Are you cold, my shrew? I'll fetch a blanket to wrap round you."

She shook her head. "It's just that I am—so very frightened."

"Little wonder," he thought. To banish the distress in her sweet face, he told her some of Mitchell's adventures, winning her back to gaiety until he mentioned the duel. He saw at once that he had erred and sought to change the subject, but she questioned him intently, becoming so pale at last that he teased, "Just like a woman! You abhor duelling yet must know every last gory detail! Cheer up, little one! The sun is coming out. Look—already the fog is thinning."

It was, and soon a brisk breeze blew away the remaining wreaths of vapour. They were traversing a copse of sun-dappled young trees when Mitchell returned, proclaiming exuberantly that he'd found a likely looking tavern a few miles ahead with "some of the juiciest looking roast beef you ever saw!" Having set all their mouths to watering, he admitted he had not brought any of this deliciousness with him since he'd been unable to locate his purse. By the process of elimination they discovered he had last seen it after breakfast. The thought of riding all the way back to the clearing infuriated Harry, but since the purse held all that remained of their funds, he decided the journey must be undertaken. Nanette, however, prevailed upon him to first search the cart. For half an hour they waded through Diccon's incredible collection of belongings and 'trade-ables,' then suddenly realized Mitchell was not among them. Harry tore around to the far side of the cart and discovered his brother comfortably sprawled against a wheel, engrossed in a translation of Virgil. All but gnashing his teeth with fury, Harry advised him that they would bury the book with him! "Does it not occur to you, hedge-bird, that *we* have all been searching for what *you* were so besotted as to misplace, while *you* lounged at your ease?"

"But, I found it. Do you take me for a cocklehead? I had put it where I'd be sure to find it—in the breadbox. Here!" He shook the fat purse under Harry's nose, then leapt to his feet and backed away in alarm.

"Then why in the *devil*—" grated Harry, advancing on him in a crouching menace, "could you not have the sim-ple decency to—"

Mitchell made a mad sprint for his horse, vaulted into the saddle and, reining about, grinned, "Behave, gaffer, lest I bring you porridge for lunch!"

"Dare you return with less than a splendid repast, and, by God, we'll have roasted Mitchell!" Harry strode for-ward, but Mitchell was away, riding like a centaur, his laugh floating back after him. The irate Harry stood and watched him, hands on hips, unable to hold his anger as he noted with pride what a splendid seat his exasperating brother possessed.

A grinning Daniel took up the reins once more, Harry helped Nanette to the seat, mounted his good natured but poorly gaited hack, and they were off again, following the lane under a canopy of branches, the sunlight turning the young leaves a pure yellow green. The air grew warmer and was sweet with the fragrance of blossoms. They rounded a curve and came out onto the rolling velvety slopes of the South Downs, with just ahead a small stand of birches rising from a carpet of bluebells. Nanette clasped her hands at the sight. "Oh, Harry! It is so pretty! May we camp and eat luncheon up there by the trees?"

He agreed that this was a capital idea and led the way up the rise, asking that Daniel keep a weather eye out for Mitchell. By the time they had made camp, unharnessed Mr. Fox, and set him to graze, however, there was still no sign of either Mitchell or their lunch. It was long past noon, and knowing both Nanette and Daniel must be as hungry as he was, Harry at last sent Daniel after his wayward brother. "You'll probably find he spotted some likely looking tome through a cottage window and is haggling with the owner over price!"

Daniel went riding off, and looking around at this pleasant Down country Harry thought how lovely it was. But turning, he saw something lovelier. Nanette was gathering bluebells. She was kneeling, looking down at the bright blossoms she held, and he crossed to her, tenderly watching the dance of one curling tendril of dark hair that the breeze fluttered against her temple.

She gave a little cry and raised a distressed face. "Oh! How thoughtless! I have no vase for them. What a wicked waste!"

"So few," he consoled. "And they grow wild, after all."

"They are perfect living things! I could not make one— but I have destroyed them—needlessly."

Smiling, he went over to unearth a rather battered tin from the cart and pour into it some of the water from the bottle they carried. Returning, he bowed, "A vase for my lady's bouquet."

Nanette was delighted and decreed that they should grace the luncheon table, and when Harry had lifted the folding table from the cart, she covered it with the oilcloth 'tablecloth' and placed the 'vase' in the centre. She stood back, eyeing the effect admiringly, and he loved her the more because she was undismayed by the worn old cloth and battered tin and saw only the beauty of the flowers. This, he thought, was how she would travel through life—surmounting the heavy ground with her steadfast gaze turned always to the new hope that followed every sorrow. She looked to him for comment. Despite his silence, his eyes were very eloquent; and because she had learned to read his moods there, she became tongue-tied also. Then she noticed how his hand gripped his injured arm and she all but flew to his side and started to unbutton his cuff. "Oh! I did not change the dressing this morning, and it is paining you. No, do not pretend otherwise! I can tell by the . . . the way . . ." And she stopped speaking, her busy hands stilled by his strong clasp. Trembling, she gazed down at those long, slim fingers, not daring to look up.

Harry touched the funny little bun on top of that so-precious head and breathed, "You are sadly . . . unchaperoned, ma'am."

She raised her head slowly, her eyes meeting his with the sweet shyness that whispered to him of a promise he must not acknowledge. "Yes, Harry."

"And . . . all alone," he sighed.

"Yes—Harry."

Surely one little kiss would not be so very improper . . ? But conscience said sternly that it would be most ungallant, wherefore he muttered, "I must not—take advantage of you, little one."

"No . . . Harry," she whispered, her voice incredibly caressing.

"I . . . will not," he vowed, taking her by the arms.

"Nor I . . . Harry," she breathed, lifting her face for his kiss.

He bent toward her.

"Sir Harry! Sir Harry!"

The familiar bellow blasted that enchanted silence. Nanette jerked under his hands, her languorous eyes opening wide.

Astounded, Harry released her and swung around. *"Anderson!"*

CHAPTER XIII

THE SERGEANT WAS TOILING BREATHLESSLY UP THE SLOPE, a gig drawn by a grey mare standing in the lane below him. He thrust out his hand and, as Harry ran down to take and wring it gladly, gasped out, "Oh, sir! How . . . how glad I is to see yer!" Puffing hard, his gaze slipped to where Nanette had returned to the table and in some confusion was toying with the flowers. Amazement and dismay chased one another across his rugged features, but he said nothing.

"How in the devil did you find me?" Harry demanded. "I thought you had gone to Cancrizans Priory. Did you receive my letter?"

"No, sir. I did go to Cancrizans but you wasn't there; and Lord Bolster was fair aside of hisself, thinking as— Cap'n . . . ?" he scanned Harry's face anxiously. "You all right? You look a bit pulled."

"A small accident. Nothing much. Is the Marquis at the Priory?"

"No. And it don't look like 'nothing' to me," muttered the Sergeant uneasily. "Lord Damon got it into his head you'd up and gone to Monsewer Sanguinet's house in Kent, so he drove off yestiday like the devil was behind him."

Well aware of Camille Damon's driving habits, Harry chuckled. "Good old Cam! Did Lord Bolster go with him?"

"No, sir. I think *he* went to the Grange to see if you was there. And I went to Beechmead Hall, thinking you might've got there by now, or gone to Lord Moulton's house. But I'm very glad—that is—I . . ." The honest eyes lowered. He snatched off his old beaver and began to turn it, staring down at it wretchedly. "I don't hardly know how to—to tell yer. You *knows*, Captain, as I'd give all I got not to cause you no grief."

"Of course I do. But never grieve, man. If this is about my—"

Shoulders squared, the Sergeant drew himself to attention. "Let you down, sir. Proper. I ain't never forgive Mr. Mitchell fer—fer that there spill you took in '13." A bleak look frosted Harry's eyes and his chin lifted slightly. The Sergeant's heart fell, but he went on doggedly. "I allus held that no man could get so lost in a book he didn't rightly know what was going on about him. But . . ." anguish crept into the dark eyes. "*I* done it, S'Harry! I let yer brother go orf with a pistol in his pocket! One o'your Mantons as he'd told me just the day afore he didn't plan to pull the trigger of. *Pull* the trigger, sir! And that there duelling pistol with the finest hair-trigger you don't hardly have to breathe on! It was a bloody miracle he didn't get hisself killed calling out that Sanguinet! The poor Count de Roule said as he done right well, but just the—"

"You've seen de Roule?" Harry interposed eagerly. "He was not treated roughly, I hope?"

Puzzled by the Captain's lack of concern for his brother, Anderson answered, "Matter of fact, he was knocked about a bit, but—tough as nails, that'n! Even if he *is* a Frog. No—it's Mr. Mitchell, Captain! Lor'—what a dance he led me! What with milling kens, and hanging from winder sills by his finger nails—"

"Mitchell?" Harry ejaculated. "Oh, come now, Andy! My brother a housebreaker—a prig? That's doing it up rather too brown!"

"True as I stand here! I tell you, Captain, we'd the Runners after us in town, and the watch in Hampstead; and then he drug me onto a perishing ship, what was pure horrid, and me so sick as a dog! But—I got to admit it, S'Harry. He's a plucked 'un! And I was as wrong about him as ever I could be. But—Gawd knows where he is now or . . . what's happened!'' And his voice broke.

Overcoming his amazement at this further revelation of his brother's wicked antics, Harry clapped him on the back. ''Never worry so, you old war horse! He was here with me only a minute ago, and looking amazingly well, moreover!''

''W-With . . . *you* . . . sir?'' The downcast head shot up, hope brightening those remorseful eyes. ''Does ye really mean it? Mr. Mitchell's safe? Not hurt, nor nothing? He's—home?''

''And up to his old tricks,'' smiled Harry. ''He's supposed to be fetching our luncheon but has completely forgotten us, I have no doubt.''

''Thank . . . Gawd!'' Anderson gulped. ''Oh, sir, you don't know how I blamed meself! It was all on account o' that there book! Mr. Michell got me interested in it on the packet, and I brung it with me. I got so wrapped up in the tale I couldn't hardly set it down. That night your brother went orf with the Count, I didn't even look up when he came back fer the pistol. I couldn't forgive meself when I realized what he'd took, and me doing *nothing* to stay him! The very thing, sir—the very thing what I'd held agin *him*!'' He beamed mistily. ''Might say as how I got taught a lesson, eh, sir?''

''I'd say you obviously benefitted from it, for I think it splendid that my brother interested you in books.'' Recalling the implication in Mitchell's letter, he added curiously, ''By the bye—which one are you reading?''

''It's called *The Mysteries of Udolpho*,'' said Anderson cheerily, ''and it's all about this poor young woman what—''

''*Mysteries of Udolpho* . . . ?'' Harry gazed upon this old soldier, upon the craggy features, the broad shoulders, fierce mien, and upright carriage that not even the loss of his leg had been able to change. ''The—the one by—*Mrs. Radcliffe* . . ?''

''S'right, sir. You might think it's just fer the ladies, but never you believe it! Reg'lar exciting, it is! Scary castles, and open graves, and—''

''By . . . thunder!'' blinked Harry, struggling manfully to overmaster his mirth. ''Forgive me, Sergeant. I forget my manners. I'm escorting a lady to Devonshire and must make you known to her.''

Anderson darted a stern glance at Nanette. ''Oh, I know her, sir. Spotted her right orf.'' He hesitated briefly and, his long years of service giving him the right, scolded, ''I'd've thought as how you'd got enough trouble, Captain. The whole countryside's a'looking fer *that* lady! If you're caught with her—well, I hopes you know what you're about, and that's a fact!''

Harry grinned and, with one hand loosely clasped on his shoulder, led Anderson toward Nanette. ''What a worrier! I'm hopeful of getting her to Devon unrecognized. Otherwise, I fear her reputation will be—somewhat tarnished.''

''And your neck somewhat stretched, sir!'' nodded the Sergeant grimly.''A great lady like *her*—and all the rewards as is posted! Lor'! Awful chancy!''

A terrible apprehension gripping him, Harry interrupted in a strained voice, ''*Great* . . . lady . . ?''

''Well, I know she ain't got no title, but still—S'Harry, if Miss Carlson's *father* chances ter come up wi' you . . . ! Cor luvvus!''

Harry all but staggered. A roaring in his ears drowned Anderson's stern warning. Miss *Carlson*? His beloved little shrew? It *could* not be! Yet in that crushing moment he knew somehow that it *was*. That his poor, terrified waif, the persecuted girl whose 'wicked stepfather' had demanded she ''marry for money'' was in fact one of the wealthiest heiresses in all Europe! And worse—the tender, fiery, warm, and wonderful little lady to whom he had given his heart was the same fiendish madwoman who had dared suspect his beloved father of complicity in a murder!

''S'Harry . . ?'' Anderson was peering at him anxiously. ''If I said summat as I shouldn't've . . ?''

Harry somehow managed to reassure him, and when Anderson persisted that he looked ''like a shirt what's been run through the mangle,'' he barked a laugh, said that he was starving merely, and sent the Sergeant hurrying back to the gig to join the search for Mitchell.

Nanette was adding some greenery to the flowers. She glanced up as Harry approached and asked lightly, ''Who was—'' One hand flew to her throat. ''W-What is it? Why—do you look at me . . . so?''

He advanced to seize her arms in a merciless grip—so different from the way he had held her only moments before. ''And—why,'' he grated, ''why did you lie to me? Miss *Annabelle Carlson.*''

Her face became as white as his own. Briefly silent, she recovered to quaver, ''L-listen. I beg of you to—''

''To listen to *more* lies? More nonsense about 'wicked stepfathers' and lecherous uncles? You deceived me from the first! Why?''

''Y-You . . . l-lied, too. You s-said you were Harry Allison.''

''Only because I'd no wish to advertise that I was quite in Dun territory! Now let us have *your* excuse, madam!'' The scorn in his voice flailed her, and when she did not reply, he shook her savagely and demanded, ''Why did you hold men to be worthless animals? Because they dared court the lovely heiress?''

She struggled vainly to break free. ''I was besieged! Some pursued me honestly, for myself. But most of my devoted suitors scarcely saw me for the lure of gold that dazzled them!''

Releasing her, Harry's lips curved to a pale, humourless grin. ''So that is why you grimaced and acted the idiot. To escape the fortune hunters.''

''Yes. Partly. But—''

''And you *dared* believe that of *me*?'' he thundered. ''You thought I stayed with Diccon purely to get my greedy hands on your *damnable* money?''

''Harry! I did not—*know* you,'' she choked out pantingly. ''When you first came, I thought perhaps—''

''*What* did you think? Oh, but this is rich! For the love of God! Did you imagine I arranged to be beaten so as to

213

win your sympathy? *Did* you? Of course you did not! Now, let us have some plain speaking for once! You knew very well I'd no notion who you were and that I believed your lies about your mercenary sire.''

''But—I really was—''

''You *knew*,'' he overrode harshly, ''how desperately I wished to speak with Annabelle Carlson, yet you chose to keep silent and mock me with your grimaces and contortions! I'll own you played your part well, ma'am! You should've trod the boards, by God! How you ferreted and dug and wheedled information out of me! 'Tell me about your *dear* papa, Harry! Tell me about Moiré. I *love* to hear of your happy times . . . !' Faugh! What trickery and deceit!''

Reaching out her hands to him, Nanette half sobbed, ''Can you not understand? I was alone and utterly desperate. I had run away in defiance of all . . . convention. Risking my good name—my future. At first, I sought only to—''

''To discover what manner of savage I was? What the devil did you take me for? When had you to fight off my unwelcome advances? When did I behave dishonourably towards you? Did I *once* hold you against your will, and—and kiss you?'' Longing even now to kiss away her tears, racked by despair, he raged, ''*Did* I?''

''Please—*please*,'' she begged. ''Let me explain!''

''Oh, you will explain, ma'am!'' He took her by the shoulders again, grating, ''By thunder, but you'll explain! You shall tell me why you hounded my gentle father with your nonsense! Why you'd the consummate gall to accuse him of—''

Vaguely, he had been aware of the distant drum of hoofbeats. Now, Mitchell rode up, flung himself from the saddle and ran to tug at Harry's gripping hands. ''You're hurting her! Are you run mad? Let her go!''

His face murderous with rage and pain, Harry whirled on him. ''Where in the *devil* have you been?''

In all his life his brother had never employed such a tone toward him, and glancing from Nanette's tears to Harry's

214

ashen-faced despair, Mitchell stammered, "I'm . . . sorry. I-I met a French émigré, and we fell to talking about the Revolution. I'm afraid I simply forgot—about our lunch."

"Oh, to *hell* with our lunch!"

Mitchell's eyes took on a look of shock, and Nanette's head lowered. Harry spun away, battling for control, and looked blindly out across the Downs, at the morning that had been so beautiful and was now bleak and empty. The ache in his head seemed to join with that in his arm; but the ache in his heart was deeper yet, the more savage because even whilst he had loved her with such reverence, knowing at last what real love meant, she had believed him to be a scheming fortune hunter. With a dull sense of bewilderment he knew that in just these few seconds his every dream for the future had been wiped away, with no hope of retrieval. His path was clear, however, and must be followed with some semblance of dignity. He took a deep breath, pulled himself together, and turned back to say with frigid politeness, "I do apologize, ma'am. I was behaving like a boor. But whatever else, you are a woman. Alone."

Aghast, Mitchell caught at his sleeve. "Harry! Do not talk to her like that! You're ill, old fellow. Your arm—"

Harry wrenched free. "And you are late, Mitch. But—allow me to present you to—" He bowed with mocking grace. "Miss Annabelle Carlson."

Speechless, Mitchell stared at her.

"Do not," Nanette whimpered. "Ah, do *not*—look at me like that."

"Forgive us, Miss Carlson," said Harry. "We loved our father, you see. And he is dead. So we must ask you a question or two. Very politely."

Nanette flinched to that cold tone, and Mitchell frowned and set out the stool for her.

She went instead to stand beside the table and faced them with hands folded as though she were on trial. "I loved my brother also, gentlemen. He was all—I had left. The gentlest, most warm-hearted boy . . ." Tears hung on her lashes. She brushed them away impatiently and, her little chin high, said in an only slightly quivering voice, "During his last leave, your father saw him foully murdered. And would say nothing. I implored him to speak, but he insisted I was mistaken. And so that evil man went free!''

"If my father said he saw nothing—Miss Carlson,'' said Harry softly, "then be assured—he saw nothing.''

"I can be assured of one thing,'' she flashed with a return of her old fire, "that your father lied to protect his friend.''

"By Jupiter!'' frowned Mitchell. "Forgive me, but—that is not so!''

Harry's eyes were a narrow glitter in his white face. He lifted a restraining hand. "The lady will, I am certain, have an explanation for so vicious a statement.''

Nanette flushed and began to speak with slow reluctance. "I became very ill after the Enquiry into my brother's death. My stepfather sent me to a cousin in Buenos Aires, and I remained there for over a year. When I returned, my friends, thinking to protect me, spoke of anything but my bereavement. I was unaware of your papa's death until quite recently, when I discovered how totally he had deceived me.''

A stifled exclamation escaped Mitchell at this; but Harry, his cold gaze fixed on Nanette, made no comment.

"The night Frederick was killed,'' she went on, "there was a full moon. Sir Colin admitted at the Enquiry that the murder vehicle passed his own so closely that the wheels almost scraped. He was, in fact, incensed and leaned from the window to berate the other driver. Yet he denied having seen the crest on the door panel—a crest I *know* was there! I taxed him with the lie!'' Ignoring Harry's sharply down-drawn brows, she hurried on, "I told him that I *knew* who had murdered my brother—and why. He pretended to pity me and said he had *never* met the man and that the other carriage had, in fact, been quite *empty*! Such wicked untruths!''

His fist clenched, Harry said, "If you really believed that, ma'am, why did you not testify yourself? It would certainly have been allowed.''

"I *begged* to do so! But my solicitor would not hear of

216

it. I would be disgraced, he said, and judged mad." She tossed her head angrily. "Much I cared. He was just afraid—as everyone is afraid!"

"Afraid?" sneered Harry. "Of whom?"

"Why—my papa, of course."

Mitchell's jaw dropped and he gaped at her.

Harry murmured cynically, "Oh, you've not heard the half of it, Mitch. Miss Carlson's papa, having murdered *her* brother, is so depraved as to wish her to marry *his*!"

"His . . . brother?" echoed Mitchell. "Her own *uncle*?"

Nanette's lower lip began to thrust outward and her eyes to spark.

Harry nodded. "For—money." And the corners of his mouth lifted into an unpleasant smile.

"Your brother, Mr. Redmond," said Nanette stormily, "has the very fine sense of humour, no? He finds it droll that a helpless girl is bullied into wedding someone against her will; that her adored brother was murdered—cut off at the beginning of a so promising life! That her stepfather, urging his brother to wed her, looks at her himself with eyes that . . . that . . ." And she stopped, bit her lip, and shook her head as if refusing a thought too horrible for contemplation.

The mockery vanished from Harry's face. He stepped closer to her and breathed an aghast, "Little one—what are you implying?"

"That . . ." she looked up at him with pathetic entreaty, "That—heaven help me! I think he—desires me . . . himself!"

"Now—by God!" whispered Harry.

"It cannot be so!" Mitchell cried. "You do not describe a human being, Miss Carlson, but a—a veritable monster!"

"I describe a handsome and distinguished gentleman," she said, her sorrowful gaze still upon Harry. "The man your papa insisted he had never met—who was *not* his friend. Whom he, in fact, *dis*liked, if only by repute. And yet whose hospitality he enjoyed—knowing I had named him my brother's murderer! I describe my illustrious step-father—M. Parnell Sanguinet!''

"To justice!'' said Harry with taut intensity. The three tin cups clanked together. "To justice!'' echoed his companions, and the toast having been drunk, they all sat down; Mitchell, cross-legged upon the blanket; Nanette on the stool; and Harry perched against the table, close enough to catch the fragrance of her, yet not quite touching her.

The wild jubilation that had followed her disclosure had both delighted and astounded Nanette, for when her true identity had been revealed she had supposed them also to be aware she was Sanguinet's stepdaughter. There was no questioning her story now. Elated because at last they had a clue to the mystery surrounding their father's death, the brothers had whooped and embraced and pounded at one another before apologizing most humbly for having doubted her. Mitchell's face had been alight and open as he bowed to her. Harry's had contained an element of reserve, and if she trembled at what that reserve might imply, she was too relieved to dwell on it. For the time being it was sufficient that they believed her.

Mitchell's initial suggestion was that they at once proceed to Chichester, and Nanette enthusiastically endorsed such a course of action. Harry, however, pointed out that neither Daniel nor Andy had as yet returned from the tavern.

"Andy?'' said Mitchell in astonishment. "But—he's at Cancrizans.''

"He was. He found us and left here only moments before you arrived, seeking you. And Daniel went after you earlier. Did you meet neither?''

A flush burned Mitchell's cheeks and he admitted shamefacedly that he had "sort of wandered off'' with his émigré and forgotten the tavern entirely.

"No matter,'' Harry nodded. "They'll be back directly, I daresay. Meanwhile, may we beg that you tell us your story, ma'am?''

"Very politely, Sir Harry?" Nanette twinkled, praying for an answering smile.

He bowed. "Very politely—Miss Carlson, or may I say Miss Annabelle?"

"My name is Annabelle," she said, her hopes fading as she met his grave regard. "But Mama preferred the French version—Nanette."

"I see. And when you told me that Parnell Sanguinet sought to force you into a marriage for money, you meant for *your* money, *n'est-ce pas*?"

She nodded, her small hands gripped tightly together because this cool, judicial air was frightening her. "That was one of the reasons, at least."

"And you believe your brother was killed because he sought to prevent your marriage to Guy?"

"Yes." Her eyes darted from one to the other of them. "Always, I feared it might happen, for my stepfather has a—a way of dealing with those who oppose him."

Mitchell frowned, and Harry said slowly, "I'd think he would have kept you in France and not allowed you to attend the Seminary, did he intend to wed you to his brother."

"I doubt he so much as thought of me then. He despises children and stayed away from us for years after Mama's death. Which was as well because Frederick loathed him—and as for his brother, Claude . . !" she shuddered. "I used to dread lest my brother would say something—or even *look*, merely. Frederick had such a way with his eyes." Her own became sad and nostalgic, and for a moment she was silent, then went on, "My aunt Amelia in Devonshire had loved Mama dearly and wrote to ask that I be sent to the same Convent school she had attended. Frederick was at Eton by that time, and I missed him terribly and was wild to come. Papa's man of business agreed; so I came, and we were able to see one another occasionally, until he bought a pair of colours."

"*He* did?" Harry interjected shrewdly.

"Well, Papa bought them for him. It was one of the few

times he had ever agreed to anything Frederick asked. We were, in fact, surprised.''

Harry was not in the least surprised and, glancing up, saw in Mitchell's grim expression an echo of his own conclusion. "Nan—er, Miss Carlson," he said quietly, "forgive me, but—your mama was a lady of vast wealth, I understand. Did her fortune pass to her husband—or to her son?''

"To Frederick. and then, if he left no heirs, to me. But Parnell Sanguinet was far more wealthy than Mama. I don't think he married her for her fortune but because she was very lovely and much sought after and admired.''

"When I was at the chateau," Mitchell interposed thoughtfully, "I gained an impression of great wealth. They look to be living as high as coachhorses. Do you believe the fortunes of the Sanguinets have been depleted by such extravagances, Miss Nanette?''

"I don't know. Something happened.'' She shrugged expressively. "I hard that Claude—he is the eldest brother— had some disastrous financial ventures. And I knew his political connivings were terribly costly, for he was always into this or that intrigue. Also, he bought a huge old manor house on one of the Scottish islands and poured money into it, though I did not know of that until recently.''

Mitchell's fine brows lifted. "That's odd. What on earth would a French aristocrat want with a Scottish manor house?''

"Does Claude control the family coffers, then?'' asked Harry, impatient with this digression.

"Yes. I have very seldom met him, thank heaven, for he is most horrid. I heard him once talking to Guy. He spoke so softly, and laughed many times; but Guy was white as death, and me—I was purely terrified!''

She looked as if even the memory frightened her, and Harry at once changed the subject. "Did you have a comeout? I don't seem to recall hearing of it.''

"I was to be presented and have a London Season when I turned seventeen. I was—oh, so excited, and Frederick enormously proud of me. But then . . .'' The animation

220

faded from her vivid face, and she shook her head. "Papa came."

And Parnell, thought Harry, found that the child he'd virtually abandoned had blossomed into a beautiful girl. A girl undoubtedly judged the finest prize in the matrimonial sweepstakes. Frowning, he said, "I wonder you didn't accept an offer before he began to interfere. Girls marry at sixteen, often."

"Well, I was at the Seminary, you see—or with Aunt Amelia, who is very strict. Still—there was one boy of whom I became quite fond. Aunt Amelia approved, but— Papa would have none of him. He told me it—it was the gold that put the shine into his eyes. Not love for me."

Harry swore under his breath, and Mitchell uttered a scornful, "What fustian! I'll wager the poor fellow was scared off, if the truth be told!"

"No, Mr. Redmond," Nanette contradicted in a sad, small voice. "He was bought off. Papa paid him quite a large sum to—remove his attentions. And then boasted to me of it."

She kept her eyes lowered, but Harry sensed how much that piece of deviltry had hurt her, and his right hand clenched tight.

"Good God!" Mitchell ejaculated. "Surely your brother could have done something?"

"When he came home from Spain and learned what was going on, he was enraged. He went roaring into Papa's study." Her eyes looked back into the past and she said softly, "I heard Papa tell him I would marry Guy. Frederick became even angrier, and Papa played with him . . . laughed at him . . . mocked him, in his cruel, clever way. When it was over at last, Frederick came up to my room. I expected him to be in a passion, but instead he seemed almost elated. He said that I was not to worry any more, because at last he had found a way to put a spoke in the wheel of M. Diabolique."

Harry asked intently, "What did he mean?"

"Would that he told me. I suppose it was some scheme to prevent my marrying Guy. He went out, in a great hurry. . ." Her voice cracked a little. "He was killed—that very night." She blinked up at Harry and said beseechingly, "Can you wonder I suspect my papa? But—I have no proof! Nothing! And—no one will listen."

The brothers glanced grimly at one another. Mitchell said with indignation, "I would have thought one of your many admirers would—" but his words faded before the stricken look that flashed across her face.

"While I was in mourning," she said, "there could be no thought of marriage, of course. When I came home, Papa saw to it that only the—what Frederick used to call the 'raff and chaff' were allowed near me. He knew that I'd have none of them. I became the target for every fortune hunter, military rattle, and libertine at large . . ." Mitchell darted a startled glance at his brother, but Harry's face remained expressionless. "A naval officer I'd met abroad persisted in courting me," Nanette went on. "Papa disliked him intensely. I knew . . . I *knew* how dangerous it was . . . but—I was so lonely, and afraid . . . I told him all I suspected." She drew a hand across her eyes. "He was shot to death one night. By a highwayman—or so they said."

"Jupiter!" gasped Mitchell. "Parnell turned to the High Toby!"

"Or bought the services of such!" Pale with anger, Harry exploded, "God! It defies belief!"

"The Sanguinets are all-powerful," Nanette sighed. "Papa can be very charming and persuasive, when he wishes. If people began to question, he told them that I was 'very ill'—the grief had caused my intellect to become disordered. It was hopeless. And so at last I refused all gentlemen callers and went about only with my school friends, or Guy. Papa was out of the country for much of the time, and although I was not allowed to live with my aunt any more, gradually, I began to be happy again. He had . . . given me a little rope, I suppose. But last month he came back. And very soon I—I saw how . . . he looked at me . . ."

Enraged by her sorrow, yearning to comfort her, and

222

loathing the man who had so victimized her, Harry grated, "And so you ran away."

She nodded. "I ran to Sister Maria Evangeline. She is a good, brave woman. But Papa's men found me, and I knew that if they took me back, he would never again let me out of his sight. I was half out of my wits with fear. And then Sister Maria Evangeline herself took me to Diccon—not the clergyman, as I told you, Harry—because she knew him and said he could be trusted to escort me to my aunt. I put on my maid's dress and tried to make myself look so that no one would recognize me. I know it was—a dreadful thing to do, but—I was so desperate, I was beyond caring." She paused, then finished in a scratchy, pleading little voice, "It really *was* . . . quite dreadful . . ."

Again the eyes of the brothers met in a mutual rage; then Mitchell said frowningly, "But—if Guy becomes your husband, *he* will have control of your fortune. From what I saw of him, I'd not judge him a weakling. Parnell would likely get short shrift."

"Guy loves me," Nanette acknowledged. "But—Claude and Parnell have some hold over him—I do not know what. Only that he fears them."

"Even so," Harry argued, "if he really loves you I very much doubt he would allow Parnell to steal your fortune."

Nanette stared down at her hands and muttered, "My fortune . . . My *mis*fortune, rather. I hate it, for the grief it has brought upon me and those I love."

"Yet would find life bitter, indeed, without it," Harry thought cynically, and asked, "Does Guy know—that his brother, er, desires you?"

"No! This is what I so dread, for he is, as Mr. Redmond discovered, an honourable man. If Papa so much as laid a hand on me, and Guy learned of it . . . Dear God! I know what he would do. and—one way or another, he would be killed. I could not—I just *could* not . . . bear . . ." Her voice broke and she turned away, her lips trembling.

Stunned by such shocking revelations, Mitchell lifted incredulous eyes to his brother and caught his breath. The look was there now—the same tender, worshipful adoration he had glimpsed in the eyes of St. Clair and Camille Damon. His horrified comments were forgotten and he watched in breathless silence, feeling that he intruded upon something both private and sacred, yet not daring to destroy the spell by moving away.

Harry was oblivious to all but the grief of the girl he loved. The nightmare she had lived through would, he knew, have reduced most gently bred ladies to total, terrified submission. But Nanette had not submitted. God love her valiant soul, she'd fought as bravely as she knew how! A dozen impressions of her flashed through his mind. He could see her railing at him, laughing at him, ministering to his hurts, caressing Mr. Fox, wielding that ridiculous oar, singing her husky little songs by the campfire . . . A lump rose in his throat and his eyes misted. How indomitable she was—how warm and sweet, and unutterably beloved. And—how rich. One of the richest ladies in Europe, while he was just another 'military rattle' . . . another fortune hunter. He fought despair away and his jaw tightened. Whatever else, he could serve her. He could protect her from that evil, twisted man. And somehow ensure that she find happiness.

"Little shrew," he said huskily, having quite forgotten the presence of his awed brother. "I swear to you—upon my honour—that so long as I live Parnell Sanguinet will not lay a hand on you!"

Sergeant Anderson returned from the tavern alone, Daniel having left a note with the proprietor explaining that he had been summoned to join Diccon but that he and the Trader would likely come up with them in Chichester, and to look for them at the Market Cross at three o'clock. The Sergeant greeted Mitchell with scowls and scolding, while his eyes betrayed the joy his words denied. He had purchased bread, cold ham, a fragrant and still-warm apple pie, ale for the men, and a mug of lemonade for Miss Nanette. He was the hero of the hour and, having happily satisfied the pangs of hunger, they journeyed on in great good fellowship.

They reached Chichester in mid-afternoon. Taking no chances, Harry gave the quaint old town a wide berth, skirting the environs until they came upon a pleasant glade some way off the road and hidden from it by a large clump of poplars. They all agreed it was a perfect campsite, whereupon Mitchell went into the town armed with a firm resolve not to be diverted, a list of necessary supplies, and instructions to locate Diccon and return as quickly as possible.

Very aware that a certain anxious gaze was fixed upon him, Harry proceeded to become very busy indeed. The moment Nanette had been assisted with the unloading of her various boxes of 'vital necessities,' however, Anderson, while ostensibly helping Harry locate the most suitable spot on which to erect the tent, growled a soft, "I'm coming with yer!"

"The devil you are!" flashed Harry, but just as softly, and with a weather eye on the girl. "My brother would do splendidly alone here under normal circumstances, but he's not ready to take on Parnell Sanguinet!"

"No, and not likely to, hidden away in the wilderness." Anderson gave a derisive snort. "Anyone has to face Monsewer Diabolick this arternoon, I don't reckon as how it'll be Mr. Mitchell. And well you knows it, Captain."

"Well, you just bear in mind, my lad, that *I'm* the Captain and you're the Sergeant!" grinned Harry. "Which has nothing to say to the purpose, since we're both of us civilians at the moment." No answering smile lit the craggy features, and clapping a hand upon Anderson's shoulder, he said, "Was there ever such a worrier? I wonder you've not succumbed to an irritation of the nerves long since— you're worse than a little old lady with your fidgets! Come now and help me free Mr. Fox from his poles."

Within the hour, Mitchell rode in. He had accomplished his shopping and strolled about town for a while, then rested in the Market Cross and watched the various comings and goings without catching sight of either Diccon or Daniel. Harry was disturbed by this intelligence. He would have welcomed the presence of at least one of the men, for he

225

could then in good conscience have allowed his brother to accompany him to Howard Hall. His every instinct urged him to remain with Nanette himself; but one of them must see Cootesby, and if there should be trouble at the camp-site, he, with his injured arm, would be the least effective. Besides, despite his scholastic abilities, Mitchell was still inclined to be shy and awkward when faced with polished, worldly men. If Cootesby was the conniving and treacherous scoundrel Harry suspected, the boy would be no match for him.

Troubled, he tucked his hand in Mitchell's arm, and they wandered to the edge of the glade together. For a moment they gazed in silence at the tree-clad slope beyond; then Harry said a grave, "I'm sorry, Mitch."

A look almost of relief sprang into the grey eyes. "Yes. I am, too."

"The thing is—we cannot both go, can we?"

"Certainly not." Mitchell put out his hand and, with a trace of shyness, said, "No more military actions, if you please, gaffer."

Gripping that hand hard, Harry's eyes were very serious for a moment, then he grinned. "Look to your own command, bantling!"

Anderson had the sorrel gelding saddled and ready. Harry swung easily astride the animal and leaned to take the small hand Nanette reached up to him and assure her he would be back well before dusk. He started off with Mitchell's cheery, "Don't be late for dinner!" ringing in his ears. "Keep yer eyes open, Captain!" exhorted the Sergeant glumly. "Do be careful! Oh, *do* be careful!" called Nanette, and even Mr. Fox sent a vaguely anxious bray after him.

Clad in his ill-assorted garments and worn shoes, Harry rode out feeling as though he wore chain mail and carried not Diccon's baton but a lance of shining steel.

CHAPTER XIV

HOWARD HALL, THE COUNTRY SEAT OF LORD HOWARD Cootesby and the home that most often saw him in residence, was situated a mile or so west of the town. It was a tall, narrow house of red brick and nondescript design, perched on a hill that rose like the dome of a bald head from an encircling band of woodland. It was towards these trees that Harry now rode, his thoughts upon the people he had left behind. Usually, the more hazardous the endeavour the higher the quivering sense of excitement that would grip him, his reaction to any challenge invariably one of eagerness to confront the unknown, to test his own mettle to the fullest. Today he felt tense and plagued by apprehension. Perhaps, even with Andy and Mitchell to guard her, Nanette was in jeopardy . . . And surely, even to entertain such thoughts was disloyal; the Sergeant was magnificent in a scrap, and Mitchell had certainly proven himself to possess both nerve and stamina.

He shook off his gloomy forebodings and urged his hack to a faster gait, but almost immediately slowed again. A short distance into the woods, a man lay stretched out, shoulders propped against a tree. He was clad in sombre black, but mindful of his encounter with Devil Dice in just such a spot, Harry's fingers closed around the baton in his pocket. Gargantuan snores were emanating from the sleeper. Amused, he prepared to ride on, wondering that the nearby trees did not sway. He knew of only one other gentleman capable of such powerful resonance. Old Maude, it would seem, had a rival. Unless . . ? He dismounted and stepped closer. It couldn't be! The shape was sufficiently pear-like to be that of his uncle, but— By gad! It was! Now why on earth was the Reverend Mordecai Langridge napping in Lord Howard Cootesby's Home Wood?

"Langridge" quoth Harry sepulchrally, about a foot from the sleeper's ear.

The Reverend burst into a frenzy of convulsed movement. His arms flew out, he uttered a yelp, and, scrambling to his feet, peered about in bemused dismay, gasping, "Yes, my love . . ?"

Harry gave a crack of laughter. Langridge stared in disbelief, then came to grip his nephew's hand delightedly. "We were correct, then! I am glad . . . to . . ." His smile died into stark shock. "Good gracious me! Poor lad! What ghastly—er—attire! And—what's this? Blood stains? Have you fought Sanguinet? Is he dead then? They are an evil clan, my boy, and will enact full vengeance, I fear!"

"Do not bury him yet," Harry chuckled. "I ran afoul of an honest Welsh bull, merely. Nought to worry about." He glanced down at his ill-assorted raiment and muttered a rueful, "Forget about my hand-me-downs, though. Blast! Well, at least you are presentable, Uncle. You can get me past the butler."

The Reverend led the way to a stolid-looking mare who was comfortably devouring a nearby shrub. "My horse threw a shoe, I'm afraid. but—as for getting you into the Hall, dear lad—out of the question! Quite."

Harry ignored this daunting prophecy but was forced to admit the mare could not be ridden. "We'll walk," he decided. "Come on, Uncle Mau-decai. Tell me why you are here."

If Langridge noted the small slip, he gave no sign of it, and still insisting that their journey was pointless, was drawn along by his nephew's more forceful personality and as they went, explained his presence. Harry's absence had smitten him, he said, to the point that he had finally ridden to Three Fields in hopes of finding him there. "But you were *not* there," he said redundantly, "and Lord Jeremy was from home, so I followed him to Cancrizans and had no sooner arrived than the Marquis returned from Sanguinet Towers in a positively towering fury. Such language!" Considerably in awe of Camille Damon, he shook his head. "Seldom have I seen so violent a temper in such a young man, though he curbed it upon learning of my calling and apologized most humbly, while all the time those strange eyes of his were positively shooting out sparks of rage."

Harry laughed. "He received a rude reception from Sanguinet, did he? Good old Cam. I can all but see him fuming. I hope he didn't seriously offend you, sir. He's a hell of a—er, that is, he's a splendid fellow, you know. Was Jerry there?"

Lord Bolster, it appeared, had indeed been present, and the three had decided that Harry would undoubtedly attempt to question the gentlemen who had taken part in the fateful card game. "So the Marquis drove to Hampstead to see if you had yet visited Mr. Sprague Cobb, and Bolster and I came here and have been taking turns watching the road so as to warn you." Here, the Reverend halted, flung up one hand dramatically, and exhorted, "You *must not* go on with this, my boy! It is quite useless, and—"

"To the contrary." Walking on, the laughter that habitually lurked in Harry's eyes vanished entirely. "I have reason to suspect that Parnell Sanguinet had a more compelling reason than I'd dreamed for arranging my father's death."

"But—my boy, you do not understand. There is no possible way that—"

"It is of no use, sir," Harry interposed. "I know what you believe, but Mitch and I both think—"

"Mitchell? You have seen him? Now heaven be praised! Sergeant Anderson came to the Priority quite overset with anxiety. I scarcely dared tell you of your brother's rash conduct in Dinan! What the *ton* will make of it I cannot guess! How fortuitous he was not facing Parnell as he surmised!"

"The *ton* may make of it whatever they wish," said Harry, bristling. "And Mitchell would have done just as

229

splendidly had he faced Parnell rather than Guy Sanguinet! Now tell me quickly, if you will, what you meant when you said you had come to . . . warn . . ." His words died. They were close to the house now, and the front doors were swinging open. Three men armed with cudgels sauntered onto the small area atop the sweep of wide steps. One wore the green of a gamekeeper, but noting the black and gold livery of the others, Harry's eyes narrowed. "Aha . . . I have it."

"They will not let you in." Langridge plucked nervously at his sleeve. "When we first enquired for Lord Cootesby, they were so insolent it was all I could do to restrain Lord Bolster. Come—before there is a vulgar confrontation."

Harry had detected a familiar face. "Why, Uncle," he murmured, his eyes beginning to sparkle. "A little vulgarity is good for the soul." He shook off the Reverend's pudgy hand and strode forward. "Well, well! My friend, Mr. Fritch."

Hatred glowed in the small eyes of the gamekeeper who had manned the gatehouse at Sanguinet Towers. "I hoped as you'd come," he leered hungrily. "Oh, but you don't know how much I hoped it!"

The butler trod timidly into view and stood just outside the doors, wringing his hands. "You there," called Harry, ignoring the menacing advance of Sanguinet's men. "I am Harry Redmond. Is your master at home?"

" 'E don't know," sneered a red-faced, heavily built ruffian with deliberate impertinence. "Come and 'ave a spot o' tea wiv me, Sir 'Arry! I got a nice crumpet 'ere wot you can try yer teeth on!" And he smacked his cudgel into the palm of one beefy hand.

His companions let out loud guffaws, and the Reverend whispered, "They're ugly customers! Come—you are in no condition to—"

"Have you a pistol about you, sir?" enquired Harry softly, keeping his attention on the sneering bullies.

"No. And lad—hasten! They are too many, and you—"

"Yes, blast it all! Oh, well—cannot always play fair, I'm afraid!"

With a lithe spring, he was in the saddle. Langridge fell back with a startled exclamation. Harry wheeled the gelding and galloped back down the drive, followed by shrill hoots and shouted profanity. When he'd enough distance, he turned about and slapped the sorrel's flank hard. The animal fairly leapt toward the house. The three stalwarts, who had converged upon a dismayed Langridge, now flung themselves for the charging horse. Not without courage, Fritch raced to intercept Harry at the steps and sprang forward, club upraised. The sorrel stumbled and almost fell. The club whistled past Harry's ear and landed glancingly on his mount's flank. Screaming, the sorrel bucked. The other hirelings retreated from those flailing hooves with commendable alacrity, but Fritch, caught off balance, was tardy. Harry's boot shot out and connected with his narrow jaw. Fritch flew backward and lay unmoving. Harry jumped the hack up the two remaining steps and through the front doors, even as the butler sprang clear, uttering a shout of excitement.

The foyer of Cootesby's ancestral hall was a good size, but it had not been designed to accommodate a large, plunging, and thoroughly frightened horse; and as two more men wearing Sanguinet's livery ran from the rear of the house, it became very crowded, indeed.

Harry gave a whoop and guided the hack to the stairs beside which a tapestry hung on a long iron rod. He seized the rod and whirled the sorrel towards the eager group who charged him, the rail—tapestry and all—held like a lance in his right hand. He caught the first bully squarely in the chest, and the man zoomed backward carrying a comrade with him. The other two separated. The horse screamed, its terrified prancing hindering both Harry and his attackers, the tattoo of hoofbeats deafening in that enclosed space. A door flew open at one side of the hall and an elegant, grey-haired gentleman paused on the threshold, staring in astonishment at the mayhem. To add to the uproar, a Pekingese dog, having halted beside his master as though similarly stunned, was galvanized into indignant reprisals and yapping shrilly, tore around the horse's hooves. Eyes rolling, the sorrel danced, the dog yapped, Harry laughed, and Sanguinet's men dodged frantically to avoid the thrusts of the makeshift lance and the cavorting gelding.

A wiry fellow, bald save for two small tufts above his eyebrows, made a dash up the stairs and launched himself downward. Harry sent the gelding sideways, and the flyer missed his target but sailed into a grandfather clock, accompanying it to the floor amid a clanging crash and the chink of breaking glass. The clock began to chime, adding its mellow and incessant voice to the turmoil.

"If you're Cootesby," laughed Harry, "call your louts off before we wreck the place!"

The gentleman spread his hands helplessly. Mordecai entered at the same instant that Harry was attacked from either side. One end of the lance doubled the first man nearly in half. The tapestry slid from the other end of the rod as Harry almost dropped in. The oncoming bully was enveloped in its voluminous folds and disappeared from view amid a plethora of muffled curses. The redfaced individual who'd been on the front steps now made a lunge for the swinging end of the rail, caught it, and wrenched powerfully. Half torn from the saddle, Harry reeled back, still clinging to his 'lance' with stubborn determination. Fritch, his jaw swelling, staggered up and made a savage swipe at this hated opponent. The long club missed Harry's head by a whisper but caught his left arm fairly. He choked back an involuntary cry and was dully cognizant of a great deal of confusion, but the only true reality now was the white-hot pain that seared through him, reducing all else to insignificance . . .

Cold marble was pressing against his cheek . . . He was sprawled on the floor. Distantly, Maude's voice was upraised, a shrill and unfamiliar quality to it that angered him. They'd better not hurt gentle old Maude! He crawled to his hands and knees. His eyes were dim, but he could discern his uncle, crouching between his own helplessness and the gloating advance of four of the defenders. As Harry stumbled to his feet, his hack galloped madly out of the front doors and down the steps, the Pekingese in full-throated pursuit. The red-faced man jumped for the Reverend. To Harry's amazement, his uncle struck out. In some strange fashion he was armed with Dicon's baton, and the red-faced one yowled and reeled away.

"Stay back!" roared Mordecai, brandishing the baton with sinful delight. "You are not blind! You know what manner of man you challenge!"

The eyes of Red Face fastened to that baton, and he hesitated.

"Rush him! Damn you! Rush him!" screamed Fritch, clutching his jaw.

Harry, half immobilized by the pain that radiated from his arm, knotted his right fist. "Come on . . . then . . ." he invited thickly.

They came on. With a squeak of excitement, Mordecai gripped his baton tighter. Four clubs, wielded by four expert hands, swung upward.

So did one musket.

"Out!" commanded a crisp, cold voice.

Lord Cootesby stood halfway up the staircase, the musket aimed steadily at Sanguinet's men. His head was held proudly, his face pale but stern with resolution. "You have terrorized my servants, insulted my guests, and intimidated me," he itemized. "No more!"

"You wouldn't dare," Fritch taunted, sidling forward a pace. "You know what Monseer said." He jerked a thumb at Harry. "He wants Redmond. Bad."

"That's enough of your impudence!" Cootesby snapped. "Out! Or—" The musket swung to point squarely at Fritch's middle. "Shall you be the first to discover I would indeed dare . . ?"

The red-faced man had evidently lost his aggressive spirit and was backing away. Fritch turned on him furiously. "You going to let him run you orf? He doesn't dare shoot. Monseer's got him—"

"Ar," said his cohort. "But his lordship's got a musket. And that'n—" he indicated Langridge, "he's got a baton wot I don't like the look on. Not a'tall! I ain't going up agin no perishing Runner!''

He beat a path to the door. His companions, alerted by his ominous words, turned their attention to the weapon clutched in Mordecai's chubby hand and vacillated. The butler trod into the side hall. He held an enormous blunderbuss whose gaping muzzle was levelled at the intruders. It was the last straw. They snarled dire threats but backed away. The last to go was Fritch. On the threshold, he levelled a malevolent glare at Harry. ''When my monseer comes up with *you*,'' he snarled, ''you'll wish you never bin—''

The musket roared. Glass shattered in the window beside Fritch, and the wall became peppered with shot. With a shriek he galloped after his fellows, urged on by the ribald comments of grooms and gardeners, who had appeared as if by magic to support the belated stand taken by their employer.

''See them off the premises, lads!'' shouted the butler, hastening to the door.

''By Jove!'' exclaimed Cootesby, walking swiftly down the stairs. ''I feel halfway clean again!''

''Thank you, sir'' said Harry feebly. ''Jolly . . . jolly good've . . .'' As from a great distance he heard his uncle ask anxiously if he was all right. He attempted to reply, realized with horror that he had used the hated nickname, but could not seem to complete his apology. The room was becoming quite dark, which was odd because the sun had not yet gone down. An arm was firmly about him, and Maude's voice echoed, ''. . . game . . . to the last . . .''

''There, I think he's coming round now, sir.''

Harry sighed and looked up into the kindly eyes of a white-haired, motherly lady wearing a lace-edged cap, who was bathing his brow with a damp rag. He was sprawled in an armchair in a large, pleasant library. Nearby, Cootesby stood watching him anxiously, and the Reverend Langridge, hands clasped behind him, was surveying the proceedings, an aghast expression on his face.

"Deuce take it!" said Harry, sitting up in dismay. "Did I make a confounded fool of myself, then?"

Cootesby smiled, crossed to a table, and poured a glass of wine. "You did exceeding well, Redmond," he contradicted, returning to give Harry the glass.

"Indeed, I cannot see how you could fight at all, sir," the lady put in gently, "with such a dreadful gash in your poor arm."

Harry glanced down then and discovered that his jacket had been removed and fresh bandages applied to his injury. "Good Lord!" he gasped. "How long was I unconscious?"

"Only about a quarter of an hour," Langridge said reassuringly. "We made no attempt to revive you, dear boy, until Mrs. Hart was finished."

Harry stood rather unsteadily to thank the woman, obviously Lord Cootesby's housekeeper, for her efforts. She warned him gravely that he must consult a physician at the earliest possible opportunity, and upon his promising to do so, she called to her maid to remove the tray of medical paraphernalia, and left them.

Lord Cootesby opened the door for his two servants and returned to take a chair beside the fireplace, his calm features reflecting no trace of his inner curiosity.

"I'm sure you must be wondering why I look such a fright, sir," said Harry, sitting down again since his head still spun in an unsettling fashion.

"Not at all," his lordship lied politely. "I am instead most grateful that you—" he gave a whimsical smile, "dropped in."

Harry laughed. "An unorthodox arrival, wasn't it? I'm afraid my hack may have damaged your floors, and I'm dashed sorry for the destruction of that fine old clock." The brandy was commencing to make him feel steadier, and he took another swallow from the glass.

"There!" cried Langridge triumphantly. "Don't sound like a bloody vendetta, does it, Cootesby? You should never have listened to Sanguinet's lies."

His lordship agreed. "The man was so deuced convinc-

ing. And when I heard your brother had shot Guy, I thought
. . . perhaps . . .'' He shrugged ruefully.

"If you thought we seek vengeance upon the man responsible for our father's death, you are perfectly correct,
sir," said Harry. "But I've gained the impression you were
not to blame."

Cootesby's gaze lowered. Staring at the finely embroidered fireplace screen, he sighed, "I was, though." He
looked up and said remorsefully, "I should have stopped
it, Redmond. We all of us should have stopped it! Poor
Cobb took it almost as hard as did Schofield. I told him
we were not responsible—but we were. I own it. Your
father was in no state to play."

Harry's hopes plummeted. "Then—he really *did* play?"

Cootesby stared at him, then flashed a troubled glance
to Langridge.

"But—my dear boy," said the Reverend uneasily, "I
told you that he—"

"Yes, I know you did. But I was sure there must be
some mistake. I've lately discovered that my father had
reason to mistrust Sanguinet, so why—"

"Mistrust?" Cootesby intervened. "No, no—I assure
you he did not. I would say, in fact, that they were fast
friends. Extremely attached."

Harry was shocked into a brief silence. Then he asked,
"How well did you know my father, sir? Had you often
played cards with him?"

"I'd not met him prior to that evening. I am seldom in
Town, you see, and not well-acquainted at the clubs. Schofield was a good friend of mine." He shook his head
regretfully. "He never got over it. He was the one
who—who reached the room first . . . After . . . we heard
the shot."

It seemed to Harry as though that fateful last word
stopped time, as though all movement was suspended. He
no longer heard the tick of the clock, the rustling of leaves
outside the open windows, the calls of homeward-bound
birds. His very breath felt frozen in his throat.

"Poor lad!" Langridge came to slip a compassionate

hand onto his shoulder. "All so unprepared, alas! And who must bear that cross but myself? Oh, may God forgive me, but I have made wretched work of it!"

Scarcely hearing the words, Harry thrust him away, sprang to his feet, and confronted the startled Cootesby. "You . . . lie!" he accused in a murderous half-whisper.

"No!" cried Langridge frantically. "He don't mean it, Cootesby!"

His lordship stood at once but, instead of hurling the challenge the Reverend so dreaded, said a distressed, "Indeed, I wish I did, my dear fellow."

"It is truth!" Langridge moaned. "I lacked the courage to tell you, Harry. But—your . . . your poor papa, having lost all . . . Oh, merciful heavens! He—he shot himself!"

With a sob of rage Harry leapt forward, his hands darting for his uncle's throat. Langridge staggered back, choking, sputtering, striving vainly to tear away that merciless hold. Maddened, lost to all thought or reason, Harry tightened his grip, conscious only of the need to kill anyone who dared voice such an accusation against his beloved father. Cootesby fought desperately to loosen his hands, peering into the contorted young face and shouting, "Redmond! Let be! Are you run mad? Your uncle was not even here! I was—I *saw* it!"

Gradually, the words penetrated his anguish. The red mists that clouded mind and vision began to fade, and he saw Langridge's face, the eyes starting out in terror, the pudgy cheeks purpling. With a muffled groan he relaxed his hold, and his uncle reeled to the nearest chair and collapsed into it, wheezing and clutching at his throat. For an instant, Harry glared ragefully down at him. Then he strode to the window and stood holding his throbbing arm and staring at a tabby cat cleaning itself on the terrace. The gallant gentleman who had sired him would never have used a pistol to escape the consequences of his folly. Even at what must surely have been the darkest hour of his life, when his adored wife had died in his arms following a riding accident, Colin Redmond had somehow come through it without surrendering to despair. Surely, the loss of home and fortune—terrible though it would have been—could not compare to the loss of his lady? Surely his father had not so changed as to—

He whirled to a touch on his elbow. Lord Cootesby blinked but did not retreat before the savage crouch, and held out a wineglass in silent sympathy. Harry accepted the brandy with a hoarse murmur of thanks, but set it aside and crossed to where Langridge huddled, regarding him with stricken eyes.

"My apologies if I hurt you, sir," he offered curtly.

"A small . . . and well-deserved punishment, dear boy . . ."

Still very white, Harry frowned down at him, then turned to make his apologies to Cootesby. His lordship giving a slight, grave inclination of the head, Harry took up his glass and, returning, asked, "Would you be so kind as to tell me how it all came about? As much as you know, that is."

Cootesby marked the narrowed, deadly eyes and the jut of the firm chin, and knew with deep regret that he could only hurt the intrepid young man before him. Still, perhaps when he knew all the facts, he would be better able to adjust to the tragedy . . . And so he began slowly, "I've known Sanguinet for some years. Must admit I never cared much for him, but his brother Guy and my son Roger fought together in Spain and were inseparable. When Roger was killed at Vittoria, Guy—brought him home. He was wounded himself, but was . . . very kind." His eyes became sad and remote, but recovering himself, he apologized and went on. "At all events, Sprague Cobb and I were at White's one evening when Parnell Sanguinet came in. He and Cobb were soon plunged into a discussion on art—a subject in which I have an intense interest. Schofield joined us, and before I knew it, we were all invited to spend the next weekend with Sanguinet. Would to God I had refused! I'd heard little good of the man, but—" He gave a small, shamefaced shrug. "I was curious to see his collection of ancient crowns. You have heard of it, I daresay? For that foolish reason, I allowed my better judgement to be swayed."

"Was my father at White's that evening?" Harry asked tensely.

"Not while I was there. In fact, I was somewhat surprised to discover him at The Towers when we arrived. I deduced that the three of them were the very best of friends, although Cobb told me later he'd only met Sir Colin a time or two, at Sanguinet's."

Taken aback, Harry said, "You had the impression then, that my father had visited Sanguinet Towers on *several* occasions?"

Cootesby answered reflectively, "Yes. At least, Cobb said—no, begad! I am quite sure of it, for Sir Colin knew his way about the place, and it is a regular rabbit warren!"

"I'll be damned . . ." muttered Harry.

"We were treated royally," Cootesby went on. "Sanguinet was, I now comprehend, in an expansive mood, for I've since seen him in a far different light. However, the house is spectacular, the crown collection truly fascinating, and the chef—superb! We enjoyed a good game after dinner—for a time. Then the wine began to flow rather too freely, I thought, and the stakes climbed higher and higher. Your father . . ." He shot a worried look at Harry's drawn, intense face, "—was drinking heavily. Schofield urged him to refrain and when he refused, became more and more troubled. At length, Barney himself withdrew but was unable to induce your father to do so."

It was all wrong, thought Harry angrily. No matter what Cootesby, or anyone, said, it simply was not Colin Redmond! "I assume Sanguinet persuaded my father to continue?" he grated.

"I'm sorry, Redmond, but it was quite the reverse. Sanguinet suggested we retire, but your papa would have none of it and—ah, accused Sanguinet of refusing him a chance to recoup." He avoided Harry's glittering stare and said unhappily, "I'll own I was much embarrassed."

"And such behaviour totally at odds with my father's impeccable manners!"

"Oh . . . quite . . ." murmured the Reverend sadly.

"The wine, no doubt," soothed his lordship. "Cobb

239

also was quite put about and declared the play too steep. When he withdrew, I followed suit. Twice Sanguinet attempted to halt the game, but your father . . . well, in all fairness, it would have been most difficult to refuse him.'' He paused and said heavily, ''I hate to go on . . .''

''My father lost everything. This I know. All I ask is—was it fair and aboveboard?''

''It was, sir. I'd stake my life on it. If your father lost, it was his own doing.''

Through a taut pause, green eyes challenged brown and, finding those eyes steadfast, Harry's heart sank and he asked, ''And—afterwards?''

Cootesby went to pick up the decanter and refill their glasses. Not until he had replaced the decanter upon its silver tray did he speak again, and then remained with one white hand on the stopper, and his eyes fixed blankly on the tawny liquid. ''We went up to bed. I think we were all terribly shocked, although your papa, I must say, took it very bravely. It must have been about two hours later that I was awakened by the shot. I knew at once what had happened . . . I ran into the hall and met Cobb, and together we went to your father's bedchamber. When we . . . got there, he was slumped across the table. The . . . pistol was—still in his hand.''

Harry's right hand was gripped so hard that the nails bit into his palm. He had managed to control his emotions, but at these words his reserve broke. He swung around and stood with hunched shoulders and head downbent.

''Sanguinet was most distressed,'' Cootesby sighed, wandering back to the fireside, ''and feared he would be held accountable. He insisted that Cobb at once ride for the Reverend. Poor Schofield was . . . absolutely beside himself and had to be laid down upon his bed. All the servants were kept away, and we touched nothing until your uncle arrived some three hours later.'' He went to his chair, sat down, and stared glumly at his boots through a silence broken only by the tossing of the trees outside.

''You know the rest,'' said Langridge. ''When I saw poor Colin, all I could think of was to spare you—to spare the family the . . . shame . . .'' Harry half turned and threw him a withering look. Mordecai spread his hands. "Dear boy, I *know* how you must feel. I am—more than sorry."

He was more than sorry, thought Harry, blinking mistily at the carpet. Sorry for what? For the embarrassment that would be occasioned the family did it become common knowledge that Colin Redmond had shot himself? As if that mattered in the face of the tragic, pointless ending of that fine life! As if anything could fill the void left in the lives of his sons! Mitch! Dear God! How was he to tell Mitch? Rage seared through him. It simply did not fit his father's inflexible sense of right and wrong! There *had* to be a reason! Struggling to gather his wits, he asked, "My lord, were you aware that Schofield died recently, under most peculiar circumstances?"

Cootesby murmured, "A foolish accident, I grant you. But poor Barnaby had been very low in spirits since his son was—"

"No! Your pardon, sir, but Schofield knew what his son was—he'd known for years! His devotion was to his wife. That he grieved for Bertram's blindness, I do not doubt. That it destroyed him? Never! And as for my father—friends they were. Loyal, devoted friends. Barney would mourn him, of course. But not so deeply as to drive him into his own grave. There was something else! Some punishing sense of guilt—or remorse. I know it!''

A crease appeared between Cootesby's brows. He set his glass down and leaning back in his chair, propped his chin in the palm of one hand, and said, "Who knows what troubles may have plagued the man? Perhaps he was in failing health, or financial difficulties. Or his wife ailing in some way."

Harry bit his lip and paced up and down wrestling furiously with the facts as opposed to his unalterable faith in his father's character. "Why did Sanguinet wait so long?" he muttered. "he has not the compassion of a crocodile. Why would he let us go in our fool's paradise for almost two years?"

"Perhaps he felt responsible," Langridge reasoned. "He

241

agreed willingly enough that I wait until your health was restored before divulging the truth to you and your brother.''

''And yet,'' flashed Harry, ''our kindly Frenchman suddenly becomes so alarmed by the prospect of my coming here that he forces his men upon Lord Cootesby for his 'protection'. Why? Unless . . . Unless you *do* know something, sir. Perhaps without even being aware of it. Something that Sanguinet is determined to prevent me discovering.''

''But—what . . ? I know nothing that was not known by all the men in that card game.''

Harry gave a bleak smile. ''Precisely so. My papa— dead. Schofield—dead. Cobb—disappeared. And yourself, your pardon, but—known to be of rather reclusive habits and now all but held captive upon your own estate!''

''By . . . George!'' Cootesby stared his dismay but, reluctant to credit this grim implication, argued, ''If I am so dangerous to him, why not have me killed? He certainly has men who'd not balk at such a deed. Shotten, I'll wager, would whistle while he choked the life from a man!''

''Shotten . . ?'' echoed Harry, lost in frowning thought.

''A beastly rogue who is often with Sanguinet. But— *surely* you exaggerate, my dear fellow? Sanguinet is arrogant and ruthless, I grant you. But—three *murders*? I cannot believe that he is as—''

''Merciless?'' flared Harry. ''But he is! And if my suspicions are correct, mark how clever he has been. Three men, either dead or missing, yet not one word—not a whisper, of murder. Our diabolical gentleman leaves no possible link to himself, or that damnable card game.'' He intercepted the uneasy glance that flickered between the two older men and said impatiently, ''Well, perhaps he dared not kill every player save himself—or perhaps he felt you posed the least threat to him. Who knows?''

Langridge pointed out very gently, ''But—dear boy, your papa was *not* murdered. And Schofield overturned his carriage . . .''

The tone was such as one might use to reassure an hysterical child. With a surge of anger, Harry realized that they probably supposed him irrational from grief and worry. He began to have some concept of what Nanette had endured and, throwing his head back, asserted with stern defiance, "Barnaby was driven to his death, Uncle; I am certain of it. And as to Papa—there is only one logical answer. He must have been drugged!"

"Drugged?" gasped his lordship. "In front of a roomful of other men? I'll admit your father behaved as though he was a little up in the world, as the saying goes, but—nothing more. And in heaven's name, why would Sanguinet stoop to such a thing? Whatever else, the man's lineage is good; he is vastly well breeched, and I'd not think . . ." He hesitated, and said uncomfortably, "Forgive me, but—would your estates offer sufficient inducement to . . . ah . . ."

"From what my brother tells me, I must admit they would not," scowled Harry. "But nor do I believe that greed lay behind my father's murder. The truth is that Papa chanced to witness a dastardly killing, which thereby rendered him a serious threat to Sanguinet." And he knew with helpless frustration how far-fetched and inconclusive they would judge that allegation.

Sure enough, Cootesby was courteously silent yet darted a covert glance at Langridge, who squirmed about and muttered, "You refer to the Carlson affair, of course. But, Harry—my brother knew nothing of it. Under *oath* he swore repeatedly that he saw nothing to indicate foul play and that Sanguinet was not even *in* the other carriage! You surely do not doubt your papa's word of honour?"

Harry flushed but argued stubbornly, "My father may have overlooked something—some detail that later came to mind."

The Reverend stood and, wandering up and down, muttered, "It is all so chancy. I fear you merely grasp at straws; but suppose Parnell Sanguinet *did* drug poor Colin—though I must admit I can only think such an event wildly improbable—how could you *possibly* hope to prove so outlandish a thing?"

"I don't *know*!" Harry ran a hand through his hair distractedly. "Dammitall! It is so clear to me—yet might as well be gibberish! If only— Wait! I have heard that drugs affect a man's eyes. My lord—I know it is a lot to ask, but—did you notice anything odd about my father's eyes that night? Were the pupils abnormal in any way?''

''Alas!'' Cootesby groaned. ''I must crush your hopes again, poor fellow! I wish you had asked that question of any other man, but—I should explain that I've a hobby, a rather compelling one. I paint portraits.'' He gestured shyly to a fine painting above the fireplace. ''That is of my late wife. I am quite . . . proud of it. But I'll admit I find the eyes most challenging and am therefore especially interested in them. In point of fact, Redmond, when you came today, my first thought was that I'd have guessed you were his son even though your own eyes are a so much deeper green than were Sir Colin's.''

Harry's breath hissed through his teeth and his heart missed a beat. ''B-But . . . sir! My father's eyes were *not* green!''

Paling, Cootesby came to his feet.

''That is true!'' Langridge clasped his hands and said in a voice that shook, ''Natural enough you'd forget, Cootesby. After nigh onto two years . . .''

''No.'' Cootesby denied in a half-whisper. ''I distinctly recall that Cobb made some silly remark about green eyes bringing him bad luck. And—and somebody . . . Schofield, I think, said something about it—running in the family.''

''I inherited my mother's eyes, so I'm told,'' said Harry breathlessly. ''My brother Mitchell has my father's eye colour. Grey!''

They stared at one another, the ramifications stunning to all of them. Even Harry, his worst fears confirmed yet his hopes realized, was speechless.

Cootesby groped blindly for his chair and sank into it again. ''Have I been . . . duped, then? Was I party to so hideous a scheme? My God! But—I . . . I *saw* him!''

His mind racing, Harry said, ''You saw this—this green-eyed man, whom you were led to believe was my father. After the shot, did you see his face?''

Cootesby drew a hand across his suddenly sweating

brow. "The clothes . . . were the same . . . I remember so well that . . . when we got there, the door stood wide. Schofield was bending over him. With Sanguinet. Schofield came to the door and urged us not to go inside. It was . . . too horrible, he said. He looked like death himself and was in tears . . . poor fellow. So—" he shrugged helplessly. "I'd no wish to see such a sight, I must admit."

Harry drew a deep, trembling breath and turned to Langridge, his eyes holding a question.

"It was Colin," confirmed the Reverend, plucking at his lower lip in his perturbation. He shuddered and added, "And he was shot at that very table. God help me, I wish I might say otherwise."

Harry muttered savagely, "How monstrously clever! Only Sanguinet and Schofield knew my father, and you and Cobb had no reason to suspect they were foisting an imposter on you. After the game was over, the imposter fled. My father was brought in and callously murdered. Uncle Mordecai's identification was positive, for he never saw the man with whom you played, only my father's body!"

Langridge all but fell into a chair. "Not *Barnaby* . . . ?" he groaned. "Harry, *surely* there must be another explanation. Good old Barnaby . . . would never . . ."

"He did!" rasped Harry. "I am as sure of it as I stand here! And God help him, I believe that is what drove him to his own death! In some way, Sanguinet forced Barnaby Schofield to acknowledge an imposter as my father. And having established his identity and provided grounds for what was to be *kindly* disguised as his best friend's suicide, Barnaby could not live with his guilt!"

Langridge leaned back, his face white and twitching. "And I . . . helped them! By covering up what I deemed a—cowardly suicide, I *helped* . . . my brother's murderers!"

Harry said nothing, but his hand dropped to where his sabre had been used to hang and his slow smile was a terrible thing to behold.

CHAPTER XV

THE SUN WAS LOW IN THE SKY AS HARRY GALLOPED DICcon's hack down the drive, Langridge beside him on a borrowed grey mare, and Howard Cootesby's farewells and promises of all possible assistance still ringing in his ears. His mind whirled with speculation. He had convinced Cootesby, at least. The man would testify for them though the chances of such testimony being credited after so long a time were not good. He thought with a stab of guilt that he should have stressed the need for Cootesby to protect himself. Sanguinet would not hesitate to murder him now, and he himself had mentioned a possible killer who . . . What was it he'd said? ". . . who would likely whistle while he choked the life from a man." For some reason the remark haunted him. "Who would likely whistle . . ." Why should that be so tantalizing? He knew no Shotten, nor anyone who— But he did, by God! *Dice*! Devil Dice had whistled constantly! He had thought at the time it sounded like an ostler . . . His heart began to pound with an excitement that was increased as he remembered what Nanette had said of the naval officer who had persisted in courting her despite Parnell's dislike of him. "He was shot to death one night . . . by a highwayman . . ." "By thunder!" Harry exclaimed aloud, and urged the sorrel to greater speed.

The wind was coming up and clouds were building, but the sunset was exquisite, the tumbling clouds blushfully pink and edged with gold against deep turquoise skies.

Blind to such aesthetic beauties, Harry rode ever faster, only dimly aware that Langridge was falling behind.

He was spurred now by a strange unease, a nagging sense of something amiss that grew until it gradually displaced rage and the grim lust for vengeance. Plagued by this deepening fear, he leaned forward coaxing the sorrel on, and the animal responded with a bunching of powerful muscles, as though its reserves had been held for just such an emergency. They thundered along the country lanes, under wind-whipped trees. The miles flew and the sun dipped lower. Langridge was far behind now, and Harry encountered no other travellers save for a large black carriage that crowded him off the road, its reckless speed the more remarkable in view of the fact that as it flashed by he saw it was unoccupied.

The tired sorrel laboured up the last rise, and it seemed to Harry that he traversed a scarlet world, the lurid glare like an omen of disaster. He shouldn't have left her! Yet Anderson was there, and Mitch would die to protect her, for he was more than half in love with her himself . . .

He topped the rise. Below, all was peaceful. The small stand of poplars tossed whisperingly in the wind. There were no tethered horses in view, no ruffians loitering about, no signs of activity on the wooded slope beyond the copse. Heaving a sigh of relief, he rode downhill at a reduced pace and was starting into the trees when a sound came to him: a soft but repetitive whimpering that turned his blood to ice. He vaulted from the saddle and began to run.

For as long as he lived, the scene that met his eyes as he burst into the clearing would haunt his memory. There was no sign of Nanette, Mitchell, or Anderson. The tent was collapsed, the contents strewn about as though there had been a desperate struggle. Mr. Fox lay nearby, and it was from the little donkey that the whimpering emanated. Harry started for him, shouting a scared, "Nanette . . ? Mitch . . ?"

"Captain? That you?"

Andy! Harry's heart jumped. But—where in the devil . . ? And then he saw a hand wave a rag from the far side of the cart, and the vivid stain on that rag sent him racing toward it to halt once again, struck dumb with horror. Sergeant Anderson sat on the ground, blood streaking his cheek from a deep cut above his right ear. His wooden leg was gone, his garments rent and dusty, his face twisted with anxiety. Of all this, Harry was aware but vaguely. Mitchell lay sprawled on his face, both hands gripping the spokes of a wheel. He wore no jacket, and his shirt was cut to ribbons, the torn fabric hideously stained and clinging to the lacerated flesh of his back. Harry's stunned gaze returned to the Sergeant. Anderson strove to speak but could not. Mitchell's white-knuckled grip on the wheel shifted. His dark head was raised to reveal an ashen, sweat-streaked face, and eyes frantic with pain and humiliation. "Harry! I . . . failed you! He . . . took her. You—you *must* go . . . after—" The panting utterance ceased, the white lips drawing back from teeth tight-clenched.

Recovering his wits, Harry dropped to his knees and touched his brother's damp hair caressingly. "My poor old fellow . . . I am—so very sorry!" His narrowed eyes flashed murderously to the Sergeant. "Sanguinet?"

Anderson nodded, but before he could speak, Mitchell gasped, "He . . . *whipped* me!" The fine young face was horror-filled, and Harry was half choked by the fury that welled up in his throat. "As if—I were . . . a *dog*, Harry! I couldn't believe . . . he would . . . really do it. And—and even when Miss Carlson . . . came back, he . . . he *wouldn't stop!*"

"Sir," Anderson put in huskily, his head bowed as though he was ashamed to meet his Captain's eyes, "if you could please fetch me some water."

Harry sprang up, sprinted to the cart and, grabbing the water jug, glanced to Mr. Fox. The donkey was bleeding at the shoulder, but the wound did not look too serious. He called a few words of comfort as he seized a bowl and tore back to Anderson. He poured some water into the bowl, handed it to the Sergeant and, returning to the cart, unearthed a flask of brandy, then ran to kneel once more beside his brother. "Try and take a mouthful or two," he urged gently, "It—"

Mitchell turned his head away. "I *tried*, Harry! You *must* believe me!"

"Of course I believe you." Harry set the flask down and took the hand that came out to him. Holding that hand strongly, he said, "I am sure you did splendidly. We'll get her back, never—"

"She . . . she *saw* him whip me!" Mitchell groaned. His grip tightened convulsively, his voice rising to a shrill cry of despair. "As if . . . I were . . . a *dog*!"

"Easy . . . easy!" Harry soothed. He was shaking with rage, possessed by such a longing to do bloody murder as he'd never known. Andy's big hands were peeling away a sodden remnant of shirt as tenderly as any woman could have done. The sight of that ravaged back sent terror lancing through Harry, but with a tremendous effort he managed to speak calmly. "Do not try to talk now, Mitch. We'll have you feeling better in—" He gave a gasp and cried a terrified, "Mitchell!" as his brother's taut body sagged and the hand he held relaxed its crushing grip to rest limply in his own. Scarcely daring to breathe, he sought a pulse and gave a long-drawn sigh of relief as he found it at last, rapid and uneven, but lacking the terrible threadiness he'd met from time to time on the battlefield. He whispered a grateful, "Thank . . . God . . !"

"Better give him some brandy, sir," gulped Anderson.

"Heaven forbid! He cannot feel anything now. Good God, Andy! Whatever happened? No—never mind, you shall tell me later. I'll take over here. You go and look after Mr. Fox."

"Can't do it, sir." His rugged features flushed with shame, Anderson gestured toward the trees. "I think . . . they throwed it . . . that way."

Harry clambered to his feet, ran to the trees, and sought frantically about, his mind a whirling chaos. Mitchell was badly hurt, to say nothing of the terrible blow to his pride. As for Nanette . . . "I'll come, my darling girl! Just as soon as I have Mitch in the hands of a surgeon, I'll come for you!" He found the wooden leg at last and, placing it beside the sergeant, took the rag and began to minister to his brother. Anderson, meanwhile, restored his mobility and without a word stood and clumped over to Mr. Fox.

"*Harry*! Oh . . . my dear . . . God!" The Reverend rode up, leading the sorrel. His flabby face pale with dread he started to dismount, only to be restrained by Harry's upflung hand and crisp command that he ride into Chichester and find a doctor. "Mitchell has been most savagely whipped. Please be as quick as you can!"

For once the garrulous Mordecai was shocked into silence. He stared from Mitchell's still form to Harry, to Anderson, to Mr. Fox. And shaking his head as if all of it was totally beyond his comprehension, dropped the sorrel's reins and rode away.

In the stark waiting room of Dr. Jonas Twickenby's surgery, Sergeant Anderson, his head neatly bandaged, started up from the wicker chair as Harry opened the inner door and entered. "Sir! Is he— Will he be—"

Harry said tersely, "They kicked me out, but Twickenby's working hard."

The Sergeant drew a deep, quivering breath. "Did Mr. Mitchell say anything, Captain?"

"Only—about Miss Carlson." A muscle in Harry's cheek twitched nervously, and in a voice suddenly hoarse, he said, "He begged me to leave and go after her."

"Just like him . . . Pluck to the backbone! Not one single sound outta him—all the way in that perishing old chaise with not a decent spring to it! You should've been the one to hold him, sir! Not me!"

Harry crossed to slip one hand onto the broad shoulder, pushing him back into the chair again. "You great chawbacon! You were in no case to ride. How do you feel now?"

"God love the man!" thought Anderson, and said gruffly, "It'll take more'n a whack over the brainbox to put a period to this old Army mule! Sir—what about this here Twickenby? He looks an awful sour prune! The woman who tied up my head says he's a good enough doctor, but d'you think he's—"

"I think we're damned fortunate that my uncle found

250

him. He seems to know his business, and his wife is a splendid nurse.''

''What—was that fat lady his old woman, then?''

Harry nodded, his expression hardening. He had stayed beside his brother when the doctor began his task, but the white-faced agony of the gentle, scholarly boy had brought his rage to the boiling point, and he'd vowed softly, ''I'll find her, Mitch. And before I kill Sanguinet, he'll rue the day he laid that whip across your back! I swear it!'' The doctor's large wife, who had seemed undismayed by the sight of Mitchell's injuries, had uttered a cry of horror at those grim words, and her dour husband had folded his arms and refused to proceed until the barbarian was ejected . . .

Andy was watching him anxiously. Harry glanced around the dusty little chamber and asked, ''Where is my uncle gone?''

''He's trying to find a farrier to go and help Mr. Fox. Kind in him, I thought, sir, for he was wanting powerful to stay here. But—it's coming on to storm, and he says if it gets much darker he'll never find the way. He knowed you wouldn't want us to just leave the poor little devil lying there.''

''No, of course not.'' Harry's eyes flickered anxiously towards the closed door beyond which his brother lay.

''Captain . . . I feel so . . . I mean—if only I could've *done* something!''

''Stupid hedgebird! D'you think I do not know you did all you could?''

Anderson blinked speechlessly, then managed, ''You must be fair aside o' yerself, sir—wanting to get after that madman!''

It was true. The need to go to Nanette was a frenzy within Harry, but he could not leave yet. He pulled up a wooden chair, straddled it and, sitting with arms folded across the back, said, ''I shall go as soon as I can. Now— for God's sake tell me what happened.''

''It was about twenty minutes afore you come back, sir. Miss Carlson was poking about in the cart, getting dinner ready, as I thought, and me and Mr. Mitchell was sitting by the fire. He was telling me about that there Urey-Pidies of his, and—well, I suppose we lost track o' the time. I looked round and she'd up and gone! I went to the cart and all her things was gone, too! "Mr. Mitchell!" I shouts. "Miss Carlson's run orf agin!" He come over smart-like, and we decided we'd best get arter her. We turned round, and . . ." He spread his hands helplessly. "There they was. Big, mean-faced coves; five or six on 'em, along o' that there Monsewer Diabolick, and another bruiser riding a mare might've been twins with our Lace, sir."

"Dice . . .!" breathed Harry through his teeth.

"Gawd! *Devil* Dice? Then it *was* our Lace? But—she'd got no white stockings."

"Dye. But never mind that now. Go on, Andy."

"Well, that there Dice had a pistol aimed steady at Mr. Mitchell's bread basket, so we just stood there. The Frenchy (all in black he was sir, like the rest of 'em), he come drifting over, very lazy-like, and asks Mr. Mitchell where was Miss Carlson. Cool as a cucumber, Mr. Mitchell says as how since they hadn't been proper interduced he didn't think he could rightly give a answer. Then along comes another swell riding on a beautiful Arabian mare the like of which I never did see. Looked like she was made out of gold. But the gent's got one arm in a sling and don't look quite up to the rig. Mr. Sanguinet said he had no business following them, and called him Guy, so I knew it was his brother. Well, he gets orf his horse and says he'd got *every* reason to follow, and he'll be glad to do the honours, and he interduces Mr. Mitchell. Diabolick puts up his eyeglass and looks Mr. Mitchell up and down and laughs. "You allowed that *baby* to best you?" he says. "*Really*, Guy!" Then he asks Mr. Mitchell again where Miss Carlson went, and Mr. Mitchell says as he wishes as how he knowed." The Sergeant hove himself out of the chair at this point and began to thump restlessly up and down, while Harry, eyes very grim, waited.

"I didn't like the way he looked at Mr. Mitchell," Anderson went on somberly. "He was halfway laughing, but with a—a sort've hungry look. He says in that soft voice o'his as how she couldn't have got far because he'd had a report as she was with us when you rid out. 'I'll lay you odds, Guy,' he says, 'as she's up there somewhere on that slope over yonder. Watching. If we go after her, it might take some time. So I think we'll just ask Mr. Redmond to bring her down here to us.' I begun to edge a bit closer to Lace 'cause I thought we was fair in fer it. Mr. Mitchell didn't say nothing, but he give a little grin, and Diabolick says as he can see Mr. Redmond thinks it's all some kind of game, but it ain't, and he don't like it if one of his family gets set upon. His brother says the duel was fair and to let the boy alone. Sanguinet acts like he hasn't even heard him and tells his coachman to go and fetch his whip. I'll tell you, S'Harry, me blood run cold when he said that, but I never thought he'd do it. His brother knowed him better, I expect, because right orf he goes up to him and says as how Mr. Mitchell's a gentleman. 'You must *not*!' he says. Diabolick, he just tells his men to tie Mr. Mitchell to the wheel o' the cart. Well, S'Harry, I could see as he means it all right. And poor Mr. Mitchell, he's staring at him as if he can't believe his own ears. Very pale he is, but—what a plucked'un, sir!''

''Yes. He is, indeed,'' said Harry tautly. ''So you made your move, did you?''

''Yus, sir.'' Anderson gave a small sigh of relief that the Captain had known he would put up a fight. ''I reckoned as it was now or never. You'll mind as I allus kept a needle and thread stuck under me collar, just in case you lost a button orf yer jacket or something? Ain't never lost the habit. I gives the mare the needle—right in the rump. Cor! You shoulda seen her go! Straight up! And the bully keeps *on* going, like a ugly fat bird! Mr. Mitchell makes a dive fer Diabolick and I takes on the cove nearest to me. We was going at it hot and heavy fer a little bit, but then— someone whacked me over the head and I sort've lost track o'things fer a minute. Next thing I knowed they'd took orf me wooden leg, sir. I just had ter lie there and . . . and watch. I wasn't no use ter poor Mr. Mitchell. None a'tall!''

For a moment Harry said nothing, visualizing the scene

with painful clarity. Then, holding the chairback very hard, he grated, "Who did it? Sanguinet himself?"

The Sergeant nodded. "And loved every minute, Captain. I'll say one thing, his brother tried to stop him. When that perisher shook out the whip, he grabbed hold of his arm. Diabolick looked him straight in the eye and said something. Not much, but I could tell it was enough. And Guy give up."

Harry swore bitterly and rammed his fist against the chair. "How soon did Miss Carlson come down?"

"Very quick, sir. I was a'thrashing and a'cussing. Mr. Mitchell didn't make one single sound, but the donkey was crying something awful. You'd a thought the whip was coming down on *his* back! Miss Nanette come running up, white as a sheet, and begged Diabolick to stop. She'd do whatever he wanted, she says. He smiles at her and says a'course she will—he never doubted it. And in he starts again! I think even his own men was fair took aback!"

Harry stared at him in unseeing misery. Had it been only this morning they'd talked in that misty clearing? Only this morning that Mitch had said shyly, "I do not think I would care to be—all alone in the world." He'd not dreamed then that he himself might be the one to be "left all alone". If Mitch died . . . A smothered groan escaped him, and his head bowed onto his arms. At once the Sergeant was beside him. "Don't sir! Don't you never give up! S'Harry—you done the best you knowed!"

The best he knowed . . . Perhaps. But if only he'd sent Mitch to see Cootesby and had himself remained with Nanette. He might have known that Sanguinet, desiring her, would have tracked them down! How glibly he had offered her his protection. How nobly he'd sworn that whilst he lived Sanguinet would not lay a hand upon her! Well, his hand was upon her now! That thought made him writhe. For the present, his one hope lay in the fact that Guy Sanguinet apparently bore some resemblance to a gentleman and, despite his loathesome inheritance, might shield her . . . at least until he himself could come up with them. Meanwhile, there was nothing to be gained by brooding over how much better he might have handled matters. He had done all in his power to elude detection and, believing he had succeeded, had left her as well protected as possible. He'd had an obligation to his father as well as to his brother and the girl he loved. He *had* done his best. He said a husky, "Thanks, Andy," and pulled back his shoulders. "What of Miss Carlson? He didn't abuse her in any way?"

"No, sir." The Sergeant returned to his chair once more. "She's got plenty o' spirit, that little lady. She run and grabbed hold of the whip and hung onto it, but Sanguinet just pushed her away." He paused, an odd little smile appearing as he said slowly and with relish, "His brother shot the whip out of his hand."

Harry's eyes opened wide. "Jove! That must have been a fantastic shot!"

"That it were. Diabolick didn't say nothing. He just stood there staring at his brother. Lor'! I don't never want no one to look at me like that, Captain! Then he pulls a little pistol out of his pocket. Miss Carlson runs to Guy and throws her arms around him. I thought as he was done fer, I can tell yer. And so did he, I reckon, 'cause he pushes Miss Carlson away from him." Anderson shook his head condemningly. "A lovely bunch they is, eh sir?"

"For God's sake!" Harry exploded. "Don't keep me in suspense! Did he shoot?"

"He aimed very careful and let him sweat for a minute. Then he says. 'Blast that animal and its beastly noise!' and up and shoots the poor donkey!"

"Devil take the miserable hound! I'd fancied that a mistake! Better he had rid the world of one of his own vicious clan!" Harry stood, stalked to the uncurtained window, and peered outside. The evening was dark and stormy, and it was beginning to rain. Where would Sanguinet take Nanette . . ? Would he dare to beat her . . ? A cold sweat sprang out on his brow and he had to battle the terror of it. He swung back into the room abruptly. "Which way did they go, Andy?"

The Sergeant peered curiously at him. "Why, you

must've passed 'em, sir. They'd not been gone above five minutes when you come. And they took the same road.''

"The only coach I passed bore no crest and was quite empty. They—''

The door opened. Twickenby came into the room, followed by his wife, and Harry went quickly to meet him. The doctor raised a lugubrious countenance and said sadly, "I did—the best I could, sir . . .''

Harry felt sick. "My . . . brother . . ?'' he said in a far away voice.

"Twick . . . en . . . by . . .'' warned the lady in a low undertone.

He shot her a malevolent glance. "He's asleep now. Thanks to laudanum. I wish I could say he will recover. But—it's been a terrible shock, you see. I will do my best, of course, but—he's not very physically hardy.''

Harry wet his lips, tried to speak, and could not. Mrs. Twickenby moved closer and looked searchingly into his drawn face. "My dear young sir,'' she murmured, "pay him no heed. He's only trying to get his price up.'' Her husband cast her a glance of pure loathing, and she chuckled and, patting Harry's arm, said kindly, "Your brother's going to have a nasty week of it—I'll not lie to you. But we'll take good care of him—of that you *may* be sure. My sheets are aired and free from fleas, and if he starts to run a fever, Twickenby will bleed him. He's a hard man for the pennies, but a fine doctor for all that. Now—ten shillings for tonight, and a guinea on deposit, if you please . . .''

Harry drew the collar of Andy's greatcoat higher about his chin and leaned to the blowing mane of the hack the Sergeant had found for him. The wind was out of the north and the rain drove into his face, the drops cold and stinging. As well he'd insisted on the Sergeant staying with Mitch. Andy had been furious, but was in no state to ride fast and far as Harry must do. He prayed his decison to follow this familiar road had been well founded. Sanguinet might have been heading for the main London turnpike, or perhaps had intended to journey as far as Guildford before

256

turning east to Kent and Sanguinet Towers. But Harry was gambling on the sadistic nature of his enemy. If Parnell Sanguinet suspected he entertained a *tendre* for the girl, it would afford him tremendous enjoyment to hold Nanette at Moiré: to gloat over her in the very house of the man who loved her.

He smiled humorlessly, and spurred harder. If his intuition proved correct, his enemy might have dealt him a better hand than he knew. Moiré Grange was an old house, with a priest's hole and secret escape route dating back to the days of Henry VIII. It should be a simple matter to get into the Home Wood, and from there to the butler's cottage, the larder of which contained the entrance to a tunnel that led directly to the pantry of the Grange . . .

His thoughts and the blackness of the night were disrupted by a flash of lightning. The mare jibed and neighed her fear. She was an unlovely creature with a hammer head and a jolting gait that caused Harry's arm to throb ever more wearyingly so that he thought with longing of his so-missed Lace and her sweetly smooth and untiring gallop. The hack had bottom, at least, for he'd set a wickedly dangerous pace through the storm, drawing heavily on his knowledge of the road. He'd no sooner had the thought than the mare shied. A carriage was halted at the branching of the road ahead, the guard holding his lantern so as to read the signpost which informed the traveller that Horsham lay ten miles to the northeast, and Haslemere ten miles northwest.

A shout from the carriage was followed by a small scream. The lantern drew a blue gleam from the musket the coachman levelled at Harry. He reined in at once, holding up his right hand, and shouted over the clamour of the wind an offer to be of assistance. Apparently reassured by his cultured accents, the coachman howled, "How's the road to Horsham, sir?" to which Harry replied, "Awful, I don't doubt. Take it slowly or you'll lose a wheel at the least."

A feminine voice called, "Sir! Pray come here!" and he walked the mare to the carriage, narrowing his eyes against a flurry of wind-driven rain. "Oh, sir," the voice was pleasant and sounded to be that of a mature lady in some

257

perturbation of mind. "Are we safe upon this road? I've heard Devil Dice preys upon those who journey hereabouts." She leaned to the open window as she spoke, the guard's lantern illuminating her plumply pretty face.

"Why, you look to be well-protected, ma'am," said Harry. "But were I you, I'd slip that necklace under the squabs."

Her white hand flew to her bosom and the diamonds that sparkled there. "Oh, but I should feel unclad without them!" She moved closer, saying flirtatiously, "Such a charming smile as you have, dear sir. We've met before—no?"

"I fear that pleasure has been denied me. Do you travel alone, ma'am?"

"No, my sister is with me." She drew up the fur-lined hood of her pelisse. "She is under the seat, foolish creature! We should have reached Horsham long since but were delayed by first one piece of trivia, then another. And finally were forced off the road by a most cloddish crew and all but overturned!"

Harry tensed. "I wonder could it be the coach I am striving to come up with. Were there outriders?"

"Several. And a more surly lot I never encountered. Not the type you would associate with, I am very sure! Are you . . . quite positive we have not met before, sir? Good gracious, my mind must be getting addled, for of late I seem to see you everywhere! Could it have been in Paris? I would swear . . ."

Her bright eyes searched his face uncertainly. Harry assured her he could not have forgotten so charming a lady and was favoured by a rippling laugh, the notification that he was a saucy rogue, and the extension of a small, gloved hand through the open window. He kissed it impudently, bade her farewell, and rode on. "A more surly lot I never encountered . . ." It *had* to be Sanguinet's party! He had guessed rightly!

The rain did not fall as drenchingly in the Home Wood, but all about was the thrash and rattle of tossing branches; leaves and debris filled the air, and the occasional muffled crash of some great limb falling bore witness to the fury of the storm.

Leading the frightened mare, Harry progressed steadily and could not but be grateful for the uproar. When he had come to the top of the hill he'd watched the lodge gates for some time and thus discerned an occasional glow that spoke of a cigar or pipe. Guards were posted, probably armed with orders to shoot first and question later. He had made a wide detour therefore and now, knowing every inch of these woods, came at last in sight of the butler's cottage. A light gleamed in the parlour window, but he saw no sign of movement inside. Joseph was no longer here, of course; but before he left, would he have bothered to remove the key from under the loose brick by the step? The audaciousness of entering through the front door was appealing. He tied the mare, strove to quiet her jumpy nerves for a minute, then started forward only to be staggered by a mighty gust. From somewhere above him came a deafening crack and a dark mass smashed to earth scant feet away. The mare screamed, bucked and reared frenziedly. Running for her, Harry was too late and she tore free and fled into the night. If she was seen, his presence would be made known. Still, she'd run off to the north, away from the main house. With luck she'd go clear to the boundary and onto Westhaven's preserves with none the wiser. Meanwhile, the sooner he was about his business the better.

He leapt the small picket fence, ran across the debris-littered patch of lawn, and flattened himself in the shadows of the tall yew hedge beside the door. Lightning flared in a brilliant betrayal that laid bare his place of concealment; but after long, tense seconds there was still no sign of reprisal and he crept to the doorstep. The key was there! He snatched it up, breathed a triumphant, "Aha!" and peered in through the parlour window. A scrawny-looking woman was asleep in the armchair beside the fire. Harry fitted the key very carefully into the lock and raised the latch. The door creaked a little as it swung open and his eyes darted to the sleeper; but despite that small sound and the blustery rush of air, she made no movement, continuing to snore softly. He closed the door, wiped his muddy boots thoroughly, then tiptoed to the kitchen.

By the faint light from the parlour he discerned muddle and disorder, with many unwashed pots and pans lying about. The shelves lining the larder were no neater. Harry carefully lifted out the lowest of the shelves against the rear wall, revealing the narrow blackness of the aperture beneath. This was the entrance to the priest's hole, that ancient escape route thanks to which many youthful indiscretions had been committed. As he started to put the shelf down, the end struck the wall with a crash he'd have thought would wake the dead. He stood tensely, cursing his clumsiness, his ears straining; but the soft rasp of the woman's snoring continued smoothly, and he could breathe again. He balanced the shelf carefully on a pile of empty bottles, then crept into the kitchen to appropriate a candle and tinderbox from the table. He slipped them into his pocket, went back to the larder, and deposited a piece of currant cake into his other pocket. He was taking up the shelf again when the front door slammed wide and a man's voice bawled, "May? Are ye awake, old woman? I'm cold and wet and starved!"

The kitchen began to brighten to the approach of a lamp. His heart pounding, Harry knelt, snatched up the shelf, and backed down the remembered old steps, groping his way and lowering the shelf into place over his head as heavy footsteps thumped into the kitchen. He heard a rattle of crockery and the woman whining her mystification over where the candle could've got to. He fumbled for the tinderbox, lit the candle and, shielding the flame cautiously, scanned the shelf above him. One of the threadbare cleaning rags it held was hanging through! It might not be discovered for weeks; on the other hand, did anyone seize it, the tunnel would be found and his life might well be forfeit. He tiptoed down the narrow steps, poured some melted wax onto the lowest step, and settled the candle into the puddle. Creeping upwards again, the man's coarse voice was clear.

". . . won't never escape him again, I can tell ye! Stupid

chit! And if that there Redmond shows his nose, we're ready for *him*!"

"D'ye suppose the Frenchy'll kill him, Shotten?"

Shotten! So Devil Dice lived in Joseph's cottage! Harry lifted the shelf a fraction, dreading it might scrape and betray him. Light glared into his eyes and he saw to his horror that Dice stood scant feet away.

"I hope he does!" barked the highwayman. "Monsewer never has forgive me fer saying I put a period to him and then him turning up alive where we didn't dare dish him!"

Dice halted before the shelves and began to rummage about. Holding his breath, Harry edged his way downwards.

"One of these days," said Shotten, "I'll get loose o' that damned Frog, and— Hey! What's this?" Harry's heart jumped into his throat. He eased the shelf into place and pressed back against the mouldering wall. "Why—dang ye, May! You went and et my piece o' that cake! Here I come home after a hard day . . ."

Staying for no more, Harry sighed with relief and started off. The low, narrow passage, doubtfully reinforced here and there by rotting timbers and bricks, was shrouded by webs that assured him nobody had passed through for a long time. He ate the cake as he went; it was dry and heavy but took the edge off his hunger, and he grinned, picturing Shotten's rage had he but known the man they sought was dining at his expense. He hurried on through the chill, musty gloom, crouching low and encountering only spiders and a solitary mouse during his journey. Surely he now held the advantage of surprise, for most of Sanguinet's men were guarding the grounds and no one would expect him to suddenly appear inside the house. With luck he might be able to find Nanette and win her away without being detected, though he would likely have to wait until everyone was abed. It shouldn't be too long a wait, for it was already long after midnight . . .

It never occurred to him that he was rushing headlong into an enemy stronghold, that he had no weapons and was hopelessly outnumbered. He thought only of his love, and vengeance.

CHAPTER XVI

THE GREAT HOUSE WAS VERY QUIET WHEN HARRY AT LAST judged it safe to open the panel. The shelves no longer contained the large bread bins but were crowded with dairy products, some of which had been carelessly propped against the rear wall and were displaced by its motion. He heard something topple and even as his eyes rested upon the middle shelf, several eggs sailed past to land with soft crunches on the floor. He listened tensely, but aside from the kitchen cat who at once investigated this fortuitous event, there was no disturbance. Harry began to clear the shelf, but the space was small and the Sergeant's coat cumbersome. He slipped out of the coat, deciding he could reclaim it on the way back, and crawled through the aperture. The pantry door was partly open; lights still burned in the kitchen but he heard no sound as he closed the panel. The cat looked up at him warily but, when he stooped to stroke her, resumed her self-imposed task of tidying up the eggs remaining. His eye caught by a pitcher of ale, Harry bore her company for a moment while he drank thirstily, thinking that it was dashed considerate of whomever had designed the tunnel to begin and end it in a pantry. Distantly, a clock chimed the hour. Three. By now most of the servants would have retired . . . He tiptoed to the kitchen door and pushed it open a crack. The familiar room stretched before him, neat and empty. He strode swiftly across it, running one hand caressingly along the tabletop. Entering the flagged corridor, nostalgia tightened its grip on him. Home . . . The home where he and Mitch and his father had been so happy. He was dazzled then by a lightning flash. A reverberating peal of thunder drowned his footsteps as he hastened towards the stairs. A few feet ahead, the door to the small saloon swung open suddenly and a footman backed out carrying a tray piled with teacups and a teapot. Harry made a dive for the open door of the main dining room. He flattened himself against the wall in the darkened room, and the footman grumbled past en route to the kitchen.

Harry uttered a sigh of relief, then ran lightly down to the saloon. He leaned to the door, but could detect only male voices—no little shrew . . . Across the wide central hall, light glowed from under the library doors. At any moment the footman might finish in the kitchen, but with luck would go straight to the rear stairs. Harry made a dash for it, down the corridor, across the hall, and to the sweep of the curving staircase, where he halted abruptly. A gentleman was sauntering down those stairs. A dark, well-built, elegant young man of moderate height, one arm carried in a sling, who paused also, took in the intruder's shabby garb but intrepid manner and, with an amused lift of well-shaped brows, enquired calmly, "Have I perhaps the honour to address Sir Harry Redmond?"

"Damn!" thought Harry. He bowed. "M. Guy Sanguinet?"

Sanguinet bowed in turn, contriving to make the gesture graceful despite his injury and his position on the stairs. With a twinkle in his hazel eyes he observed, "You are of an impudence, sir!"

"All in the point of view," Harry pointed out coolly. And thinking that Guy bore little resemblance to Parnell, added, "This happens to be *my* house."

The thin lips took on a cynical twist. "And you have come home to die, *enfin*?"

"I have come in pursuit of the murderer who killed my father."

Sanguinet restored his hand to the railing and shook his head. "*Mais non.* Your papa shot himself, as I told your brother. I regret to have to—'' Amazingly, a long-barrelled pistol of gleaming silver seemed to leap into the hand in the sling and was aimed steadily at Harry's heart, wherefore he checked his forward plunge. Sanguinet nodded gravely. ''The quarrel with you, Redmond, I have not. Give me your word to leave Moiré as you came, and—''

''The devil I will!'' Surprised nonetheless by this leniency, Harry exclaimed, ''Do you seriously expect me to leave Miss Carlson to your brother's tender mercies?''

''Ah . . .'' The Frenchman's eyes became very still. ''Our triangle becomes a quartet. The lady have tell you, perhaps, that I too love her?'' Harry nodded and Sanguinet said with a wry shrug, ''But not, *tristement*, that she return my affection. Even so, you may be assured I do not permit that she is abused.''

''May I? Yet you stood meekly by and watched your brother flog a helpless boy half to death!''

Sanguinet all but cringed. He said nothing, however, and moved down to the next stair.

The wind outside was so fierce now that Harry had to lean closer to make himself heard. ''I am told you are a gentleman. Your brother is not. And you certainly know what he intends for Miss Carlson.''

Brief but stark despair flashed across Sanguinet's face. ''Permit that I say this—but you risk your life if—''

''No more than you, apparently, since you creep about concealing a pistol! Did you intend, perhaps, to use it on—''

His words were drowned in a bellow of thunder that shook the floor and rattled the windows. Simultaneously, the kitchen cat shot from the corridor, skidded in the hall, and tore up the stairs. Sanguinet's eyes widened in surprise. Harry sprang up the few steps separating them and grabbed for the pistol. He knew somehow that Guy would not summon aid—that this was purely between the two of them. And it was so. Struggling desperately, they stumbled downward. Both men were young, and each hampered by an injury. Evenly matched, therefore, they strove in grim silence for possession of the weapon, the ravening storm drowning the sounds of their efforts.

"Fool!" gasped Guy as they reached the lowest stair. "You will be . . . discovered . . . at any moment! Now go—and I swear—I shall not betray you."

"But—you are a Sanguinet," panted Harry. "Wherefore . . . your word is without value."

Guy swore and heaved mightily. Gasping with pain, Harry staggered, but Sanguinet was swaying, his face convulsed, the pistol wavering. Harry released his hold on it and struck instead for the jaw, connecting true and hard. Sanguinet's head jerked back; he crumpled, and Harry caught him and eased him to the floor. He ripped off the sling, untied it and, taking the fabric between his strong teeth, wrenched with his right hand until it tore. Working rapidly, he bound Sanguinet hand and foot, using the remaining strip for a gag. He then dragged the unconscious man to the well beneath the stairs, cursing under his breath at the pain this caused him. Returning, he snatched up the pistol and strode to the library doors. Lightning glared vividly. He waited for the peal, then opened the door.

The two who faced each other before the fire were too intent upon their discussion to be cognizant of his coming, and he shot the heavy bolt carefully and strolled toward them.

". . . anything in this world—only name it," Parnell Sanguinet was saying grandly. As usual, he was clad in black relieved only by the white gleam of his cravat and the lace at his cuffs, his sombre garb accentuating the vivid beauty of the girl who drew back from his outstretched arms. A very different lady this, Harry thought with a pang, from his little shrew. She was elegant in pale green sarsenet, emeralds glowing at throat and ears, an emerald comb among the shining curls upon her head, and that head flung back, her attitude reflecting loathing. "There is *nothing*—in this entire world—that could induce me to share life with you," she said clearly. "Sooner would I be dead! And Guy will never allow you to—"

Undeterred, he paced closer. "Buy Guy, dear child, will do as I wish."

"You underestimate him," observed Harry, the pistol very steady in his right hand.

"*Sacré bleu!*" The ejaculation was hissed out as the Frenchman whipped around to crouch, unmoving, before the menace of the pistol. Nanette uttered a gasping cry, her locked hands held before her mouth, her eyes reflecting a mingling of joy and terror. Lightning flashed once more, and Harry's skin crawled as the glow seemed captured in the pale slitted eyes, so that for an instant it was as if he faced a wild beast rather than a man. Without glancing to Nanette, he asked gently, "Are you all right, little one?"

"Yes, yes! Oh—but you should not have come!"

Sanguinet straightened. A small pulse beat beside his jaw, but he smiled and murmured, "*Vraiment!* You have walk into my web, Redmond. Most unwise."

"Oh, but I do believe you have spun your last web, monsieur."

"Mitchell!" exclaimed Nanette. "Harry—he is not—"

"He's alive. No thanks to this carrion." He gestured contemptuously to her stepfather.

Sanguinet's eyes widened at the epithet. "I think," he murmured, "you will regret that insult. And I think also that you dare not shoot, poor fellow, for my men they would hear."

"Perhaps you should not refine overmuch on that either." The drawl was lazy but the glitter in the green eyes almost gave Sanguinet pause until he recalled that he held all the cards in this deadly game. "You can do nothing," he shrugged. "*Délicieux*, is it not? Even have I do everything you and my lovely Annabelle suspect, I am the diplomatist. I represent a government with which your Foreign Office is of an anxiety to improve relations. They do not risk the international incident for merely the foolish little tragedy you tell them."

"Governments be damned!" Harry flashed. "You'll answer to me for your crimes! And your sword can speak for you—not your glib tongue!"

"*Allons, donc! Allons!* How may you accuse me of a crime when *you* are already totally without the credit? Can it be possible, monsieur, you have not yet see my posters? Your England is very full of them—all having your likeness and naming you the kidnapping rapist who have steal my so-loved daughter." He chuckled softly. "Ah, but how pale you are become, *mon ami*—and with reason—for truly you are a marked man. Do any of your so-upright British peasants lay the eye upon you and you are hung by your heels before two words you may speak!"

Cold fingers shivered down Harry's spine, but he said scornfully, "Gammon! You'd not do so, for it would ruin Nanette completely, and—"

"And do but think, Redmond, how gallant I shall then seem in the eyes of the world—to take this shamed girl and give her my noble name."

"You filthy scum!" Harry's finger tightened on the trigger. "You *would* ruin her—just to force her to—"

Perceiving belatedly that his gloating had carried him too far, Sanguinet said sharply, "Kill me, and it shall but lend the credence to my posters!"

Nanette, who had stood in stunned silence, now intervened, "Harry! Do not! I think I have found a way to prove some of our suspicions, at all events! Papa's coach has folding inner walls which can be closed to conceal the centre. They are very cleverly painted so as to indicate empty seats and a far window, and to anyone casually glancing inside, the carriage would be apparently unoccupied. We have only to tell the Bow Street people, and—"

"By God!" Harry exclaimed exuberantly. "So that's how it was done! We—"

A branch crashed against the windows and glass shredded into the room. The draperies billowed inward, the wind blowing out all the candles. Nanette gave an involuntary cry of shock, and Harry's anxious glance flashed to her. Untroubled by a concern for any but himself, Sanguinet snatched up a candelabrum and with a savage swipe, smashed the pistol from Harry's hand. In an instantaneous reaction, Harry's left hand clamped around that flailing wrist and twisted; the candelabrum went clattering down. Sanguinet wrenched away and darted for the long library table. A smallsword lay on that table, the jewelled hilt winking in the fire light. He whipped the blade from the scabbard and spun about, the steel whistling through the air in a deadly arc that forced the pursuing Harry to leap desperately aside.

"*En garde!*" cried Sanguinet, and advanced, the sword circling.

Harry retreated, his eyes probing the dimness for something with which to defend himself.

"Papa! I beg of you!" Nanette implored. "He has no weapon!"

Her stepfather stopped at once and, slanting a teasing glance at her, asked, "You will wed me, then, do I spare this one?"

"Yes . . ." she said in anguished helplessness. "Anything! Only—"

"Only—*hell!*" grated Harry and, vaulting the sofa, snatched a poker from the hearth, then flung himself clear of the blade that flashed not an inch from his ribs.

"*Sottise, mon petit chou!*" cried Sanguinet gleefully. "You will wed me irregardless!" Even as he spoke he was swaying away from Harry's powerful thrust. "How sad— is it not sad, Anabelle? His weapon is ill chosen—it is too short. *Voilà!*"

Like a streak of white fire his point shot for Harry's chest. Harry twisted with lithe ease, and if the sword ripped through his sleeve, his poker struck home also, slamming down across Sanguinet's outflung left hand so that a shout of pain was drawn from the Frenchman.

A thunderous barrage rang out. The door to the hall shook, and anxious voices cried, "Monseigneur! M. Guy has been beaten! Monseigneur!"

"Break down the door!" shouted Sanguinet. The amusement had vanished from his face, for what he had imagined a comfortably one-sided game had lost its charm. His hand hurt, and M. Parnell Sanguinet did not like to be hurt. "I have deal with your papa," he snarled, "and your so-foolish impertinence of a brother. With you, *Monsieur le Capitaine*, I shall be less kind!''

He was no mean swordsman and his fierce attack sent Harry reeling back, deflecting the flurry of thrusts as best he might. A sustained pounding from the doors rivalled the occasional peals of thunder, but those doors were old and solid . . . With luck they might hold until he triumphed—for triumph he would, by God! He was at a slight disadvantage, perhaps, but he *must* win, for Papa, and Mitch, and to free his beloved from this insane satyr!

Appalled by the ferocity of the fast-moving struggle, Nanette disregarded both the cacophony of the mounting storm and the assault upon the doors, her entire concentration on that murderous smallsword and Harry's hopelessly ineffectual poker. She marvelled at his skill, his sure and agile movements, his unyielding defence and occasional attack. Time and again he eluded death by a whisper. Time and again the sword was beaten aside, the fierce lunges evaded. She pressed her hand to her mouth, praying the outcome was not inevitable, and running clear when the deadly battle swept towards her.

Sanguinet fought mostly in *sexte*, only occasionally shifting into *quatre*. He was very skilled, but had they been equally armed, Harry felt he would have had a good chance. He soon discovered, however, that his opponent possessed one inestimable advantage: He could see in the dark! The strange eyes that had been so narrowed by day were wide now, the movements swiftly unerring, whereas Harry was unfamiliar with the new furniture placement, and the flickering light of the fire cast deep shadows, which added to his peril. Again Parnell was attacking, the thrust almost catching his side. At the last instant he struck the blade upward but, leaping in for what might have been a telling blow, tripped over an unseen footstool, tumbled heavily, and only saved himself by a frantic roll to the side. He sprang up on the instant, but he was panting; and scanning his face, Sanguinet laughed softly. ''You have hurt your arm, yes? And only look at how the hand it is swollen. I wonder, *mon ami*—could it, do you think, have . . . mortified . . ?''

Thunder shook the house and a new barrage rattled the doors. Sanguinet's lunge was blindingly fast, and a long rent appeared in the side of Harry's jacket, his jump back having been just a shade too slow. Nanette thought frenziedly. ''My dear God! He is getting tired!''

The flash of lightning was very close and a vivid blue-white; Sanguinet blinked, his eyes squinting. Harry jumped forward; his poker smashed the blade down, then rammed hard under the Frenchman's ribs. Sanguinet's mouth flew open, his eyes started out, and he doubled up and went to his knees, the sword tumbling from his hand.

With a cry of triumph, Harry tossed the poker away and scooped up the smallsword. He was breathing hard, sweat streaked his face, and his arm throbbed mercilessly. But he was elated, and as Nanette ran to him, sobbing her relief, he swept her into a brief, fierce hug.

Both arms folded across his middle, choking for breath, Sanguinet straightened slowly, to find the point of his own blade at his throat and beyond it the pale, grim face of a man who had every reason to kill without mercy. ''Please!'' he gasped. ''Please . . . do *not*! I will pay . . you . . !''

''Fool! What price would you put on my father's life? My brother's self-respect? You are a murdering, slimy apology for a human being—*say* it!''

Sanguinet wet dry lips. ''I am . . . a murdering . . . slimy apology for . . . a human being! *Anything*! What do you want? Name it! I do not wish . . . to be dead.''

Harry had not expected such a craven display and said with a curl of the lip, ''You whining cur! My brother has more courage in his little finger than—'' He checked as a shot roared above the howl of the wind and the wood of the door splintered, but the bolt held. ''Devil take you,'' he gritted. ''I would dearly love to watch you hang, but— I'd just as lief kill you by my own hand! And I will—does that door fall!''

Death glared in his eyes, and Sanguinet yowled a frantic command so that at once his men ceased their efforts.

"Paper and pen, little one," said Harry. "Quickly, now." She ran to obey, and he went on, "I want a written confession, Sanguinet. Everything! My father, and Schofield— How *did* you entrap Barney?"

"He w-was devoted to his wife . . . May I please get up now?"

Harry said inexorably, "We were, I believe, discussing Grace Schofield."

Sanguinet whimpered, "She—she adores that . . . miserable weakling of a son."

"Yes. Probably even more now that he is blind—poor devil."

"He—m-misappropriated funds . . . from the Officers Club.—No! Do not! I have help . . . Schofield! I swear, by *le bon Dieu*! I help him keep it quiet!"

"And your price was my father's life!" snarled Harry. "You damned nail! That scandal would have destroyed Grace, and Barney worshipped her! I *knew* it had to be something like that! By thunder, but you don't deserve to live!"

Sanguinet cringed back, but was reprieved as Nanette brought a Standish and paper. "Up—foulness!" Harry gave the kneeling man a hard prod. "We—"

The lightning this time lit every corner of the room with an unearthly blue glare. There was an ear-splitting explosion. The house shuddered to a tremendous shock, and the entire front wall burst inward. Harry was conscious of a heavy odour of sulphur, and glass and bricks raining down. In that split second he knew that the great oak had been struck and was crashing into the room. His reaction was instinctive. He grasped Nanette and pulled her away from the hail of branches and debris. In an equally instinctive reaction, Sanguinet whipped a small pistol from a desk drawer, only to be sent sprawling as the room became a ravening chaos.

With arms tight about his love, Harry saw a dark mass hurtling at them and shoved her violently away. Icy wet leaves whipped about him; twigs raked down his face. A

271

staggering shock; a great weight driving the breath from his lungs. The darkness became absolute.

The smell of smoke was heavy in the room, and Sanguinet's voice, shrill and hysterical, keened through the darkness. "You *cannot* escape me! This I swear!" Dazed, Harry muttered, "Are we . . . in your realm then? Don't seem . . . hot enough . . ."

"Harry!" A soft hand slapped gently at his cheek. "Oh, Harry . . . please . . . I cannot move it. *Please*, wake up!"

He responded at once to the note of panic in that dear voice and strove to rise, but in vain. A branch across his shoulder pinned him on his left side and something was grinding into his back so that he could scarcely breathe. The lightning's next flare revealed Nanette bending over him, her hair tumbled and thick with dust, the dirt on her face channelled by tears. He also caught a glimpse of Sanguinet digging himself from under a pile of rubble and the sheer disaster that was his papa's so-loved library, with books and furniture scattered and buried under branches, splintered wood, and bricks. When the thunderclap died away, he commanded, "Nanette, go quickly! Is the door clear?"

"No. They tried to get in, but it is quite blocked. And I will *not* leave you!" She tugged at the branch desperately.

After a wracking effort, Harry panted, "It is—no . . . use. If they've half the brains . . . God gave 'em, they'll come in through . . . the wall. Nanette—stop! Can you not understand? If we are both caught, we are both doomed. If *you* get away, he will not dare—"

"I won't! I won't! Harry—try! I beg you! Try!"

"He will but waste the time!" yowled Sanguinet, scrabbling frantically about. "Do not imagine, Redmond, that you live to boast of tricking me into have kneel at your feet! For that you die slowly—by my soul, I swear it!"

A muffled sob escaped Nanette. "There! It gave a little, I think! Push!"

Harry's back was commencing to regain some feeling,

which was miserably unfortunate, but he strove until the sweat ran into his eyes. "For the love of God—go!" he gasped out. "We're fairly at Point Non-Plus, little shrew. Get to Cancrizans Priory—it's near a village called Pudding Park, in Dorset. I have . . . good friends there. They'll know what to do."

She put one hand to her brow, weeping in so distraught a fashion that he forced a harsh, "Blast it all! Do you *want* him to murder me? With you safely away, he won't dare! Go!" She bent above him and he caught a faint vestige of perfume as her lips brushed his cheek; then she was gone. But the next flash revealed Sanguinet staggering to his feet and beginning to search about, and knowing for what he sought, Harry gritted his teeth and fought madly to escape.

"Do not so distress yourself . . ." A lurid glare was beginning to flicker through the darkness, and by that glow Sanguinet looked quite crazed, covered with grime, hair awry, lips drawn back from grinning teeth, eyes gleaming redly. And in his hand, a small black pistol.

Harry abandoned his futile efforts. "Another—perfect crime?"

"More, shall I say—'tidy' at the least. Permit that I tell you, Redmond. To the very last I think your papa he will elude me. My scheme, he is *meticuleux*, but almost I am foiled! At the finish, I have him, though! He was, dear my friend, quite aware when I aim the pistol. Just as I now do. He is paralyze from the drug, but he have watch me and see what is coming . . ." His giggle sent a blazing rage through Harry, but sensing that such an emotion would gratify his tormentor, he said with cool aplomb, "Poor chap. Your loft is really full of maggots, isn't it."

The hand holding that black and deadly pistol jerked. Sanguinet said purringly, "*Insouciant*—how admirable. But think on this while you lie here and wish to be dead—I shall find my Annabelle . . . Ah, that take away your smile, no?" His finger tightened on the trigger. "In the spine, I think, will give you sufficient time to repent . . ." He took careful aim. Harry felt sick; he had seen men die from such a wound and could only pray he'd not make too much of a cake of himself.

The explosion was sharp and deafening.

Sweating, his teeth gritted tight, Harry felt nothing more than the misery he presently endured.

An expression of unspeakable dread was on Sanguinet's face. He coughed and, striving to raise the sagging pistol, choked horribly, sank to his knees, and pitched forward.

For a long moment Harry gazed disbelievingly at his huddled shape. Then he looked up. Nanette stood very still amid the wreckage, Guy Sanguinet's silver pistol dangling from her hand.

The wind howled, the rain drummed, and from somewhere outside, fire sent an ever brighter glare filtering through the smashed wall to play upon three people who moved not at all.

A crash and a flurry of distant shouts roused Harry. Nanette must not be found here! He called her name, but she made no response, continuing to gaze with that awful concentration at her stepfather. "Nanette!" he pleaded. "little one . . . my shrew!" The last term drew her wide gaze to him, the horror in the big eyes giving way to an agony of despair that wrung his heart. "My brave girl! Never look so—he was not worth one instant of your grief!" But her expression was unchanged, save that now she shuddered violently. "Help me," he cried urgently. "Little one—I need you!"

She came at once to stand looking down at him, keeping her head turned from Sanguinet. Harry waited out a deafening peal of thunder, then asked her to find something to use as a lever. She obeyed numbly and, returning with a bookshelf trailing behind her, heaved at it until she was able to thrust it under the branch, then threw all her lithe young strength against it. Harry strove mightily, and at last, with a twist that made him groan under his breath, was able to crawl clear.

The branch crashed down as he scrambled to his feet, but Nanette stood unmoving, her eyes once again upon her stepfather. Harry tottered stiffly to take the bookshelf she still held and toss it aside. He pulled her into his arms and she clung to him, whimpering, "What a ghastly, ghastly . . . thing . . !"

He had expected the shot to result in an immediate resumption of the assault of the door. That it had not done so he attributed either to the fact that Sanguinet's men were making their way around to the front of the house so as to enter through the wreckage, or that they were all occupied with the burning tree. In either case, to leave the library by way of the break in the wall might well be to walk into a vengeful reception. He glanced to the hall door, but it was hopelessly blocked. Certainly, to stay where they were would be disastrous . . . He knew the girl was watching him and, not wishing to further frighten her, replied calmly, "Yes. Well, I rather think we should toddle off, little one. We have likely outworn our welcome here . . ."

She neither responded nor followed as he turned away, but when he reached back and took her hand, accompanied him meekly. He guided her carefully through the rubble, his way lighted by the lurid glow that grew ever brighter. When they reached the shattered wall, he told her to wait in the deeper shadows while he reconnoitred and was inwardly astounded by the placid quiet with which she obeyed. He clambered stiffly through the ragged aperture and was at once plunged into a maelstrom of wind and rain, the howling gusts interspersed by a deal of confused shouting. The oak tree had always seemed large, but stretched on the ground it was enormous. It was not burning as he had supposed; the upper floor of Moiré was ablaze. Mitchell's room must have been struck by the same bolt that had felled the tree. A bucket brigade had been organized, and many men strove frenziedly against the roaring flames. For a second, Harry stood motionless, his heart twisting; then he swung quickly back to lift Nanette over the wall and into the fortuitous screen of the branches.

She made no attempt to protect herself from the lash of wind and rain, and he wrapped his jacket about her and gently placed her hand on the front to hold it closed. Peering at her through the leaping red glow he saw a faint, remote smile on her dirty little face, and fear touched him. He slipped his arm protectively about her and, shivering, led her down the slope toward the Home Wood. For as long as he was able, he kept the bulk of the downed oak between them and the fire fighters, but soon they were crossing the pleasure gardens, the glare of the fire all about them, and no concealment at hand. With every step he expected they would be seen, but their luck held from one taut moment to the next. They were almost to the river when he heard a howled, "*Murder*! Monseigneur's been shot in the back! Look for Redmond! Murder!" He swore under his breath and pulled Nanette into a run over the old stone bridge. " '. . . shot in the back . . !' Lord! What a mess!"

They were down the far side of the bridge, then running through sodden fern and bracken and, at last, into the Home Wood. If only he had his hack! Still, they'd a good chance now. Perhaps—

A bell began to ring urgently, awakening new shouts, distant but ahead of them. Harry stopped, and Nanette halted at once. He glanced down at her, this precious small shape in the darkness, waiting, trusting in him. He patted her hand encouragingly and led her to the west, and she stumbled along, making no complaint when she fell to her knees, nor thanking him when he helped her up. The rain was icy, and even beneath the trees the wind was exhausting in its endless buffeting. Harry's shirt clung wetly against him and his teeth began to chatter with the cold. Excited voices were coming from all sides now, the bell having summoned men in from the gatehouse and the road. With utter desperation, he knew that whatever else, he *must* get Nanette clear; but as they stumbled around a fallen branch, a man sprang out before them. A broad-shouldered individual clad in a long driving coat of multiple capes. He was hatless, his wet hair shining a dull gold in the shielded beam of the lantern he held, seeing which, Harry's thundering heart eased and he gasped out an incredulous, "Jerry? How in God's name did you find us?"

"Andy said you had c-come here," advised Lord Jeremy Bolster. "And I heard an insolent fellow at your lodge-gate whining about keeping a weather eye out for you." The beam of his lantern played briefly on Nanette's face and was lowered. "Guessed you was already past the gudgeon, so I p-p-paddled in after you. Thought I heard a shot a minute ago, but probably mistook it, eh?"

"No," said Harry. "Nanette, this is my good friend Jeremy Bolster."

She turned a mild smile upon his lordship, and Harry added swiftly, "She's too upset to talk."

"Jolly sensible," said Bolster unhesitatingly. "Ain't the time nor place. My chaise is hidden on the north side of the hill." He directed another brief beam at his friend and as they started off said severely, "Really, old pippin, you look as if you'd been teasing a B-Bengal tiger!"

Harry touched his scratched face. "Worse than that, I'm afraid. I just shot Parnell Sanguinet."

"Very public-spirited," said Bolster, with only the barest of pauses.

"In the back," Harry added.

This time his lordship's aplomb deserted him, and despite the voice of the storm, his gasp was audible. "Now that was d-dashed clumsy, Harry! Not the thing at all. No wonder his people are a trifle annoyed!"

The searchers were coming closer. They sounded very annoyed, indeed.

"Blow out your damned lantern," said Harry gruffly.

"R-r-run!" Bolster urged, having hurriedly obeyed.

"There is not the need to run," Nanette remarked in a matter-of-fact way. "You were perfectly justified, Harry. He would have killed you."

He bit his lip, then said very gently, "Yes, m'dear. But I don't think we'd best try to explain that now."

"What we'd best do," said Bolster, "is r-run like the devil!"

They ran, each man holding one of the girl's cold hands. She would be all right once she was warm and safe, thought Harry. And how very typical of Bolster to come and help. Dear, loyal old Jerry.

"Whoops!" breathed the object of his thoughts, and they darted for a sodden clump of fern, having all but run into the arms of several enthused searchers. They knelt there, scarcely daring to breathe while the men stamped and shouted past, then scrambled up and fled again. But soon, whichever way they turned, voices were before them, so that they had constantly to double back or hide, tense with apprehension, until they were at last surrounded and hopelessly cut off from the side of the hill where waited Bolster's chaise. In desperation they took refuge behind dense shrubs in a small hollow against the hillside that years since had been one of their 'caves'. Harry's good arm tightened about Nanette as a loud altercation broke out within yards of them. Still wrangling, the men moved off at last, but a new enemy was approaching; dawn was starting to brighten the east, and by that faint gleam, the eyes of the two friends met over Nanette's downbent head.

"Good chase, by God!" observed the dauntless Bolster.

"Damn near over," Harry whispered. "They almost have us. I'll lead 'em off."

"Don't be a f-fool! They won't find us here, and—"

Harry glanced down and inserted a regretful, " 'Fraid they might . . ."

"What?" Bolster grabbed for his wrist. "Good Lord!" His eyes flew to his friend's face, pale in the dimness. "Why the devil d-didn't you say something?"

"I thought it had stopped bleeding. At all events, it has now." He took his arm gently from about Nanette. "Get her away at once, Jerry. No hanging about waiting for me. Lord only knows which direction I'll finally—"

"Bacon brain!" hissed Bolster furiously. "You'll not get a mile! Sanguinet's stirred up a pr-proper hornet's nest. Says you kidnapped her and have sworn to kill her unless you're paid ten thousand in g-g-gold. You can imagine the public reaction to that tale! You're the v-villain of the century!"

Harry's lips set into a grim line, but he argued, "Miss Carlson will deny it. Take her to the Runners, and she'll clear my name."

"You'll be cold meat before we get her there!" Bolster thought unhappily that the chit looked incapable of recalling her *own* name, and said, "I shall go! That vicious herd out there will not dare put a period to me! Besides, even did you get clear it will take weeks to counteract Sanguinet's mischief and tear down his dashed posters. *No! Wait*, Harry—for heaven's sake! There's a thousand guineas on your head! *Dead or alive!*"

"Is there, by God! All the more reason Miss Carlson must not travel with me! A fine set-to *that* would be! And she is utterly exhausted, poor soul."

Thunder rumbled distantly and the rain seemed to be easing, but the hunt sounded ever fiercer and was sweeping back toward them. Harry pressed a kiss upon Nanette's cold brow, knowing he would probably never see her again, and she smiled up at him placidly.

"Dammit, Harry!" the distraught Bolster clamped a hand onto his shoulder. "Think, man—*think*! Sanguinet was shot *in the back*! When that's abroad, on top of all the rest, you will be fair game. There'll be no willingness to l-listen to the true facts, whatever they may be!"

"I t-told you what they were, d-devil take you," Harry shivered.

Bolster groaned. "If you don't mean to deny it, you're as good as dead! If you ain't lynched by some public-spirited rabble, you'll be— Oh, hell! What's the use! Here," he stripped off his coat. "B-best put this on. You s-sound worse than I do, and you're like a blanc-manger. She shot him, I collect?"

Harry flashed a startled glance to Nanette, but because of his own long battle with the effects of shock, Bolster knew the girl was far from this time and place, her mind cushioned from an event too horrible for endurance. A renewed crashing through the nearby undergrowth put a stop to any more talk. Then a voice Harry recognized as that of Shotten howled triumphantly for "Tom" to come and rest his ogles on "this here!" Harry gripped Bolster's hand. "Jerry, he was her *father*! She *must* not be seen near me, with them believing I killed him. Can you not see the

newspapers, the crowds, the trial? For God's sake, man—
help her! Promise!''

"Of course—but, oh damme, you're in no condition
to—''

"Gudgeon—I've come through worse than a scratch on
my arm! Now stay quiet until I'm well away.''

Bolster pressed a fat purse into his hand and snarled,
"Birdwit! Head for the Priory, or Beechmead. We'll do
whatever we—''

A flurry of approaching shouts chilled them both. Cautiously, Harry slipped through the shrubbery and moved
off a little way. Through the trees came Shotten, holding a
lantern low to the ground and leading a group of men inexorably towards the 'cave'. Harry reached up and pulled on
a branch. It broke with a loud crack and he began to run,
making no least effort to be silent. A howled chorus of
"There he goes!'' was followed by more excited shouts,
the thud of many feet, and then a shot and the wham of
the ball driving into a tree he passed. There would be more
shots he knew, wherefore he dodged about constantly during his flight. Nanette would be safe now, thank God, for
they were all pounding along behind him like so many silly
sheep. But he knew that they were not sheep: They were
angry men, lusting to kill . . . Rested men, who'd likely
enjoyed a good supper before being called upon. Whereas
he'd had a long and wearing day, and was not just at the
top of his form.

"Redmond,'' he thought wryly, "if you survived that
mess at Rodrigo only to be hung because of a stupid damn
bull, I shall take a very dim view of it!''

He ran faster, the vengeful crowd clamouring after him.

CHAPTER XVII

ONE THOUSAND GUINEAS REWARD!
WANTED—DEAD OR ALIVE
FOR
KIDNAPPING AND ASSAULT

WHEREAS, SIR HARRY ALLISON REDMOND, BART., LATE OF HILL STREET IN THE City of London, did upon the night of the Twelfth of May last, brutally steal and kidnap a certain unmarried lady of Quality, holding her CAPTIVE against her will; and having torn her from the bosom of her loving father and family, did cruelly Abuse, Terrorize, and Assault said young lady, thus causing her to suffer great Mental and Physical Anguish; the above REWARD, namely ONE THOUSAND GUINEAS, will be paid to such person or persons who shall APPREHEND or cause to be Apprehended said Sir Harry Allison Redmond. To the furtherance of which is hereunto added a close description of the same DANGEROUS KIDNAPPER: Viz. He stands five feet and eleven inches, and is of powerful build. His hair is near black; his eyes narrow and of an unusual green; his complexion sallow and his demeanour hostile. He is believed to have a wound in his left forearm. When last seen he was clad in a torn brown corduroy jacket, grey pantaloons, and worn brown shoes.

APPROACH WITH CAUTION! This Criminal is known to be Armed and DANGEROUS!

Harry ripped the poster from the signpost, limped to the doubtful sanctuary offered by the crumbling arch of a ruined bridge and, settling himself against the stones beneath it, contemplated the poster with revulsion. Each time he saw one of the things he damned Sanguinet bitterly. How even such as he could have deliberately subjected Nanette to public humiliation was beyond believing, and anyone who had read the first notice of her kidnapping could not but realize she was the lady referred to. The likeness of himself that was sketched below the words was, he had to admit, skillfully rendered. His expression had been changed somewhat—at least, he hoped it had been changed and that he did not habitually go about wearing such a cynical leer. A short final paragraph contained information for collecting the reward and advised that the kidnapper had last been seen in Sussex and might be expected to head for the coast. Harry's lips curled mirthlessly. Unhappily, his every attempt to do so had been thwarted.

The morning was damp and chill, and he wished he still had Jeremy's fine coat. He'd had to shed it hurriedly the previous dawn when a farm wife had come upon him in her chicken coop and had been so courageous as to seize one of the capes and hang on, screeching bloody murder. He'd attempted to point out that he had left more than sufficient cash to pay for the three eggs he'd gathered, but his protests had gone for nought. The woman had recognized him, and her yowls were for the innocent lady he'd brutalized—not for the products of her flock. Fortunately, her valour had not gone beyond hanging onto his coat and, having slipped out of that garment, he'd escaped just barely ahead of the charge of shot her husband had sent after him.

He crumpled the poster, leaned back his head, and closed his eyes; and his sigh was not because his arm throbbed so, or because he was cold and hungry, but for his love. Three days since he'd seen her—only three days, yet his heart felt bruised and his spirits were low. How could he endure a lifetime without the sparkle of those mischievous eyes, the ripple of the lilting laugh, the challenge of her seeking mind, the warmth of her generous heart . . ? Well, he must, somehow, for it was quite hopeless, even were he not a hunted fugitive, even if Sanguinet was not dead.

Many people lived out a lifetime denied the joy and companionship of love—yet they survived. If he could reach the coast and take ship . . . if he could escape without dragging his friends into his predicament, would he prove less resilient, less able to meet the challenge Fate had flung at him? Pride answered a fierce "No!" but love whispered, "Nanette . . . my little shrew . . ." and he sighed again.

He had learned a good deal these past three days; notably, that there was nothing more ghastly than to be despised by one's own countrymen, and that not all his combined privations in Spain could compare to the horrors of this brief time of being ruthlessly hunted. He had escaped Moiré by leading his pursuers in circles until he was reasonably sure that most of Sanguinet's men were hot on his heels, at which point he'd headed for the marshy ground at the foot of the hill and left them floundering in the mire. He'd doubled back to the road then and stolen a ride first on a passing cart of turnips and later in the day in a hay wain. He'd snuggled deep into that fragrant cargo and slept from pure exhaustion, only to be rudely awakened by the tine of a pitchfork slicing through the hay an inch from his nose. He had sprung up to find the wain halted in a farmyard bathed by a brilliant sunrise. Three muscular farmhands had gaped at him, then confirmed his impression of unfriendliness by sending a second pitchfork streaking for his chest. Not staying to rebuke them for such unmannerly conduct, he'd taken to his heels, the farmhands following suit with lusty enthusiasm. He had eluded them at last, but the incident had served to convince him that Jerry had spoken truly—Sir Harry Redmond was sought throughout the Southland.

After that he'd not dared travel during the daylight hours. The posters were everywhere and his description too accurate. For the first time in his life he was grateful that his beard grew rapidly and within a day or two would be sufficiently luxuriant to change his appearance. On Saturday he'd hidden through the daylight hours and spent the night trudging towards the sea, yet barely avoided a cluster of hunters watching the road from a hilltop, having apparently decided their valuable quarry would resort to nighttime travel. Sunday morning he had to run for his life from four hefty youths who recognized him despite his beard, and at dusk he was reduced to digging up carrots and potatoes to ease the pangs of hunger. That night he appropriated a threadbare woollen jacket from a barn, leaving two shillings to pay for it. He'd lost Bolster's purse when he abandoned the coat, and after paying for the jacket was reduced to a grand fortune of two shillings, a sixpence, and a groat. By Monday he was so changed in appearance he again attempted daylight travel, but was soon deterred by the several eager bands he dodged who were very obviously seeking him. To continue in the face of such odds would be foolhardy, and he'd hidden in a church-yard until dusk, then struck westward for Cancrizans Priory in Dorsetshire, stopping here when his enemy, dawn, began to light her celestial lamps.

His thought lingered on his beloved little shrew. Hope-fully, she was by now recovered from the effects of shock . . . in which case he thought with a tender smile, poor Bolster would have his work cut out to prevent the valiant girl from rushing headlong into some impulsive attempt to shield him by confessing her part in Sanguinet's death. Mitchell also haunted his reflections: That his brother would recover he was certain, but he dreaded the effect that vi-cious whipping might have on so highly strung and sensi-tive a young man.

Thus, Harry Redmond, Baronet. A few short weeks ago one of London's most admired Corinthians, now a ragged, hunted fugitive accused of hideous crimes, with little of hope and none of joy. Yet whose musings were perhaps less crushing than they might have been, if only because they turned so often not upon himself but on those he loved.

He fell asleep and awoke in early afternoon to warm sunshine. While washing, he saw so heavily bearded a stranger reflected in the stream that he was encouraged to step out bravely along a flower-bedecked lane. He came upon a pedlar who, having failed to sell him a hammer, a set of croquet mallets, or a device for extracting the juice of lemons, was overjoyed to trade his lunch for Harry's groat. The bread was a little stale, he confided (once the groat was safely in his purse), and the cheese might be a trifle mouldy, since it was his *yesterday's* lunch what he hadn't et since he'd been give a pie in exchange for a pair of scissors. Nonetheless, no meal at Watier's had ever pleased Harry more, and having consumed bread, cheese, and a dry currant bun, he felt renewed in both mind and body and went upon his way whistling cheerily.

He was soon on the borders of the New Forest and, entering that leafy retreat gratefully, stopped at the first stream he came to and attempted to bathe his hurt. The bandages were soiled and tattered and the gash much swollen, frighteningly angry looking, and so painful it was difficult to tend. He was concentrating on his task when he sensed the presence of others. He crouched, prepared for desperate combat, but looking up found himself surrounded by solemn-eyed gypsy children. They seemed unafraid, and when they addressed him in the Romany tongue, he guessed they believed him to be of their own people, which was not surprising in view of his tanned skin and abundant dark hair. He had always had a way with children, and his easy grin and gentle manner did not fail him now. Soon they were gathered around, helping as best they might. A small, motherly girl, shaking her head as she retied the bandage, told him sadly that it was "a very nasty place" and added that he would surely die within the week unless he came and let 'Gammer' heal it for him. Harry was possessed of a growing fear that the wound was mortifying, but was more afraid he would be recognized. He thanked her but refused, his explanations that he must get on his way being interrupted by a thoughtful boy, slightly older than the rest, who intervened to demand that they return home. Their resentment eased into laughter when Harry made a great show of kissing the hands of the girls and bowing with elaborate flourishes to the boys. His small nurse was, in fact, so captivated by this procedure that she returned to offer him her other hand, as well; and upon his properly saluting those little fingers, he was advised that if he would wait "a year or nine" she would marry him. He escaped this *contretemps* by confessing the prospect delightful but claiming the existence of a 'wife,' and since his lady love giggled and skipped blithely away, could not suppose she would grieve excessively. He watched her go, smiling at her sweet innocence, but when he turned, found the older boy frowning at him.

Suspecting himself rumbled, he said lightly, "Don't think she'll wear the willow for me, do you?"

The boy said nothing but brought from his pocket a much-folded sheet of paper and held it out, his eyes large with importance.

Taking this document, Harry unfolded it and looked upon a far grimmer poster, ominously headed with a royal 'G.R.' The reward stood now at an unprecedented Two Thousand Guineas, and to the crimes of Kidnapping, Assault, and Brutality, were added the cowardly murder of the gallant father of his victim. The details must wring the hardest heart in the land, and his description now included the item that his face was severely scratched, wherefore he would very likely grow a beard to cover those telltale marks. His heart sinking, Harry muttered, "Not much doubt who I am, is there?"

"They've took the niceness out of your eyes, sir. And made your mouth turn down 'stead of up."

"Thank you." And all too aware that his life was held in this child's hands, he pointed out quietly, "Two thousand guineas is a great amount of money."

"It be," the boy acknowledged with an odd dignity. "But we Romanys do know Devil Sanguinet. He served our people crool. Me granfer says they've made him out good, and if they'd lie about that, the whole lot's likely wrong."

This evidence of sagacity cheered Harry, and he asked for advice on the state of the hunt. He was warned not to go near the seacoast and that the country from here to Devonshire was being beaten for him by both the populace and the military. "Ye'll be took and hung in a hour, sir, does ye not turn about for Lunon—or the north."

If Harry was sure of anything, it was that his friends were fighting for him; but it was very evident that Bolster had been all too correct when he'd said it would take time. The murder, of course, had brought in the full power of the King's justice . . . and there would certainly be inter-national ramifications. His one chance was to get out of the country—to start life anew . . . "Them scratches," the boy was muttering uncertainly. "You didn't never *really* hurt the gentry-mort?"

"Good lad! No, I never so much as raised a hand . . ." Harry stopped, his thoughts on a sunlit clearing, the scene coming so vividly to mind that the boy wondered at the wistfulness in his eyes. "Well, and I'm a liar," he admitted, "for I boxed the lady's ears."

A broad grin spread over the small, dark face. "Were she obstrep'rous, sir? Me dad boxes Mum's ears be she obstrep'rous. Not as she minds nohow, for they always cuddly-kiss afterwards."

"She was . . . just a mite obstreperous," Harry smiled. "Yet I dare to think she forgave me, though we did not— ah, cuddly-kiss."

They shook hands, man to man, and calling, "I hope ye gets clean away! Kooshti divvus!" the boy ran lightly after his companions.

The woods seemed very lonely when all sounds of the children had died away. Staring at the sparkling riffles of the stream, Harry at last faced the truth. He could not hope to reach either the coast or Cancrizans Priory. Nor could he very much longer journey alone. His arm must have medical attention, for the dry burning of his skin was not, he feared, from the sun. Reluctantly, he put pride away. The time had come when he must call on his friends for help.

It grew very warm in the late afternoon, but Harry pushed on, having decided to attempt a wide northerly loop and swing south again towards the homes of Lucian St. Clair, the Earl of Harland, and Lord John Moulton, at any one of which he was sure to find sanctuary. Of the three great houses he preferred Lucian's Beechmead, for he knew the Viscount and his bride would still be away and thus unanswerable for shielding him. He was commencing to feel oddly confused at times, however, and with the advent of dusk, blundered clumsily into a large group of searchers

287

he should have easily avoided. For the next two hours he played a desperate game of least-in-sight with them. Only the darkness saved him; and as their shouts faded, he was forced to rest until the frantic hammering of his heart and the searing in his lungs eased. Huddled among the reeds beside a turgid stream, he gripped his throbbing arm and panted heavily. Never again would he be able to enjoy the hunt, for he was commencing to know too well the helpless panic of the hunted. When he started off once more, he was periodically shaken by chills though his skin seemed on fire. He stumbled on until the lights of an isolated farmhouse loomed before him. A cart covered by sacking stood under a rickety lean-to, a large black dog snoring beside it. To venture closer was to risk discovery, but he was too exhausted to care. He headed for the cart, stepped over the dog, crawled inside and, pulling the sacking over him, was lulled to sleep by the snores of the inept canine sentry.

"What d'you mean—killed him?" exclaimed the apothecary indignantly, putting down his saw. "Ain't s'much as laid a finger on him yet!"

His accuser, a short, round, balding individual given to innocently raised brows and a meek hesitancy of manner, peered more closely at the man who sprawled in the chair of the dusty little shop, right arm trailing over the side, bearded face sunk onto his chest, and long legs extended before him. "Looks t'me," he blinked, "like ye've lost the customer I brung ye, Stanley Crimp. Gentleman's been and gone and died on ye, sure enough!"

"A sight you know of it, Bert!" Mr. Crimp's thin claw of a hand reached for his customer's wrist nevertheless and, having located a pulse, mirth lit his cadaverous features as he proceeded to straighten his greasy hair, then tie a soiled apron about his middle. "*Gentleman*—is it? That's a laugh!"

"Gentleman," reiterated Bart, folding his hands over his round little stomach and regarding his tall companion solemnly.

Mr. Crimp deposited needles, thread, lint, a large

wooden hammer, and various other surgical supplies on the battered table beside the chair. "If you think a 'gentleman' would be caught dead in those shoes—or that jacket . . . then you ain't seen many of the breed!"

Seating himself on a nearby chair and rocking familiarly back and forth on the uneven legs, Bert said an aggrieved, "I seen enough to find one for you though, didn't I? Resting on the step o' Macauley's fish shop he was—along o' all the cats in Winchester."

Pausing in his preparations, the apothecary enquired if 'old mother Macauley' had seen this ungentlemanlike behaviour, whereupon Bert nodded. "Out she come, a'clobbering at him with her broom, and screeching as he's gin raddled, which he wasn't."

Crimp chuckled. "What'd he do?"

"He bowed," shrugged Bert loftily. "Wotever would you of expected?"

"Bowed . . . ?" gasped Mr. Crimp. "To . . . old mother Macauley?"

"Very flash," Bert nodded, jumping up and emulating the bow with exaggerated drama. "Gent born—ain't no doubt." Returning to his unstable perch, he mused, "P'raps he's lost his fortune at play . . . or killed his man in a dooell, or . . ." He broke off, his rheumy eyes widening, and meeting that scared look, Crimp's own expression became alarmed. "Here!" he whispered, "You don't think . . ?"

Bert stood and tiptoed nearer to the chair. "He *could* be, Crimp! Oh . . . Gawd . . . ! They do say as he shoved a knife clean through the poor cove's liver and lights! And the poor Frenchy—a fine, high-born gent, furriner or no! Pertecting of his ravaged child!" He bent to scan the suspect, breath held in check. "But—they say in them posters as how he's got scratches on his face."

"Well so he might have—under that beard. And—see here . . !" The apothecary crept to the far side of the chair and, lifting a rag from the bared arm that rested there, beckoned to his friend.

Bert looked and grimaced, and for a moment they stared at one another.

"Two . . . Thousand Guineas!" breathed Bert, eyes bright with avarice.

"Hurry up!" urged Crimp. "If he ain't the guilty party— no harm done. If he is, he'll be slowed down considerable when I'm finished, I can tell you!"

Bert was already scurrying away but turned at this, to call in an urgent stage whisper, "You won't never do him in?"

The apothecary pursed his lips doubtfully, then brightened. "It makes no never mind. Reward's the same, warm or stiff."

Heaving a sigh of relief at this happy reminder, Bert was gone.

Mr. Crimp eyed his patient curiously, reached forward, and with great caution parted the short dark beard that curled about the pale features. Slight as it was, the touch roused Harry. He blinked up at the man who crouched over him and demanded an indignant, "What the deuce d'ye think you're about?"

Mr. Crimp jumped back and, snatching up his saw, gulped, "I—I was . . . forgetting, sir, whether or no you s-said you would be wanting a shave!"

"Shave?" Flinching, Harry hauled himself upward. "With—*that*?"

The apothecary glanced down at his saw and uttered a nervous laugh. " 'Course not! That's for—"

"Good God! You dirty blackguard! You were going to hack my arm off!"

"Well now, it's got to be done, ain't it?" said Crimp reasonably. He lifted the straps at the side of the bolted-down chair. "You just rest easy and tell me where you want us to take you after I—"

"Devil I will!" Harry waved him off. "You're not going to strap me down, cut my arm off, nor take me anywhere, confound you!"

The apothecary patted his shoulder in a consoling way, but his cunning eyes slid to the side. Following that glance, Harry jumped up, grabbed the hammer, and tossed it across the room. "I prefer laudanum, if you please! Not that I'd give you the chance to administer either!"

"Don't often have to use my hammer," sighed Crimp, his thousand guineas receding rapidly. "They usually faint when I get to the bone."

"Or die, more like!" Harry shuddered.

Crimp protested this statement with vigour and then assured his patient that it was his own welfare that was being considered. "Can't run from a thing like *that*." He indicated the injury with the travesty of a sympathetic smile. "Longer you leave it, worse it'll get. In a day or two, it'll be much too late, even if you was to take it to the shoulder!"

"I'll tell you what I'll take, and that's my leave of you, sir!" Harry picked up his jacket and strode purposefully toward Crimp and the front door.

For a wild second the apothecary contemplated brute force. His patient was far from being in plump currant—still, he *was* tall, and the set of his shoulders such as to dampen any valorous inclination to uphold law and order. Crimp compromised, therefore and, seizing a bottle from a side table, adjured Harry to toss off a couple of balls of fire and he'd scarcely feel a thing. Harry declined this offer, but submitting to the logical advice that the wound *must* be cleaned and rebandaged, reluctantly sat down again. At once the crafty apothecary, not one to give up without a struggle, warned of the dangers attendant upon refusing to be strapped in. "The least wriggle," he said earnestly, "and one slip o' my hand—" The glitter in the Ravisher's nasty narrow eyes silenced him, however, and he set about his task. He possessed a marked lack of either skill or compassion, with the result that Harry held his breath briefly, then let it out in a blistering review of Mr. Crimp's antecedents. Bert, the apothecary realized, had been correct after all. Only a gentleman could swear with such fluency!

Watching him, Harry lapsed into a weary silence. He had been fortunate in his choice of overnight accomodations, for he'd woken to find the cart jolting along the sunlit lanes toward Winchester. He'd slipped out some distance from the old town and, finding a stream and sheltering trees, had bathed, endeavoured to make himself look somewhat more respectable, and walked through the sparkling morning until he'd sat on the doorstep of the fish shop and met Bert—which he began to think a mixed blessing. His doubts solidified as Crimp tied the ends of the bandage agonizingly. "Damned clumsy dolt!" he raged. "Did you spend your time attending to what you're about instead of constantly gawking out of the window . . ."

The apothecary gabbled a defence, but Harry, his own glance having shot to the murky casement that overlooked the street, suddenly realized that all the sights and sounds attendant upon a busy market day had ceased. Suspicion tightened his nerves. He left the chair and stalked to the window. Not a soul was visible, yet he could swear he heard voices in a subdued murmuring that contained a hint of excitement. He swung around even as the apothecary rushed him, the heavy hammer flashing at his unguarded head. He jumped lightly to the side and, as the hammer whizzed past his cheek, slammed home what Lord Bolster would have acclaimed 'a leveller'. Mr. Crimp's feet almost left the floor as he arched backward, coming tidily to rest in his treatment chair.

"Very obliging of you . . . old fellow," said Harry. He swiftly buckled the straps about the unconscious man and snatched up a grubby towel to serve as a gag. They were waiting for him to come out, of course. That miserable little toad-eater Bert must have gone for the Watch. He ran to a half-open door at the side of the room and entered a small, littered parlour. The few articles of furniture were stained and sagging, and a grey piece of sheet, tacked over the one window, filtered out the daylight. A curtained opening gave onto an odorous kitchen, to the right of which was the promise of a bolted door. Harry started to it, but paused and sprinted back to the parlour. Cautiously, he peered around the edge of the sheet. He was looking into a narrow alley between the buildings. To the left several men crouched, one holding a rake, and the others variously armed with clubs, farm tools, and muskets. To the right, where the alley joined the street, he could glimpse the fringe of a crowd, the men peering eagerly toward the front door of the shop. Even as he watched, he caught sight of the crown of a hat moving below the window and drew back, grimly aware that he was surrounded.

A voice outside rose in a hoarse whisper. "Peel! They want—" And another voice hissed, "Quiet! Dang ye!"

For an instant Harry frowned at a greasy hat that adorned the sorrowful sofa. "Nothing ventured . . ." he thought, and with characteristic zeal for this hopeless challenge, raced into the front room. Crimp was uttering gurgles and thrashing about. Harry pulled free his grimy apron, tied it over the apothecary's head, then tied a drooping jacket over that. Taking up his own jacket, he eased into it and grabbed the lopsided chair. Howling at the top of his lungs, he heaved it through the front window and raced into the parlour again, spurred by a great shout of excitement from the front. He jammed the greasy hat onto his head, ran to the back door, and shouted, "Peel! Peel! Be ye thar?"

"Aye!" An eager fist pounded at the door. "What's to do?"

Harry shot the bolt even as the front door crashed open. He flung the door wide. "We got him!" he roared. "Come quick!"

The first upstanding citizen peered at him and hesitated momentarily but was borne along by the eager tide. They poured into the front room, where total chaos appeared to prevail; shouts of "There he is!", "Kill the ravisher!", "Hang him!", intermingling with adjurations to "get him outta that chair!" and a lone but more practical, "Where's Crimp?". In a flash the small house was a mass of striving, shouting, cursing men. Harry allowed them to sweep past and edged unobtrusively into the alley. Running to the corner, he all but collided with a muscular individual in an embroidered smock and, seizing his arm, shouted triumphantly, "We got the perisher! We do be fixin' to hang him!" The stranger gave an enthused cry and rushed on.

Harry breathed a sigh of relief, but as he walked along the wider cobbled thoroughfare he heard the sound he had dreaded, the terrible, mindless yowling of an angry mob. His heart thundering, he pulled the greasy hat lower over his betraying green eyes and turned down the next alley.

Only a few people were visible here; a man who ran by, dragging on his coat, his face alight with anticipation; a vendor hawking brooms; a woman far to the end of the alley, lackadaisically sweeping a worn doorstep. Longing to run for the trees that beckoned so invitingly beyond the old buildings, Harry dared not even hasten for fear of attracting attention. God! How they howled! He began to sweat as the sound came nearer. When he passed the woman, she lifted a tired, wan face and bade him good day . . . He mumbled a response and raised his hat. It was a mistake, and a bad one. She stared, shrank, then let out a piercing shriek. The far end of the alley was suddenly filled with a surging tide of enraged humanity. Harry essayed a mad dash for the trees, the shouts behind him rising into a bestial roar that made his blood run cold. He was almost to the last house when three men raced around the corner ahead, three men wearing a familiar black and gold livery, and each carrying a serviceable-looking cudgel. They slowed, and sauntered toward him; and Harry halted, panting, "Treed . . . by God!"

From behind came the pounding of countless feet; the ravening clamour that was death cruel and shameful. "Better to go quickly," he thought and, advancing on Sanguinet's men, was met by one who sprang ahead of his fellows. Harry easily eluded the flailing club and struck once with all the power of his legendary right. The face disappeared, only to be replaced by another and a fist like a ham, shooting for his jaw. He tripped over the fallen man and thus the fist whistled past, and he seized that muscular arm and pulled his assailant into a profane collision with the onrushing third man. A swift sense of danger and he spun around desperately, but a descending hand clutching a rock caught him above the right temple, and he was on his knees, half blinded, his head exploding. Vaguely, he was aware of rough hands dragging him to his feet; a stifling, lunatic confusion; a sharp agony as someone wrenched at his left arm; a shrill voice shouting for a rope. He struggled feebly, but a fist drove at his face and, powerless to duck, he reeled to the impact and sank again, consciousness fading.

"Murderer! . . . Filthy woman stealer! . . . Hang the dirty bastard!"

Through the sick weakness and pain, he knew a dull regret. Who'd ever have thought he would finish like this? Hanged in some wretched little alley in the dear land of his birth . . . Whatever would Mitch think . . ?

"Let him up! Outta my way! Move, you coves! Let him up!"

He was hauled upright and strove mightily to lift his head but, even when he achieved this, could discern only a vague blur. Yet the voice had sounded oddly familiar, like a half-remembered dream. He blinked and was able to see a horseman with broad, powerful shoulders and a coarse-featured face, the small eyes glinting mockingly down at him.

The man leaned forward in the saddle and, his thick lips twisting into a leer, enquired, "Wanta confess your sins afore you die—sir?"

A rough hooting and shouts of laughter, and Harry was shaken and buffeted so that speech failed him and he was unable to utter his defiant response.

"You don't know who I be," sneered the rider, "so I'll tellya as I works fer the Sanguinets. And Monsewer Claude wants to know—number one, where you put the lady. And—number two, how you fired that there pistol when you—"

"It's not . . . too difficult," Harry interposed thickly. "You—just curl your finger . . . 'round the trigger, and—"

Blows thudded upon him, and a voice growled in his ear that he'd best act civil to the gent. The rider grinned, a soft hissing escaping his stained teeth as he waited. A small sound—that brought with it the blinding flash of recognition. "He's not a gent!" Harry croaked. "He's Devil Dice!"

There was an instant of stunned silence. Shotten froze, his features becoming livid as all eyes turned to him. Then he threw back his head and laughed raucously. "That's a good one!" He glanced around, but M. Sanguinet's staunch retainers had melted into the crowd at Harry's words, not to be seen again. "All right now," he barked, "here's yer rope, me bullies!"

Harry's desperate attempt to speak was stifled as his head was jerked back and the noose—already tied, he noticed—was thrust towards him. He wished anguishedly that he'd died after Rodrigo, honourably. But then Nanette's piquant little face flashed before his eyes and he knew this was worthwhile . . . Only he so yearned to have seen her, just once more before—

"Wait a bit!" A new voice and a pale young face frowned into Harry's dazed eyes. That he commanded some respect here was evidenced by the way the eager tumult quieted.

"Get on with it!" cried Shotten. "You gonna let him orf? The Runners'll cover it all up if they get him, 'cause he's Quality, and—"

"And you bean't, eh? Very far from it, I'm sure," the newcomer retaliated scornfully. "Redmond will hang—don't ye never doubt that. We doesn't hold with murdering kidnappers in Winchester!" A clamour of agreement supported his statement, and Shotten glared vindictively at him. The brief respite was allowing Harry a chance to gather his scattered wits. His vision was clearing, and with a leap of hope he recognized the newcomer as Tim Van Lindsay's soldier— the fellow with 'two first names' he had helped a little that afternoon at Maidstone. Billy somebody . . . Billy Ernest!

"We all knows what this'n done," Ernest was saying. "But, by grab, we knows a sight more o' what Devil Dice done! It won't hurt to hear what Redmond's got to tell us— knowing as he's at the gates o' hell, as you could say." The clear eyes bored steadily at Harry. There was no trace of recognition in their depths, yet that long look convinced him that the youth meant to help insofar as he was able, his harsh words merely a cover for whatever he had in mind.

The large man who held Harry's left arm demanded he "spit it out," his grip tightening unbearably. "If you will shift . . . your blasted paw a trifle, fellow," Harry rasped, "I shall endeavour to do so!"

There were a few chuckles, not unmixed with reluctant admiration. He was gaunt, his face streaked with blood, his beard and hair shaggy, his clothes tattered; yet there was withal a proud tilt to his head, an indomitable light in his eyes still.

"He do be a game-un, you gotta allow him that!" observed a rotund little man wearing a butcher's apron.

"He's a murdering liar as you shouldn't give a ear!" Dice contradicted. "I'm a respectable gent, and no one can't prove no different!"

Harry's gaze was fixed on that belligerent face. He'd likely not be able to prove anything at that, but— His breath caught as he saw at last the superb bay mare that Dice struggled to restrain. Lace! His peerless Lace! And she was trying to come to him, snorting her eagerness although Dice held her with a hand of iron. Her snowy fetlocks were gone, but he'd know her anywhere in the world! "I can prove what I say!" he claimed ringingly. "A few weeks back I was shot by Devil Dice—or Shotten as he calls himself—and my best mare stolen. Your—ah—'gent' there rides her now!"

Dice's denial was vehement and well larded with oaths; but fear glistened in his little eyes, and he edged the mare a few paces away.

Harry called an imperious, "Watch!" and whistled piercingly. At once, Lace spun about and reared, whinnying and pawing the air. A shout of excitement went up. Dice panicked, tore the mare's head round, and galloped off.

"Stop him!" screamed Billy Ernest.

Several men sprinted in pursuit. Harry whistled again. A loud, clear warbling note. Lace did not fail him. She swung back immediately, and when Shotten sought to wrench her away, she bucked, coupling all the power of her sleek muscles with her rage that she should be kept from her beloved master. Dice shrieked and soared from the saddle, an eager group running to apprehend him.

"Look out!" warned Ernest, jumping clear. The mare's ears flattened and the crowd scattered madly from her headlong charge as she thundered to Harry, teeth bared. The man holding his right arm yelped and retreated. The large individual to his left was made of sterner stuff, however, and swung his captive so that he himself was protected from the mare. Lace reached across her master's shoulder and sampled his captor. The large man let out a howl and relaxed his grip. Gasping with pain and desperation, Harry drove a right jab into his midsection and leapt for the saddle. He urged Lace away. How smooth was her stride, and how lightning fast! But as he sent the mare galloping to the woods, he saw from the corner of his eye a levelled musket. He flung himself down and, clinging to the pommel, glanced back. Young Ernest was limping after him, shouting threats and waving his arms, while a great grin spread over his face as he effectively blocked the musket owner's aim.

"Remove your hands from my body at once, Sir Harry Redmond!" Harry straightened in the saddle and opened his eyes eagerly but saw only a tracery of branches against the orange sky. A moment ago the sky had been grey and it had begun to drizzle . . . He reached for the trailing reins. It must be late afternoon . . . but was it still Wednesday . . ? He caught himself in the nick of time, having almost tumbled to the ground. Mustn't fall again . . . last time he'd barely been able to remount. He wound the reins about the pommel and lifted his left wrist carefully. Tucking the hand into his buttoned jacket, he flinched as pain lanced excruciatingly from the swollen fingers to his armpit. Damn, but he'd be put out if they had to amputate! Was that Mitch calling him? He shook his head, angered that the fever was clouding his mind so. "Damn you, Sanguinet," he muttered fretfully, "You *shall not* beat me!"

He took up the reins again and rode on through countryside that was a veritable paradise of lush greens, the meadows begemmed with wildflowers, the air sweet with their fragrance, and everywhere the chestnut trees, standing proudly in their pink or white crinolines like arboreal ladies waiting for the dance. Aware only dimly of these sylvan beauties, Harry turned Lace southeast and, in a dogged refusal to yield to pain and weakness, sang softly the most ribald Spanish song he knew.

CHAPTER XVIII

"MITCHELL!" THE REVEREND LANGRIDGE HURRIED across the entrance hall at Greenwings, both hands outstretched to the young man who had burst through the front doors of the gracious old mansion, pushed past the startled butler, and was running towards the stairs.

His face strained and grey eyes dark with fear, Mitchell gripped his uncle's hands, his own trembling. "Hello, sir," he managed, in a brave attempt at self-control. "Bolster told me that you and my aunt visit the Moultons."

"Well, John's away, m'boy, but his lady has made us welcome, bless her! And thank God she did not accompany him, for Salia was ever a splendid nurse, as you are no doubt a—"

"Harry!" Mitchell interpolated tersely, "He—he's not . . . ?"

"No, no, lad," Langridge soothed. "He goes on nicely. Good gracious, but you look ready to drop. Did anyone see you come here?"

"What? Oh, I don't know! Bolster said Harry is very near to sticking his spoon in the wall! I must go to him!"

"Calm yourself, I beg. He's sleeping now. I was the one who found him, you know. It was dusk, and I'd not have seen him had I not chanced to spot a horse standing in the park. Poor fellow was fighting frantically to drag himself back into the saddle; likely thought we were more of those damnable bounty hunters! I ran up and took the poor lad in my arms. He lay there, trying to smile, like the brave fellow he is, and with tears of joy in his eyes to see it was me. "Hello, sir," says he. "Did I get all the way to Wimbledon, then?"

Mitchell's face twisted, and Langridge shook his head sadly. "Poor, poor Harry. Salia has been caring for him. She is very skilled, you know, and—"

"For the love of God! *Will* you tell me straight out! Can he live?"

"Of course he can! Now pray do not struggle so. Your brother is not upstairs, at all events."

Mitchell, a nightmare ride behind him, lifted one hand to his brow and said a bewildered, "Not . . . upstairs? Then—where . . ?"

" 'All they that take the sword shall perish with the sword!' "

Mordecai started as that resonant quotation rang out. Under his breath, Mitchell whispered a furious, "Hell and the devil!" and, turning, smiled tautly. "Aunt Wilhemina. How do you do?"

Mrs. Langridge towered behind him, her turbaned head high, the lofty ostrich plumes waving, and her large dark eyes grave. She wore a robe of mulberry velvet edged with pink brocade, over a rose pink slip; a not-unattractive combination, but spoiled by the great bishops sleeves that contributed to an impression of vastness.

Mitchell bowed dutifully over the hand she extended and, having scolded him for his disgraceful behaviour in France, she allowed him to kiss her cheek, while remarking that he did not look at all himself since he had been so brutally whipped. He stiffened and flushed darkly, but his attempt to speak was drowned as his aunt proceeded to point out that most of the present woes of the Redmonds sprang from their refusal to heed the wisdom of the Bible. " 'Vengeance is mine; I will repay, saith the Lord!' " she cried, one plump hand upswung.

The set of Mitchell's jaw alarmed his uncle, who hastily suggested that they adjourn to Lord John's study. Mitchell bestowed a frigid bow upon his aunt; but her hand fastened upon his arm, and in a display of kindness she said, "Harry has been magnificent throughout. You may be very proud of him.''

''I am,'' he said simply. ''Thank you, Aunt,'' and followed Mordecai.

He might have known, thought Langridge, filling two glasses with Moulton's best Madeira, that Bolster wouldn't be able to break the news without scaring the boy half out of his wits. Best fellow in the world was young Bolster, but not the soul of tact. ''I shall take you to Harry directly,'' he smiled. ''But we cannot have you looking as though you are come for his funeral, can we? Sit down now—that's better. Drink up. You have had a nasty shock.''

The potency of the wine began to relieve some of the terrible tension that had scourged Mitchell since Bolster had miserably told him to hasten to his brother's side, ''before it is too late . . .'' ''Sir,'' he said, ''do you know what happened? Where he's been?''

''He doesn't say much of it. For the first few days, save for a brief interval or two, he was out of his head completely. All he spoke of was his 'little shrew'—and yourself. He says he had 'a spot of pother' in Winchester. It was a good deal more, I'd imagine, for when I found him he was weak as a cat, had hold of the stirrup and came all those miles when he must have been suffering the most hideous agonies, I cannot—'' Tardily becoming aware of the horror in his nephew's eyes, he said in a rallying tone, ''Splendid constitution, of course, else we would have buried him the first day!'' Mitchell whitened at this, but again perceiving his blunder, the Reverend went on, ''Never look so anxious, boy. Danger's over now, praise God! Lucky I found him, though. I did tell you it was me that found him? And lucky I'd the presence of mind to have escorted your aunt here. She and Salia are bosom bows, you know. Odd, isn't it? They are not at all alike. But . . . schooldays, that kind of thing. Indeed, it is quite astonishing how Salia can handle—'' He coughed, reddened, and finished, ''Well, enough of that! How are you, my boy? You got into quite a nasty muddle yourself.''

. . . quite a nasty muddle . . . Mitchell smiled a shade too brightly. "Perfectly fit, thank you, sir. My back's almost healed."

Perhaps, thought Langridge regretfully. But your spirit ain't.

The day was not warm, the sun hiding behind a hazy overcast, while a brisk breeze riffled the leaves on the old trees that stood majestically about Greenwings's velvet sward. Mitchell was aghast, therefore, to be conducted to the rear terrace where a youthful maid kept vigil beside a bed. Astounded, he strode to look down at his brother. Harry lay on his side, sleeping peacefully, the coverlet pulled high around him, but his left arm bared to the elements. Glancing at the wound, Mitchell gasped, and he jerked scared eyes to the haggard features, clean shaven now, but very white save for the dark hollows about the eyes. Aching with sympathy, he reached out to lightly touch the tumbled hair.

"Now burn you, Mitch!" grumbled Harry, turning onto his back and opening his eyes. "I *knew* you'd come rushing here like Horatio to the gate, or whatever in the hell it was he rushed to."

A brilliant grin gave the lie to his scolding. The hand he stretched out was cool and firm, if rather bony, so that gripping it between both his own, Mitchell blinked rapidly and, fighting for control, said a choked, "Blast you! What a deuce of a fright you . . . gave me!"

"No, did I? Well, I understand just how you felt." Harry's fingers tightened and he added, "You look splendid, young cub."

Mitchell was quite powerless to respond, and for an emotion-charged moment they maintained that strong handclasp while their eyes conveyed the love their lips could not speak. Then Mitchell swung away and, having made a show of blowing his nose, grunted, "And it was not Horatio but Horatius; nor a gate but a—"

"Water closet," interposed Harry irreverently. "As you

say, Sir Erudition. You've all the brains in the family. I own it.''

"And you—none at all!'' Turning back, Mitchell's frown was sterner than Harry had ever beheld it, the set to his mouth so forbidding that he seemed suddenly older. "What the devil were you about? There was no logical reason for you to panic and run. No one could have suspected you.''

Harry's eyes slid away. So Bolster hadn't told him. Good old Jerry . . . reliable, as always. "Could they not?''

"You?'' Mitchell perched upon the side of the bed, neither of them having noticed that their uncle had departed, taking the amused maid with him. "Shoot a man in the back?'' He gave a derisive snort. "But of course! Typical! Only you were raving about having been pinned under a branch.''

"Blast!'' thought Harry, and staring fixedly at a blackbird hopping on the lawn, he ventured the account he had been conjuring up these past few days. "Yes—well, that was the whole thing. Sanguinet saw the tree coming down, and—''

"In the darkness,'' Mitchell nodded.

"He could see in the dark. He had those . . . odd eyes . . .'' He saw the grim tightening of Mitchell's mouth and said swiftly, "Besides, it was struck by lightning, terribly bright, you know. So he ran, and I—''

"Did *not* see the lightning? Terribly bright, you know.''

Harry's eyebrows drew down slightly and he said with firm deliberation, "It was behind me. Well, I mean—the *tree* was behind me. And when it took me down with it, the pistol in my hand went off. Accidentally.''

"My God! You surely don't expect anyone to believe that gibberish?''

"It occurs to me, my good youth,'' said Harry awfully, "that the respect to which I am entitled is noticeably absent!''

Mitchell frowned, his easy good nature as 'noticeably absent' as his brother's much-vaunted respect. "It occurs to me that I am either too young, too fribbleish, or too little thought of—to be told the truth!''

That acid tone had never before been directed at Harry. Some of his consternation was reflected in his eyes and, cursing these new moods that so bewildered him, Mitchell changed the subject. "Why in the world are you out here?"

"Salia," said Harry succinctly.

"Won't have you inside, eh? Cannot say I blame her."

"He was a most impossible patient!" Lady Salia Moulton walked gracefully across the terrace, a shawl clasped around her shoulders and one white hand extended for Mitchell's kiss. "Wherefore, in a fit of pique, dear boy, I forbade him the house." She at once detected the hardness in the eyes that had always been so gentle. Logical enough, but she prayed it might disappear when this nightmare was done with . . . "How are you, Mitchell?"

"Overwhelmed, dear ma'am." He smiled at her, thinking her beauty ageless despite the silver that streaked her black hair. "With animosity! Since you have prevented my scapegrace of a brother from going to his just reward."

"Villain!" laughed Harry. "Always knew you coveted the title!"

"But—of course." Mitchell's eyes slanted to the injured arm. "And just how close was I to achieving me foul ambitions, ma'am?"

The words were lightly uttered, but his gaze was searching. Meeting it, Salia answered gravely, "You would have been less close, Mitchell, had he allowed us to amputate."

So Bolster had been right . . . Chilled, he said with unprecedented harshness, "You should have had Lord John knock him over the head and done it anyway!"

"John is not here, else I most certainly would have done so. He visits Harland in Paris."

Mitchell directed an alarmed glance at his brother. "Yes," Harry said ruefully. "A fine bumble broth I've pulled her into. You must get me away from—"

"Were it not for the sun," interrupted Salia, shutting off his words by the simple expedient of placing her cool fingers over his mouth, "he would have lost the arm, Mitchell." She slapped Harry's lips gently as he kissed her fingers, and added a quiet, "Perhaps—too late."

"It was infected, then?"

"Gangrene had set in. Ah, no, my dear! Never look so terrified. The title is quite lost to you, rest assured."

"My lady," he said unsteadily. "I do not know how to thank—"

"Pooh! The remedy is not mine but has been handed down for generations among my people. My grandmama was a gypsy, don't forget, and their lore is very much a part of me still. Likely you thought us quite mad when you found Harry out here, but between the sun and my herbs and fomentations—"

"And the fact I'm such a deucedly virile chap," contributed the irrepressible Harry.

"Cling to that thought," advised my lady, twinkling at him, "for it is time for another poultice!" She chuckled at his wailing protest, then left them, having first warned that her patient must not be tired.

When she was gone, Mitchell resumed his seat on the bed, conscious that his brother had been covertly scrutinizing him and dreading lest he refer to the abasement he shrank from discussing.

Harry, however, had no intention of commiting such a *faux pas* and instead asked, "How is Mr. Fox?"

"Up and about again. Camille sent a cart for him, and some of his grooms conveyed your four-footed friend to the Priory. He's still there, for I didn't know what to do with him and have heard nothing from Diccon."

They talked for some time—largely of their chances of proving that Sanguinet had been responsible for their father's death, and then Mitchell said that Camille Damon had insisted he should be taken to the Priory as soon as he was sufficiently recovered, and that a very capable midwife from Pudding Park had aided immeasureably in his recovery.

Wondering how complete was that recovery, Harry murmured that he'd heard Damon speak of her, and then, with forced nonchalance enquired, "Who . . . else was at the Priory?"

"Gad, who was not! Camille, of course, though he was gone most of the time—seeking you, I later discovered.

305

And Bolster, stammering so badly we could scarce understand him, wherefore I *knew* he was up in the boughs! And both of 'em telling me the biggest whiskers imaginable so I'd not suspect what my maniac of a brother was about! Andy—grumping about and telling me of Mrs. Radcliffe until I wished I'd never let him so much as lay eyes on a book!" With superb innocence, he went on, "Oh, and Miss Carlson, who— Hey! Lie down!"

Harry had started up, his face flushed with eagerness. "How does she go on? Have the Sanguinets been hounding her? Is she safe? Does she talk? Is—"

Mitchell thought a relieved, "At last!" and put in dryly, "She is frantic, naturally, but quite recovered. She stays with her aunt, and I collect the Sanguinets have made no attempt to take her back—dare not, probably, for fear of what she might say. She's in the deuce of a taking to discover where you are and makes no bones about accusing us of keeping the truth from her. She forces her servants to haunt the offices of the constables and the Watch, and accompanied us into Town several times to tell the Runners you had been trying to protect her and that Parnell Sanguinet had attempted to murder you."

"And—they believed her?"

Mitchell looked down, not answering, and Harry knew that Parnell had done his work well. "They believed her short of a sheet, more like," he muttered.

"She told them you were pinned under the tree when you shot him . . ." Mitchell glanced at him obliquely. "We live in a modern age, *Sauvage* . . . The surgeons say the ball hit Sanguinet's back—level. No angle. So you see, it makes no sense."

Harry was silent. Then he reached out to clasp the slim, nervous fingers that twisted so endlessly at the fringe of the coverlet. "Mitch . . . dear old lad, you know that of all men I'd keep no secrets from you. Were they my own."

Mitchell nodded. Then, standing, asked, "Does Bolster know?"

"He guessed. He'll say nothing. But I shall involve you

by asking that you get me out of England as soon as possible. And—alone.''

Mitchell stared blankly at the pleasant sprawl of the old house. "It will break her heart, Harry. Surely you could at least write to her?''

"Of course. As soon as I'm able.''

After a long, troubled silence, Mitchell said, "Aside from the fact that she is overset with worry for you, she is her own sweet self. Do you suppose—can she have . . . forgotten—what really happened?''

"I pray so. And, God willing, will never remember.''

Through the days that followed, Harry mended steadily. His athletic pursuits had kept him in top condition, and his basic good health enabled him to gradually throw off the effects of the infection that had so nearly claimed his life. He maintained throughout his customary air of lazy good humour, but inwardly he chafed at the delays. That he had reached Greenwings at all was miraculous, and Salia had undoubtedly saved his life; but she and John Moulton had known their present happiness for a comparatively brief time, and Harry fretted bitterly against being the possible means of casting a shadow over that joy. He paced his room endlessly, fighting the weakness that clung with such infuriating persistence, and had so far progressed as to be allowed downstairs to prowl the library one morning when a familiar voice called his name. He swung around to find Bolster hastening towards him.

"Jeremy!'' he cried, seizing his friend's outstretched hand. "Deuce take it, but I'm glad to see you! Sit down! Sit down! And tell me what's afoot. I'm so pampered and coddled I have no idea what's happening. How does Mitch go on? I see you've managed to keep him away. And—''

"He's not the only one we've m-m-m- kept away. Your lady imagines you safely in France, else—''

"Where I *should* be by now!'' Harry flashed, his heart having given a painful jolt at the mention of Nanette. "Jerry—I *must* get away from here! I cannot guess why I've not been discovered these past three weeks, but heaven forbid the Moultons should be involved! Is there any chance it can be arranged?''

"All done, d-dear boy. That's why I come down. Damon has re-re-re cousins all over the Continent. Place must positively ooze 'em! His yacht will carry you to Cherbourg on Friday, and he's m-made arrangements for you to be met.''

Greatly relieved, Harry next and rather diffidently enquired if it was possible Lace might be taken along. This, it seemed, was also arranged. Marvelling at their thoughtfulness, he lapsed into a long silence.

Glancing up, he found Bolster watching him with a sympathy that brought the colour burning into his cheeks. "I've written Nanette a letter,'' he said awkwardly. "If you—would be so kind as to deliver it.''

"Of course—be delighted. Jilted her nicely, I t-trust?'' His lordship strolled nonchalantly to sprawl on the deep window seat and, meeting Harry's steady stare, assumed an expression of saintly innocence. "Lay you odds you made a mull of it. What did you say? Were you c-cold or n-n-noble?'' He raised one languid hand. "Do not dare strike me! I can afford to lose no more teeth. Besides, I've known you since we was in sh-short coats. I have every right to be told what—''

"Devil you have!'' Harry strode closer.

Bolster sighed, closed his eyes, and raised his chin resignedly.

Forced to a reluctant grin, Harry demanded, "How did you know, damn you?''

"Obvious. You're a hunted man and must leave the country.''

"I could have asked her to accompany me.''

"Could.'' Bolster's voice dropped a little and he finished with the oddly judicial solemnity that occasionally marked him. "Except—it was in the *back*, my bold knight.''

Harry turned away and walked over to the window. Watching him, Bolster sighed heavily. That poor little Miss Carlson was head over ears in love with his friend was very obvious. That she was too blinded by the tender emo-

308

tion to realize how hopeless was that love was equally obvious. But Harry knew. The dear old boy was smitten at last; and Cupid, having waited so long, had loosed his arrow with cruel perversity. For despite his laughing eyes and apparently light-hearted view of life and its foibles, Harry was a product of his upbringing. He would live and if need be die by the Code of Honour, without question. And none knew better than he that however villainous, however depraved Parnell Sanguinet had been, it was unthinkable that his daughter should wed the man believed to have murdered him. As if that weren't bad enough, he was so dashed proud . . . the little gal was a great heiress, whereas old Harry . . . God! What a horrid mess! Bolster glanced up from under his lashes. Harry was staring into the garden. What did he see—his empty future? The man loved England devotedly and would be fortunate did he ever set foot in it again . . . always granting they could smuggle him safely to France! After that, what hope for him? No fortune, no properties—and he'd certainly be too damned high in the instep to accept any help!—torn from the woman he loved; universally despised for a treacherous shooting . . .

"If you're going to cry, old sportsman, I'll be dashed if I'll dry your tears for you!"

His lordship jerked his yellow head up and was slightly stunned to find a twinkle in the eyes that met his own.

"It ain't *that* bad, you know," consoled Harry, smiling despite his own heavy heart.

"C-Course it ain't!" Bolster confirmed, adopting a manner so joyous one might think he'd just come into a fortune. "And—after all, you *have* often said you'd never marry."

"I have, indeed."

"And—you *always* had more than your share of opera dancers. To say nothing of your Spanish barques of frailty. And then there was your l-little ladybird in—"

"Yes, well, may we please omit the inventory, Jeremy?"

"By all m-m-means. Point is—you've often been in love—eh?"

Harry winked, but his thoughts turned wrenchingly to a sun-dappled woodland clearing and a girl in a plain round gown, with flour on her pert nose and her brow wrinkled with concentration as she offered her definition of love. So apt a description of how he felt these days . . . "an empty picture frame"—only complete when she was near . . .

From outside came a blast of sound, an ear-splitting cacophony as welcome as it was familiar. With a whoop he was through the open window and calling, "Diccon! Mr. Fox! Jove, but I'm glad to see you!"

Left alone, Lord Jeremy Bolster ran one square, powerful hand through his straight yellow locks and, undeceived, swore long and fluently.

"A very close shave, friend Harry. Lucky I was to get out've it!" Having already exchanged handshakes with Redmond, Diccon now watched the reunion of man and beast, as Mr. Fox leant his head against his friend's waistcoat and, with closed eyes, chomped ecstatically upon a note from Mitchell which Harry had generously offered.

"I'm most sorry to hear it." Harry pulled the little donkey's ears, glanced up, and asked, "Your amateur smugglers?"

"Aye. Got me into a proper bumble broth, they done. But," the lugubrious features reflected anxiety. "I hear as how you got into a worse mess."

"Yes, but never mind about that." Harry turned from Mr. Fox and, facing Diccon squarely, asked, "Why did you not tell me who she was? Why all the business about her having been given a ride with a cleric, and you coming upon her by chance?"

"We-ell . . . I ain't much at being a gentleman—or nob, as y'might say. But I ain't much at breaking me word, neither. And I give it to her, Sir Harry, when that there Sister Maria Evangeline put her in me care. The Sister and me, we've had—er, dealings before . . . Speaking o' which, I'm very grateful to you fer dealing so kind with my friend here.''

Harry patted the donkey. ''That was largely my brother's doing. I suppose you're aware of how Sanguinet served Mitchell?''

''Yes. A nasty customer, that one. I hopes as how yer brother's full recovered?''

''He seems . . . very fit.''

Diccon noted the troubled look in the green eyes and said kindly, ''Why, he's a sensitive gent, sir. And to be flogged like that—in front of the lady as he cares fer—why it's enough t'make any proud young buck feel a bit less'n a man, I 'spect.''

It was the very thing Harry feared, and he stared at the Trader's gaunt face wonderingly. ''I've not surprised you with anything, have I? Do you know everything that's happened to us since last we saw you?''

''Why, it's the Fellowship o' the Road, Harry. Word travels far'n fast. Le' see now . . . I knows as ye went to see Lord Cootesby. And how they hunted you down over to Winchester—almost had the noose about yer neck that time! But . . .'' He took himself by the chin and, shaking his head wonderingly, muttered. ''What I *cannot* come at is how a fine, upstanding young chap like yerself would happen to shoot even so mad a dog as Parnell Sanguinet . . . in the *back*. Now that there's really got me scratching out me cock loft, as y'might say, for there's them as it fits—and them as it don't . . .'' He waited, an expression almost of pleading on his face.

''It was—an accident, really,'' Harry offered lamely.

''You mean . . . as ye *did*—do it?''

How incredulous those pale eyes—and God bless the man for his incredulity!

''Yes. But—he wasn't much to grieve for . . . was he?''

Diccon sighed and took from his pocket the snuffbox Harry had given him. He proffered it and, being courteously refused, took a pinch himself, inhaled, sneezed, wiped at his eyes with his copious handkerchief, and sighed again.

Harry sensed he had been judged and found wanting. Disturbed by that fact, he said, "I see that you still have the box. Not traded yet, eh?"

Diccon polished the snuffbox on his sleeve. "I been offered for it. But I don't trade what's give me by—special folk. This here, f'r instance . . ." He rummaged about in the cart and turned with the baton of the Bow Street Runners in his large hand. "Remember this, Harry?"

"I do indeed . . ." And with a pang he remembered also how well Nanette had wielded it. "Was it given you, Diccon? You promised to tell me of it someday."

"Aye—I did." The Trader hesitated. "It ain't a story as I dare tell many folk—or I'd've been worm bait long since . . . Still—" He gave a slow grin. "Seein's you and me got more in common now than what I thought—I'll tell you. This here's only half the story." He began again to hunt through the miscellany and at length exclaimed "Aha! You won't never believe this! Close yer eyes and hold out yer hands . . ."

"Is it heavy?" Harry enquired, eyes obediently closed.

"Lord love ye—no. No heavier than . . . that!"

A sharp click. A coldness about his wrists. And with a spasmodic contraction of the muscles under his ribs, Harry knew—too late. Opening his eyes, he stared down at the twin steel bracelets and the chain that looped between his wrists.

In stern and cultured accents, Diccon proclaimed, "Captain Sir Harry Allison Redmond, in the name of the King, I arrest you for the wilful murder of M. Parnell Sanguinet!"

CHAPTER XIX

HARRY'S HEAD CAME UP SLOWLY, AND MEETING THAT stunned look of disbelief, Diccon said a regretful, "In the old days, Sir Harry, that nasty piece of business would have been accomplished with less embarrassment for such as yourself. I am truly sorry. But grace and *finesse* are, alas, going by the board."

How different he looked, thought Harry numbly; his shoulders erect now, the lazy grin displaced by a look of power and purpose. "And . . . I . . ." he stammered, "m-must be the . . . sorriest fool of all time. For—I fancied you . . . my good friend."

"Had you seen fit to confide in me, sir, you would have been told the truth. Had you sworn you did not murder him I should have accepted your word. Indeed, I still will do so." He searched the thin face narrowly, but receiving only the same shocked stare, shook his head. "There is a time, you see, for friendship. And a time for duty."

"And—a time for smuggling?"

The bony shoulders shrugged. "I have many callings, sir. Wandering minstrel, tinker, trader, smuggler. All part of the overall policeman."

Recovering his wits gradually, Harry riposted, "Or is 'policeman' also a masquerade?" Diccon made no answer and his expression changed not one iota, yet Harry experienced a sense of extreme danger. Heedless, leaning forward he said, "Do you know what I think, Mr. Bow Street

Runner—or international spy—or whatever in the devil you *really* are . . ?''

Diccon's voice had taken on a purring quality as he murmured, "My, but you have a rare imagination."

"Together with a belated perception! It was all planned, was it not? From the very beginning!''

"If you refer to the death of your father . . ."

"No—but you *knew* of it, didn't you? All the time, you knew exactly why my papa was killed. And by whom!''

"There is a deal of difference, Sir Harry, between 'knowing' and proving. Your father was killed because he witnessed the death of Frederick Carlson. Another killing was undesirable and he was allowed to live, but only for so long as he believed it accidental. He sent a note to Bow Street, saying that he had recalled a detail that might be of import and asking that an officer be sent 'round to talk with him. Regrettably, his note was intercepted. He was interviewed by an imposter, and later lured from Town—to his death."

"And was it to track down his murderer that you followed me? Oh, pray do not trouble to deny it. Our first meeting I ascribed to chance, but I thought it odd that I kept encountering you. It was not coincidence. You had me watched!''

"Every instant," Diccon admitted coolly. "I was waiting to intercept you on the night Dice shot you down. My men erred, else I'd have put a stop to that business . . ." He frowned a little, then said judicially, "though it worked out well enough . . . While you were at Sanguinet Towers, Miss Carlson was brought to me—also prearranged, although she did not know that."

Stunned, Harry fought to appear calm. "You left a lot to chance. When I went to Maidstone I'd every intention of taking the stagecoach—*then* what would you have done!''

"When you returned from your Good Samaritan efforts on behalf of the young soldier, you would have found the seat already taken. Oh, do not look so chagrined. I don't think you were entirely deceived—you suspected the call of the cuckoo . . . did you not?''

He had suspected, but only at the back of his mind. His

stupid brain had wondered at the fact that Diccon wandered away from time to time, and that the cuckoo's call had sounded so clearly; but he'd been so preoccupied with his own problems he'd not put the two together. Seething, he burst out, "You deceive very well, Diccon! Why? Because Sanguinet wanted me dead? Did you thereby think I knew something?"

"Sanguinet feared you might stir things up if you sought retribution for your father's death; but, for many reasons, he could afford no more scandal. You did not constitute an immediate threat. At first, there was still the possibility you would die of your wounds. When you did not, your passion for racing and sports, your involvement last year in that nasty business with Lord St. Clair, your entire, somewhat hazardous way of life promised to take you out of the picture for him. And meanwhile, he was very busied with other matters. Your uncle played into his hands by concealing the truth from you."

"If you were aware of all this, why was none of it brought out?"

"Unhappily, I was not aware of it all. I was in France then, on—another matter. Still, Parnell was watched, and he knew it. When I returned to England having quite failed my assignment, I was—er—indisposed, but I began to tie some loose threads together, and it seemed to me that if I could not catch this tiger for his major crimes, I might snare him for the minor ones."

"Minor . . ?" Harry half whispered, his eyes glittering behind their narrowed lids. "My father's death was . . . *minor*?"

"Comparatively. But Sanguinet could not afford to let you meet his ward; to allow you to—compare notes, as it were. You owe me your life, really, for the only reason you were not killed at his estate was that he knew I was close by."

"And hoping he *would* have me killed, of course!"

Diccon shrugged. "I knew he desired his daughter. It was my hope, and a very chancy one, that being hit in so vulnerable an area, he would become emotionally involved and make a mistake.''

''And—*we* were to be his mistake!'' said Harry through his teeth. ''We were the bait for your tiger. You set us out—and gave not a tinker's damn whether he destroyed us!''

With cold hauteur, the Runner corrected, ''Say rather that I would sacrifice the Household Cavalry—to the last man—would it destroy Claude and Parnell Sanguinet.''

''Why—you cold-blooded devil!'' breathed Harry. ''You could have warned me! You could have given me a fighting chance! Instead, you abandoned us. Knowing his men were all about, you stood by and watched him force Nanette to—my God! Did you watch him whip Mitchell, hoping *he* would die? Now *damn* your merciless soul!''

Wild with fury, he sprang, his arms swinging up, the chain between the handcuffs flashing for Diccon's throat. The Runner moved also, lightning fast. One sinewy hand shot out to catch the chain. The heel of the other struck once in a vicious chop across Harry's throat, staggering him.

A lithe figure ran from the steps. Strong arms swept around Diccon, pinning him from behind. His head smashed backward, but Bolster was not without experience in encounters with the Watch and, ready for just such tactics, he evaded the manoeuvre. One of Diccon's heavy boots kicked savagely, but again, was avoided.

''Step back, my lord!'' The Reverend Langridge stood beside the drive, the hunting gun in his hands tremblingly pointed at the Runner. ''Do not be lulled to a false sense of security by reason of my cloth, sir!'' he warned shrilly. ''Sir Harry Redmond is the head of my house. Further, you trespass on Lord Moulton's property, and I have a perfect right to shoot a trespasser!''

Bolster stepped away, eyeing the clergyman with astounded admiration. ''J-Jove! You're a prime gun, sir! You all right, Harry?''

Holding his throat, Harry wheezed, ''Diccon claims . . . to be . . . from Bow Street!''

''Does he, by God! Can he p-prove it?''

Looking to Lady Salia who had also come out and

watched them with fearful anxiety, Harry nodded. "I—rather suspect . . . he can."

"Sounds d-d-deuced smoky to me." Bolster eyed Diccon truculently. "Thought you said the silly a-a-a fella was a smuggler? Here Diccon—you just take those ha-ha-ha manacles off Sir Harry!"

"Gladly, my lord," Diccon agreed with a faint inclination of the head. "If your friend will tell me he did not shoot M. Parnell Sanguinet—in the back."

Bolster slanted an uneasy glance at Harry but said loyally, "Had he been shot in the no-no-nostril, he'd be just as dead."

"*Mordecai Langridge!*" Wilhelmina sailed around the corner of the house, a formidable figure, feathers swaying with the speed of her approach, her stentorian voice at full volume. "Put that hideous thing down at once!"

"N-No! Pray—do not!" Bolster pleaded.

The gun wavered and Diccon, well aware of the peril of a loaded firearm in nervous hands, paled a little.

"This—person," quavered the Reverend, paling even more, "says he intends to haul our Harry off to gaol, m'dear."

His life's companion was only momentarily disconcerted. "Harry is a grown man and must take the consequences of his actions. I warned him. Besides, if he is innocent he will be spared, for does not St. Matthew tell us, 'if ye have faith as a grain of mustard seed . . .' "

"The Colosseum," pointed out the ever-practical Bolster, "was likely f-filled with folks who had faith, ma'am. Lions ate 'em up. Sorry, but—there 'tis."

"Enough!" she roared, lifting her hand dramatically. With a sort of leap Bolster retreated a pace behind Lady Salia. Turning to her shivering husband, Wilhelmina reminded, "Langridge, you are in Orders! Put that weapon down this—"

"Oh . . . be quiet . . ." gulped the Reverend.

Four stunned pairs of eyes turned to him.

"*What . . . did . . . you . . . say . . . ?*" demanded his lady, terribly.

317

His bridges burned behind him, Mordecai went the distance and, keeping his gaze on the Runner, said, "Pray be still, madam." Wilhelmina's jaw dropped, and taking advantage of the awed silence, he went on, "I shall hold him here. You get to the stables, dear boy. The grooms will strike those fetters from your wrists in a trice!"

"By . . . George . . !" said Bolster, enormously impressed. "Courage above and b-beyond, sir! Come on, Harry!"

The twinkle faded from Diccon's pale eyes. "I really *am* from Bow Street, Reverend, and it is only fair to warn you that this is a very special case with international ramifications. Your calling will not help you—no more than Lord Bolster's rank will protect him. If I am in any way interfered with, you and your lady, together with Lady Moulton, must be judged accomplices."

Wilhelmina recovered sufficiently to turn a stern frown on the Runner. "How *dare* you threaten my husband, sir?" she said with somewhat dubious logic.

Harry, his eyes locked with Diccon's, swallowed pride and pleaded, "Five minutes start? For friendship's sake . . ?"

"By force only," answered the Runner inexorably. "In which event these people will have no choice but to flee the country."

"Much would we care for that!" Lady Salia came to slip her hand in Harry's arm and smile fondly at him. "You surely cannot believe, my dear, that we could be happy, knowing your life was the price of a short sojourn abroad? Besides, John has grumbled incessantly that we have not yet had a proper honeymoon. We shall travel, and have a lovely time. And at all events, you will be acquitted very soon, so that we can come home again."

"Very soon . . ." *Never* was more probable. Watching her sweet face, Harry thought of how long she and John Moulton had been kept apart by a capricious Fate. And now at last they were joyously together in the home they both loved. He glanced at Bolster. His friend's grin was as bright, his loyalty as true as ever. And Jerry was to be married to Amanda as soon as she returned from Belgium. How would little Mandy like living in exile? His aunt was watching her husband, an expression in her eyes he'd never seen before and that he now realized was admiration. As if sensing his regard, she turned to him and smiled, and he knew that she too would stick by him, whatever the cost.

Bolster saw hope die from his eyes and cried furiously, "You cannot prove your innocence, you great g-gudgeon! They will surely hang you!"

"Oh, no they will not!" Langridge repudiated hotly, but as Diccon gave a grim smile and stepped forward a pace, he blenched.

Bolster whipped the gun from his shaking hands. "Your pardon, sir, but—not quite in your line, y'know. Toddle off, Harry. And good luck, d-dear old boy! I'll hold this Trap 'till you're away safe."

Diccon said a quiet, "I trust you are prepared to fire, my lord," and again paced forward.

A deadly glint lit Bolster's usually mild hazel eyes. "One more step," he gritted softly, "and I will blow your miserable head off!"

"No, you won't," Harry intervened. "It is of no use. He's only following orders, and—"

Bolster's jaw set, and the angle of the gun shifted. Recognizing that this intrepid young man had every intention of crippling him, at the very least, Diccon threw up one imperative hand.

Three stern-faced men armed with pistols stepped from the shrubs beside the drive, and although the weapons were not aimed, their eyes were fastened steadily on Lord Bolster.

"Oh . . . damme!" groaned Jeremy, and lowered his weapon.

Her calm breaking, Lady Salia gave a sob and, running to throw herself into Harry's arms, was balked as the handcuffs came between them. "*Must* you put those horrid things on him?" she wept.

"I wish I could remove 'em, ma'am, I do assure you. But, I've reason to know how handy he is with his fists."

Diccon gestured to his men, one of whom whistled, and a black coach rumbled around from the front of the house.

Lady Salia pressed a hand to her lips, and Harry jerked his head to Bolster who at once came over and drew her gently away. "You're never going to haul him off in *that* monstrous thing?" he raged, patting Salia's shoulder. "Deuce take you! He's a baronet!"

"A baronet who has murdered a foreign diplomat of noble birth," Diccon pointed out. "However, I will not take Sir Harry to gaol in the coach. He can ride with me."

Two saddle horses were brought forward, at the sight of which Langridge cried an aghast, "*Ride*? Through the streets? With those—damnable shackles for all to see?"

Diccon smiled faintly. "Are you ready, Sir Harry?"

Harry was assisted into the saddle. Langridge and Bolster came to clutch his hands, to stammer out promises of aid and support, and to watch, grieving, as Diccon mounted and took up the bridle of the other horse.

One of the Runners climbed into the cart. The other two entered the coach.

Harry bent to kiss Wilhelmina and Salia, and with his head well up and his face paper white, began the journey to gaol.

Convinced the Surrey Gaol would be a likely destination, Harry's heart sank when they passed through that pleasant county and came to the outskirts of the great city. But long after the countryside had given way to cobbled streets and ever denser buildings, long after the clear air was sullied by the smoke from countless chimney pots, and the sweet songs of birds replaced by shouts and turmoil, by jostling crowds and the unceasing rumble of wheels, he would not believe Newgate. They passed through slums and the black coach pulled up very close to protect him from the hail of bottles, stones, and refuse that greeted the appearance of a flash cove—a nob—and in bracelets! But not until he saw the great glooming pile rising above the shacks and nightmare dwellings of the poor could he credit it. Not until they rode into the yard and he was ordered by a stern Diccon to dismount, and then was gripped by each arm and hauled unceremoniously into the terrible old building did it finally burst upon him in all its horror. Captain Sir Harry Allison Redmond was no more. In his place was the villain in the poster—an accused murderer and kidnapper, who would be despised by the upper strata of those who inhabited this hell on earth, and hated by the lower.

Once inside the building he was subjected to a brief interrogation. Stunned and exhausted, he no longer saw faces and knew only that he passed under a succession of eyes, variously stern, sneering, or hate-filled. He was dully aware of tramping along noisome, narrow, and odorous corridors; of a dim door flung open to reveal a dark, tiny cell, the murky slot that served for a window, a sagging cot. A sardonic voice informed him he was "too hoity-toity t'be in with the rest of 'em!"; a hand shoved violently at the small of his back. He staggered forward, heard the door clang shut, and crouched, head bowed, trembling, in the near darkness.

"Sit down in it, sir! Do not step over it! *Sit down in it . . !*"

The voice was so real it might have been in the room with him. His head jerked up and he peered around dazedly. General Craufurd had been used to scream that adjuration at his men did they dare step over a puddle in the line of march . . . Harry sank against the dank wall. He was not in Spain surrounded by his indomitable troops. He did not hear the tramp of countless feet, the hoofbeats of horses and mules, the shouted ribaldry of the men. He heard instead a drunken yowling, the rattle of a tin cup across bars; a song without melody or decipherable words that told of despair, and the sobbing of some poor woman, God help her!

He closed his eyes and bowed his forehead against the stone. "My father was Sir Colin Redmond," he whispered, "and my grandfather, General Lord Harry Allison . . ." He repeated it time and again until at length the crushing sense of being buried alive faded a little; until his pride reasserted itself, and he pushed panic back whence it had sprung. He looked up at the 'window' again and squared his shoulders. A grim smile curving his mouth he

321

muttered, "Thank you, sir. I may have to sit down it it—but, by God! I'll not step over it!"

"So you shot him," said the dispassionate voice, "because you were struck by the falling tree. And you did not see the lightning."

This time, the questioning seemed to have lasted for several days, with each question more asinine than the last. Harry was very tired and longed to lean against the wall of his cell. He sighed, knowing that would not be permitted, and raising one hand against the glare of the lantern, said wearily, "I *did* see the lightning. I did *not* see it strike the tree. *Bonjour*, Diccon."

"You were pinned by the tree," Diccon went on relentlessly, "yet you managed to free your arm, and fire—"

"You, sir," Harry observed regretfully, "are bacon-brained, that's what it is. The gun went off *as I fell.* I wish to see my solicitor. I have had no visitors since I came to this spa. It has been—" he thought a minute. "Two weeks . . ?"

"Ten days, Redmond. And you have had visitors. The newspaper people . . ."

"Egad! They have seen me, and sketched me, and talked their stupid damned heads off. And they do not listen any more than do you!" He peered vainly into the light. "Mr. Fox would be better company!"

"When you were lying there upon your right side, was it—"

"My left side, dear Diccon. My *left* side."

"Ah, yes—you were trapped upon your injured arm—yet managed to free yourself—unaided. What an astounding stoic."

"Man of iron, sir. Had you not realized?" His laugh sounded a trifle shrill, and he bit it back abruptly, repeating, "I wish to see—"

"These . . ?" Diccon tossed some newspapers at him. Catching them, Harry swore. He was on the front page of the *Gazette*; the *Morning Post* featured a large sketch of him on Page Two; and he rated the third page of *The Times*. The captions seemed gigantic: 'Aristocrat to Hang for Brutal

Murder!' 'Titled War Hero in Newgate!' 'No coddling for Baronet Fiend!' The sketches showed him unshaven and gaunt, yet with a hint of jauntiness about him, as though even in this ghastly place he retained some remnant of pride. And that same pride flailed him. What must Mitch be suffering before such public disgrace? And Nanette . . ?

Diccon was jabbering again—pounding at him, as he had done day and night seemingly, since his arrival. Allowing his tired eyes to skim a grossly dramatized article, Harry learned that although he was weak from injuries incurred while rescuing his victim from a maddened bull, he had been denied any special treatment. It seemed an odd report, and reading on, he learned that the Authorities were merciless by reason of the international aspects of the case and their fear of offending the French. Puzzled, he could only assume this to be blatant sensationalism. In actual fact, a doctor had visited him several times and pronounced himself well satisfied with the state of the arm. The next article had him chained to the wall in a mouldering dungeon reminiscent of the Middle Ages, yet in good spirits, though he stubbornly refused to answer any questions concerning the Brutal Crime, and denied adamantly that he was, in fact, Protecting Another! "Oh, my lord!" thought Harry. And imagining Nanette in this hellhole, felt sick.

A truncheon prodded him gently. "Horrified," he mumbled, scarce knowing what he was answering.

"You are quite sure of that?" purred Diccon. "When Sanguinet was hit he looked—horrified . . ?"

"What?" Still absorbed by the article, Harry muttered, "Oh, yes—yes. What would you expect, you jackass?"

"I would expect it to be rather difficult for you to know that, Redmond. Since he was hit—in the back! My, what a long neck you must have!"

Comprehending too late, Harry stumbled, "No! I—I was paying no attention, that's all. I—"

"You spoke the truth for the first time since we brought you here!" Diccon's voice was a snap of steel. "Sanguinet was shot *after* you were downed! By someone striving to prevent your own mur—"

323

"No!" cried Harry, dropping the newspaper. "He—it was—"

"It was a pack of lies!" thundered Diccon, standing, his face eerily highlighted by the glow of the lantern. "You *watched* him killed by somebody else!"

"No! Damn you! No! *I* killed him! I was holding the pistol when the tree fell, and—"

"*This*—pistol . . ?"

Into the brighter beam from the lantern came Diccon's hand, holding a black pistol. It was the first time Harry had seen it since he'd lain there helpless during that ravening storm; shocked into silence, he stared down at it. Almost, he could hear Sanguinet's gloating laughter, the voice of the thunder, the howling of the wind . . . He fought to think clearly . . . Diccon was trying to trap him, no doubt. They probably knew which was the correct weapon. "No," he muttered, drawing back instinctively, "not that one."

Now those lean fingers held a weapon that gleamed silver in the lamplight, just as it had gleamed in Nanette's little hand. Harry swung his eyes away and nodded.

"Admit it, then! You killed Parnell Sanguinet with this. You shot him in the back with this silver pistol! Do you confess?"

The black-hearted devil was after Nanette! Well, he'd not drag her into this, the slimy, damned trickster! "How many times must I say it?" he raged. "Are you totally caper witted? Yes! Yes! Have *done*, man!"

"Well, damn your eyes and limbs! Why in the devil didn't you tell me that at the start?"

The lantern was raised to reveal Diccon, tall and astoundingly elegant in a long-tailed black jacket and grey pantaloons, his cravat a masterpiece, his features contorted by anger. "You miserable, blasted hedgebird! If you had only trusted me, none of this would have been necessary!"

For an instant Harry merely blinked at him. Then he leaned against the wall and this time was not forced to stand upright. "Trusted . . . *you*?" he echoed. "Why you slippery serpent! You've deceived and manoeuvred and confounded me from the first instant we met! I'd have to be *looby* to trust you!"

"Well, I hope you're satisfied! Ten days of purgatory you've put me through! Keeping you in here, wearing you down until I could tear the truth out of you! Is *that* what she shot him with?" He tossed up a hand as Harry crouched, ready to spring, and the guards moved forward. "Why, you cockaleery doddipoll! It ain't *possible*! Can you not understand? *No one* could have shot Parnell Sanguinet with this pistol! It's brand new. It has never—*ever*—been fired! When my men finally found it yesterday, it was not even *loaded*!"

"But, if I did not shoot him," said Harry slowly, massaging wrists from which the loathed chains had just been struck, "and Miss Carlson did not . . ."

"Who did?" Diccon's thin fingers drummed briefly on the top of the battered old desk. His office was a cluttered little room not much larger than Harry's cell, sparsely furnished, and with only two wooden chairs for visitors. "I rather fancy we'll have a deuce of a time to learn that. Many men had reason to hate him, any one of whom could have crept into the room in the darkness and confusion, without being seen by either you or the lady."

Tensing, Harry leaned forward. "Damn you! Have you known all the time I did not shoot him?"

Diccon gave an amused chuckled. "You begin to know me too well. No—" he gestured placatingly, "do not add my murder to your—unsavoury reputation."

"Devil! Yet you dragged me through the streets like some—some common filth, kept me in this—hell . . ! And all the time—blast your eyes! *Why*?"

Staring inscrutably at the ravaged young face, Diccon read rage there, and suffering and sorrow, but not hatred. Even now Redmond was too much the military man not to understand the demands of duty, too intelligent to be shabbed off with pure nonsense, and too innately decent to warrant such. It was, in fact, damned difficult not to be fond of the quixotic gudgeon . . . "I suspected," he admitted, "that you were not the killer. You, however, were named by M. Claude Sanguinet." He frowned, and again his narrow fingers did their nervous beating on the desktop. "A very powerful man. You ran. Miss Carlson disappeared. Your friends brought all the force they could muster to your defence, and made life blisteringly hot for me, deuce take 'em! Miss Carlson came forward then and attempted to clear you of kidnapping her, of course, but that charge was obscured by the greater one."

"But—*you* knew!" gritted Harry. "And you also are—a powerful man."

"Not that powerful, else I would award this nation's highest honour to whomever did pull that trigger!" His eyes glinted briefly, then he gave a wry grin. "I'm just a poor public servant, unfortunately. And I was faced with a shrewd campaign by a man with unlimited funds. The populace was stirred to a frenzy by allegations that you would be acquitted because of your rank. Versailles was furious because one of her top diplomats had been murdered. The Foreign Office and the Horse Guards . . ." he shuddered. "They were berserk! Prinny was in a ghastly squeeze, and when you ran and would say nothing to clear yourself, they all hove a sigh of relief and said, *en effet*, 'So be it!' I had no choice but to—"

"To haul me half across England in manacles?" blazed Harry.

Diccon said lazily, "My masterstroke. It worked rather well, I thought."

The wind taken out of his sails, Harry stared at him blankly.

"Suppose," murmured Diccon, "we had allowed you to stay in the Surrey Gaol as Leigh-Hunt was permitted to do? Suppose you'd been decently fed and housed? You'd have appeared at your trial with your proud head high, as elegant and defiant as you could stare, would you not?"

"Be assured of it!"

"Birdwit! And you'd have been hanged!"

Harry's eyes widened and, silenced, he leaned back in his chair.

"I'll tell you this," Diccon imparted, scowling, "Much of your misery was self-induced! Had you allowed yourself to be taken by my bubble-fingered men, and God knows I'd enough of 'em seeking you!—you'd have fared better and not come so nigh to having your neck stretched."

"By God . . !" gasped Harry. "You mount a subtle campaign, sir. But—I could wish I'd been allowed to know of it!"

"Had you been of a different stamp, you would have. But—you're a hell of a poor actor, Redmond. I thought—when we put you in that little box . . ." He saw Harry's eyes narrow again and waved his hand apologetically. "Yes. Your brother told me that you feared small places. My regrets. But—I'd to choose between letting you hang—or trying to break you."

Harry fought back an all-but-overmastering urge to smash his fists into that suave countenance. "And—did your scheme work well enough that my innocence will be believed?"

"Don't be a fool. There are those who will always cherish the notion that the aristocracy won again!" He smiled, but there was no answering smile in the eyes that watched him. Redmond, he thought, had detected a break in the rope . . .

"You said," Harry observed slowly, "Sanguinet has 'unlimited funds'. If that is so, then—why was Carlson murdered? Had Sanguinet already appropriated his step-daughter's fortune?"

"Not to my knowledge. He's vastly well breeched. But nobody needs money like a rich man, you know."

The light tone failed to banish Harry's frown. "My father's murder," he muttered, "was in some way connected with that damnable coach!"

Diccon's expression changed not in the slightest. Only a faint flaring of the thin nostrils accompanied his puzzled, "Coach . . ?"

Harry stood and, leaning forward, placed both hands on the desk. "Frederick Carlson was not murdered so that Parnell could appropriate his daughter's fortune—you said so yourself. Yet he *was* murdered. Dreading scandal, or any investigation, Sanguinet had my father brutally killed. Why? Because he saw the first murder—or was it because of something else he saw? Something Sanguinet dared not have revealed . . .'' He saw a flicker in Diccon's eyes and swept on triumphantly. "It *was* that coach—wasn't it? If Parnell was troubled by daylight, he could simply have installed dark curtains. Instead, he went to elaborate lengths to make his coach appear to be unoccupied! Why?''

''What matter?'' Diccon opened his drawer in bored fashion and began to pare his nails with a knife he found there. ''He was a madman . . .''

Harry slammed clenched fists on the desk. "You *lie*! Tell me, or I'll—''

''That will do!'' Diccon's eyes were a blue flame, his mouth a hard, thin line. He put away the knife and snapped, ''Sit down, Captain!''

Harry's jaw set, and his own eyes blazed, but he felt suddenly as though he stood before his Colonel's desk, and he sat down.

''I have used you,'' Diccon said curtly. ''And will make no apologies for having done so. Nor should you feel abused, since your father's death has been avenged. To all intents and purposes, Colin Redmond was killed because he saw murder done. Because I have—er—deceived you, I put myself to the bother of attempting to bring you off from this. But be aware, friend, that I could just as easily have thrown you to the wolves and let your heroics reap the full penalty! *Be still!*'' The silence that followed those thundered-out words was absolute. Then Diccon leaned forward, a smile leaping into his eyes, a warmth softening his voice. ''Harry—confound you, you're a pest, if ever I was saddled with one! But you are also an honourable gentleman and entitled, I suppose, to an explanation. I will have your word though, that you will speak of this to no one . . ?''

''You have it.''

''Very well.'' Diccon settled back in his chair, frowned through a thoughtful moment, then said slowly, ''It is believed—it is *known*—that there is a conspiracy afoot that threatens both the life of the Prince Regent and the future

328

of England.'' He raised one hand to quiet Harry's startled utterance. ''We fight a group of fanatics. Power-mad, ruthless financial giants. The Sanguinets are up to their necks it it; not for France, but for themselves. The coach was a crucial factor in a coup that we managed to circumvent. Parnell later used that same coach for his own schemes, much to his brother's wrath.'' He shrugged, and went on in a milder tone, ''More I cannot reveal, save that we lack the evidence to charge them . . . Take my advice, friend. You've run your race. You're free. Live. And do not concern yourself with matters best left to those of us whose business it is to handle them. You are exceedingly fortunate to have made the acquaintance of Mrs. Penderly.''

Taken off-stride by the abrupt remark, Harry knit his brow. Mrs. Penderly . . . the name sounded so familiar . . .

''I understand,'' Diccon murmured, ''that she met your brother during his assault on the Chateau Sanguinet, and later, encountered you near Horsham on the night Parnell met his just desserts.''

''Jove! Was it the same lady, then? Now I come to think on it, she *did* mistake me for someone else.''

''Your father,'' nodded Diccon, and in response to the surprised pucker of Harry's forehead, added, ''Yes. Interesting coincidence, eh? She was with your father on the night of *his* death. I gather that in Dinan she took a great liking to Mitch—''

''*With*—my father?'' Harry interposed, totally mystified. ''But Sir Colin was at Sanguinet Towers that night. How could he have had a—er . . .''

''Romantic assignation? Oh, no. It wasn't that. They met purely by chance. A wheel had come off the lady's coach, and your papa was so gallant as to prevail upon his companion to stop and assist her.''

Harry stared at those impassive features. ''I don't understand. If my father was at Sanguinet Towers, and—Besides he couldn't— *What* companion?''

''Good gracious, Redmond, you do muddle your phraseology. Why, the gentleman who accompanied your father, of course. Mrs. Penderly said he was most reticent, and wouldn't lift a hand—or even come near her. It was your papa who conveyed the ladies to the village inn, and your papa who rousted out the blacksmith and had the wheel repaired. He even paid the reckoning, since the lady had lost all her pin money playing silver loo at her party.''

His heart pounding madly, Harry came to his feet. "For God's sake man—what are you saying? Have you found a witness who says she was with my father on the evening of his death? *How* did you find her? Can you be *sure* she knows it was my father who—''

Diccon thrust a miniature at him. Taking it, Harry stared down at his sire's beloved features. The last time he'd seen it, the miniature had been on Mitchell's bedside table at Moiré . . . His eyes lifted wonderingly to Diccon's bland smile.

"I showed it to Mrs. Penderly," the Runner nodded. "She's positive about the date because it was her sister's birthday party she'd been attending. And she's positive your father is the man who helped her. And—no, I do not propose to go into the details of how we were able to find the little lady.''

Harry slipped the miniature into his pocket, his tired mind groping . . . "Then . . . he must have been with her for some time that night . . .''

"From at least half-past nine o'clock until after midnight, she claims.''

"My . . . God . . !'' Leaning forward, both hands on the desk top once more, his face flushed with excitement, Harry gasped, "Do you realize what that means? Diccon—if my father was with Mrs. Penderly, he could not *possibly* have spent the evening with Parnell Sanguinet! He *could not* have gambled away Moiré, and his fortune!''

A twinkle gleamed in those deep eyes. "Well now,'' drawled Diccon. "Ain't that a—as y'might say—interesting . . . development?''

CHAPTER XX

DANIEL'S BLAST ON THE YARD OF TIN WOULD HAVE WOKEN the dead. And Moiré Grange was, it would seem, very much alive. Even as Harry marvelled at the excellence with which the fire damage had been repaired, the front doors were swung wide and before the carriage had halted a lackey ran to open the door and let down the steps. Joseph, openly weeping, followed. Not trusting himself to speak, Harry slipped a hand onto the old man's shoulder. "You're home . . . sir," the butler choked. "*We're* home!" Harry corrected gruffly, walking with him into the house.

In the hall many of his former servants were drawn up, but the ranks broke and they greeted him emotionally, each one eager to seize his hand. Mrs. Norah Bacon curtsied, then threw her arms about him, sobbing, "I *knew* you would be cleared, Master Harry! I *knew* it!" Mrs. Thomas rushed to embrace him, lifting a wet cheek for his kiss. The loved and familiar scents of the old place filled his nostrils . . . Flowers and furniture polish . . . and a cake baking . . .

The door to the main salon crashed open and Mitchell ran forward, hands outstretched. Harry strode to take them, regarded his brother's twitching mouth mistily, then swept him into a fierce hug.

Joyful shouts rang out. "Welcome home!" "Good old Harry's back!" "Our gaolbird!"

He had to draw a sleeve across his eyes hastily as they crowded around him. Bolster, beaming with joy; Camille

Damon, his smile a white gleam in his dark face; Sergeant Anderson, blinking through a glitter of tears. John and Salia Moulton watched smilingly from the open salon doors, and Harry went quickly to kiss Salia and shake hands with Lord John. "Sir, I pray you will forgive the trouble I caused—"

"Nonsense, boy," said Moulton kindly, slapping him on the back. "I am only delighted we were able to be of help."

Harry turned to his brother. "Mitch . . . Is it—truly ours again?"

"Lock, stock, and barrel, *Sauvage*."

"Claude Sanguinet was—ah—prevailed upon to . . . deed it back to you," nodded Moulton, his brown eyes alight. "Together with your fortune."

"He had no choice when Mrs. Penderly told her story." Lady Salia squeezed her husband's arm fondly and, smiling up into his pleasant, ruddy features, added, "John and Harland were prepared to take it to Prinny himself had he not done so."

"Harland? I thought the Earl was still in Paris."

"Came back specially," said Mitchell. "You'd not have believed the fury he and the Duke of Vaille turned on Bow Street!"

"And my honoured sire," put in Damon with a mischievous grin, "can be a terror when aroused—as I can testify."

"D-Did you know your smuggler is a c-c-confounded *major*?" asked Bolster. "Do not ask me of wh-wh-what . . . Free Traders, most likely! But when he found that Penderly woman, it turned the trick."

"Ah, but Claude Sanguinet tried to wriggle out of it!" Mordecai Langridge hurried to clasp Harry's outthrust hand and wring it hard. "But I would have none of it! 'My nephews,' said I, 'have suffered enough at the hands of your murderous clan, sir!' Far be it from me to speak ill of the dead, for it goes against my calling, as well you know, dear boy, but Parnell Sanguinet was a monstrous evil creature, and there comes a time to call a spade a spade!'' He turned to his wife who had followed majestically. ''Ain't that right, m'dear?''

'' 'Remorseless, treacherous, lecherous, kindless villain!' '' she quoted, beaming as she turned from wrapping Harry in her large embrace.

''Gad . . !'' Bolster whispered in his ear. ''What's that?''

''Sounds like *Macbeth*,'' breathed Harry.

''Hamlet,'' Mitchell corrected softly.

Lady Salia came to take Harry's face between her hands and, smiling fondly up at him, said, ''Welcome home, my dear.''

Home . . !

The fire in the pleasant panelled lounge was dying now, and neither of the brothers was willing to disrupt his comfortable occupancy of the deep armchairs to add another log since it was well past midnight. ''Y'know,'' murmured Harry sleepily, ''we scarcely ever use this room . . . Pity.''

Half to himself, Mitchell said, ''I still cannot credit it! When Diccon said that those blasted newspaper articles had proven 'quite useful' I was ready to strangle him.''

Harry sat straighter in his chair. ''You were at Newgate?''

''What the devil d'you mean by that? Of course I was at Newgate! Every damned day! As were Bolster and Cam!''

''I should have known, of course,'' apologized Harry, and by neither look nor word betrayed his inner consternation at that swift boil of anger, so foreign to his hitherto mild-mannered brother.

His very gentleness, however, was a rebuke. Mitchell coloured up and drew an impatient hand across his brow. ''I'm sorry.'' He gave a taut smile. ''Frightfully hot at hand these days, am I not?''

Harry acknowledged that they'd both had a bad few weeks and paused, the new tensions between them causing him to choose his words with care. Before he could utter them, Mitchell said hurriedly, ''Speaking of the Sanguinets, the thing *I* cannot understand is that silver pistol. Why in the devil did Guy carry it in his sling? Why was it not loaded?''

A small crease appeared between Harry's brows. He had lost his opportunity to try to talk out the problem. But quite obviously the questions had been tossed in so swiftly because Mitchell did not wish to discuss his troubles. Respecting that, he answered, ''I cannot but feel sorry for the fellow. He was properly caught. Loving the girl his brother was hounding; too much of a gentleman to countenance it, too loyal to his brother to fight him.''

''He certainly tried to help me, irregardamnless!'' Mitchell's eyes were very grim. ''Considering I'd put a ball through his chest, it was pretty decent of him.''

The fine hands were tight clenched, and sensing how hard it had been for him to refer to the matter, Harry said easily, ''I think he had decided to get Nanette away somehow. He took the pistol but daren't load it for fear he'd actually shoot Parnell. He bluffed me with it fairly. When I saw it in Nanette's hand later, I was sure she'd shot her stepfather, to save me.'' He added with a wry smile, ''And I suppose *she* thought *I* had shot him.''

''Don't you *know* what she thought?''

The unease that had been gnawing at Harry all day deepened. There was a coldness now to Mitchell's handsome features. The eyes were hard; the mouth set in a sardonic line. Had Parnell's whip so changed the boy? Or was it that he, too, loved Nanette and was grieving . . ? ''I suppose,'' he evaded, ''you will be returning to your little schoolhouse?''

If Mitchell was vexed by that evasion, he gave no sign of it. ''I think not,'' he said slowly. ''If you've no objections, I mean to spend the summer in the south of France, with Jacques and Bolster.''

Bolster? De Roule was to be expected; he and Mitch had formed a deep attachment shortly after that dreadful mess Lucian St. Clair had become involved in last autumn, but— Bolster? ''Are you sure? Since Jerry will be shackled soon, I should have thought he'd—'' Harry broke off, Mitchell's grave expression recalling several hints that had come his way and that he'd ignored, unwilling to believe anything could go wrong with so ideal a match. "Oh, the devil!" he groaned. "Mandy has cried off!"

Mitchell nodded. "Bolster knew you would worry for his sake. And he had no wish to add to your burdens."

"Damn and blast!" Harry stood, paced to the fire, and kicked angrily at the smouldering log. "It's because of her murdering hound of a brother, I collect?"

"She feels, so I hear, that she is unfit to become Lady Jeremy."

"That curst gudgeon!" Harry spun around. "He said not one word of it! I thought, once or twice, he seemed a trifle glum, but—oh, dammitall! How could Mandy be so feather-witted? He adores her! She must be mad to throw away every chance of happiness for both of them just because of her high-in-the-instep pride! And what in the deuce are you grinning about?"

"It would appear," Mitchell shrugged, "to be the onset of an epidemic."

A slow flush darkened Harry's face. He turned away and stared down into the dying fire.

"If you do not offer for Nanette, you're a prize fool."

"Then . . . I am a prize fool."

"Yes indeed!" Mitchell's lip curled his scorn. "Merely because she chances to be an heiress?"

"One of the richest heiresses in all Europe."

"And one who loves you—for reasons unknown."

Harry gave a wry smile, though the acid cynicism was bewildering. "I wonder. Or was it all part of Diccon's plot . . ."

Mitchell's frown became thunderous. "By God! If you were any other man . . !" But realizing that his fist had clenched, he turned from Harry's wondering stare and said hurriedly, "Moiré is a fine old place, with a splendid park, and—"

"And would fit into a corner of Carlson Terrace and be lost."

"For lord's sake, Harry! You do not care about her

money—you've never had the least sense in such matters! Instead of considering her happiness, you choose to immolate yourself like some stupid noble knight of old! Why in the name of God don't you forget that stuffy pride of yours that is as outdated as—"

"I think, Mitchell . . . that you have said enough." Harry's voice was level but warning, and anger flashed in his eyes.

For an instant an answering glare shone in Mitchell's eyes; then he walked to the side table, slammed his glass down, and stared at it in fulminating silence.

Harry watched him frowningly. He felt shut out now, as though Mitchell had withdrawn and brooded in some distant place, clutching his hurts to himself and allowing none to approach. There had been many differences between them through the years, but never such bitter rage. Deeply disturbed, he came up behind his brother and placed one hand on the taut shoulder. "Forgive me, old fellow. I know you mean to help, but . . ."

Mitchell turned at once and, cuffing him gently, said, "It's just . . . I cannot bear to—to think of her knowing any more grief."

"And do you think I enjoy it? Mitch—try to understand. All her life she's been hounded, fawned upon, victimized. And all because of that blasted fortune! When I first met her she was like—like a wild thing! Ready to do battle at the least hint of friendliness, convinced any such overture was for one purpose only—to win her affections, and thereby—her money."

"But you knew nothing of her fortune then. She must surely be aware that you fell in love with her *before* you knew."

"Perhaps. But how can *anyone* really know what is in the heart of another? I think she still believes all men are predators. And thus her only chance for happiness is to wed someone like Camille Damon, or Hawkhurst, or young Hilby. Men so wealthy her own fortune would be of no consequence."

"Fool!" Mitchell exploded. "You've not seen how she looks at you when you do not know it! I have!"

"Don't get on your high ropes again," smiled Harry but as Mitchell threw up his hands in exasperation, said haltingly, "Don't you see, Mitch? She would never be sure. If I lost my temper, even once, she would think—'Did he offer for love . . ? Or—' "

Mitchell spat out a furious epithet. Harry sighed and for a moment said nothing. Then he asked softly, "How many times did she come to see me? She surely must have realized when she read the newspapers why I wrote to her as I did. She undoubtedly knows Moiré has been restored to us. If she loved me as deeply as you say—would she not have come here, and—"

"And done what, Sir Arrogant Puffery?" sneered Mitchell. "Gone down on her knees to your all-hallowed nobility?"

Harry smiled a haunted, wistful smile and, mindful of Nanette's fiery pride, said sadly, "On the day my little shrew stooped to do *that*, my haughty cub, I would indeed wed her."

The next month swept by. Required to testify at several hearings and with the Bow Street coach becoming a regular visitor to Moiré Grange, Harry was also engulfed in the business of his estate and the mass of correspondence that had accrued during his absence. He performed the latter task in leisurely fashion, since his eager search through the pile had discovered nothing addressed in the feminine hand he so longed to see. Over two months since he had last laid eyes on his love, with no word—no sign . . . She had written him off, obviously. Perhaps it was as well.

Mitchell had left for Brussels, where he was to join de Roule and Bolster. Jeremy had fled directly after Harry's homecoming, unable to confront his friend with the news that he had been jilted. Ten days after his departure, a long letter of explanation arrived at Moiré, but since his scrawl was all but illegible, his spelling outrageous, and the phrases hopelessly disjointed, Harry was only able to guess at most of the contents. That Jeremy was totally grief-stricken was very obvious, however, and he at once dashed off a letter to Mitch begging to be kept advised of Bolster's state of mind.

Diccon drove down one morning and, during a brief visit, idly let fall the news that Devil Dice was now being sought in connection with the murder of Parnell Sanguinet. Dice, it seemed, had been a very unwilling tool for the Frenchman, his services secured by Sanguinet's knowledge of his true identity. He had escaped soon after being apprehended in Winchester and thus far had avoided recapture, although posters were up from Land's End to John o'Groats. Harry shuddered, knowing all too well the nightmares of such a flight; and having remarked dryly that such sentiments were wasted on 'that vermin', Diccon took his leave.

His departure emphasized a fact that Harry had been seeking to ignore: He was lonely. Mitchell and most of his friends were either abroad or in the country. Jocelyn Vaughan had written, inviting him to spend the summer at a "jolly fine house" he'd rented on the Steyne at Brighton, but although he was fond of Vaughan, Harry's spirits were downcast and the thought of a stay with that dynamic young Corinthian lacked appeal. He was in no mood, either, for the social whirl offered by Lord Edward Ridgley. The Earl, an old and dear friend, was the best of company, but so warm hearted he could not fail to be dismayed by any trace of low spirits, and to be obliged to feign cheerfulness was more than Harry could undertake. He apprehended at this point in his reflections that he missed his friends—yet did not wish to be with them. He decided, therefore, that this was the perfect time for him to go into London, for he must sooner or later do something about acquiring a house there, and although he could leave the matter in Anderson's capable hands, it was a task he preferred to attend to personally. To this end, he ordered his curricle prepared for the following morning, and having infuriated both Anderson and Jed Cotton by saying he would be driving himself, instructed the Sergeant to pack a valise with sufficient clothing for a few days in Town.

Next morning he was on the road before noon. The greys were fine steppers and eager to go, and he gave them their heads whenever traffic permitted, flashing along the turnpike at speeds that brought shouts of wrath ringing out behind him. It was a fine day, the air brisk and a stiff breeze blowing. He concentrated upon the beauties of the field and hedgerow, of deep blue skies, the invigorating smell to the air, and how extremely fortunate he was to be here at all. He could, he told himself determinedly, have been killed in Winchester, or died when his arm became gangrenous. Even now he might be slowly going mad in that nightmare slot of a cell in Newgate, or perhaps at this very moment mounting the steps of a scaffold. He had so very much for which to be thankful. He sighed and urged the greys onward, waving his whip gaily at an infuriated heavyset gentleman who shook a fist in response, his whiskers all but sticking straight out from purpling cheeks as the curricle shot past with a good inch to spare.

Harry lunched at a favourite old tavern outside Dorking, unable to pass by the place where he was assured of receiving a warm welcome. Sure enough he was bowed to, beamed upon, and ushered to his customary table with so much pomp that one might have suspected the Regent himself had arrived. They had never doubted dear Sir Harry—not for one single second, the host's good wife imparted, *sotto voce*. Others had, thought Harry, beyond a doubt. Even now a young lieutenant of hussars was surveying him furtively. He would, he realized, for a time, at least, be a target for curiosity wherever he went. There was only one way to handle it . . . His friendly grin brought an immediate answering smile and the two young men were very soon not only sharing a table but an animated discussion of how Blücher should have brought up his troops at Waterloo. When it transpired that his new acquaintance was journeying to Tunbridge Wells and a mill between Gentleman Thorpe and the Tooting Terror, Harry's plans underwent a radical change.

At four o'clock he was sitting atop the Lieutenant's chaise in a field outside the Wells, lustily cheering the efforts of two blood-spattered, muddied and perspiring pugilists whose efforts having been considerably prolonged by much wrangling among their seconds, seemed likely to be halted by the weather. Heavy clouds were building, and Harry was irritated by the knowledge that he should have brought his chaise, as Andy had urged. He was not so enchanted by the mill as to allow his greys to stand in the rain and, having invited the Lieutenant to visit Moiré, returned to his curricle. Many other gentlemen were attempting to leave. Harry jockeyed his team expertly through the near-impossible tangle of vehicles, only to be backed into on the very fringe of the crowd by an exceedingly youthful would-be Corinthian driving a high-perch phaeton.

An hour later, his right rear wheel badly sprung, one of his greys limping from a sprained knee, and his temper considerably frayed, Harry reached the nearest livery stable. It was full dark before he was sufficiently satisfied with the condition of his horse to summon a hackney and venture into the by-now teeming rain, and his mood was not lightened by the jarvey's disclosure that the Wells was crowded to overflowing by reason of the mill. His vexed insistence that the man must know of *something* brought only the mournful verdict that there was nought as would befit 'his honour'. Harry smiled faintly and thought that the jarvey, at least, had not recognized him! He was about to return to the livery stable and attempt to hire another team when the route they followed brought a jog of memory. He instructed his driver to turn right at the next corner and, disregarding the firm observation that "there ain't nothing fitting down there!" peered eagerly through the downpour.

A weeping willow that drooped beside the lane . . . a wide sweep of lawn, and at the edge, a sign, rain drenched and creaking in the wind, that proclaimed, "Mrs. Burnett's. A Refined Boarding House for the Genteel Traveller." In a voice rendered hoarse by nostalgia, Harry told the jarvey to pull up and wait. He sprang lightly down and, with the collar of his splendid six-caped coat upturned and his hat tilted jauntily over one eye, ran to the door.

The angular lady at the counter looked up in no little astonishment as the tall young Corinthian closed the door on a flurry of wind and rain and, doffing his hat, revealed a head of thick, slightly curling dark hair and a pair of fine eyes that not only brightened her own but brought a dubious recognition.

"Aha," smiled Harry, relieved that she had not exclaimed in outright horror at the sight of him. "So you remember me, ma'am."

"Well now, sir," she said uncertainly. "Seems as if I do—and then again, I doesn't. I don't usually forget eyes . . . But—the only young gentleman I can recollect with eyes like yourn was a naughty rascal wot fair turned this old place upside down with his pranks and mischief!" She leaned across the counter, imparting zestfully, "You wouldn't never believe it, sir, but I'd a nun staying in the house that night, and—"

"Sister Maria Evangeline," nodded Harry.

Much shocked, Mrs. Burnett drew back. "Oooh!" she gasped, pointing a bony finger. "You're . . . *him*! You're that naughty rascal! Oh, my stays and shoelaces! Oh, goodnight!"

"Now *that*," he grinned, leaning closer to pinch her blushing cheek gently, "is exactly what I wish to discuss with you—*dear* Mrs. Burnett . . ."

CHAPTER XXI

HARRY AWOKE TO THE UNFAMILIAR CLATTER OF A COACH passing underneath his windows. The chill of his nose told him the morning was brisk, but the mattress was a soft billow of feathers and the sheets seemed almost perfumed . . . He lay there, fully awake, but keeping his eyes closed, remembering the last time he had occupied this very room, wishing he could turn back the clock, and achingly aware that despite all the perils, the happiest days of his life had been spent wandering the pleasant lanes and by-ways with Diccon and Nanette . . . "Little one . . . my beloved . . . how I miss you . . ."

A soft knock at the door announced the arrival of the maid with the early coffee he'd ordered. Sighing, he opened his eyes and summoned a smile as the girl trod into the room, tray balanced on one hand.

"Good morn—" he began in his polite way.

Her reaction was not quite what he had expected. Her eyes became round as saucers, her mouth taking on the same shape as the tray dropped from her hands. "*Oh*! Oh, my *lor'*!" she gasped, taking a hurried step back, oblivious of the wreckage at her feet. "Well, I *never*!" And she fled, turned at the door to peep back in, and with a squeal, vanished.

"I'll be damned!" ejaculated Harry.

"Ravishers usually are," murmured a soft feminine voice.

Captain Sir Harry Allison Redmond sat up faster than

he'd ever moved in his life. A vision stood beside the modest dressing table. A vision clad in a wrapper that was a misty blue cloud of gauze; a vision with huge hazel eyes full of love and mischief, and flecks that echoed the lacy blue cap tied demurely over her shining black curls.

"Wh— Wha—?" croaked Harry.

"The last time we were alone together in this boarding house," said Nanette yearningly, "you called me a—er . . . what was it? Oh, a 'Puss'! And you told me you were 'not a bad sort' . . ."

"It—it was . . . *you*?" he gulped, idiotically.

"Then and now, beloved. Only this time—willingly."

Her eyes were limpid, her mouth soft and inviting.

"See here!" Harry remonstrated, pulling the sheet primly around his chin. "What—what the deuce are you . . . doing in my bedchamber?"

Nanette smiled, loving him so much it was a pain, and loving him the more because although he trembled with longing for her, yet even now he strove to protect her. "Why, I am compromising you, of course. My own adored tyrant . . . my so-gallant gentleman who was willing to risk his dear life—to endure suffering and shame and danger for my sake. And yet is too proud to offer for me because of my so-hateful fortune."

A ripple of subdued but excited chatter broke out not too far distantly. Discerning Mrs. Burnett's outraged tones, Harry groaned, "Oh, my God! What am I to tell the woman? Nanette, you naughty vixen, turn around! Quickly!"

Dimples peeping, she obeyed. He jumped out of bed, threw on his dressing gown and fastened the buttons hurriedly, then told her he was respectable.

She turned shyly, and noting that his rumpled hair was twisting into elf-locks she was reminded of the happy journeyings with Diccon. A tremulous smile pulled at her lips and her eyes blurred.

Gazing at her, Harry thought her exquisitely lovely. She was all he would ever want . . . all he would ever need, and in her face a worship that set his heart to thundering.

343

The thundering was echoed by a low but persistent rapping at the door.

"Sir Harry! Sir Harry! Have you got someone in there?" Mrs. Burnett's voice was discreetly soft, yet shook with righteous indignation. "This here is a respectable house, I'll have you know!"

"I don't . . . understand," said the bemused Harry, retaining sufficient of his wits to ignore this interruption. "Did you follow me here?"

"But, of course. Nerina's brother was coming to that ridiculous mill, and she insisted we accompany him so that we might shop in the Pantiles. I have been praying for weeks that you would come for me . . . and trying to build up my courage to come to you, in spite of that very foolish letter you sent. But—I was afraid you would send me off again. 'This,' I thought, 'must be handled very much with *adroitement*, for he is clever and I may lose him forever! We chanced to pass when you were leaving the stable, and I begged that we follow. When you came here, I knew what I must do. Nerina nearly fainted when I took rooms also, although it was silly because my dear Lindsay—the abigail who gave me her dress when I first ran away—is here with me."

"And doesn't know you are in *here*, I'll wager," he said, still struggling. "Nerina was right and it is—most improper, as you must—er, certainly . . . be aware."

"Terribly improper," she agreed. "But very necessary, all the same. I crept in here before anyone was about and waited for you to wake up so that I might entrap you! I am shameless, *oui*, but . . ." She held out her arms, "Ah, my dearest one, how could I resist so golden an opportunity?"

Dizzied with love and a joy he scarce dare acknowledge, Harry yet clung to his unyielding Code. "Are you—er, I mean—do you wear a . . . a nightdress under that—wrapper?" he stammered.

Blushing adorably, Nanette discarded the wrapper. She was fully clad in a charming gown of pale primrose crepe, with a low, squared neckline and the bodice fastened with tiny mother-of-pearl buttons. "I am not so abandoned as to appear before you in . . . my nightrail," she said breathlessly, only to add with an incorrigible twinkle, "The maid, however, assuredly thought I wore only a nightgown under my wrapper, so you are fairly disgraced, you know."

"Wretched little shrew . . ." he said in a choked voice, and reached out to her. With a muffled sob, she ran into his embrace. He caught her tight against his heart, and with his cheek against her hair and his eyes closed, murmured rapturously, "My darling . . . oh, my most precious vixen. Are you—*quite* sure?"

"Quite sure," sighed Nanette.

Wherefore he bent his head at last and kissed her thoroughly with a love that seemed more of heaven than earth.

"I'll give you a 'alf hour!" hissed a very earthy voice at the keyhole. "And then I'm a'calling of the Watch! Such carryings-on I never did hear in all me born days! Twice! Don't you *never* set foot in my house again! Barrynet, green eyes, or no! *Imagine!*" Still muttering her outrage, the good lady took herself off, her rapid footsteps fading into silence.

Harry deposited a kiss in the softness of Nanette's palm. "You must return to your room at once. I'll go down as soon as I'm dressed and try to calm her . . . somehow!"

"Will you? I wish I might hear it," she giggled, and nursing his hand to her cheek, murmured, "There is just . . . one thing, Harry . . ."

"What is it, my own, my heart?"

"I am afraid," said Nanette demurely, "You shall have to . . . marry me, now . . ."

ROMANCING ADVENTURE...
by Patricia Veryan